# STORM SHATTERED

# STORM SHATTERED

## THE DARKEST STORM - BOOK 3

### PATRICK DUGAN

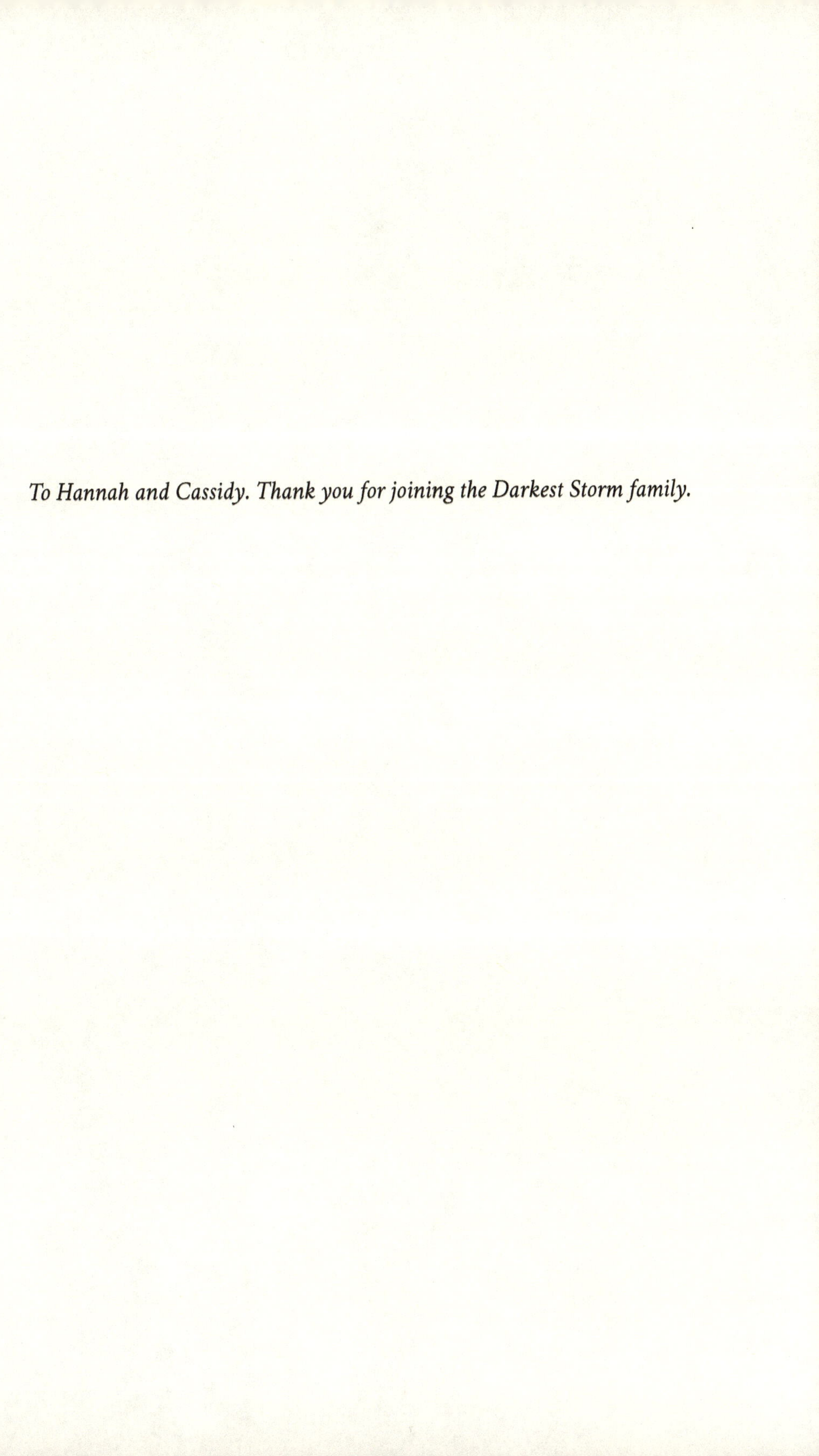

*To Hannah and Cassidy. Thank you for joining the Darkest Storm family.*

There are days you jump out of bed, ready to tackle the world. There are other days where pulling the covers over your head and hiding makes a lot of sense. Then there's today where I'm not sure what happened.

"Tommy, can you hear me?" Pepper said in her thick New York accent. Pepper died at the hands of Reaper years ago, but her spirit had come back with me when Reaper's scythe sliced into my back. "We're at Harker, and you pushed me into my body a few hours ago."

*Pepper. You there?* I asked, confused because she sounded different.

She didn't respond. I couldn't feel her presence in my head.

"Come on. You've gotta wake up."

I realized Pepper spoke from next to me, not in my head. The memory of the music that had led me to return her to her body seeped into my brain. "You're alive?"

"Well, no duh," Pepper said in my ear. "Nice of you to notice."

"Tommy, are you okay?" Mom asked.

As my brain cleared, I started putting the events of arriving at Harker into place. The drive into the mountains, finding the hidden base, and Blaze, my mentor and friend. We'd put him in the machine to cure his cancer.

I blinked, partially to clear my vision, partially because a bright light shone in my face.

More memories of Marcel finding the tube. No, it was a stasis chamber with Pepper's naked body preserved inside it.

The music. I'd heard a melody as I touched her, and then she came back to life. How the hell had that happened?

Mom's voice penetrated the fog. "Tommy, you with us?"

"My diagnosis is Thomas fainted. All neurological scans are normal. Medically speaking, he is operational." The sound of Gabriel, Harker's resident holo-doc, talking brought me fully back.

The light clicked off. I opened my eyes to find Mom, Dad, and Marcel standing around me, as well as the hologram Gabriel. A now-covered Pepper Spray sat in a wheelchair next to my head.

Memories flooded back in. My best friend, Marcel, had found Pepper's body in the cryogenics facility. Somehow, I'd managed to put her back into her body. She lived again after being trapped for years in Grim Reaper's scythe

I closed my eyes. "I'm fine. What happened?"

"I'll tell you what happened. You took one look at my boobs and passed out," Pepper said. "I've never had anyone hit da floor from looking at me naked before."

"Well, you're ancient. Nobody wants to see that."

"Thomas!" Mom sputtered. "Gabriel, are you sure he didn't strike his head when he fell? He's been taught better manners."

"Yes, ma'am. I did a full brain scan—"

Marcel laughed. "And it found nothing, bruh."

Pepper chuckled. "I was in there, and there's a lot of empty space."

"That's enough from you two," Mom said, though she wore a smirk on her face. "So, what happened?"

I tried to rise, and the world tilted.

Dad caught me before I toppled off the exam table. "You should wait a bit before sitting."

"Yeah." I thought back to the minutes leading to my blackout. "Marcel found Pepper's body in a tube thing."

Marcel gasped. "Tube thing? Tube thing? Bruh, that is a self-stabilizing, molecular-level stasis habitat. It is one of the most amazing machines I've ever seen, and you call it a thing?" He realized everyone stared at him. "So, you found the thing…"

I shook my head slowly so as not to damage my brain any more than it already was. "So, we found the machine, and Gabriel confirmed Pepper was inside, as Marcel had said." I fumbled around for the right words. "When I touched Pepper, an instant connection formed. It felt like music running through me, and the stronger the song got, the more connected we became. It felt like our hearts beat as one, taking up the rhythm of the music as it poured through me into her. Then the music faded, and she opened her eyes. I guess I passed out at that point."

Marcel rubbed his stubbly chin. "If you subscribe to the theory that human consciousness is formed from energy—"

"Gabriel, stop recording," Dad said before Marcel went on. "Glenda, cease all internal monitoring."

The holo-doc faded from view. Glenda, Harker's AI system's identity, spoke over the hidden speakers. "All internal monitoring has been turned off. You can resume through the main command console."

Dad shook his head. "Marcel, I need you to erase any stored conversations from Glenda and Gabriel once we finish here. Should have thought of it sooner. No sense leaving a record if we have to escape from here."

Mom rubbed Dad's arm. "You had a couple of things on your mind, I'm sure. What were you saying, Marcel?"

"Well, Tommy absorbs energy, so basically, if Pepper's essence was energy, he absorbed it, then transferred it back into her body. Fascinating. I wonder what other forms of energy Tommy can use, and how many ways he can modify it? I need to build a simulation to…" He wandered away, talking to himself as he left the medical bay.

I closed my eyes. Metaphysical theory gives me a headache.

As I woke up, this time in a bed instead of the medical ward, I glanced around the room. My backpack and pants sat on a chair in the corner. It was much smaller than my bedroom at the Castle base, but a comfortable bed made me happy, regardless. Climbing out of bed went better than expected. After a shower and getting dressed, I felt halfway human again.

Once I exited the room, I followed the blue guide lights down the hallway, past closed doors on either side. I heard voices coming from the kitchen area as I walked toward it.

The commissary, as Glenda had termed it, might have come out of any movie's lunchroom setting. Eight circular tables arranged around the room, each with four chairs. A long white counter with stools tucked under the overhang divided the eating area from the kitchen. With a microwave, sink, and refrigerator surrounded by dark gray cabinets, the kitchen more than fit the bill. If this place was like Castle, there would be more surprises to find once I explored the place.

Abby sat at one of the white and chrome tables with Pepper, who held a coffee cup in her hand, though she still used the wheelchair she'd been in last night. Abby shot a look my way as I entered. I doubted anyone ever snuck up on her.

"Hey, guess who I found when I got up this morning?" Abby asked, indicating Pepper, now dressed in surgical scrubs instead of the patient's gown from yesterday.

"Nice to be found. I'd never have believed I'd ever be back in my old body." Pepper smiled at me. "Thanks for the assist."

I grabbed a chair and dropped into it. "Are you okay?" I asked, motioning toward Pepper's wheelchair, an automated one from the looks of it.

She gave me a wry grin. "I'm fine, but the extended absence has atrophied my muscles quite a bit. Now that the systems are all online, I'll be able to work my way back."

Abby looked her over. "Weren't you a member of Stryke Force with Blaze?"

"I was, way back when," Pepper said. "Reaper removed me from the position."

"According to Marcel, you're a cyborg. Thought you'd be all robot parts, like Marcel's dream girl."

I winced. Pepper laughed awkwardly.

"No robot parts. The doc who worked on me replaced my eyes and junk like that."

This wasn't a good subject. Pepper had told me the story of being given to the doctor who carved her up and sold her to the Cartel. She'd been used to transport drugs before they forced her to become an assassin. "Is anybody else up yet?"

Abby looked at me, a puzzled expression on her face. "Not yet. Mimi and Waxenby are still in the med lab. Marcel programmed the food synthesizer thing for you."

I hopped up and walked across the commissary to the kitchen proper. The door I'd taken as a microwave wasn't. A palm-shaped outline sat next to it. I placed my hand where it indicated. A computer voice chirped. "Order, please."

"Um, Mountain Dew and a Wildberry Pop-Tart?"

"Processing." A low hum sounded as the machine did, well, whatever it did. The door slid open, and there sat my order. The pastry was warm to the touch but not hot enough to burn. I happily returned to my seat with the breakfast of champions.

Abby shook her head. "Still don't get how you eat that crap."

"It tastes better than you'd think," Pepper said. She rolled back from the table without touching any controls. "I'm gonna grab me some too."

"Oh my god, you've corrupted her. I guess being stuck in your brain sac would mess anyone up." Abby glanced at Pepper. Once she was out of earshot, Abby asked, "You okay?"

I nodded since my mouth was full of wildberry goodness. I swallowed before saying, "It was so weird, but I'm glad Pepper is whole again. Having a second person in your head is strange."

She snorted. "I'm sure having any thoughts up there is weird." She smirked at me. "I wonder if Marcel has gotten any sleep since we got here. He headed down to the master control room after we dumped your sorry ass in bed last night."

"I doubt it." I took another bite of pastry and washed it down with ice-cold Mountain Dew. This, I could get used to.

Pepper returned to the table, placing a glass and four Pop-Tarts down in front of her. She slid two across to me. "I figured you'd still be hungry, you know, after pushing me back into my body."

I realized I'd devoured the two I had, and my stomach growled for more. She'd been in my head for so long there was a wrongness to her not being there. I watched as she slowly ate. Her hands shook with fatigue as she raised them to her mouth. I wondered just how long it would take her to work back to full speed.

"Good morning," Mom said, as she and Dad entered the commissary. He strode purposefully into the kitchen on his routine coffee quest.

"Hey, Mom," Abby and I echoed as she approached our table.

She wore an old sweatshirt over yoga pants. Her blond hair was pulled back in a ponytail, reminding me of pictures I'd seen of when she was a kid. She slid into a chair next to Pepper.

"Pepper, how are you feeling?" she asked, concern etching her features.

A twitch of a smile played across Pepper's face. "I'm fine. Hey, anything's better than being on the slab in there."

"Gabriel recommended you stay in the med lab so they can help build your muscle tone back. Maybe the process would help," Mom said.

"The robo doc don't know nuthin' about this. Eating real food will do me good, and once my systems have recalibrated, I'll be ready to go." Pepper took another swig of Dew as if to prove her point.

Mom wasn't going to lose the trail. She was in mama bear mode, and Abby's bemused expression showed she knew it too.

"Recalibrated?" Dad asked as he set a pot of coffee and a cup in front of Mom. "What's going on?"

Pepper sighed. "I don't wanna talk about it." The word *talk* sounded more like *tawk* the way she said it.

I'd gotten used to Pepper's accent while she resided in my gray matter, but it took a bit of readjusting to it in the real world.

"I understand, but under the circumstances, I'd like as much information as you are comfortable providing." Dad took a chair next to me. His eyes locked on Pepper's, who stared right back in defiance. I wondered who'd blink first.

After a long moment, Pepper spread her hands out in front of her. "Fine. Tommy could tell you since we don't have many secrets from each other after sharing a brain." She paused and glanced at Abby, as if she expected a smart-ass remark. When Abby didn't say anything, Pepper continued. "Abby called me a cyborg, which is technically true, but I don't have no bionic parts or any of that bullshit. The doc augmented my existing parts so I'd avoid detection. There is a micro-computer of sorts to coordinate all my systems. It allows me to do things an ordinary person couldn't. Kinda mimics a Gifted's abilities as far as speed and strength."

"Your limbs haven't been replaced?" Dad asked quietly. "Before the Darkest Storm, the prosthetic engineers had developed limbs that interfaced with the user's neural systems."

"Nope. Doc didn't want parts falling off. As part of Stryke Force, I wore overlays on my skin to make it appear I was made of metal, but it was for show."

"Why would you do that?" Mom asked. She still bore the signs of worry, but I think curiosity had gotten the better of her.

"Kinda seems stupid now, I'll admit." Pepper fidgeted in the wheel-chair for a second before she continued. "Stryke Force was a non-Gifted team, and after a few incidents where there were high collateral casualties, we decided to make sure I didn't look Gifted. Plus, it screwed with the techno-wizards when they couldn't control me." She laughed. "Man, freakin' Mechno had a nervous breakdown when his Gift didn't work on me."

"Who's Mechno?" Abby asked, looking to Dad.

"He controlled robots with his Gift and was part of the Evil, Inc., group. They were a half-social-activist, half-terrorist group. Made a lot of noise but never did much. TV news loved them, though." Dad said. He poured another cup of coffee.

"They were jokers, alright," Pepper said with a snort. "They would go on and on about corporate greed. Then they'd hack a bank and rob 'em blind."

"They weren't the strongest opponents we ever faced." Dad said as he stirred his coffee. "Would you mind if we had Marcel run a scan on you?"

Pepper's face flared red. "No way. I'm not your freaking lab rat to be poked and prodded."

"No poking or prodding. It would be good to know if the Dark Brigade modified you in any way while they had you. They destroyed half the Earth. I doubt they'd think twice about manipulating your systems to use as a weapon."

"So, you callin' me a traitor? There's nuthin' wrong with me. You can stick it up your ass for all I care. Once I'm functional, and Blaze is better, we're outta here."

Mom spoke before Dad could. "Pepper, Michael doesn't doubt you. You and Tommy are closer than any two people could ever be, so we trust you. What he's saying is the people who had your body did horrible things, and he wants to make sure you are safe."

The redness hadn't lessened any, but she took a deep breath before speaking. "I'll think about it. Tommy knows I'd never hurt any of you."

I nodded. "Pep, I know you wouldn't, and I wouldn't let anyone hurt you. I've got your back, and that won't ever change."

Abby made an awful sound like she'd vomited. "You two make me sick. Nobody is hurting anybody. Ranger wants to make sure we are all safe. That includes Blaze, who's in the tank in med lab." She sounded annoyed.

Mom started to say something but stopped as she spotted Marcel running in, tablet in hand. His hair was wild, and he had a frantic energy about him. "Marcel, honey. Did you get any sleep?"

"Mom, no time for small talk. We have a major problem." His hair bobbed as he stopped before the table. To his credit, he wasn't winded. Blaze's training had gotten him into better shape.

"What's the issue?" Dad tensed, ready to move at a moment's notice. "Have we been discovered?"

Marcel's shaggy head shook. "No. We put Blaze into the cellular regeneration chamber, and we shouldn't have. We need to get him out."

A crowd of confused looks met his words. We'd fought our way here to use the machine as a last resort to save Blaze's life. I didn't understand. "Why would we take him out of the machine? He'll die otherwise."

"I was wrong. The machine was the prototype for the weapon they used to attack Earth. Essentially we stuck him in a person-sized death ray."

And just like that, my quiet day dropped into bizzaro world.

<br>

Mom recovered first. "Marcel, what are you talking about? Gabriel said the machine would save Blaze."

"According to the specs I found in the command systems, the death ray they used to attack Earth shouldn't have killed everyone. It was supposed to mutate the Norms to Gifted. The Dark Brigade wanted to build an army of super-soldiers, not eliminate the population of Earth."

Dad rubbed his eyes. "They realized after they hit Tokyo, the ray didn't work as they planned. Why would they continue if it didn't work?"

"I'm still running queries through the system to verify my guess." Marcel pushed his glasses up his nose as he read off his tablet. "A couple of the messages I found lead me to believe that once the test had failed, the Dark Brigade decided if they removed the world's governments, they could impose their will. I don't have enough data to get the whole picture. One thing is clear. The cellular regenerator was the prototype for the death ray."

"Let's go ask Gabriel." Dad stood and strode across the commissary, headed toward the med bay.

We all followed along. Abby spoke to Pepper as she pushed the wheelchair, her low voice trying to reassure her Blaze would be fine. A glance at Pepper's face told me it wasn't working.

"Bruh, this is bad. What if I killed Blaze? I double-checked the data from the Lair, and they listed it as a healing machine. Whoever entered the information for this place didn't leave any fingerprints. I don't know if they intentionally entered it wrong to kill whoever used it." Marcel's bloodshot eyes and slumped shoulders testified to how tired he was. Someone could have put bogus data into the Lair's system to hide what this facility was. It was impossible to know what had happened, but we needed to take care of Blaze first.

I nudged Marcel. I kept my voice low so no one else heard. "Blaze would have died if we hadn't gotten him here. If the machine does kill him, we tried our best."

I thought I heard a soft gasp from behind me, but when I looked back, Abby and Pepper were still speaking. I increased my pace until we caught up to Mom and Dad as they entered the med bay.

"Gabriel," Mom said, bringing up the holo doc. "The machine where we placed our injured friend. What does it do exactly?"

The shimmering form of Gabriel floated before us. "The cellular regenerator rewrites the DNA in the host body to eliminate abnormalities as well as recessive genes in an attempt to eliminate future health problems."

Marcel grunted. "If the DNA is rewritten, it would eliminate the cancer our friend has. Is that correct?"

"In 64.29 percent of subjects, the cancer was eliminated." Gabriel flickered as he moved to the side of the machine. "From the readings I've received, we will know the full extent of the procedure in approximately nine days, four hours, and sixteen minutes assuming a steady rate of substitution. This can vary by fifty percent, depending on the patient."

I thought back to when we had placed Blaze in the machine. Gabriel had kept repeating something, some warning we'd been too tired to acknowledge. It beckoned just out of reach of my memory.

Mom asked, "What happens if our friend isn't part of the sixty-four percent who are cured? Can he be treated again?"

"Some subjects have had remaining abnormal cells but suffer no other lasting effects. Most, however, died within five days of the process."

"Side effects!" I shouted as I remembered. "You mentioned side effects when we put him in. What are they?" I realized everyone was staring at me after my outburst. "Sorry, it came to me suddenly."

Gabriel's answer cut off any remarks, snarky or otherwise. "During the process, as the DNA is mutated, it can cause unexpected side effects. Some subjects did not exhibit the desired outcomes. Some of the mutations were severe enough to cause death. Overall, the program was considered a success, but there was a risk in undergoing the process."

"So, it might not work." Mom and Dad shared a look. They were probably thinking the same as I was. Blaze would have died without it, so anything had better odds than doing nothing.

"I have been programmed to seek optimal results while minimizing the sub-optimal results for my patients. I still obey those directives and will monitor the situation and, if anything changes, will notify you."

Marcel sighed. "Sorry. I guess I overreacted. When I saw the connection between the death ray and this, I kinda freaked."

Mom rubbed his arm. "Honey, we're all worried about Blaze, and you need some sleep. Come on. Let's get you back to your room. Things will be better after some rest."

He let himself be led away. Mom would take care of him as she always did. For about the millionth time, I realized how lucky I was to have her.

Images of Wendi slid into my thoughts. This time they were good ones of us hanging with mom, eating pizza in the living room on movie night, and of the picnic by the river. I could still see her smile, feel the touch of her hand, hear her laugh. We'd lost a lot the day she died but hadn't lost everything.

I wandered around, looking at all the devices and machinery in the med bay. I'd never understand half of what these things did. My feet took me past the small room where Mimi sat with Waxenby. He laid on the bed, head lolled to the side. Mimi, her eyes unfocused, had her hands on his arm. I cleared my throat to get her attention.

Her head twisted toward me, and she smiled her normal, impudent smile. "Hey, Tiger." She sounded tired. "Decided to come visit? Sounds like you were busy yesterday."

I dropped into the chair next to her. "Yeah, it was a weird sort of day. How is Mr. Waxenby?"

She shrugged. "The body is working, but the engine has thrown a piston. I've been trying to reach him, but all I get are flashes of his experiences. A sight here or a voice there. It's like his memories have been in a huge crash with the parts thrown in all directions."

I hated seeing Waxenby like this. He'd stood by us as we tried to rescue Dad and fought Powell. Waxenby had used his power to its fullest advantage and kept us together when things got tough. He deserved better than to be a shattered remnant of himself. "Can you help him?"

She pursed her lips as she considered. "Maybe. With me still learning my Gift and the amount of damage he has, it's hard to know. I'm a better grease jockey than some sort of psychic surgeon. I've been able to put some of the pieces together, kind of like a puzzle. Might be I should slap him upside his head. Works with most guys."

I laughed 'cause I'd seen her do it on numerous occasions. "Not sure it would work, but if all else fails…"

"Naw. Ollie is one of the good guys. Never a mean word for anybody. Plus, he was a good tipper when he came into the Lair. I want to help, not just get dragged around with you guys." She punched me lightly in the arm. "Plus, Mandy would kick my ass if I let anything happen to you."

That caught me off guard. Mandy hadn't crossed my mind for a while now. Our initial meeting hadn't been so great, with her setting me up to get pulverized by her boyfriend and all. She had apologized and was my first kiss. Wendi had eclipsed everything in my thoughts and my heart. The idea of another girl set my palms sweating, and my stomach churned. I stood up a bit too fast to act casual. "You're helping Mr. Waxenby. He wouldn't stand a chance without you."

Mimi cocked her head, studying me. She held my gaze, her eyes widening a bit. Calm flooded over me. It was nice that Mimi could help me through the rough spots. "You're okay, Tiger. Go get a Dew and talk with Pepper. Come see me later."

I nodded and went to find Pepper. Something upset me, but it wasn't important enough to remember. I retraced my steps to the commissary. Pepper wasn't there, but Mom was.

She smiled when she saw me walking toward the table. "Hi, honey. In all the commotion, I didn't get to talk to you much this morning."

I got a Dew from the food dispenser and took a chair across from her. "It's been a crazy couple of days. Did Marcel get to bed?"

"He was asleep before he hit the pillow. You both have come a long way since we picked up Marcel for his first weekend visit. I'm really proud of you."

I felt heat in my cheeks. "Thanks. You aren't doing so bad, Snapshot." Who knew my mom would turn out to be a sniper? It seemed forever ago that my biggest worry was Brunner and his constant hassling and Powell's criticism and endless detention.

I should have been closing in on graduation, planning on working at the Lair, and taking Wendi out on weekends for pizza and movie dates. I'd have never chosen this life, but there weren't many other options that didn't involve me dying.

"My dad taught me to shoot when I was a kid. I was kind of a tomboy growing up. It wasn't until I started studying law that I even owned a skirt."

"Do you miss our old life?"

She thought for a minute. Her eyes scanned my face like she might find the answer there. "Yes and no. I lied to myself about you being safe in Redemption. You were never safe, and there was nothing I could do about it. Our new life is an adjustment, but I still love your dad, and we are working things out. As long as I've got my kids, I'm good. You?"

"The only part I miss is Wendi."

She clasped my hand in both of hers. "I know, sweetheart. We all do. There isn't a day that goes by I don't wish things were different, but everything happens for a reason, even if the why isn't apparent."

I wanted to trust her instincts; I really did. The thought that someday I'd understand why Wendi had to die seemed impossible to me. I'd have a better chance of landing on Mars. The pain had become part of me—the sharp edge worn down to where sometimes I forgot it was there until it sliced me open again. "Let's go with that."

"All you can do," she said with a smile. "Well, it's early. What are you going to do with your day?"

I shrugged. "Don't know. I'll wander around and see what's here, though I'll probably wait for Marcel since he can get us access to the other floors."

"You should take your father along to explore." She frowned as she continued. "This was a Dark Brigade outpost. We don't know if they stored anything dangerous here."

"You mean besides frozen bodies and healing devices?"

"Exactly." She had a wry smile on her face. At least I'd done something to lighten her mood. The race from Dallas to Atlanta, and then escaping from Castle to Harker, had taken a lot out of everyone. Add to it her watching over Blaze and Waxenby. She was tired, and we needed to rest and regroup.

"You should get some extra sleep," I said, noticing the dark circles under her eyes. "I think I'm going to crash while Marcel is down."

She stood and took my arm. "Good idea. Who knows how long we'll be here? I don't like this place. I can't help feeling like the Dark Brigade will return at any minute."

We walked together to the living quarters. I hugged her and headed into my room. I fell asleep before I got comfortable on the bed.

---

The clock's red LED readout said eight-ten. I'd slept all day, but I'd needed it after going days on limited sleep and expending a lot of energy. Restoring Pepper to her body had drained all my reserves and left me feeling groggy. Even after a charge, my levels were off, though it was worth it to give Pepper her body back.

It was oddly quiet in my head. It was a fact Abby and Marcel would be glad to comment on and why I wouldn't be mentioning it.

I flipped on the overhead reading lamp. After a minute of stretching and listening to my body complain, I forced myself out of bed and into the bathroom. I took a long shower, shaved, and found clean clothes to put on.

Feeling better than I had in a week, I made the bed, put my dirty clothes in a pile, and went off in search of dinner. I entered the common area and saw Mom, Dad, Abby, and Marcel at the table. Empty plates sat in front of everyone, except Abby, who was still eating a bowl of spaghetti. Mom and Dad had coffee cups in their hands.

"Hey," I said, heading for the food dispenser. I ordered a hamburger, fries, and a Mountain Dew. A couple of minutes later, the door opened, revealing my dinner. Dad had pulled out a chair for me.

I sat, placing my tray on the table. "Thanks. Did you guys just get up?"

"Yeah," Marcel said, looking from his cracked tablet. The roll down the hill in the Reclaimer's personnel carrier hadn't been kind to it. "I got into the base's systems. I think I can bypass the door locks to get us to the lower levels."

I tore into my hamburger. It was good, but nothing special. I doubted a machine could replicate actual cooking. It was hot and juicy, but it lacked the consistency of a burger done on the grill. I was so hungry I didn't care enough to complain.

"Michael, I think you should lead these three through the lower levels. Who knows what could be down there?" Mom said, worry thick in her voice. "I don't like being anywhere the Dark Brigade used as a staging base."

He nodded. "Marcel, can you pull up the schematics for Harker?"

Marcel's fingers tapped on his display while Abby and I kept eating. There were two more empty bowls in front of her. My Gift took a lot of food to maintain; hers took twice as much.

Abby placed her current bowl on the pile. "That was good. Man, I was starving after all the fighting. I hope there's a training area since I need to keep in shape."

"I think I can get the schematics," Marcel said as his fingers kept going.

The lights in the kitchen turned red. "Attention," a voice I hadn't heard before announced over the speakers. "The molecular reassignment weapon will fire in ten minutes. This is not a drill."

What the *hell* was a molecular reassignment weapon?

3

arcel's tablet clattered on the table as he held his hands up. "I didn't do anything, I swear. I was accessing the file storage is all."

"Glenda, what is the molecular reassignment device?" Dad shouted above the message repeating over and over as the red light flashed.

"The device was installed on the International Gifted Detention Station or IGDS. The Dark Brigade deployed it there to enact the Darkest Storm Protocol."

"The death ray is on the prison space station?" I blurted out, along with what was in my mouth. I took my napkin and cleaned up the mess. "Why the hell would it fire now, and where is it aiming?"

Dad shook his head. "I don't know, but we need to find out."

"I thought you destroyed it when you stopped the Dark Brigade?" Marcel asked, staring at Dad. "It was all a lie?"

"Not now, Marcel. We need to find out what's going on." Dad raised his voice. "Glenda, can you display the Protectorate's FNN news feed?"

What the hell was that? I looked at Mom, who wore a shocked expression that reflected how I felt. How do you brush off a direct question like that?

"Of course." Marcel sounded annoyed, and I couldn't blame him. A light flickered on the far wall, and the FNN news desk appeared on the display.

A bland-looking white dude in a blue suit and gray tie reported the news to the camera. His bored expression mirrored the headlines. "The Protectorate announced today that citizens in the Southern American Zones would face shortages on beef and other meat products due to the heatwave which has caused massive livestock losses—"

"Glenda, mute the feed," Mom said. She sounded angry. "Michael, answer Marcel's question. The government assured us the death ray had been eliminated."

"It wasn't. We failed to eliminate it. We vented the IGDS's holds, killing all the terrorists who were on board where they had the weapon. The station's automated defenses destroyed any ship that came into range, making it impossible to finish the mission. The government covered it up."

"What the hell were they thinking?" Abby asked. "More lies by the government to keep us stupid."

"People were panicked and on the verge of an armed uprising, is why, Abby," Mom said, her lawyer voice back in place. "After all the losses, the world would have gone up in flames if they'd admitted the weapon still worked."

Dad nodded. "Nothing could get close enough to enter the station IGDS, so they decided it was as inactive as it would get. They called a press conference, handed out medals, and let people grieve in peace."

"How did your team open the airlocks?" Marcel asked. He still hadn't retrieved his tablet. "We might be able to access the same system."

"I doubt it," Dad said, holding up his hand to stall Marcel's reply. "We got Dominion close enough, and she mind-controlled a Dark Brigade member to open the hatches. As far as I know, they are still open."

"Oh. I can't do that." Marcel grabbed his tablet. He resumed tapping on the screen.

"No one besides Dominion could have. She was extremely powerful." Dad paced as the voice counted down to the death ray firing. "We are in the only safe spot on Earth."

"How do you figure?" Abby asked. For once, there wasn't a hostile tone in her voice. When things got tense, she butted heads with Dad a lot.

"They would have blocked firing on any Dark Brigade sites," Marcel said. "If the ray malfunctioned and started firing, you'd have a fail-safe to stop it from wiping out your own people."

"Do you think this is a malfunction?" I asked. The computer voice grated on my nerves as it reached the four-minute mark.

The talking head on FNN sat next to a photo of a Reclaimer General. I recognized him. General Mahady had done the press conference after the destruction of the school buses. I returned my attention to the conversation at hand.

"If this is a malfunction, what would the target be?" Mom asked as she rotated her coffee cup in her hand. "Where is the IGDS located?"

Marcel looked up from his device. "It's positioned over the East Asian sector. That's where the attack started in 2012. Do you think it's repeating the same pattern?"

Dad stepped over so Marcel could show him the intel. "It's possible. Tokyo is in the fire pattern from where it is."

"Aren't satellites in a geo-synchronized location?" Mom asked as the cup revolved faster. "Why would it need to move?"

"The IGDS is fully mobile to make it harder to coordinate a break-out. They detained the worst of the worst there." He paused for a moment to point at something on the tablet. "The Dark Brigade used its mobility to punish any country that stood against them after the initial attacks took out the major capitals of the world. India was wiped out after they fired nukes at the station."

"I lived through it."

Dad caught her eye. "But the kids didn't, and they need to know what to expect."

"Expect?" Abby asked as she leaned back in her chair. "You think this will happen more than once?"

"If what I'm seeing is accurate, in just over three minutes, Tokyo will be hit again." Marcel's head whipped around, so he faced Dad. "We need to warn Warden."

"How? All the gear is under tons of rubble at Castle," Mom said, as the color drained from her face. "Do they have people in all the destroyed cities?"

"No info, but I agree with Marcel," I said. The Underground had people living in every destroyed city around the globe. An attack would kill anyone there, just like the initial attacks had. "Can you contact them?"

Marcel's fingers flew over the keys, and the countdown announced three minutes. "There is a comm hub on the floor below us. I popped the locks. Let's go." He ran across the commissary to a steel door halfway to the med bay. It opened as he pushed, and we all followed him down a flight of stairs and through the next door. He led us to the right, past a large gym, and into the comm hub.

Monitors covered the walls, displaying feeds from around the globe. Some of them were from TV stations; others were official government channels. Marcel dropped into a large, black desk chair and pulled on the headset. The voice announced the two-and-a-half-minute mark.

After a few seconds of punching buttons and turning dials, Marcel said, "This is Mr. Wizard. We have an emergency and need Warden now." He listened as the other voice spoke. "I don't care. Get her now. Pull her off the toilet if you have to. In two minutes, it will be too late."

We waited with the warning message endlessly repeating. Finally, Marcel spoke again. "It's Mr. Wizard. I'm with Cyclone Ranger and—" His face flushed red. "What do you mean I need to prove who I am?"

I grabbed the headphones off Marcel's head and jammed them on mine. "Warden, this is Tommy. Molecular Molly is your daughter, and Salvo died in Dallas. Now listen, in two minutes, the death ray is going to wipe out Tokyo. Get your people out."

Warden's voice was firm and strong, but I heard the twinge of panic. "What do you mean, the death ray is going to fire? Omega Squad destroyed it."

"No, they didn't. We can discuss details later. Move your people."

She didn't argue. "Roger that. Out." The line went dead.

I pulled off the headphones and tossed them to Marcel. I looked at Dad. "You owe her an explanation."

"Yeah, I do." He patted me on the shoulder. "Good work. Maybe we'll actually save some lives if they listen to us."

Marcel tuned in to one of the monitors. FNN came on the set. We sat in silence as the countdown penetrated the still of the complex. I wondered what Mimi and Pepper were thinking with the blaring warnings.

The voice launched into the final countdown as we watched. "Ten, nine..." Even knowing what was coming, my heart raced like a gamer on his eighth Mountain Dew.

The newscaster droned on, unaware of what was about to happen. I wondered if the Protectorate would even announce it on FNN. When Pepper didn't respond to my internal question, I felt lonely. I'd gotten used to her being my onboard sidekick.

"Three, two, one. The molecular reassignment device has achieved successful deployment."

Marcel canceled the mute on FNN's feed as the alarm went silent. "And that's why Cheetos are—" His face paled as he heard the news over his earpiece. "We have breaking news. The abandoned city of Tokyo has been fired on by the orbital death ray. It was previously thought destroyed, but the Protectorate is now in control of the weapon. FNN will be broadcasting the Protectorate press conference in fifteen minutes." A bright red banner appeared at the bottom of the screen.

"What?" I asked, shocked by the blatant lie. "How can they say they have control over it?"

"We don't know if the Protectorate is in control or not," Dad said as he got up and started pacing. "If they found a way to operate the device, they could knock out the underground once and for all."

"Do you think the Protectorate is telling the truth?" Abby asked. She leaned forward, elbows on knees as if waiting to launch herself into action.

Dad shook his head. "I doubt it. They'd have used it on Darkest

Storm Day or Freedom Day to demonstrate their control over the populace. I'm sure they are spinning the narrative to blame the Gifted and prove that we deserve to be caged."

"Does anybody need anything?" I said, standing up. "I'm going to go talk to Mimi and Pepper, so they know what's going on. I'll be back to watch the announcement."

Abby stood. "I'll chat with Mimi while you get Pepper. That way, you'll be back in time."

"Cherry Pepsi," Marcel said without looking up from the console where he worked. "As big as you can get. It's going to be a long day."

"I'll bring a pot of coffee," I told Mom as she was about to ask.

I followed Abby out the door. "This is crazy."

"Just goes to show you can't trust any government," Abby said as we reached the door to the stairs. "The American government lied about the death ray being destroyed. The Protectorate is all set to lie about the Gifted causing this. No matter who's in charge, we get screwed."

I opened the door and motioned Abby through. We climbed the stairs in silence. Without Pepper's internal banter, I felt abandoned. We re-entered the commissary level. "You'd think they'd put elevators in these places."

"It's good for you, Sparky," she said, with a not so gentle pat on the back. "Mimi's in with Waxenby. I bet Pepper is still waiting by Blaze."

I nodded. "It's going to be a long eight days until the machine is done."

Abby and I followed the corridor to the med bay. She turned into the room where Mimi and Waxenby had been since we'd gotten here, and I continued into the central part of the med bay and found Pepper. The long tube of the regeneration machine glowed with a soft yellow light. The device had a window to monitor the patient. Still in her wheelchair, Pepper had her face against the now frosted-over window. Nothing could be seen, but there she sat.

"Hey, Pepper," I said. I approached, not wanting to scare her. Her orange hair was pushed back over her ears. She'd borrowed a sweatshirt and leggings from Mom, having removed the scrubs she'd worn when she returned to her body.

I saw the tiredness in her eyes, and then it was gone, replaced by an impish glimmer. "Do you miss me?"

"What?" I didn't need clarification, but the question caught me off-guard.

Her eyes dug into me. "Do you miss having me floating around in your head?"

I started to reply with a joke, but the intensity of her gaze stopped it. "Yes. I feel like I lost my best friend and my conscience at the same time."

"Me too." She ran her hand over the outside of the machine. "I'd been alone for so long, and then I was sharing space with you—hearing your thoughts, experiencing your memories. Now, I'm alone again."

"Are you saying you didn't want me to restore you to your body?"

After a second, she shook her head. "Naw. Just tryin' to deal with all this at once. I just was wonderin' if you felt the same."

"Yeah, but at least now I can shower without worrying about you looking."

"There were some weird parts. I wouldn't trade being close to you ever." She laughed. "You brought me back from the dead and all."

"I didn't know if it would work. The pieces fell into place, and before I knew it, you were alive," I said, and then realized I hadn't told her why I was here. "I came to tell you what's going on. The death ray fired on Tokyo a few minutes ago. We're all watching in the control room downstairs. I didn't know if you wanted to watch the Protectorate explanation."

She turned back to the machine entombing Blaze. "Thanks, but no thanks. My life is here until the door lifts, and we see what comes out."

I had to let her make her own decision. "Can I get anything for you?"

"Not unless you can speed up time," she said, flashing me her mischievous smile. "You're a good kid, Tommy." She leaned her head against the device and continued her watch.

I returned to the commissary and got a pot of coffee, two cups, and a cherry Pepsi from the food replicator. With everyone's orders handled, I headed back to the control room.

Mom took the cups and poured coffee while I delivered Marcel his drink. The scene on the monitor had changed to a podium in front of a blue curtain adorned with the Protectorate symbol. I grabbed a chair and sat next to Marcel, who had a second screen up and was flying through code of some sort. It gave me a headache to even look at it.

Mom and Dad took seats as General Mahady stood behind the lectern.

"Good morning," he said, pausing to set his hat on the lectern before him. His brown hair showed streaks of gray, and he looked tired as he stood to address the FNN cameras. "At nine p.m., Tokyo local time, the Protector himself ordered the firing of the Electromagnetic Burst weapon from our orbital station. The public refers to this as the death ray."

"What a crock," Marcel said, looking up from his code. "They have no idea what happened. I've gotten into one of their command frequencies, and they are running around with their hair on fire."

Dad grunted, pausing the feed. "We don't have any more answers than they do." He caught Marcel's glare and quickly added, "Yet."

"If you two are done, I'd like to hear the man lie," Mom said, shutting down Marcel's response. She reached over and pushed the play button and the feed resumed.

"As you know, we are in a fight against the Underground. A Dissident, who calls herself Warden, was behind the collapse of a major portion of the Dallas metro area after a failed weapons test. We have it on authority the Underground is planning a massive strike against the people of the Protectorate in an attempt to restore the Dissidents to power." The video in the corner showed a view from one of the Reclaimer cameras. People ran toward the fence, trying to escape the upcoming blast. In an instant, they were vaporized, leaving nothing behind. My heart stopped.

After a few muttered words from off-camera, the General continued. "The Protector decided last night to eliminate the Underground, by striking at their weapon stronghold in the ruins of Tokyo. Further firings may be necessary as we review data on Warden's whereabouts. Thank you." He replaced his hat, turned on his heel, and walked from the room.

Just when things couldn't get any stranger, blue light filled the room as a portal grew in front of the door. Alyx the Summoner, member of the Council and magical protector of Earth, walked in on phantom legs. "The Brotherhood is on the move, and we're going to need your help."

## 4

Dad got to his feet and shook hands with Alyx. "Does this have anything to do with the death ray firing?"

"Everything," Alyx said with a grimace. "It took me longer to pinpoint your location than normal. Whoever built this place hid it from the magical spectrum as well as the physical."

"Well, it is a Dark Brigade base," Marcel said. He spun in his chair to face Alyx. "From the little I've been able to access so far, this was the R&D lab. There are other bases, but they're behind some serious encryption, and it'll take a while for me to break it. I wrote a new tool that should crack it in a week or so."

Dad ran his hand through his hair. "We don't have a week—"

"I'm clued in, but that level of encryption should take six hundred and fifty years to crack. A week is a fair compromise."

"Whoa. Dude, that is amazing." I said.

He grinned. "I built a brute force hacker, but then cloned it off on the Protectorate…" He stopped and looked at each of us. "Sorry, I'm doing it again. I basically put a virus on the Protectorate servers, which replicated across their systems, so they are all trying to break it at once. Even if the Protectorate techs find the virus, there is no connection back to us."

Dad put his hand on Marcel's shoulder. "We'd be lost without you. You're right. A week will have to do." He turned back to Alyx. "So, what has the Brotherhood done?"

It was Alyx's turn to look ashamed. The Brotherhood of Midnight was the eternal enemy of the Council. "We don't know. I was hoping you had information on the unexpected firing. I can open a portal to the station, but after the Kra-kelal came through the doorbell portal, I realized it might be good to have backup."

"I'm ready whenever you are," Dad said, stepping around Marcel.

"Absolutely not!" Mom said, inserting herself between Dad and Alyx. "Are you crazy? What happens if you get stuck in space? It's not like we can fly up there and get you."

"Actually, I need Tommy," Alyx said quietly. He must have been aware of the fury he was unleashing with his statement. "His Gift—"

"Over my dead body." Mom spun on her heel as precisely as General Mahady had. "Tommy is a minor and has fought through more than anyone his age ever should. I will not subject any of my children to that kind of danger."

Dad touched her arm. "Susan. You should—"

Tears raced down her cheeks as she confronted Dad. "No, Michael. I'm done listening. It's bad enough they could have died in the Gauntlet or in Atlanta or under Dallas or at Castle. We are safe here. Safe. I can go to sleep and not worry the Reclaimers will come in to take him off to the Block, or Powell will kill him for being Gifted. I'm done."

He pulled her into a hug and let her cry. His gaze caught mine. I read the conflict in them. Did he honor the wishes of a wife he thought he'd never see again, or resume the role of humanity's protector he'd walked away from all those years ago? He'd argued we should make a normal life for ourselves, but the stakes were higher now than ever.

Alyx cleared his throat. "Susan. I have no right to ask, but the fate of the world hangs in the balance. If we don't stop the Brotherhood, they'll destroy everyone to gain the power they need."

She didn't pull away from Dad but turned her head to answer. "Alyx, we've paid enough. Let someone else risk their children."

"I need Tommy's unique Gifts if we are going to stop the Brotherhood," Alyx said softly, as if the words might provoke another outburst. "I have a solution that might work." He held out two silver necklaces, each with a blue stone pendant attached. "I will have Tommy wear one, and you will wear the other. You'll be able to experience what is going on as if you were there. If at any point it gets too dangerous, you say the code word, and it will summon him back."

She pulled away from Dad and took one of the necklaces, sliding it over her head. Alyx handed me the other one, and I did the same. Other than a tingle when it touched my skin, nothing happened. Mom's eyes glazed over with a milky whiteness.

*I don't think this is working.*

I heard her voice in my head. It was like having Pepper riding shotgun.

*Is this thing on?* I thought to her.

No response.

"Mom, can you hear me?" I said again, out loud this time.

*I can't hear your thoughts.*

It was unlike how it was with Pepper, whose emotions and thoughts I could feel.

"If you say, 'return to me,' Tommy will teleport back to the same place you are." Alyx shrugged. "It may still be dangerous, but you'll know what's going on, and if things go bad, you can pull him back."

"No, I won't risk it. We have no way of getting Tommy back if something goes wrong, and this thing doesn't work. I'll not lose another child."

It shocked me when I realized she meant Wendi and maybe Jon. "Mom, I'll be fine. You'll be watching over me just like you always have."

"No, Tommy. I can't bear to watch. If something happened to you and I failed, I'd never be able to live with it. The answer is no." She removed the necklace. A moment later, her eyes returned to normal.

Abby set her hand on Alyx's shoulder as if to keep him from talking. "Mom, I'll ride along with Sparky. You know I'd never let anything happen to him."

Tears raced down Mom's cheeks. "But, Wendi…"

Abby hugged her hard. "I miss her too, but we have to stop these people from hurting anyone else. Let me take the necklace."

Mom kissed Abby's cheek, though she had to stand on her tiptoes to do it. She passed the necklace to Abby. "Yes. I trust you, Abby. I know you'd never let anything bad happen to Tommy. You are one of my kids, after all."

Abby blushed, and I saw how much Mom's faith in her meant. "I won't let you down, Mom." After the Reclaimers had killed Abby's parents, she'd struggled with trusting herself.

Her eyes locked on mine, and we shared an understanding. By watching over me, she could fulfill two promises, one to Wendi and one to Mom. At that moment, Abby couldn't have been more my sister if we'd been twins.

"When do we go?" I asked, hoping the answer was "now." Mom was tired, stressed, and worried about us. I hated to add to it, but a quick up-and-back would take it off the pile of things that worried her.

"Now, if everyone is cool?" Alyx looked at Mom, who nodded.

I went and hugged her, and she returned it at full force. "You be careful," she said. "I can't lose you."

I felt guilty for wanting to go, but I had to do this. People died in that attack, and I needed to protect those I could. "I will. Love you."

"Love you too, sweetheart." She let go, and I crossed to stand next to Alyx. Abby took a seat and settled the necklace around her neck. "Can you hear me, Sparky?"

I winked at her. "Roger that, Goose." Her growl sounded in my head, and I laughed, drawing a couple of odd looks.

Alyx opened the portal onto the station. "Stay close. The airlocks are open, and I'll keep air around us until we seal them again."

We stepped through the portal and onto Omega Squad's greatest failure.

The station's flight deck reminded me of the aircraft carriers I'd seen in movies. According to the schematics Marcel had found, the prison, living quarters, and other essentials were a level down. The only other thing up here was a huge storage area and the flight control center.

Three yellow-marked lanes led to the transport exits of the landing bay. The walls, perforated with grates, and the ceiling were a dull gray color from what I could tell in the low light. Pallet jacks, rolling carts, and other equipment had withstood the vacuum of space since they were attached to the walls by cables. Some had flipped over, but the artificial gravity had held most upright.

The control room, with its windows set in riveted metal cases, sat in one corner. The rear wall had a double-sized cargo door that led back into the storage areas and to a lift to the lower level. The metal podium next to the door was our target. We could have gone into the control room, but the panel in the bay had what we needed. It could have been the Megadrome's detention cells, and that didn't do anything to alleviate the feeling that this was a trap.

Overlooking the Earth through the transport bays, surrounded by a translucent globe of energy, stood the molecular reassignment device, or as we called it, the death ray.

It looked like a cross between old-fashioned anti-aircraft guns and a robot. Multiple arms jutted from the sides of the metal body. A transparent sphere, at least ten feet in diameter, rested at the end of the weapon barrel. Most likely, it focused the beam's energy into the pattern Marcel had described. Another larger sphere hung from a metallic arm below the orb.

This weapon had killed billions of people, and here I was in the same space as it. Part of me wanted to puke at the thought of so many deaths.

With the artificial gravity on, we walked across the steel floor like we were still on Earth. The emergency lights gave the open space an eerie glow. The shadowed bulkheads made me think of a bad horror flick.

"Stay close. I can only keep the air in for so long," Alyx said, as we moved across the bay. "The override controls are there."

We headed toward the control room. I stuck right behind him as I looked around, not wanting to step out of the pocket of oxygen he held around us.

We reached the control stand beside the rear doorway. I wondered how many criminals and Dark Brigade members died when Dominion opened the hatches and launched them into the vacuum of space. Given what I'd seen of justice, I wasn't sure if they'd deserved their fate or not. Were there people confined here like in the Block back on Earth? Caught up in events out of their control and branded a criminal? I doubted I would ever get an answer.

The lights intensified, and a blue field formed over the open bay door. Air hissed through the grates, as the station's life support kicked on.

"In a half-hour or so, we should have a breathable atmosphere," Alyx said.

I nodded. "We should look at the death ray while we wait. What is the white energy surrounding it?"

"It looks like a magical shield, but there isn't a mage in sight maintaining it." Alyx led us halfway down the bay before stopping. "I want to try something. Just stay close."

He sat on the floor, mumbling words I couldn't hear. I dropped down next to him and felt the energy flowing. He sat like a statue, only his mouth moving, as he studied the docking bay.

The force field sealed the area to keep in the pressure and air. They must also have allowed ships to take off and land through it. Having to deal with decompression of the landing area every time a ship came or went wouldn't make much sense. I wondered what other technological wonders the abandoned station hid.

With the lights on, I saw all the signs of damage around the room. Stains covered parts of the walls and floor, though I couldn't tell if it was oil or blood.

The inflated tires of the cargo baskets had blown out, along with part of the forklift's exposed motor. Debris collected in the corners of the bay closest to the force field, not that I wanted to know what the piles contained.

Alyx spoke a few words, and a blue nimbus encased the white field surrounding the massive weapon. Inside the protective sphere, a conduit as thick as my thigh ran down to vanish beneath the steel floor.

The blue light brightened as Alyx continued to mumble under his breath. Did the white protective shield completely encircle the machinery, or was it possible to go under the floor and up inside the white light? For that matter, if we cut the conduit, would the weapon cease to function? For once, this might be an easy mission.

I fought not to get my hopes up.

Alyx finished casting whatever spell it was and looked around. The blue light winked out as he returned his focus to the situation at hand. "What a colossal waste of time. I don't know any more about the protection sphere than when I sat down."

"I had a thought," I said, as he stared at the death ray. "What if we cut the power supply to the weapon? No power, no shooting."

He stood and walked to the orb, his phantom legs barely visible under him. On the list of strange things, watching an amputee walk at full height with no lower legs hit the top ten, for sure. Since I didn't think there was breathable air yet, I stayed close. He paced in front of the protection sphere, his hands tracing patterns in the air. Another spell?

"Well?" I asked, impatient to know what was running through his wizard's brain. "Do you have a plan, or will mine work?"

He shook his head. "I'm not sure, but you might be able to burn through the steel plates and cut the power. We'll need to let the atmosphere come up to full. Let's check the monitor."

I followed him to the control panel. The readout confirmed full atmosphere in ten minutes. "So, when we've got air, I'll try to burn through the floor and sever the power, and we're done."

He smiled. "Not quite. We still have to destroy the weapon, or the Brotherhood can repair the damage, and they are back in business."

"Oh." I hadn't thought of that. Another idea occurred to me. "Once we cut the power, I can amplify the current coming in, use it to overload the death ray, and boom, no more gun."

"It might work," Alyx said, a big grin crossing his face. "Even with all the protection, we could fry it. Excellent idea."

We waited until the air pressure readout showed green. Alyx let the bubble we'd been in go, and I found where I thought the conduit would be from the direction it came off the device. "I think I can cut here." I pulled the energy together and was about to fire. "Alyx, you might want to back up. Accidents tend to happen around me."

"Good point." He jogged away and stood by the door. Twenty feet or so was a good enough buffer.

I let loose a stream of lightning into the metal floor. The spot glowed red and then orange until it grew to white. I cut off the juice and fired a concentrated blast into the center of the glowing metal. Nothing happened. I tried again with the same result.

*Third time is the charm.*

The floor around the site I was cutting shattered, throwing shrapnel in all directions. Red-hot pieces hit me in the legs and torso. A rush of misery and a fresh burst of energy flowed into me from the impact. Acrid smoke wisped from where the hot metal had torn and burnt my clothes. Being Gifted is tough on your wardrobe. The rattle of metal scattering across the floor filled the air. I looked at the death ray to see if there'd been any change and was not let down.

Chunks of shrapnel hit the protective sphere. The barrier turned from white to red, and the pieces of the floor dissolved. I turned to look at Alyx as alarms clattered over the loudspeakers. He tried to run to me. His face had lost all color as the scene unfolded. A bolt of red energy flashed out of the doorway behind him, dropping him to the floor.

He didn't move.

5

Yelena, mage of the Brotherhood of Midnight, entered the room wearing a form-fitting black gown. She was even lovelier than I remembered from before. Her long silver hair hung loose down her back. Two twisted braids ran from her forehead, circling her head like a crown. "Thomas, so good of you to join me. I've been waiting for you, darling."

"Abby, don't pull me back. I have to get Alyx," I mumbled, as low as I could without drawing too much attention. Yelena couldn't hear me at this distance, but it left me few options for charging forward to grab him. "Just talk about anything, or she'll control me."

*Got it, Sparky.* Abby's voice was loud in my head.

When Yelena took Reaper in Dallas, Pepper had broken the spell by helping me fight until I pulled free of Yelena's mental grip. I hoped this would work now. If it didn't, I'd be her puppet. A very happy puppet, if her kiss had been any indication, but a puppet nonetheless. As I blushed, I was grateful Abby couldn't hear my thoughts.

I walked toward the beautiful but evil mage. I needed to keep her talking so I could grab Alyx and get out of here. "Where's your pet? Did Reaper run off on you? Is that why you're looking for me?"

Her laugh was low and throaty. I had to admit she was a striking woman if you got past the Brotherhood of Midnight part. "Thomas, so full of questions, so lacking in brains. How I do enjoy our rendezvous." She paused and considered me before a broad smile appeared on her face. "No passengers in your head this time. You will make an excellent minion."

*You know this bitch?* Abby snarled. *She certainly is nice to look at, but I wouldn't turn my back on her.*

*I wasn't planning on it, but I need to get to Alyx and get us out of here.* I kept walking, concentrating on Abby's voice and the distance to Alyx. "Why don't you whistle up your dog and let me finish what I started in Dallas? I'm sure Reaper is itching for a rematch."

She wagged a finger at me. "Now, now. I need many servants to carry out my plans, and Reaper has his tasks to accomplish. Your tasks would be much more pleasurable." She leaned forward slightly in a pose my mother would most certainly not approve.

My thinking fuzzed. I pushed back, knowing if she gained control I was finished. My thoughts went to Wendi and the sacrifice she made for us. I focused on saving Alyx, of stopping the death ray. Anything to keep my mind from falling under her control, but like I was in quicksand, the more I struggled, the faster I slid into oblivion.

*Sparky, pull your head out of your ass. Maleficent's hitting you with her hoodoo. You can fight her influence, like you did in Dallas.* I didn't feel Abby's emotions like with Pepper, but I heard the concern in her thoughts.

"Come, Thomas." The force of the compulsion increased as I moved in a fog toward Yelena. "A little more enticement?" Her dress shimmered before it dissolved. In its place, she wore a black gown of sheer material. It puddled on the floor, which is where I tried to keep my eyes.

It didn't work.

She smiled seductively as she pulled her silver hair over her shoulders, covering her chest. "Come closer, and I'll show you anything you want to see. Doesn't that sound fun?"

I nodded, even as my brain screamed to free myself from her. Some unspoken command stopped me from reaching Alyx. Yelena's invisible touch controlled my mind, directing me as I stood helpless. I felt a longing to hold her and protect her from anyone who would dare oppose her. I pushed against the tendrils of her influence, but as I closed off one, three others snaked into my brain.

*Wow. She is stunning, but this isn't a blind date. She freed Reaper. You need to fight her off.* Abby moved into panic mode. *Tommy, you've got to get away from her now.*

"Yelena," I said, slurring as if I were drunk. I couldn't pull my eyes off her. She was the most beautiful woman I'd ever seen. I tried to picture Wendi but could no longer find her in my memories. Yelena was all I could think about, even with Abby screaming incoherently in the background.

Yelena smiled at me. "Now isn't that better, Thomas? You can use your Gifts to further the Brotherhood of Midnight's plans. Together we can find the hidden site and destroy it before the others discover it."

"What site?" My addled mind forced the words out of my lips. I retained a margin of control, but it was slipping away.

She waved me off. "Don't worry about such things. We will talk business after we've sated our desires. Once you've destroyed the remote site, you will be mine forever."

*Tommy, she's a freaking psycho. If you don't get control, I'm pulling you back, and Alyx can fend for himself!* Abby's thoughts tore into my brain like a meteor streaking across the night sky.

The pain shattered Yelena's control over me, but I didn't react.

Before me, Yelena stood, fully clothed in a black jumpsuit. Her beauty faded until I saw she was an old woman. Everything with her was an illusion. Only her silver hair was real.

"Yelena, be mine?" I said, not wanting her to know I'd broken free of her control.

"Yes, my pet?" The cruel smile was back. As far as she knew, she'd beaten me. "We will be together forever. You won't have to worry about that troublesome Eiraf or the Council forcing you to do their bidding. Those fools don't even realize there is a traitor among them. You will be happy, my pet."

I needed to play along, but let Abby know without tipping my hand. Time to go after Yelena's weak spot: her vanity. "You're as pretty as Abby."

*Welcome back, Sparky. I wondered if I'd lost you there for a minute. Time to ice this bitch.*

The mage sniffed. "I do not know who this Abby is, but I doubt she compares to me." She adjusted her dress to better expose her breasts. "Come along. We have much to do."

I walked faster than I should have, but I'd only get one shot at this. I gathered the energy in my core and flung out my hand, throwing a bolt of lightning at her back.

A white glow flashed as the energy shattered against it.

"Foolish boy." She rounded on me, her face twisted in an angry sneer. "You dare attack Yelena Nightbringer?"

I threw another bolt at her, knowing it wouldn't do anything, but maybe it would distract her. "You're looking old, Yelena. Might be time for some beauty cream." I shot a series of blasts her way, edging toward Alyx as I did.

"Who are you to insult my beauty!" she screamed, her voice crackling with rage. "I am the most beautiful woman you have ever seen, and to think I offered you my love."

"Love? I doubt you understand the meaning of the word, you old hag." I dumped every possible ounce of scorn and pity into those words. She'd made mistakes, and her anger would prompt more.

Her mouth opened to fire back but closed instead. She laughed, her hands coming up in surrender. "Very good. You seek to rescue your fallen. Well played." With a flip of her wrist, a black portal opened. "Slither, take care of the boy and bring me the mage."

Whatever stepped out of the portal wasn't human. He stood around six feet tall with thick arms and legs like a bodybuilder, but the most prominent feature was his face. If you merged a snake and a man, this would be what you got. He had vertical nose slits and an over-sized mouth, but his eyes were human. His skin pattern reminded me of a rattlesnake. A long tail lashed back and forth behind him like an angry cat.

"Yes, mistress. I will do as told." His voice held a sibilant rasp to it, though I understood him easily. He bowed to Yelena before he fixed his glare on me.

She rubbed his bald scalp. He purred at her touch. "You may eat the boy, but don't harm the mage. He is in stasis and will not bother you." Her gaze locked on mine. "You have spurned me for the last time, Thomas." With that, she stepped through the portal.

I turned toward him. "Just let me take Alyx, and I'll be gone. You aren't my enemy, and I don't want to fight you."

Abby's voice went back to regular volume. *You aren't in court, you know. Mom might be able to pull it off, but I don't think it's working.*

Slither leapt over Alyx's prone form, pivoting in the air so his tail cracked across my chest and sent me sliding across the floor. Pain shot through me, and the impact rattled my teeth. Energy surged through me from the absorbed blow. So much for the negotiator.

*You might want to fight. Or are you waiting for Big and Scaly to tire of beating you?*

I rolled to the side. Slither's tail slammed into the floor where I'd been with enough force to dent the metal. Climbing to my feet, I flung a bolt of lightning into his chest. Instead of dodging, he spread his arms wide, head back, and hissed into the air. As I watched, Slither's shoulders widened, and his bulk increased. He now stood a head taller than me.

"On my world, we only have electrical storms. They are like your sun to my kind." He rushed me faster than anyone that large should be able to and slammed into my chest, sending me flying toward the death ray. I skidded across the floor and grabbed the hole I'd created to stop myself.

Stupid idea. The skin on my hand burned from the hot molten metal I'd cut through. I screamed as I jerked my hand away, clenching it to my chest. Still, it was better than hitting the protective barrier. I doubted I'd fair better than the shrapnel.

*You aren't doing so well, Sparky. Maybe I should pull you back. Mom knows something's up.*

"No. I'll handle this overgrown garden snake." Carefully, I climbed to my feet, waiting for the next attack. When he charged, tail lashing out mid-air, I rolled and slipped behind him. I ran to grab Alyx. No sense fighting when escaping was the goal. I made it about halfway before Slither's tail knocked my legs out from under me. The strike blurred my vision and sent waves of torment through me.

He hissed in a way that I assumed was him laughing at me. Slither blocked me getting to Alyx before launching another attack, this time with his fists. He struck me in the face, but I'd braced for the shock and the mashed nerve endings. The series of blows he delivered was strong enough to kill a normal man.

Thankfully, I wasn't normal.

The power generated by his blows hit me like a tsunami. Instead of lightning, which hadn't worked so well, I encased my fist and punched him square in the chest. He staggered back with a low hiss. I followed up with three more; the last knocked him from his feet. I moved so I had Alyx at my back and then proceeded to step toward Slither.

*Damn, Sparky. That was impressive.*

Slither didn't stay down long. Using his tail, he flipped himself to his feet and ran at me. We traded blows, but while his strikes were fast, they weren't as hard as before.

*Watch out!*

Too late. The end of his tail wrapped around my neck. I got my fingers between it and my throat before he started squeezing. My feet left the floor as he lifted me, increasing the pressure. The muscles spasmed and convulsed as he tried to crush my windpipe.

"I will kill you slowly, and then my mate and I will eat you. You are a worthy opponent, and I will honor that."

"Didn't your mother tell you not to play with your food?" I said with the last of my breath before the pressure started making air scarce. The misery intensified as the pressure grew. The corners of my vision darkened.

*I'm pulling you back.*

"No," I groaned, concentrating on converting the energy in me to heat.

My hands glowed. Heat seared Slither's flesh, cutting through his tail. He grabbed his wounded appendage, dropping me to the floor. The two-foot section from the burned end to the tip fell to the floor with a wet, sickening thud. He wailed, head back like a wounded animal, which I guess he was.

Air rushed back into my abused lungs, and I rejoiced in not being used as a squeaky toy. Air ran across the abrasions caused by nearly being strangled and set my injured throat on fire.

I looked up, expecting to see blood pumping from the wounded tail, but the heat had sealed it shut. A fact the now very angry, very large serpent dude readily grasped.

I'd just gotten to my feet when Slither pounced on me. His hands locked around my throat. His mouth pushed closer to my face and his tongue flickered across my skin. I was guessing this wouldn't be a goodnight kiss. Green liquid dripped from the approaching fangs. I kicked him hard between his legs and got no reaction.

He laughed. "I am not a weak human." His face drew within inches of mine. His breath stank like dead rodent and mold. My lungs labored to pull in air. I fought to keep the fangs away from me.

I slammed my fist into the lower part of his jaw, snapping it closed with great force. His tongue didn't fare so well. It dropped to the floor to join his severed tail. He might beat me, but he'd have a few reminders of our fight.

His grasp loosened. He grunted and renewed choking me. My next punch barely did anything as my arms began to grow heavy from lack of air. I was running out of options, and we both knew it.

Abby's voice sounded in my head. *You've got two seconds before I bring you back. Alyx will find a way out.*

I grasped his wrists. As my hands heated up, Slither did the smart thing and disengaged before I burned his arms off. I needed to finish this and fast.

Slither threw me to the ground, trying to keep my hands away from him. I fell face-first, igniting my earlier injuries. Slither leapt on my back while I was down.

Without thinking, I fired a sustained blast of energy into the floor in front of me. We shot toward the death ray, the beam acting like a jet engine to propel me across the smooth floor, taking the startled serpent with me. I kept the energy flowing, speeding us toward the weapon's protective barrier. As we reached the hole I'd blasted in the floor, I cut the power and grabbed the opening, halting my momentum.

The sudden stop threw him headlong into the shield at full speed. It acted like a paper shredder on his body. In a few seconds, the snake-man lay splattered on the floor, reduced to a puddle of green ooze.

I returned to Alyx, leaving Yelena the burned-off parts of her pet snake. Once again, I was glad Mom hadn't seen it. She hates snakes.

Come to think of it, so do I.

6

Alyx and I stepped back into the commissary where Mom, Dad, and Abby had relocated to allow Marcel to dig into Harker's systems. The unconscious Alyx lay stretched out on the floor with me on top of him. I sat up and got ready for the lectures to begin.

Mom caught sight of me and pounced like a starving cat on a fat mouse. "What happened to you?" She rounded on Abby. "You were supposed to pull him back at the first sign of trouble."

Dad put his hand on her arm. "Susan, there is a perfectly rational explanation." He shot me a *this better be good* look

"Can I have a Mountain Dew?"

Mom started to protest, but I cut her off.

"I'll tell you the whole story, but I'm really thirsty."

Abby walked into the kitchen to get my drink while Mom checked on a befuddled Alyx as he tried to sit up.

"I'm fine, just need a few minutes. I'd like to hear what happened as much as you."

Mom's face burned red. "Thomas George Ward, this better be the most convincing story you've ever told or so help me God…"

Abby handed me a glass of Dew, and I took a few gulps. While the bubbles tore at my abused throat, I needed the liquid to moisten my mouth. I sat on the floor beside Alyx, who cradled his head in his hands.

I launched into the story, telling about the sphere around the death ray, Alyx getting zapped, Yelena trying to take over my mind—to which Abby happily contributed color commentary—and the fight with the snake dude. Mom wanted to disagree with Abby's decision to let me stay.

"I tried to just grab Alyx and return here. Abby wanted to pull me back a few times but abandoning him to the Brotherhood would have been a death sentence." I finished off my drink. "Mom, we are in a war, and all of us have to fight. I can't sit on the sidelines and let the Brotherhood kill everyone."

She sighed. "I agree with what you're saying, but when I look at you, I don't see a seventeen-year-old. I see my two-year-old, holding my fingers as we walked around the old farmhouse. I see the baby I rocked to sleep every night. You're going to have to let me worry. For a long time, you were all I had."

Tears trickled from the corners of her eyes, so I got up off the floor and hugged her. "I love you, Mom."

"Love you too, honey."

I released her and got another soda. Things were different now than in Redemption, and overall, we were safer here than we ever were there. No Brunner or Powell, no trips to the Block, and no Reclaimers hassling me whenever they could. The easy choice would be to hide here and let it play out, but easy is seldom right. I would fight, as would the rest of my family. We'd already lost people, and I hoped we wouldn't lose any more, but the reality was that people die in combat.

Alyx groaned. "I'm getting too old for this." I offered my hand to help him up. He took it, but then stopped. His legs were gone. "I'll need time to restore myself."

Abby swooped in and lifted him into a chair at the nearest table. "There you go. Do you want a drink?"

"Water, please," he said, shooting her a grateful smile. "Go over what Yelena said again. I'm not sure I caught it all the first time."

I took a seat across from him and repeated her words as accurately as possible. My brain had been fogged out with her attempt to control me. Abby sat the glass in front of Alyx. I drummed my fingers on the table, trying to remember. "She mentioned me needing to do a task for her. One Reaper wasn't doing. Something about destroying a hidden site?"

Abby pulled up a chair, as did our parents. "She called it a remote site. Remote to what?"

Alyx shook his head. "I have no idea."

"I have a guess," Marcel said as he strolled into the commissary. He carried his tablet in one hand and a printout in the other. "I found notes in the death ray's specs that reference a site on Earth built to control the weapon. It was the backup in case the team failed."

"Then why didn't they use it after we killed the station's crew?" Dad asked as Marcel pulled up a chair.

Marcel caught my eye. "Usually, I prefer these as a weapon to defend my bruh, but I'll just sit in it today." Marcel never tired of reminding me he hit Turk with a chair to keep him from beating me senseless. Leave it to Marcel to throw shade at me in the middle of discussing a death ray.

I rolled my eyes at him. "Just answer the question, Mr. Wizard."

"Back off, dude. From the records, there were only about twelve people in the Dark Brigade who had classified clearances, split into two teams of six. The main group failed to get to the International Gifted Detention Station. The backup squad ended up taking the weapon to the station, assembling it, and firing it at Earth. When the Brigade backups were killed, it broke the chain-firing event, and the station returned to its default location over Tokyo." He laid out the printout, showing old photos. "These are the only images I found about the teams. I can pick out Nightingale, Twitch, and Stonewall. The rest aren't in focus enough to make them out."

Dad scooped up the pages and pointed. "That's Ignite, if I'm not mistaken. It's hard to believe all these Gifted belonged to the Dark Brigade."

"I'm still working to decrypt the file share. Hopefully, there's a lot more information on this. At least it's a start." He tapped on his tablet for a couple of seconds, then turned it to face the rest of us. "On the day of the attacks, the death ray fired at Tokyo and headed to Beijing next. At nine a.m. local time, the weapon fired at all targets in range. So far this time around, the station hasn't moved, but I don't know if that's due to the first attack being a one-shot accident, or if a new schedule is in place."

"I guess the big question is, can we find out if it moves?" Mom said as she took the pictures from Dad. "We'd at least get some advanced notice."

"Maybe." Marcel rubbed his chin, thinking it over. "If I set the console to monitor it, I might be able to get early data on the engines firing. I'll have to check into it."

Abby snorted. "Show me something techie you can't accomplish. If Mr. Fix-it were here, we'd rule the world."

"Oh, Warden wants to talk to us. I didn't mention anything about Castle or Boulder." Marcel didn't look up from the tablet as he spoke. "I wasn't sure what I should say, so I just told her I'd tell you, Ranger."

"You did the right thing, Marcel," Dad said. "I have no idea what to tell her myself." He glanced at mom, who shrugged. "Can we contact her?"

"She asked for us to come to Atlanta, if possible." He stared at the tablet as if he would bore a hole in it.

"Marcel, honey, what's going on?" Mom put her hand on his shoulder. "What are you not telling us?"

"Nothing. We're going to have to let Warden know about Boulder sacrificing himself to save us, and it's my fault. I should have wired up the self-destruct."

"It is not your fault. Boulder made the choice to push the button instead of following the plan."

"Marcel, Boulder wanted a suicide mission after Salvo died," Abby said, her voice low and menacing. "He couldn't bear the guilt, so he took the easy way out,"

Mom gasped. "Abby. That is no—"

"Let her talk." Dad's face had gone rigid, like he'd been turned to stone. I realized he'd snapped into soldier mode. "Go on, Abby."

"When Wendi died, it would have been easy to go after the Reclaimers and kill as many as I could, but I couldn't do that to my family. It was selfish. Boulder lost his family. He had nothing left, so he chose to die. If it hadn't been at Castle, it would have been somewhere else."

"Abby's right," I said, lightly punching Marcel in the arm. "There was nothing any of us could do to change the outcome."

"Marcel, I've known the Underground for a long time," Alyx said. "They are a loose-knit organization, not a family like yours is."

"Ours is," Mom corrected him. "You and Nico are as much family to us as Blaze and Pepper are. You better remember that, oh high and mighty wizard."

Alyx cut in. "Pepper? Pepper Spray died years ago. What are you talking about?"

Mom's face flushed and her eyes grew wide. The look was mirrored by the rest of us around the table. "Tommy, you might want to explain this one."

"Sure." The sudden change in topic threw me for a loop. "In Dallas, Reaper used his scythe on me."

"He what?" Alyx's face reflected my startled expression. "How aren't you dead? He killed Pepper that way."

"Well, dead isn't quite accurate." I fumbled for the right words. "When the scythe hit me, it pulled me into it, but it didn't sever me from my body. I found Pepper's spirit in there, and together we broke out."

"You broke out? So, Pepper came back to life?" Alyx looked confused, and I couldn't blame him. Metaphysics was way over my head.

"Not really. I returned to my body and brought her with me. For a while, she shared my brain." I glanced at Abby and Marcel, waiting for a smart-ass comment. They both shook their heads at me. "When we got to Harker, Marcel found her body."

"Wait a minute," Alyx said, holding up his hands. "We buried her. I was at the funeral. This makes no sense."

"I know it doesn't, but it's what happened." I took a deep breath and plunged into the rest. "Reaper removed her soul, but her body survived."

"After a while, her body would have died, but someone put it into a stasis capsule," Marcel said, in full professor mode. "Don't get me wrong. The technology is next-gen badass, but who would store soulless bodies? Totally creep-o-zoid."

"When I opened the chamber, I felt a connection. I used my Gift to push her spirit back into her body. It worked, and now she's here and watching over Blaze."

"She's alive?" Alyx's expression warred between joy and disbelief. "What's wrong with Blaze?"

Aw, man. I guess we didn't do a very good job of keeping Alyx informed with the collapse of Dallas and fleeing Castle. Does Hallmark make a card for "Your friend is dying, and your dead friend is alive again.?" I didn't think so, but in this case, it would have come in handy.

Mom leapt into the fray. "Blaze has lung cancer. Makeda tried to cure it, but it had gone too far." She paused a moment. "We brought him to Harker after Castle was compromised. Marcel found a reference to the healing machine, so we put him into it, in hopes the device would cure the cancer."

"I found out after we got here the machine re-writes a person's DNA. It's actually the prototype for the death ray the Dark Brigade used to attack the Earth."

Alyx waved his hands. "Wait, so you put Blaze in the death ray machine? What were you thinking?"

"Alyx, Blaze was almost dead," Dad said in his no-nonsense tone. "This was the only chance to save his life, so we took it. The other alternative was to let him die. Would you have made a different decision?"

Alyx didn't respond.

"You've been hit with a lot. Let me go get Pepper. I know she'll want to see you." Mom said as she rose from her seat and headed toward the med bay.

"She's really alive?" Alyx asked, hope and disbelief mingling in his voice. "I thought I'd lost her all those years ago."

"So did Blaze," I said, knowing it would hurt, but he needed to remember Pepper loved Blaze and not him. "He didn't even get to see her before we put him into the device."

Alyx's eyes went from joyful to haunted. "I know how she feels about him." He collected himself and returned to the Alyx I knew. "Still, she is one of my best friends, and I am happy she is back." He stared down the empty hallway.

Abby raised her eyebrows at me, but I shrugged. We didn't have time to get into the romantic history of the old Stryke Force team, but here we were anyway. Alyx wouldn't be focused until he'd seen Pepper, and we needed to address Yelena's presence on the station more than we had. I felt sorry for him, knowing how it had to hurt to lose someone you love, not only her dying, but in her choosing Blaze over him.

A few minutes later, Mom walked next to the wheelchair as they came down the hall and over to our table. Pepper let out a shriek of glee as she saw Alyx. They both cried as they embraced after such a long time. Words flowed back and forth, but I'd stopped listening. My memories went to Wendi, and how I'd give anything for that to be her in the wheelchair.

I didn't know how long they'd talked. I was lost in my own world.

"Tommy," Mom said, as she touched my face. "You ready to finish discussing the situation with Alyx?"

"Yeah, I'm ready."

I put the top on the memory box and focused on the issues at hand. One day, I'd see Wendi again.

One day. But not today.

7

"Where were we?" Dad asked, as we resumed our discussion from earlier. "We were talking about Warden and Atlanta, correct?"

"Yeah, she wants us to drop by for a visit," Abby said with a snort. "Even from Castle, the trip wasn't the easiest."

"At least we don't have to wrestle the wildlife anymore." I grinned at her.

Alyx chuckled. He still held Pepper's hand like she'd vanish if he let go. Pepper didn't seem to mind, though I wondered what she thought of the whole thing. "I'll teleport you to Atlanta, if you'll let me."

"If you don't mind, we'd appreciate your assistance. It would be best to inform Warden face-to-face." Dad sounded relieved to be talking about something other than Pepper's resurrection. "If everyone can be ready, we'll leave in the morning. Alyx and Tommy need to rest before they leave base again."

"You boys can handle the trip to Atlanta," Mom said, after a moment. "Pepper and I need to get Mimi out of the hospital room for a day. I don't like her spending all her time watching over Oliver."

Dad shrugged. "I'll meet Tommy and Alyx back here tomorrow at nine. Tommy, we'll want combat gear, just in case."

"I'll be ready, but I need to talk to Alyx and Abby for a minute."

"I'm headed to the Bat-cave," Marcel said. "I need to lock down Harker as much as possible and dig into the systems more."

"I'll catch up with you in a few," Abby told him, then turned to me. "Mr. Wizard needs somebody to keep him company."

"Marcel, please notify the Underground about our arrival schedule," Dad said, before he followed Mom and Pepper out of the commissary.

"What's up, Sparky?" Abby said.

"Sorry, I wanted to discuss Yelena with Alyx and wanted you here since I was fuzzy for parts of the meeting."

"And that's different from normal how?" She smirked at me.

I refrained from flipping her off. Gotta love siblings.

Alyx waited, but he had a worried look on his face. After a moment, he prompted me. "So, Yelena?"

"Right," I said, collecting my thoughts. "She mentioned the remote station, but she also said there is a traitor within the Council."

"She said, 'Those fools don't know there is a traitor among them,'" Abby said. "Those were her exact words."

Alyx smiled. "Everything about Yelena is an illusion and lies. She was trying to sow doubt in your mind, is all."

"I don't believe that, Alyx. She thought I was under her control when she said it."

"Sparky plays dumb rather convincingly." Abby grimaced. "Tommy's right. If she believed he was under her control, why would she lie?"

A frown creased Alyx's face. "Did she say anything else?"

"Not about that. My goal was to get you and me to safety. I took the opportunity to blast her, but I ended up having to fight Slither instead." I racked my brain for any other detail, but none came to me. Should I have questioned her further? Would it have worked, given the caveman impersonation I did to keep her off guard? No sense worrying about it now, but in the future, I needed to plan more strategically. "Abby, can you think of anything else?"

She shook her head, her purple and red hair swinging side to side.

"Nothin'. If you don't need me, I'm going to go keep Marcel company. I don't want him obsessing over Boulder."

"Thanks," I said as she got up and left the room.

"Tommy, I appreciate you pulling me out of that mess. It's becoming a habit." He rubbed his face. "Yelena may have been there waiting for us. Going there was an obvious move."

"When the shrapnel hit the shield around the death ray, it turned red. It might have warned her there were intruders," I said.

"True," Alyx agreed, with a nod. "Charles isn't fully recovered from the Kra-kelal attacks, so he couldn't have betrayed us. The rest have been on the Council for so long, why would they help the Brotherhood?"

"I don't know. What do you offer a person with immortality?" I got to my feet. "Let me go get my gear ready for tomorrow, so we can talk to Warden."

I returned to my room and got my combat suit out. Until I got to Mr. Fix-it's home workshop, I'd have to go helmetless. The Harker machine lacked the ability to create them. Not that wearing a helmet had worked out very well so far.

I used the black box to zap a fresh current into me. After the fight with Slither, I needed a charge. I showered and climbed into bed. My Gift would heal all the damage Slither had dished out, but I still needed sleep after the long day.

And to think there had been a time when Brunner was the biggest problem in my life.

---

I got up and dressed. Once I put together my gear and slid the new earpiece into place, I headed out. Marcel had found older commlinks in the supply area on the third sub-level.

I finished preparing and returned to the commissary to find Pepper and Alyx talking. Even from across the room, I saw tears on his face. She looked uncomfortable as he clutched her hand. I felt horrible that we hadn't told him about Pepper, but the death ray had diverted our attention from everything else.

"Hey Tommy," Pepper said as I approached their reunion. She pulled her hand away from Alyx. "I hadn't expected to see old teammates come through our hidden base."

I shrugged. "You never know who you'll run into around here. How are you feeling?" I slid into an empty chair.

It was her turn to shrug. "Tired. Gabriel ran diagnostics, and there's no permanent damage, just some atrophy from the long stasis. It's a bit more difficult since I've got some mechanical parts. I have to watch overextending the bio parts."

Dad walked into the commissary. "You two ready to go?" He wore his black combat suit with the gold lightning bolt insignias and accents.

"Going with the Gauntlet suit? Isn't it a bit flashy?" I asked. Dad never ceased to amaze me.

"Might as well get some use from it." A sly smile crossed his face. "Your mother pointed out it looks a lot more impressive than the all-black one. Maybe the Underground will be awed."

"You look like a psychotic bee," Pepper said with a laugh. "In the Bronx, they'd mug you for the gold."

"That's why I hung out in Manhattan." Dad turned to Alyx. "Are you ready? I'd like to get this over with, so we can concentrate on shutting down the death ray."

"Sure." He swung his cloak over his shoulders and hugged Pepper again. She looked a bit unnerved by Alyx's attention. "Would it be okay if I come visit and bring Gladiator?"

Pepper nodded. "I'd love to see the schmo in person."

It was interesting that she didn't mention seeing Alyx again, just Gladiator. He didn't notice the slight if the puppy dog expression on his face was any indication.

"Great. I'll be back soon." He stood on his phantom legs and summoned a portal. We stepped through into the center of the transportation building in the Underground's Atlanta base.

The room held the translocator the Underground used to move

between the destroyed cities of the world. The tech looked up from the comic book he was reading, waved us on, and ignored us.

We left the building.

The base could have been a small town out of a movie, but it was built deep below what had once been Atlanta. Brightly painted buildings rose toward the ceiling, which was lost in the dimness beyond the lights meant to replicate the sun. A young couple pushing a baby in a stroller passed us, just like in any other town.

Molly sat outside the translocator building's door on a barrel. She had her hair back in a ponytail and wore an "I Love Science" t-shirt under a black hoodie.

"Hey. You guys certainly make an entrance," she said. A goofy grin plastered on her face. "Get it? The portal is an entrance."

I laughed. It was good to see Molly again. She'd rescued me from Dr. Goat and the Cartel when I'd been dumb enough to get caught. In Dallas, she'd fought alongside us when the Reclaimers attacked. I never knew when she'd pop up to save the day. "Hey, Molly. Are you our guide?"

She nodded, her grin turning into a pout. "Yeah, Mom is still pissed about me sneaking off to spy on the Cartel. She's threatened to snap a collar on me if I do it again."

"Where are we meeting Warden?" Dad asked.

Molly quirked an eyebrow. "Somebody have a sale on gold plating? You could be one of those statues I saw in Las Vegas."

"We're here to meet with Warden," Dad said.

Alyx cut in smoothly. "I've got a couple people I need to talk to. I'll find you once I'm done."

"Roger that." Dad turned back to Molly. "Can we get going?"

"Sure thing, Ranger." She hopped off the barrel and took us down the main street. People stopped to watch the strange progression as we went. Whispers in awed tones followed us.

The suit might not have impressed Molly, but the rest of the Underground knew instantly Cyclone Ranger was here. More people lined the street as we continued. Calls of greeting came from various members of the crowd, which Dad acknowledged with a warm smile. He was in his element: the returning hero.

We reached a long, squat, white-washed building. Sheets of metal covered the windows and two armed men guarded the doorway. They stepped aside as we approached. I heard one remark on Dad's presence with a reverent tone.

We entered a large, dimly lit foyer of an old, single-level office building. The floor was clean, but I noticed a few cracked tiles. Hallways ran off to the sides and deeper into the building. More guards lounged at foldout tables. A couple of card games were in progress, but everything stopped as the people noticed Dad.

Izanami, clad in a dark vest and pants, stepped out of the shadows. Her long, jet black hair was pulled into a ponytail that reached her waist.

"Ranger. Tommy." She nodded to each of us in turn. "Molly, I'll take it from here."

I winked at Molly. "I'll catch you before I leave."

She winked back. "You better, or I'm leaving you to Dr. Goat next time."

Izanami motioned for us to follow. She took the left-hand hallway, following it until we reached the last door. She tapped twice before opening the door and taking us in.

The room held three walls of surveillance equipment. The displays tracked Reclaimer and Protectorate feeds as well as updated from all of the Underground's sites. Warden sat with two women who worked the complex systems that protected the Underground's home base.

Warden turned to greet us. Her red hair glowed in the monitor lights. She looked tired, and I couldn't blame her. Between running the Underground, and the death ray firing at the cities her people inhabited, she had a lot to deal with. She stretched her hand out to shake Dad's. "Good to see you both. Sorry, I didn't know this was a formal visit, or are you going for the cybernetic bumblebee look?"

I stifled a laugh. Dad wasn't used to being the butt of people's jokes. With the addition of the news we had for Warden, I doubted he was in the mood. But if it irritated him, it wasn't evident in his response.

"Warden, I wish we were here under better circumstances." He glanced at the images being displayed around us. "I have some bad news—"

Warden cut him off. "Boulder is dead. We intercepted the Reclaimers' communications as they attacked your base. The troops inside reported fighting him, and then the whole place blew up."

"He died a hero."

"No. He died a selfish child. There is a time and place to trade your life for others, but his whole reason for leaving us was to avoid dealing with Salvo's death. I'm just glad he didn't take all of you with him."

"What do you mean?" I asked, confused. "Boulder triggered the self-destruct so we could get away."

Warden shook her head. "We believe he took a communications device off one of the Reclaimers and radioed in your coordinates. By the time we decoded the message we intercepted, it was too late to warn you, but it was definitely Boulder."

"What?" Shocked didn't begin to describe how I felt. Boulder had saved me multiple times and given his life to stop Castle from falling into Reclaimer hands, buying us time to get away. "That makes no sense. Parasite controlled him in Dallas. Waxenby is still dealing with the aftereffects of the mind control. Maybe it happened to Boulder as well. Can we hear it?"

Warden went to the console and played the audio clip of Boulder's voice. As he spoke, I noticed a slight slurring. Warden nodded before saying. "Tommy may be on to something. I thought the audio was distorted, but it is possible Boulder was under some sort of control."

"It is the only thing that explains any of this. There is a difference between suicidal and killing everyone because he feels guilty." I was sure I'd stumbled on the real reason of what went down.

"Well, that explains a lot. Thank you for letting us know." Dad could have been responding to a comment on the weather for the lack of emotion in his voice. "Let's get down to the issue at hand."

Warden nodded. "Agreed. We've got footage to share with you. I think we're in big trouble." She turned and approached the techs. "Can you pull up Tokyo?"

The technician on the left tapped on her keyboard and multiple camera views displayed across four large monitors over the console.

"Zoom into sector seven," Warden said.

The image, a deserted set of streets, grew to encompass all four monitors. Dead billboards hung around the square. "This is Shibuyu Crossing in what was downtown Tokyo, right before the death ray hit," Warden informed us. "Roll the footage."

The scene started and three people ran into view.

"There are a lot of vagrants who cross into the dead zones. When you contacted us, we broadcasted the warning over loudspeakers."

"I thought people who lived in the zones died?" I asked her, curious if Dr. Goat had lied to me about why they needed the drugs.

"If you stay long enough and aren't Gifted. Not every Gifted manifests power to the point you'd recognize them." She returned to the video. "This is what happened when the death ray hit."

As the three drew closer to the camera, a flash of bright light replaced the view for an instant. When it faded, two of the people were gone. The third writhed on the ground as his body dissolved into a puddle.

"According to what we've found," Dad said, after he'd taken a moment to collect himself, "the death ray's original purpose was to mutate normal humans into Gifted. Obviously, it didn't work."

"Or did it?" Warden asked. "Why did the two completely disintegrate, but the third lingered? We've seen mutations that kill the person in the process of metamorphosis. What if that's the case here?"

Dad considered her words before answering. "How many did you lose in Tokyo?"

"Over three hundred, but four lived through the blast. None of them were listed as Gifted before the attack."

Four survived the death ray. How was that possible? "Where are they now?" I asked.

Warden turned toward me. "Still in Tokyo. We couldn't risk

bringing them here, not knowing if they would manifest an uncontrollable Gift. We've evacuated Beijing, but we may have bigger problems than the death ray."

What could be worse than the death ray firing at Underground bases?

"Bring up Beijing, zone four."

The image flashed and changed to a large park. A red-roofed building sat in the background. Hundreds of Reclaimer troops filled the area. "The Reclaimers have brought in thousands of troops. They are camped out, waiting for the death ray to fire."

"They'll all die," I said, my voice a bit more panicked than I'd like. "Why throw away thousands of lives?"

Warden locked her eyes on mine. "They are willing to sacrifice as many as it takes to make their own Gifted."

Just what the world needs, more psychotic Gifted running around. Jon was bad enough. What I saw next made my heart stop.

Like an unwanted zit on your first day of high school, Yelena stood in the center of the troops.

8

<hr>

D ad, we need Alyx here, now."

He looked at me skeptically. "Why Alyx? The real question is how she got a battalion of Reclaimers assigned to her."

"Yelena is there, and she's trouble. She can control people with her magic. Alyx needs to see this. She's in his league."

The lightbulb went off over his head. "Warden, can you have someone find Alyx for us?"

"Jennie, can you find him and bring him straight back?" Warden asked. The tech on the right nodded and left the room. "So, she's one of the bad wizards? Why, of all the times, are they involved now?"

For the next ten minutes, I studied the scene as Yelena motioned for people to move boxes and equipment around on the platform. She stood in the center of the field Dad referred to as Tiananmen Square.

Most of the men wore Reclaimer uniforms, but a few had on civilian clothes. A smaller man stood off to the side, watching the proceedings without joining in. I'd never seen him before, but he bothered me for some reason. He walked off the platform and disappeared among the soldiers. Where was he going?

"Can we pull back on the camera?" I asked, suddenly needing to

59

figure out where the man was headed. The technician did as requested. Above the platform, a transparent lens hovered over the assembled men. "This is really not good. If the lens does what I'm guessing, it will turn them all into Gifted soldiers. It's the only thing that makes sense."

"But why?" Warden asked. Her brow wrinkled as she squinted at the screen. "The Gifted aren't a threat on any level. We've been jailed or forced to live in the remnants of destroyed cities. Adding more Gifted won't change anything."

"She's not making Gifted," Alyx said, as he strode into the room. She's making creatures of some sort." His legs glowed soft blue in the dimness of the office. "They must have discovered a way to use the mutagen ray to mutate humans into a form the Brotherhood can use."

Warden's jaw dropped. "This is some next-level shit. I never thought I'd miss the old days of the Reclaimers hunting us down. Why in the world would she do that?"

"The Brotherhood of Midnight's sole purpose is to end the universe and start a new one of their liking. They will commit any action, not matter how heinous, to achieve that goal. It's why the Council fights them with everything we have."

"So, what's the plan, Alyx?" Dad asked. "This falls under your purview."

"We'll have to stop them. If Yelena is successful, the Protectorate will be the least of our problems." He stepped over to get a better view of the monitor. "Warden, how close is your base to Tiananmen Square? Can we still translocate to the city?"

"Under a mile. We have an access tunnel to the back corner of the square," Warden said, exhaustion thick in her voice. "My people aren't getting into this mess. We've got to get the other bases that will be targeted ready to move to avoid the death ray."

"We'll need someone who knows the layout of the tunnels to get us there," Dad said.

Warden barked a sharp laugh. "The last person who went with you is under an avalanche in the North Carolina mountains. I'm not sure it's the best idea to lend my people to you."

Dad rounded on Warden. "The last person who went with us almost killed us all, but now is not the time to cast blame for people's deaths."

"Enough," I said, stepping between them. "What happened is in the past, and right now, we need to stop Yelena. It won't matter who did what if the Brotherhood finds a way to destroy the universe."

Warden looked to Alyx. "Can't you just open a portal and take care of it?"

He shook his head. "No, she's blocked the square off from outside magic. If I create a portal near the barrier, she'll know, and we'll have to fight our way through all those troops."

"Warden, I will accompany Ranger." Izanami stood in the entrance. I hadn't heard the door open. She was arguably the strongest of all the Underground's Gifted, and level-headed in a fight.

"No, you won't. You are far too important to my team. I'll get one of the Beijing team to do it." Warden glanced at the petite woman. "Your mind is made up already?"

Izanami nodded once.

Warden threw up her hands. "Fine. Izanami goes with you, and no one else." She directed the next statement to Izanami. "You get them to the end of the tunnel and wait there. Do not join in any fighting. You are too important to lose."

"I'll do what is appropriate to the situation, as you have taught me, Warden."

Warden's eyes narrowed. "So, you'll fight if needed." She sighed heavily. "How I'm the leader and no one listens is beyond me."

Izanami smiled. "I listen, but you taught me to do as needed, not as told. Am I incorrect?"

"Just go, and all of you be careful. Things are getting out of hand."

Dad gestured to the door. We followed him out of the building and into the street. "We're going to need Abby for this one." Dad said. "I'll have to talk to Susan. I really need her with Marcel. He hasn't been himself lately."

Alyx opened the portal into the commissary.

"I'll wait here with Izanami," I said, not wanting to return to Harker just yet.

Dad nodded. "Be back ASAP." They stepped through the portal and were gone.

"I will return," Izanami said before turning and heading down the street.

I sat on the step outside of Warden's offices. The crowds had dispersed since we'd entered, but people still walked by. Some had small children in tow or carried packages. A couple of carts drove past with repairmen going off to work.

The Atlanta bases held less than a thousand people from what Warden had told us. Their numbers were higher with the influx of people from Beijing. I wondered if this was what the frontier towns in the movies were like. People just going about their lives, helping their neighbors.

A shadow fell over me as Warden sat down. "Everybody run off on you?"

"Sort of. Getting people and gear. I thought it would be nice to sit here for a few minutes. It's not often I get to see other people anymore."

"You've had a tough run," Warden said. "I came to Atlanta to keep Molly away from the Reclaimers. There are days I'm not sure I made the right choice. It's not an easy life down here."

I laughed softly. "It's not an easy life in Redemption either. At least I had my Mom. Who knows? They might have sent you to the Block on some made up charge."

"I doubt it. Before coming here, I was a mouse of a person. Never said 'boo' to anyone. Living here toughened me up."

I looked over at her. Her eyes were focused off in the distance. Having a Gift toughened a person up these days. When your choices were imprisonment or exile, did it matter which you picked?

"I spent my days running from bullies at the school they made me go to. I'd finally gotten free with my friends, then Wendi was killed, and Jon took off."

"Jon left right after our meeting with you," Warden said. "He is one messed up kid." She pushed her hair back over her ears. "Damn fine shot with a bow and could track anything. Just as glad to see him go, though."

There were a lot of reasons I'd like Jon to go, but I was curious as to Warden's. "Why?"

She tilted her head, thinking it through. "Hate chews a person up and leaves them hollow until they collapse from the inside out. Plus, Molly acted weird around him. Either way, he won't be back here."

Jon was charming when he wanted to be. No wonder Molly acted weird around him. I had been a babbling buffoon around Wendi. "His sister dying messed him up."

"As it would anyone, but he blames you, and I saw the show. Her death wasn't your fault." She smiled at the look on my face. "Yes, we get the news feeds down here, but Mr. Wizard sent us the actual footage. We showed it to our people to boost morale."

"It couldn't have worked then," I said, half under my breath.

She put her hand on my shoulder and waited until I looked her in the face. "Tommy, you defeated the Gauntlet. No one had ever done it before. Your team took out a squad of the toughest Reclaimers around and stopped Powell. You paid a high price, but to the Gifted who are living here, you are a hero. Add stopping Reaper in Dallas to it, and you're becoming a legend."

"Some legend. I destroyed your whole base and lost Reaper." I realized I sounded like a grumpy child. Everything I'd done had just led to a bigger mess.

"You kept the transponder from falling into Reclaimer hands, freed us, and made sure we got clear before the city collapsed. Losing one base is a small price to pay. If the Reclaimers had taken the Dallas base, we'd all be dead by now."

I wanted to believe her. For so many years, Powell and the others had told me what a loser I was so many times that I guess I'd bought into it. I knew I'd done some good, but every time I did one thing right, the consequences spiraled out of control. At this point, I wanted to take my family and hide instead of fighting against the Protectorate and the Brotherhood. How had all of this become our problem to solve? I wanted to ask her when it would all end. Instead, I said, "How have you fought for so long? I'm exhausted and ready to set it down, but you keep fighting."

She considered a moment before answering. "I know the Protectorate doesn't teach history or much pre-Protectorate literature. When I'm ready to quit, I remember this quote. 'We must take sides. Neutrality helps the oppressor, never the victim. Silence encourages the tormentor, never the tormented.' Elie Wiesel spoke those words. He survived the Nazi death camps and fought against tyranny for the rest of his life. He never stopped, so how can I?"

I thought about it. Mom had told me stories about the Nazis since the Protectorate refused to teach anything close to the truth. History lessons with Powell were propaganda or fearmongering to keep the Gifted and Normals in place. Warden was right. How could I stop fighting? "How do you know we're on the right side? The Dark Brigade killed billions of people. What if we free the Gifted just to unleash another set of terrorists on the world?"

"You don't," she said, simply. "Before the Dark Brigade, the world wasn't perfect, but people were free. Their children weren't taken and jailed. Your neighbors weren't attacking you because they thought you had some power. Did the Gifted need to be reined in? Yes, but not to the point where we are despised and murdered for being different."

"Do you think there will ever be peace?"

"Don't know, Sparky," she said with a wink. "We can only do our best. Your dad is back."

The spinning blue light grew from a pinpoint until it was large enough for Dad, Alyx, and Abby to step through. Alyx dismissed it with a wave once everyone was clear. Warden and I got to our feet.

"Ranger, after a lot of deliberation, you should take this with you." She handed him a metal box the size of my hand that she pulled out of her belt pouch. He flipped it over, but there were no markings, just a keypad on one side and a glass piece set in the other.

"What is it?" he asked.

"It is a portable translocation device. If you type in the code, it will open a connection to the closest unit. From there, the Underground can transport you wherever you need to go." She handed over an inch-thick silver disc with a larger glass eye in the center. "Set this up at your base, and it will act as a translocation receiver. That way you can travel back. It will make working together easier. Just don't open either case. You'll void the warranty."

Alyx smirked. "Nothing else?"

"It will blow your face off, but the warranty is the important part."

"Good safety tip, Egon," Abby said as Dad and I groaned.

"We really need to get you away from Mr. Wizard," I said, shaking my head. He'd infected Abby with his love of old pop culture.

"What's the code to the device?" I asked

Warden's smile brightened her face. "8675309."

Dad and Abby groaned as Warden snickered. I didn't get it, but I never did.

Alyx came over to me. "I need to protect your mind from Yelena," he said. He touched my forehead, and a jolt pierced my brain. "That should keep her from taking control of you." He went to Izanami and repeated the process.

Dad stored the devices, and we headed to the translocator. Izanami arrived, dressed in a black combat suit with knife handles sticking out of her boots. Dad gave her a comm-link and had everyone turn them on. A few minutes later, we stood in the evacuated Beijing base.

"Tommy, take point with Izanami and Abby at your back," Dad said in his commander tone. "I'll stay with Alyx so we can destroy the device they're using to convert the troops. We don't have a large enough team for a prolonged fight. If we are pushed back, we get into the tunnel and collapse it behind us. Understood?"

A chorus of affirmatives answered him. "Izanami, we'll follow you out. Mr. Wizard, you've got eyes on the target?"

Marcel's voice came over the earbud. "Affirmative, Ranger." He sounded more like himself, which was good. "Strange things are afoot at the Circle K. All the Reclaimers are out cold on the ground. Yelena must have done something since they all collapsed when she waved her arms around."

"Let's hope they stay that way," Dad said as he motioned for us to head out.

Izanami nodded and took us through the empty streets of the base. Everyone who called Beijing home had fled after the death ray struck Tokyo. It felt like a graveyard, and it would have been if we hadn't figured out the next target. Yelena's presence here confirmed we had the correct place.

We followed the sewer system for a while. Things moved in the gloom ahead of the flashlights we had to rely on. Izanami stopped us until the shadows faded from view. After more time than I ever wanted to spend in a sewer, we took a set of stairs up and into a tunnel. We reached the end, and Izanami turned off her flashlight and opened the door into the back of an old souvenir shop. Glass cases held indistinct shapes in the darkness.

We crawled to the front of the store so we wouldn't be seen. I gasped at the size of the courtyard before a huge palace. Lights swept the area, showing thousands of soldiers lying on their backs, heads toward the platform in the center. Yelena gestured wildly as she screamed into the night. The hair on my arms prickled as her power washed through the air.

Alyx slid in next to me. "We are inside her barrier."

Marcel's voice came over the comm-link. "We've got a problem." In the background I heard the familiar "ten minutes until weapon fires" message.

"So much for Plan A," Dad said, and I heard him swearing under his breath.

Why should a plan work when the chaos of charging in on the fly was oh-so-much more fun?

## 9

"Alyx, how do we take the lens out?" Dad asked as he huddled inside the souvenir shop. "We've got nine minutes to destroy it and get out."

"If you can keep her busy, I'll break the spell," Alyx said, and though he sounded cool, I sensed his panic. Yelena had knocked him cold last time, and I hadn't fared much better. Her magic was powerful, and she'd had longer to wield it than Alyx.

"Tommy, you three keep her busy, I'll get Alyx close and guard him," Dad said as he readied himself. "Mr. Wizard, mark the time. We leave at t-minus two minutes, regardless. We can't fight if we're dead." He pulled Alyx onto his back.

"Roger that," I said, running out the door. Izanami and Abby followed. Dad flew overhead as he headed off to his fight. "Mr. Wizard, you got eyes on Yelena?"

"Player, she's doing some weird dance on the platform. There's giant dogs moving around her though, and they look mean," Marcel said.

I groaned. Just what I needed, more hellhounds to fight. "Watch the dogs. They can teleport."

"They can what?" Abby said as she ran next to me. "Are you serious?"

"Welcome to bizzaro world."

We threaded our way between unconscious Reclaimer soldiers. Our stealth plan was gone, so it was a full-on fight. The courtyard looked like a toddler had upended a bucket of army men on the floor. They didn't even have weapons with them. How much magic did it take to control thousands of men and women? Or had they volunteered? The Protectorate trained their troops to obey without question. Was this another aspect of the Protector's control?

As we reached the bottom step to the platform, I motioned for Abby and Izanami to spread out. Last thing we needed was to make an easier target for Yelena. I took the stairs two at a time. I caught the flash of gold across the moonless night as Dad flew Alyx into position.

"We are engaging," I said as we reached the top of the platform.

The hellhound closest to me turned, and I realized my error. These creatures weren't the hounds I'd fought with Alyx. These were closer to giant foxes with tusks coming out of their mouths, full of jagged teeth.

"Those are hell beasts," Alyx said over the comm-link. "Watch the tusks. They're venomous."

The closest one snarled at me as I approached. Abby moved to the left and Izanami to the right. Six more of the hellhounds stalked toward us.

Yelena stood in the center of the platform, waving her arms as she chanted in an unknown language. The shimmer of a new spell barrier around only her appeared. She'd been expecting us. My guess was they moved the death ray once we had arrived. Dad landed at the far end, setting Alyx down for the real fight. Time to keep the hounds busy.

"Who's a good puppy?" I asked the closest one.

It launched at me in response.

After the fight with Slither, I decided to forgo the lightning. I concentrated a mass of energy around my fists. I met it head on. I spun to the left and lashed out with a savage punch to the side of its head. The head jerked from the blow, sending the hound tumbling sideways across the platform.

Izanami struck the nearest hellhound with a dropkick, the sound of the crack sharp as her boots impacted the creature's skull. A tusk bounced across the platform. The beast dropped on its side, down for the count. Only six more to go. I hoped they'd all be that easy, even though I knew they wouldn't be.

Izanami rolled away, escaping a second creature pouncing on her. With a quick spin, she placed both feet into the monster's belly and shoved, propelling it back into the pack where it knocked over two more from the force of the landing. The snarls and yelps increased in intensity. The pack milled around, organizing their next attack.

Abby, never one to miss an opportunity, ran past me, grabbing the downed animal by the back legs. With a scream, she waded into the pack, swinging the downed hellhound like a sledgehammer, bludgeoning its packmates with its body. The dogs scattered, trying to avoid the meat hammer she wielded. Not for the first time, I was glad Abby liked me.

I followed her in, protecting her left flank, mirrored by Izanami. The hellhounds behaved like wolves, circling the three of us, darting in, testing our defenses, and then retreating as they took damage from our blows. Pack animals always went for the weakest, striking at backs and legs before they could be hit. With the three of us in a circle, they'd have to come directly at us. The howls of frustration grew louder as their attacks were met and repelled.

"T-minus seven minutes," Marcel said in my ear. We had five minutes to get done, meet up with Alyx, and get back to Atlanta. Time wouldn't stop because it took us longer than expected. I saw Dad and Alyx at the other end of the platform, trying to break through Yelena's shields.

"We need to finish these off so we can help Ranger," I said. I punched an attacking hound in the face, breaking off one of its tusks. It howled as it retreated from me, only to be replaced by another flanking attack.

This one landed a bite on my biceps. Fire shot through my arm, but the teeth didn't pierce my flesh, thanks to my Gift absorbing the force of the attack. I reached over its head and grasped it by the ears. I spun in place, tossing it into the next attacker, bowling over the closest hellhound.

Abby swung the rapidly decomposing hound in an arc in front of her. The corpse spewed flames across the other two, who snarled and snapped at her. They shied back from her improvised weapon, both showing multiple places she'd connected with them. Instead of swinging it toward the monsters in front of her, she brought the carcass up in a smooth arc behind her and launched it at Yelena's back.

The corpse exploded as it struck her barrier, but Yelena faltered from the impact. The flaming blood from the body flowed over the invisible barrier, exposing a pattern in the shield.

Alyx shouted into the comm-link. "Now I've got her!"

"Good job, Abby," Dad said. "Finish off those dogs so we can get out of here."

A hellhound launched itself against Izanami, knocking her over. She stumbled, slamming into me. I fought to retain my balance, slipped in a slick spot on the platform, and crashed down hard, more embarrassed than hurt.

The five hounds swarmed me. I punched the closest squarely in the chest as it descended on me, the air whooshing out of its open mouth from the force of the blow. Heat and a stench like a burning carcass assaulted my senses. I gagged and stumbled back.

The second one seized my left shoulder in its maw and dug its claws into me, piercing my suit and slashing my skin underneath. Without a sudden force to trigger my Gift, the claws tore into my back. Venom covered my shoulder, burning it with the intensity of the sun. I screamed as the intense fire seeped into me.

Izanami landed on the hellhound's back and used its ears to drag its head up until it dropped me. A loud crack and the thing slumped with a broken back.

She grabbed the second monster I'd stunned and threw it at

Yelena. The creature burst as it struck her shield, staggering the mage. Abby hauled me to my feet. "You okay, Sparky?"

Izanami mule-kicked the hound charging from behind, shattering most of its teeth and knocking it off the platform.

The poison ate into my skin, corroding the nerves and sending spasms down my arm. The world spun as I stood there until my equilibrium failed, and I crashed to the ground. I forced myself back up, only to stumble and fall again. I tried to right myself, but the poison had weakened my system, and my Gift was useless against it.

Izanami and Abby fought the remaining hellhound as I regained my feet through sheer force of will.

"Thomas, come here." I heard Yelena's call as if she stood by my side. Her power washed over me but failed to work as it had the other times she'd taken control. "I will heal you. Come to me."

I whispered into my comm-link. "Play along."

Pretending to obey was far easier than stumbling across the open platform to Yelena. A tremor passed through me as I crossed the barrier she'd erected. Unable to keep my balance any longer, I fell to the floor at her feet.

"You are where you belong," she said as she put her hand on my face. "The poison will consume you soon. Only I can save you. Me, who you spurned at our last meeting. I should let you die, but I am a merciful mistress. Will you serve me?"

The surge of her power hit me, but it dissolved instead of taking control. Alyx's magic prevented her from seizing my mind. I nodded and slurred out that I would serve her. My arm and shoulder had gone completely numb as the poison worked its way through my system. Hot, acidic bile rode into my throat, threatening to spill out my breakfast as I lay on the ground in misery.

Yelena spoke. Cold flowed through me, destroying the fire as it went. The vertigo lessened as the cold became more intense, to the point I thought I'd freeze solid. Suddenly, it was all gone. I gasped for breath as I pushed myself to hands and knees. I hung my head to keep Yelena from seeing my eyes.

Another pulse of magic attempted to smother my will and impose her commands. "Go and kill the others."

"Yes, mistress," I mumbled as I stood, keeping my back to her. When I felt the protective barrier, I stopped against the invisible field. With a curse, she dropped the shield.

I spun around and fired a bolt of lightning at her.

She threw up a shield to block my attack. "How?" she shrieked. "I felt it. You were mine."

"You aren't the only mage around, you know." I opened with a series of electrical strikes, forcing her to defend against them as Dad and Alyx moved in. The three of us attacked simultaneously, keeping her on the defensive as we pummeled her shields. She yelled curses at us, countering our strikes as fast as she could.

Then it happened. A single shot of lightning pierced her defenses. She jerked back as it seared her arm, and the shield dropped. An instant later, she became transparent. Her fists beat against an invisible wall, which contained her in the center of the platform.

"What did you do to her?" I asked. She thrashed inside an invisible prison.

Her mouth opened in a wordless howl, while all the while she beat futilely against the barrier containing her.

Alyx exhaled and then slumped. I guessed the spell had taken a lot out of him.

"It's a maze construct. She's between planes until she finds her way out in a day or two, but we can destroy the lens and stop her plans."

"You should have killed her," Abby growled over the comm-link. I saw her approaching. Scorch marks covered her face and hands. She'd grown to over eight feet, straining against the combat suit Mr. Fix-it had created to adapt with her.

"I'll explain later," Alyx told Dad. "But right now, I need to be above the lens to destroy it."

"Let's go," Dad said. He put Alyx on his back and then launched into the air. "Meet us at the souvenir shop for extract."

Seconds later they were above the lens. Alyx, encased in a blue nimbus of power, worked his magic as we watched. The troops below would still die in the blast, but he'd save them from being turned into horrible monstrosities. It was a mercy.

"T-minus two minutes." Marcel sounded scared as he counted us down to the death ray strike. "You need to move. You're cutting it too close!"

No need to tell me twice. Abby led the way off the platform with me following, Izanami close behind.

Yelena had stopped the poison, but I still felt weaker than normal. My stomach screamed for food, while my head wanted sleep. We reached the edge of the platform and stopped, the soldiers all around us convulsing. A seething tide of humans rippled across the stone courtyard.

"We'll just have to push our way through," Abby said, starting down the stairs.

A series of sharp impacts came from above us as bolts of blue energy streaked from Alyx's hands and struck the lens. The material rippled under the force of the blows but held.

We ran, leaping and stumbling over twitching forms. Arms flailed out to catch our legs, trying to pull us down. It was like running through a field of emerging zombies, hungry for human flesh.

With a massive concussion that drove me to my knees, the surrounding air exploded with sound, and a rain of glass shards dropped from the sky above. I covered my face. As the shard storm slackened, I got up and followed Abby and Izanami. We moved at a steady pace through the writhing mass of Reclaimers.

Without warning, the convulsions stopped, and the soldiers stood as one, surrounding us, barring us from leaving. Arms reached out, not in attack, but grasping to hold us in place. We had a long way to get to the exit point.

I punched and kicked to clear room around me, but as one fell, another took its place. "Alyx what is going on?" I yelled into the comm-link.

"The lens was a decoy; she used her magic to try and trap us here."

Their dead eyes showed no fear or pain, just a mindless drive to restrain us. I saw the brilliant blue of the portal dead ahead, but hundreds of Reclaimers stood between us and our exit.

"T-minus one minute. Get out of there," Marcel screamed into the comm-link. I could hear the background voice, warning of the impending weapon fire.

The truth of the matter was, we weren't escaping without anything short of a miracle.

Abby's back hunched, a scream roared from her like a wounded animal. Her body expanded in all directions at once, tearing apart her combat suit. Hair shot out of her skin, covering her body.

I used both hands to knock the closest soldiers out of my way. They fell like bowling pins, but others stepped on them to push against us. They weren't fighting, just trapping us in the kill zone of the death ray.

Abby's face twisted grotesquely, elongating into a muzzle. Fangs the size of my hand replaced her normal teeth as she transformed into the largest bear I'd ever seen. She lurched forward, landing hard, her front paws cracking the flagstones under her weight. She shook her huge head, roaring a challenge.

"You've got thirty seconds," Marcel said in my ear.

Abby's comm-link lay by my feet along with the shredded remains of her combat suit. I snatched the earpiece from the ground so the Reclaimers didn't get it. I turned to the giant bear. "Abby, we need to get to the portal as fast as possible."

I didn't know if she understood, but she lunged forward, trampling the men in front of her. Her massive paws gouged flesh as she tore through the human barrier. Izanami and I ran in her wake, glad that the darkness hid the results of her bull rush through the soldiers.

"Fifteen seconds."

I went as hard as I could given the terrain, pressing to keep up with Abby's incredible strides. Nothing stood in her way. We broke through the last ranks of the soldiers. I heard Alyx yell something. The portal grew in front of us. Abby bore down on the opening.

"Five seconds. Four. Three." Abby and Izanami passed though the opening with Dad on their heels. He grabbed my arm and pushed me in front of him before following. Alyx jumped and closed the portal. We all sat on the ground in stunned silence.

Instead of Atlanta, I found myself standing in the middle of a forest clearing.

We'd escaped, but where on Earth were we?

I looked around the forest that surrounded us. I wasn't sure why Alyx had dropped us in the wilderness instead of back at Harker. The stars twinkled overhead, and insects chirped in the distance. Seconds ago, we were about to die; now we were camping.

"Somebody say something," Marcel said over the comm-link.

"We're all accounted for, Mr. Wizard," Dad said.

Abby roared as she stomped around the clearing. We weren't in Atlanta. She swiped at a tree, leaving deep tears in the bark. Her head lifted as she bellowed again.

Alyx stepped in front of her and held up his hands. "Abby, we're all safe. You can return to normal." He touched her leg and kept his hand there.

She growled at him. Slowly, she shrank until her humanity emerged from the bear. Alyx pulled off his cloak and put it around her shoulders. She continued her return to human. She clutched it tight around her, dropping to the ground. I realized she was crying.

"Get away from me before you end up like my parents." She'd buried her face in the robe she held in front of her. "I killed them all. I couldn't stop it."

Kneeling in front of my friend, my sister, I said, "Abby, we'd all be dead if it weren't for you. You did what you had to do to survive."

"No, Tommy. I can't control it. When I change, I lose myself in the beast. It consumes me, and I become an animal. I don't know why I was able to return to me, but next time it might be permanent."

Alyx leaned down to whisper in my ear. "We'll be back in a bit. I'm taking the others home."

Abby put her head into my chest and sobbed. When I looked up, I realized we were alone in the forest. I held her as she cried.

Memories of the story she'd told me came sharply into view. I hadn't understood that she literally became an animal. I'd thought she'd meant she acted like one. Her parents had died at the hands of the Reclaimers, not hers, but now wasn't the time to discuss it.

Sometime later, blue light illuminated the trees as Alyx stepped through, followed by a large, round man with shaggy white eyebrows and a gap-tooth smile. I recognized him as Yutu, a member of the Council. The pair strolled across the moss-covered forest floor, Alyx carrying Abby's backpack with him.

She pulled away from me, scrubbing her face with the palm of her hand. She glowered at the older man. "Who are you?"

Yutu nodded to her. "Little sister, I am Yutu of the Inuit. I have come to train you in the ways of *amarok*. Your ability is widely held among my people. I will help you. We will hunt together, and I will teach you of the ways. No harm will come to you while under my protection."

She sniffed. "What if I can't change back? I was a jungle cat for over three years."

"Bah, once you know the ways of *amarok*, you will change your form like you change your clothes. You will adopt the way of the wolf, the bear, the cat, and the eagle. We will swim the rivers as otters and soar above the trees as hawks. You will become the master of your Gift, not the victim. Will you accept my training?"

She nodded, not meeting his eyes. "I've killed people. Will I be able to control that as well?"

"You will be as you are here and now. The beast will not control your actions, only you will." Yutu grinned at me. "Thomas, the winds of chaos have surrounded you and brought you to the strangest places, my young friend."

"Master Yutu." I nodded in respect to the mage. "It is a pleasure to see you again."

He laughed. "You are as formal as your father to greet a friend in such a way." He pulled me to my feet and bear-hugged me. I returned the hug, though not as forcefully. "Abby, Master Alyx has clothes and supplies your mother packed for you. We will be some time training, but in the end, you will make a fine *amarok*."

Alyx handed over the bag, and Abby slipped off into the woods to change. Yutu gestured and a structure rose from the ground. He continued to craft the hut, adding a door and windows. He stepped inside, and a few minutes later, smoke rose out the hole in the top. Yutu returned, grinning. "It has been a long time since I've trained a true amarok. I delight in the opportunity."

Abby walked out of the forest, her bag over one shoulder with the blue cloak folded. "Thanks, Alyx. I appreciate not being left naked in front of all the boys."

He bowed to her. "Always an honor to help a fellow warrior."

"Good save," I said with a grin. "If you had called her a damsel in distress, she'd have punched you."

Instead, she punched me in the shoulder, though not hard enough to hurt...much. She grabbed me into a rough embrace. "Thanks, Tommy."

"I'd do anything for my favorite sister."

She smiled at me, and though I could see she was still upset, there was a glimmer of hope in her eyes. For the first time, she might be able to control her Gift and not worry about accidentally hurting anyone again. "Tell Mom not to worry about me. I'll be home as soon as I can."

"Will do." We said our goodbyes, and Alyx opened the portal to Atlanta. We stepped into Warden's tech room. She sat in one of the chairs, peering at video footage on the monitor.

She pivoted toward us. "Welcome back. I think we made a mistake in going after Yelena."

"She had to be stopped," Alyx said as he closed the portal, leaving Abby to begin her training. "Who knows what evil she'd have unleashed in Beijing?"

"I'm not saying it was a waste but look at this." Warden returned to viewing the monitor. "Anyone look familiar?"

Reaper strode across the screen with four members of the Syndicate. One was his fire-throwing sidekick, Tenji, but I didn't recognize the others. As we watched, Tenji torched the locks on the doors before Reaper kicked them in.

"Where is this from?" Dad asked as he watched the scene unfold from an interior camera. Reclaimer guards rushed Reaper, but his scythe dropped the ones Tenji's fire didn't, and within a few seconds, all the troops were dead or dying on the floor.

"It's the Reclaimers' station outside of Dallas. The building is their containment center. As you can see, it wasn't fully staffed, but they did have one prisoner," Warden said, still watching the feed from the cameras. "The raid started within a minute of your arrival in Beijing. Coincidence? I don't think so."

"Who's the prisoner?" I asked as Reaper moved his way deeper into the building. A couple of lone Reclaimers tried to fight but didn't fare any better than the guards in the lobby.

"We're getting there. I want to see if you recognize the captive." She kept her face toward the monitors as she spoke. Had Reaper lost a member when they lost in Dallas? The Protectorate had sent troops to arrest him. Maybe they got lucky and captured one of his people. Of course, we had taken Reaper, but Yelena had freed him, which still pissed me off.

The final camera view showed a hallway of reinforced doors like in the Block. They must have been the detention cells any captured Gifted were kept in. The two men I didn't recognize opened the third door and vanished from view. A minute later they emerged, a struggling person held between them. As they moved closer to the camera, the technician zoomed in on the person.

Jon Stevens.

Warden swiveled her chair to face us. "We hadn't heard about Stevens being captured after the fight in Dallas. Either it was kept off official channels or the Reclaimers have figured out we've infiltrated their systems. Either way, Reaper pulled him out exactly when your team was tied up fighting Yelena in Beijing."

"Jon lived with us, but so did Reaper, until he tried to sell us to the Protectorate. Why would he want Jon? Jon hates him." Why risk hitting a Reclaimers base for a guy who wants revenge? "Yelena did say Reaper had other things to do than guard her. I wonder if this is what she meant?"

Alyx rubbed his forehead. "Yelena's cunning is difficult to penetrate. She plans three steps ahead, and her goals aren't always obvious until it's too late."

"For God's sake, Alyx," Warden said, her cheeks turning redder by the moment. "You're the Council over all magic. How the hell can't you stop one mage set on destroying the world?"

"It's not just one mage, Warden," Alyx responded without anger in his voice. "The Brotherhood has members far beyond Earth. We are dealing with an enemy whose goal is destroying the universe to recreate it in their image. Logic doesn't apply."

"Reaper knows Jon and his weaknesses. If they exploit his hatred for Tommy, he could be turned and used against us." Dad said, as he paced. He'd picked up mom's habit in the time they'd been back together. "Dresden base has been wiped, but how much does Jon know about the Underground? He lived here for a time."

"Not as much as you'd think," she said confidently. "He was blindfolded in and out of the base except when he rescued Tommy, but Salvo destroyed that entrance. We escorted him out the same way."

"He must have gone to Dallas with Turk but decided he wouldn't help the Reclaimers. How they caught him is beyond me. He could sneak past anyone in the dark," I said, wondering how effective Warden's people had been in keeping Jon from finding out how to get in and out. "Warden, you'll want to increase security around Atlanta. I guarantee Jon knows exactly where you are."

"I'll increase security, but there is no way he knows enough to be a threat. We had him under surveillance constantly." Warden stood and came over to us. "I appreciate you taking my people's safety into account, but we've lived through worse than Jon Stevens."

I hoped she was right. Among Reaper, Jon, and Yelena, a lot of power was coming to bear on us and the Underground. If Reaper gained control of the translocators, we would all pay the price.

Dad shook her hand. "Mr. Wizard can help with security, if you'd like."

She shook her head. "I'll get my people working on it. We'll leave a few nasty surprises for anyone trying to breach our perimeter."

He nodded to her. "Alyx, if you don't mind."

Without a word, the portal opened into Harker's commissary. Mom waited at a table, a paper and pencil before her. Probably a crossword.

"Warden, don't underestimate Yelena's ambition," Dad said. "She's killed more people than Atlanta holds."

"We'll be ready if she tries anything." She shook my hand. "Enjoyed our talk, Tommy. I'll look forward to seeing you again, hopefully under less dire circumstances."

I let out a quick laugh. "That would be new. It would be nice to have a day off every once in a while."

She smiled back at me. "Yes, it would. Take care."

We stepped through the portal, and Alyx closed it behind us. Mom had set the puzzle down and stood waiting nearby. She hugged me. It was good to be home. Well, as much as any place was home anymore.

Dad went over what happened with Abby, and Mom grilled Alyx on how trustworthy Yutu was, given Abby was a young woman alone with a strange man in a forest. While they talked, I got a Mountain Dew and took a seat. Mama bear worried over one of her cubs, and she'd be giving Alyx an earful for a bit.

Pepper rolled down the hallway from the med bay, but she reversed course and left when she saw Alyx's back. Not a great sign. She's been inside my head, but I didn't know why she was hesitant around the mage. I'd have to talk to her after a shower and a good night's sleep.

Alyx left once Mom finished. She came over to check on me, but I was fine. Whatever else I'd say about Yelena, she'd cleaned the poison out of my system completely. My combat suit, on the other hand, would need replacing. Tomorrow, I'd have to check with Marcel to see what supplies were hidden in the lower levels. Even though it was the middle of the afternoon, I excused myself and left for my room.

The hot water relaxed my tired muscles and after I'd changed, I climbed into bed.

My mind wanted to dwell on things, but my body told it to shut the hell up, and I was out for the night.

## 11

Two days later, Marcel showed me around the lower levels of Harker. With a layout like Castle, it reminded me of home. The second level contained the communications and supply areas. A full armory sat on the opposite end of the floor from the communications room Marcel had taken over. A large conference table with built-in monitors at each end stood in the center of the comm room. A full wall display completed the setup.

Marcel messed with the table while I walked into the armory. Whoever stocked this place hadn't spared any expense. Racks of weapons ran down the walls. Combat and sniper rifles stood at attention in custom-built racks, with bins of clips and accessories aligned around each type.

Shelves ran down the middle of the room, stacked with pistols, knives, throwing stars, and some projectiles I'd never seen. In the back of the room stood a sealed black door with a keypad lock. I'd have to get Marcel to unlock it later. I left and joined him back at the wonder table.

"Bruh, you should see all this thing can do. It's off the hook." He tapped on the screen in front of him and the wall display sprang to life. "They don't have the selection Castle had, but look."

On the screen, the Ghostbuster's logo appeared. If I held a baseball bat, I would have attacked the screen. "As if hearing you and Abby quote the damn movie every ten minutes isn't bad enough, now you're going to make me watch it?"

The screen went dark. "Sorry, bruh. I thought you liked it."

I shook my head, disgusted with myself. After a second, I said, "Sorry. Normally, I do. Right now, I'm worried about Abby. With Jon working with Reaper, we're vulnerable."

"No worries. I get it." He rubbed his chin. "When I released the collars, you stuck by me no matter what. It'll take more than a couple of harsh words to hurt my feelings."

"Thanks. Let's explore downstairs. I'm guessing we'll find training rooms."

We took the stairs to sub-level three and discovered a huge meeting room with a sizable display built into the wall. Training rooms and a gym with two locker rooms completed the floor's layout.

All the fourth sub-level rooms were coded. I wondered if they might be private living quarters, like in Castle. The fifth level contained food storage and mechanicals. We figured the other two levels would be more of the same. As we took the stairs back to the communications room, I realized I'd forgotten to tell Marcel about the armory. "In the armory, there's a keypad-locked door. Can you get in to check out what's in there?"

He feigned disgust. "Can I, the master of electronics, open a simple keypad lock? How dare you insult my skills so?"

I laughed.

"Of course I can," he said as we reached the second-level door. "Let me see what my dredge has brought back and then I'll crack the lock."

"Thanks. I'm going to go eat. I'll catch you in a bit." I climbed the stairs to the main floor and hit the food replicator. A burger, fries, and a Mountain Dew took care of lunch for me. A copy of *Dune* sat on an empty table. I dropped into my chair, flipped open the book, and started happily munching through some good junk food.

"Be careful," Pepper said as she rolled into the commissary. "You'll bite your fingers off," I moved a chair out of the way, allowing her access to the table. "Thanks. You got a minute?"

"Sure thing," I said around bites. Exhaustion etched her features. She slumped in the wheelchair like a toy without batteries. Her orange hair didn't seem as bright as before. The stress of waiting to see if Blaze would survive had taken its toll.

"What's on your mind?"

"Too many things." She put her hands in her lap. "I need to talk to you about Alyx."

I set my burger down. "Go on."

She sighed deeply. "He's worrying me. When we were a part of Stryke Force, there was a lot of friction after I chose Blaze over him."

"You were happy to see him when he first got here. What changed?"

"Honestly, I'd forgotten much of my life after all the years of being stuck in Reaper's head. Coming back made all of it confusing. I like Alyx and was happy to see him, but the more I talk with him, the more I'm sure it's gonna be bad between us." She kept her eyes fixed on the top of the table.

"I'm sorry, Pepper. Bad how? Alyx is a great guy." As soon as I said it, I realized how wrong it sounded, like I was dismissing her feelings.

Her head jerked up, a pained expression on her face. "Never mind." She put her hands on the wheelchair's controls to leave.

"Wait." I almost yelled it. "I didn't mean it the way it sounded. Please, let me explain."

Her hands came off the controls but hovered nearby. "I'm waitin'."

"He's a good guy to me, and I don't know why he's upsetting you. I'd really like to understand, I just don't right now. Explain it to me."

I held my breath as she considered what I'd said.

"The only reason you get a pass is I realize how your brain works after livin' in there." She took a deep breath. "Alyx is a good guy, but he's always wanted me. He's weirdin' me out. I guess being in Reaper's head for so long, I'd forgotten what it was like to deal with real guys. He keeps touching me and making comments that sound innocent but come off as creepy." She rubbed her forehead like it would loosen the right words. "I don't think I'm explaining it well."

"I always have your back. If something is bothering you, just tell me," I said, trying to catch her eye. "I'm not going to judge you."

Her head came up, and she smiled at me. "Thanks. It means a lot to me. I might be blowin' things outta proportion, but I've got to listen to my gut."

"Hey, I listen to mine all the time. It's usually telling me it's hungry."

She rolled her eyes. "Do you have time to help me walk around? I need to start exercising to get my balance back."

"Marcel and I found a gym downstairs. We can use it. The floor is padded, in case you fall." I put my dishes in the dishwasher after downing the rest of my Dew. "Since it's downstairs, is it okay if I carry you?" I shoved the book into my back pocket.

"Sure, though I'm heavier than I look," she said.

I pulled her out of the wheelchair and hoisted her on my back. "Wow, what have they been feeding you? Lead?" I joked, knowing her mechanical parts weighed more than the skin and bone they replaced.

"Carbinium alloy, if you must know." She pinched me as I got her settled piggyback style. "Only a goon would talk about a lady's weight. You've got no class, Tommy."

"Ow, I'll remember that." I stomped over to the door and down the stairs to level two. Marcel sat at the main table, still engrossed in the technological dream of figuring out how it all worked. He didn't even notice when we passed on the way to the gym.

The gym packed a lot of equipment in the forty by twenty space. I carried Pepper to the nearest treadmill and helped her stand on it. It had a safety harness hanging from the front of the machine. I strapped her in and started her walking. She gripped the handrails as she took her first few steps.

"My legs are fine since they're mechanical, but my balance and conditioning are off." She stumbled slightly, catching herself after a missed step. "The tops of my legs are still bio, so they need time to reintegrate with the hardware."

"I always thought you had robot legs, from the way Blaze spoke about you." I leaned against the treadmill beside her, ready to jump in if she needed help. Her gait still didn't flow smoothly, but she maintained her pace.

She smirked at me. "They built me to be a drug mule, then an assassin. People remember metallic parts when they see 'em. No sense having the customs agents looking closer than necessary. The doc implanted grafts and a neural network to mimic a Gifted's abilities."

"A lot of people would envy you."

Pepper tapped the controls and sped up the machine, keeping her legs moving as the belt increased the pace. She wasn't ready for normal walking speed, but this was more than she'd done since I'd pulled her from the stasis chamber. "Yeah, but I doubt they'd like the surgeries and everything else to get there."

"Probably not." Her steps lacked the surety I took for granted. She fell a few times, but the safety harness caught her and turned off the belt to prevent injury. Without comment, she pulled herself up and restarted the machine.

She glanced at me. "So, you doin' okay with Abby staying behind? You two are close."

With everything happening at once, I hadn't taken the time to think about Abby staying with Yutu to train. It made sense for her to learn to control her Gift, but things were off without her around. I missed her like one would miss an amputated arm. "I'm cool. I miss her, but she'd never stay here if she couldn't trust herself not to hurt one of us on accident."

"Makes sense."

I took a seat on the floor and watched as Pepper worked on the treadmill. I tried to push my concern for Abby out of my mind, but it dug in and refused to budge. I pulled out the book from my pocket. Reading had always been a great escape from my problems.

Thirty minutes later, Pepper turned the treadmill off, sweat covering her face. I stored my book and helped her down.

"Abby's tough," she said, resuming our earlier conversation. It's gotta be like me waitin' on Blaze. I hope he'll come out well, but who knows?"

Before I could respond, the all-too-familiar warning siren went off. "The molecular reassignment weapon will fire in ten minutes. This is not a drill."

*Wonderful. This is exactly what today needed.* I scooped up Pepper and returned to the conference table where Marcel sat. I placed Pepper in a chair next to Marcel and sat on the other side of him. "What's going on?"

"The space station has moved to target New Delhi. It's like the timing program has been corrupted, or someone is forcing it into this odd pattern. During the Darkest Storm attacks, the station fired at all the targets from the same orbit. Now the station moves over the target and then fires. Nothing about this makes sense."

*Welcome to my life.* Nothing had made sense since the day I'd left Redemption. I'd thought being away from Redemption would improve my life, and in some ways it had. Had things gone according to plan, by now I'd be getting ready to graduate and get away from Powell and Brunner. Mom would have moved closer to her office, and I'd have taken a job with Blaze at the Secret Lair.

All of that died when Powell attacked us in the woods. We'd been on the run ever since, fighting to stay alive and keep the world from ending. I was sure it would look great on my resume after all this was over.

Marcel had the Reclaimers' cameras they'd installed outside New Delhi showing on the wall display. I'd stopped asking how he got access to all the feeds. His Gift allowed him to interface with computer systems, and every time he tried to explain, I ended up with a headache. It was better to let him do his magic and just "ooh" and "ahh" over it.

"The Reclaimers moved away from the city's barriers," Marcel said. "Since the death ray destroyed half of Asia's Southeastern region, they aren't taking any chances." He enlarged one camera's view for a better look. Small explosions were going off near the fence.

"What's causing the fireworks?" I asked, confused. New Delhi was a "dead city" like Tokyo and Beijing. Nothing should be exploding.

"The Reclaimers mined the passages out of the city. The Cartel runs drugs through the dead zones to avoid the Reclaimer patrols. I guess these guys didn't pay their dues." Marcel switched cameras, checking each view. He settled on one where we could see a domed building.

The countdown continued on the screen before the death ray struck the city.

"I can't believe all this has happened since Reaper killed me," Pepper said, as we watched the dead city under a moonlit sky. "I wonder if I haven't been better off not knowing."

"This is the world I grew up in. It's always been this way." I'd wanted to see what things were like before the Darkest Storm hit, before the Protectorate, and before the collars. I often imagined a time where I could live where I wanted, travel without restrictions, or go about my life without incessant rules and regulations. America had been free, but the citizens traded freedom for security and had lost everything in the deal. Now the Protectorate ran it all. Maybe the Norms still felt free. I know I didn't.

Pepper shook her head. "I'll never get to stroll through New York and have a slice and a beer on a hot summer's day. All the people I knew are gone, disintegrated by the death ray. No more Broadway shows or ice skatin' at the Rock. It's like my whole life was erased."

What was there to say? We'd all lost people and places. Even the old house in Redemption with the squeaky front door had been our home, and it was just as gone to me as New York was to Pepper.

I thought about Mimi. Was being free better than working at the Lair and seeing her boyfriend? She'd gained abilities but couldn't go back to help the people she knew. If she had the choice, which path would she take? Hiding out with us, or having her old life? That life wasn't easy, but she'd always seemed happy to me.

The countdown hit the one-minute mark as we watched the dead city of New Delhi. I'd never heard of any of these cities, since Powell never taught us geography as a part of his version of history. Once the death ray had started firing at its targets again, I'd had to learn about a lot of new places.

I wondered what New Delhi had been like before the Darkest Storm. Mom said it was a beautiful city, though overcrowded. Dad had been there a few times and liked the people and the food. I'd never know—just another in the long lines of extinct places. Sure, I could translocate there, walk the empty streets, and hope not to run into any giant rats, or armorgators, or worse.

"Three. Two. One. Firing was successful. Recalculating vectors."

As we watched New Delhi be struck again by the death ray, I wondered if we'd ever be able to stop the Brotherhood.

## 12

I carried a tired Pepper back upstairs and sat her in her wheelchair. Even with half her body being mechanical, physical activity still drained her.

"Thanks, Tommy. I'm gonna get some rest before I check on Blaze."

I decided to talk to Mimi. Given how Marcel, who unlocked her collar without her knowledge, and Max, who attempted to torture her into manifesting her Gift, were both gone, I wanted her opinion on what had happened. I followed the hall down to the room Waxenby had taken since we'd gotten to Harker. According to Gabriel, Waxenby's physical condition improved daily, but mentally he was broken. Mimi tried to help, but so far, it hadn't worked.

I turned the corner to find Mimi sitting behind the top of the bed, Waxenby's head cradled in her hands. Eyes closed, she muttered under her breath. I took a seat and waited, not wanting to risk interrupting her in the process of helping him. She wore a flannel shirt with the sleeves cut off, jeans with holes all over, and a bandanna holding her hair back from her face.

For a second, I had a flashback to working with her over the summer at the Lair. We'd worked hard but had a lot of fun hanging with Marcel and Mimi, training with Blaze, and dodging Max whenever he decided to come to work.

I pushed the fact of Max being a serial killer away, focusing on the good parts. It still shocked me that Mandy had started working at the Lair. I wondered how she was doing now and if the Reclaimers had shut down the store. Other than Wendi, she was the only woman I'd ever kissed. She was a Norm, so she probably would be at college or maybe had a full-time job somewhere. I remembered her long brown hair and...

"Sport, before you need to get a room with yourself, you might want to realize I can read your thoughts, especially when you're, um, excited." The smile on Mimi's face made me blush, which got her laughing. I didn't need to worry about her reading my thoughts, since the embarrassment was plastered across my face. "So," she asked, "did you stop by for a purpose or just wandering down memory lane?"

One day, I wouldn't blush at everything Mimi said to me, but today was not that day. "I wanted to check on Mr. Waxenby and ask you a question, if you can spare a few minutes."

She rolled over in her chair, crossing her legs. Her canvas sneakers had intricate designs drawn on them. She caught my eye studying them.

"Those are cool," I said.

Her face lit up. "Ya think so? Been working on them since I can't exactly wander down to the local tattoo shop to work on my sleeves. I've got a lot of time here with Ollie, so it keeps me occupied."

I grabbed one of Marcel's sayings. "They are totally off the hook."

Mimi smirked at me. "They are awesome."

"Right. Back to your question. You don't have to answer this. It's kind of personal." I didn't know how to ask without upsetting Mimi.

She leaned forward. "Now it's getting interesting. Are we talking about Mandy?"

My face flamed again. "No," I said, way faster than normal, eliciting another laugh. "I wanted to ask you about your collar being gone."

"Oh, I'm not still pissed at Marcel, if that's what you're asking. I realize he was trying to help no matter how ham-handed his attempt was." She leaned back in her chair, arms crossed over her chest.

I was blowing this big time. "No, I wanted to ask you, if you had a choice, knowing what was coming, would you have turned off your collar?"

Her head tilted as she regarded me. "Why on Earth would you ask that?"

I explained what I'd been thinking as I watched the death ray hit New Delhi again. I dove in, sparing none of the details, hoping she'd understand where I was going. When I finished, she watched me for a couple of moments.

"I see," she finally said. "Would I go back to my old life if I could? I don't honestly have an idea, Tiger." She bounced her leg while she considered. "I miss the Lair and some of the customers. Coop and I broke up every other week, so not much to miss there. If I'm bein' honest about it, so did Jane and I. Relationships aren't my thing, I guess. Really, when you lay it all out, there isn't much to go back to."

"Jane?"

"I swing both ways, Sport. With us working together, I figured you'd realized it." She winked at me and kept going. "Now I wouldn't want to go through Max's torture chamber again, and if I knew it was a result of turning off my collar, it would have stayed on. To your point, he might have still killed me like the others, so who knows?"

At least she'd listened to me. We had a big sister-little brother relationship, and she was overprotective of me. Others had learned the lesson not to cross her where I was concerned.

"On the plus side, now I can sort of read minds and stuff. Ollie needs me, and I'm glad I'm here for him. Being with you guys is like family. I haven't had one since my mom died. I guess the answer to your question is no, I wouldn't go back."

"Thanks," I said. "I keep trying to puzzle out our responsibility to the other Gifted. Do we release them all or just some? Who chooses the ones we release, and would they even want to leave the lives they've built? When I can't sleep, I can't decide what our end goal should be."

"You've got a lot on your plate for seventeen, I'll give ya that." She leaned in and lowered her voice. "Can I try something on you?"

"Is it going to hurt?" I asked, a bit more guarded than necessary.

She laughed. "No, Tiger. It won't hurt. I want to show you a memory Ollie has been fixated on. You might be able to add context for me."

I shrugged. "Sure, why not?"

"Thanks, Sport. I knew I could count on you." She got out of her chair and moved to stand behind mine. "Sit back. I'm going to put my hands on your head. Just relax and let your mind wander."

I followed directions. Her warm hands cupped my head. I wondered what she was doing.

"Let your mind wander," she repeated. "Don't think about what's going on."

"Sorry." My eyes closed. I felt the gentle touch of her Gift on my mind. I drifted while she worked her way in and showed me Waxenby's memory.

Rough hands grasped my arms as I was carried toward an orange building. A large red-brown structure stood off in the distance. The glass windows had been boarded up, but Tenji held open a door.

A small Asian man waved impatiently at the two people carrying me. "Hurry. The Underground has eyes everywhere."

The pace increased and soon we passed Tenji and the memory ended.

A pleasant warmth held me as Mimi continued to probe my brain. The only sensation I could equate it to was when I'm on the edge of sleep, but not quite there. I floated until she withdrew from my conscious mind.

I couldn't guess how long I'd been asleep, but Mimi sat across from me, pen in one hand, left sneaker in the other. "Welcome back, Sport." She set the shoe and pen on the small table next to her chair. "How do you feel?"

"Good." It shocked me to say it, but it was true. All the tension and upset from earlier seemed far away. "What did you do?"

"After I showed you the memory from Ollie, I obscured a couple of things to help you deal with them better." She smirked at me. "I may or may not have added an impulse to chicken dance when I snap my fingers."

"Great. If I knew what a chicken dance was, it might be more of a threat." I racked my brain, but nothing seemed any different. "So, you removed my memories?"

"No, if you think about a subject I touched, the obscuring will fade, but until then, it will help you relax."

I wasn't following, and she picked up on it.

"Let's see if this helps. I could have obscured Wendi, as an example, but I didn't. If I'd obscured her, when you thought about her, you'd remember everything, but until something triggered the memory, it wouldn't come to the front of your brain."

"Got it," I said, feeling better about the whole thing. I could still see Wendi's face, taste her kiss. She'd always be a part of me. "I don't recognize the place of Waxenby's memory but Tenji, Reaper's right-hand man, was the one waving the others into the building. Mom or Dad might recognize the location."

"I'm pretty sure they are near the San Francisco dead zone, but I'm not positive. Knowing it is Reaper's outfit helps me a lot. Now I can fit it into a timeline in his head. I'm trying to reestablish context around the random memories. Given how new this is to me, I'm not much of a psychic surgeon."

"I'm sure he'll be happy to wake up and will have you to thank for it." Reaper's people had really messed him up after he'd been captured. What was so important that they scrambled his brain? I had no idea but wanted Waxenby back in one piece. We owed him at least that much after he'd saved us in the desert. "You should show Dad. He'd be able to tell you more."

"Really, if I can pull enough fragments of the memory together, Ollie will do the rest. I'm going to try to connect it. I'll let you know how it goes, Sport." She returned to where I found her. She placed her hands on Waxenby's head and went back to work.

I left the room and walked down to the regeneration machine where Blaze fought for his life inside. Pepper wasn't there. I hoped she was still asleep. I returned to the commissary for a drink and a snack. Whatever Mimi did left me with an appetite.

Mom and Dad sat at a table, drinking coffee. They stopped talking when I entered.

"I can leave if I'm interrupting."

"No, just talking about the old days. Wandering down memory lane, as my grandmother used to say."

It sounded strange to me to realize I had a great-grandmother. I'd never had more than Mom around and knew little of her parents. I pulled myself back to the present. "Mimi showed me a memory Mr. Waxenby has been stuck on. I think you should have her show you. Reaper's people were in it."

"Don't ever let a Gifted with mental powers use them on you." Dad's face grew serious and his sharp tone tore at me. "I allowed Dominion access to my mind and then she used my Gift to kill all those Reclaimers. I ended up paying the price for it along with the squad of Powell's men she killed. You've got to think before you let anyone use their Gifts on you."

I held up my hands. "Sorry."

"You're scaring him." Mom turned to him, putting her hand on Dad's arm. "What did she show you, honey?"

I relayed the memory to them. "Mimi thinks the place is San Francisco. Why would they have taken him there?"

Dad set his cup down with a dull thump. "If they were there, we need to check it out. Let's get Marcel to put eyes on San Francisco."

Three hours later, Marcel had cameras on the location I'd seen in Waxenby's memories. It didn't appear to be inhabited, but there were signs it had been before.

"What do you think?" I asked Dad as Marcel zoomed in to check out the building.

"If it could be a Syndicate safe house, it might be worth a look," Dad said. "We've only known about the one other, but there have to be more."

Mom stood over his shoulder, examining the scene, but didn't say anything.

"We're going to have to chance it," Dad said. "Get your gear. We'll move out in twenty."

"If you two are going, so am I." She cut Dad off before he could speak. "Michael, Abby is gone, and Reaper has Jon. You need backup. I'll get my rifle and be ready to go. The only way my son is going into this is with me watching out for him." She pecked him on the cheek and left the room, Dad staring after her.

He glanced at me. "Have you ever gotten your own way with her?"

"Not once." I smirked at him and got a wink in return.

"I guess the Ward men are in the same boat. We better get ready ourselves."

I ran to my room and pulled on my new combat suit. The old one had holes where the hellhound's teeth had pierced it and made it less than useful. I used the box Dad had given me to recharge my energy before sliding it into my pocket. My last piece to put on was the comm-link to keep in touch with Marcel.

I found Mom and Dad waiting in the commissary. Mom had her sniper rifle in hand and her full suit on, with helmet. Dad has his normal all-black suit, but neither of us had a helmet anymore.

The translocator had been set up on level three. Marcel unlocked an old storage room where he had installed sensors. "In case anyone activates it, we'll know." He led the way down the stairs and into the new translocation room.

The space itself was rather non-descript. The steel walls were dingy with disuse. A stack of boxes took up one corner. The silver disk sat in the center, so it didn't touch the walls.

Dad pulled the control box out and messed with the settings. He stood next to the disk. "Ready?"

Mom mock-saluted him before adjusting the sniper rifle she'd slung over her right shoulder. "Yes, Commander."

"I'm ready," I said, not wanting to tease him any more than Mom already had. She winked at me.

Dad shook his head, though he had a smile on his face. "Engaging."

A moment later, we were in the Atlanta translocation room. Warden stood at the control panel next to a guy a little older than me.

He wore glasses and had long, dark hair. Warden stepped from behind the console as she greeted us. "Good to see it works. To what do we owe the honor of a visit?"

Dad shook Warden's hand. "We have reason to believe Reaper has a safe house in San Francisco. I want to get eyes on it and, if possible, see what's in there."

"Just the three of you? Where's Abby? She's certainly handy in a fight."

Mom spoke first. "She's taking care of some personal matters. She'll be back as soon as she can. For now, we have to make do with what we have."

"That's all well and good, but I'll come along, and we can grab help from the San Francisco team."

Dad shook his head. "Warden, you're too important here—"

"Ranger, if you think you can stroll in there and get help, you're crazy. With the renewed attacks from a weapon you destroyed, your word isn't going to be worth much."

Dad gave a grim nod but kept his mouth shut. Having his integrity questioned had to be burning him.

"Besides, you don't know my people. Blaster will come in handy for this one. His powers will fit in nicely with your team, and he needs more experience." She turned to the technician behind the control desk and requested he call it in, so they'd be expecting us. "Shall we?"

"I guess I don't have any input into this?" Dad grumbled. He was used to leading and having his orders followed. A lot had changed since he'd gone into the Block.

"Not one bit," Warden said, with a wide smile. "My translocator, my rules."

"As you wish."

I swear I heard him mutter "women" under his breath. The fact they appeared to have not heard it showed he was learning.

You can teach an old dog new tricks.

## 13

Five minutes later, we stepped out of the Underground's San Francisco base translocator building. People scurried everywhere, carrying their belongings and infants and toddlers too small to walk on their own. The pre-teens toted backpacks as they made their way toward the translocation room, where a long line had already formed.

Like Atlanta, the base was a subterranean town with two-story buildings along the main thoroughfare. This base was much smaller than the others we'd visited.

Dad turned to Warden. "What's going on? San Francisco was the last city to be hit before the weapon was stopped."

"My people are all moving to Atlanta, and we're going to fight our way out. The Reclaimers are spread thin. We can move in groups into the mountains and get away. I can't let people go back to cities pulsing with the mutagenic properties of the ray's aftermath."

"You'll be cut to ribbons," I said in disbelief. "We need to find a way to stop the death ray before it strikes again. You'll make it out of Atlanta, and then the Reclaimers will decimate you. Most of your people don't have Gifts."

A grumble from the crowd silenced me. I glanced around and

noticed the less-than-happy faces pointed in our direction. Warden led us away from the line and down the road to an exit. She stopped short of the doors. "Look, I will not chance my people on a foolhardy breakout, but with no idea of how long we have, I can't risk sitting still. Three cities are already unlivable. In six months, the mutagen decay will return to the point it is now, and they can go back, but six months is a long time with no home."

Mom cut into the conversation. "Warden, after we're done here, Mr. Wizard will find an abandoned base for the Underground to claim. How many people do you have?"

"Around twenty-five thousand, give or take. Some bases like New Delhi only had a couple hundred, but the European zones encompass a much larger population. I can't imagine how you can hold so many people in an abandoned team base." Warden sounded a lot less angry. Even if the suggestion didn't work, we were trying.

"There were larger bases the old military establishments had. We might be able to use one," Dad said. "Regardless, give us a couple days to come up with a better alternative."

Warden nodded. "Two days. After that, we move the population to Atlanta and do what we have to do to survive."

Dad nodded. "Thank you. We value you and your people. We should get moving. I'd like to scout this building and get to work on your issues."

Warden pointed behind us. "We'll be needing the assistance of my associate."

We turned to catch a young man stalking up the street behind us. His dark skin mirrored the color of his combat suit. With short hair and sunglasses, he looked like a fighter pilot from the movies. The truth was, he could have been in my classes back in Redemption. He stopped just short of the group. "Warden, you wanted me?"

"I did. Blaster, this is Cyclone Ranger, Snapshot, and Sparky," I caught the grin on her face as I looked at her with my mouth open in protest. She continued. "We usually call him Tommy. This is Blaster. He has a strong offensive Gift and knows the San Francisco zone like the back of his hand."

Dad stuck out his hand to shake.

Blaster didn't extend his. "My team needs me here to ready for the relocation." He glared at us. "My first priority is to my family here."

"Blaster, you are part of my people, and until someone else wants my job, every member of the Underground has agreed to follow my lead." Warden's voice could have frozen the sun. "Now, are you part of my team, or do I need to have you removed?"

"Warden, we need to be fightin' Reclaimers, not playing tour guide to a bunch of outsiders."

"Let's get this straight," she said, her voice still ice. "These people have put themselves at great risk to help us. I find your lack of manners unacceptable. You're dismissed." She turned to Dad. "I'm sorry, Ranger. We'll proceed without Blaster."

"He'll grow out of it," Mom said. I could tell she was smiling behind her helmet's visor.

Warden led us toward a steel door set in the base's side wall.

I glanced back and caught Blaster following us. After a few moments, he called out, "Warden, wait."

She stopped while Blaster jogged to catch up. "Point taken." He held his hand out to Dad. "Ranger, it's an honor to be on a team with you. Please forgive my rudeness."

"Nothing to forgive," Dad said as he shook Blaster's hand. "We're glad to have you aboard. Hopefully this is a quick scouting mission, but we never know what we'll find." He handed Blaster a comm-link. "You'll need this. Mr. Wizard is our tech-ops guy."

After putting the comm-link in his ear, he shook Mom's hand next and then mine. "You were in the Gauntlet?" he asked as he looked at me for the first time.

"Yeah. Made a mess of it."

"Man, you blowing the car over onto those Reclaimers was legendary." Blaster's smile lit up his whole face.

"Umm, thanks," I said, feeling awkward and thrilled to be recognized for my part in the Gauntlet fight. I wonder if this was how Dad felt back before we were outlawed.

Mom fell in next to me as Warden got the door open, and we

descended to the sewers. Why did it always have to be the sewers? Once this was all over, I would never step foot near a storm drain, let alone go into the sewers, again.

We traveled by flashlight through the tunnels until we emerged in the basement of an old store. We climbed the stairs and entered what had, at one time, been a bookstore. Marcel would have cried seeing all these books toppled over and decaying on the floor. We exited the broken front window and into the fresh air.

In the distance stood the bridge I'd seen in Waxenby's memory. "We're looking for an orange building with boards over the windows." I said, remembering the details of his memory. "That's where Reaper's people will be if they're still here."

"If there's no one there, we sweep the building and gather anything we can find," Dad said, glancing around at each of us. "You never know what they left behind that might give us an advantage. If there are enemy combatants, we will retreat and assess the situation. If we do go in, the intel is the most important piece. Let anyone who tries to run go. We'll be out of there before they can return with reinforcements. No heroes today. We do this by the numbers and get out."

"What if Reaper's here?" I asked, knowing it was a possibility. I wanted to drop him in his tracks after everything he'd done to me and my family. I hadn't killed him when I had the chance, and he'd gotten away. I wouldn't make the same mistake.

"We take him down, if possible." Dad turned to Blaster. "The scythe he wields will kill you if it hits you, so keep him at range. If you can't get away from him, yell out and one of us will back you up. Understood?"

"Yes, sir, but I can fight at a distance just fine." Blaster grinned. He virtually bubbled over with excitement.

Warden said he needed field experience, and my guess was he had none. I wanted to scream at him how dangerous Reaper was, and he needed to take it seriously. I'd thought I could take Reaper down and almost died trying. The Grim Reaper was far tougher than anyone else we'd fought, and I needed to remember it as well.

"He strong, fast, and mean," Warden said to Blaster. "His team killed one of ours in Dallas and almost two more. Izanami couldn't beat him."

Blaster whistled softly. "Man, he must be a hard ass, 'cause she can dish some serious heat."

"Remember that, should he be here. We'll kill him if possible, but our goal is the intel," Dad said.

"He won't have a shield protecting him this time," Mom said.

"Let's head out. Blaster, you're on point." Dad said.

Blaster nodded. "We go this way then." He struck out across the road and up a hill covered with saplings.

Nature amazed me. The death ray had destroyed every living thing here, but now plants and animals had reclaimed the dead city. The trees twisted at odd angles as they grew—a curse of the mutagen the ray left behind.

We came out of the woods near an old group of buildings with a parking lot in front of them. Vehicles lay abandoned all around. We crossed over carefully, leapfrogging between cars until we came to a six-lane road. On the other side was a small building made up of mostly windows. Dad signaled, and we each took our turn running over and getting out of sight in the enclosure.

When it was my turn, I sprinted across the lanes and leapt through the nearest window. I landed awkwardly on an old bench that was bolted to the floor. The side walls had benches along them. Shattered display screens hung lifeless from above the windows with faded out train posters swaying in the slight breeze. I squatted next to Blaster.

"Used to be a bus stop," Blaster said as we waited. "The stairs outside lead down to the building you described."

Mom came after me. I helped her clear the wall and get down on the floor without incident.

"Your father and I visited the Golden Gate bridge," she said, a wistful tone in her voice. "I wish you could have seen it before the Protectorate destroyed it."

In the distance, the remains of the bridge loomed. The upright pillars still stood, but not much else. "Me too."

Warden came next and then Dad. Dad led us out to the concrete barrier that overlooked the target building. As soon as I saw it, I knew we were in the right place.

From my vantage point on the bridge, the target was laid out below us. A set of stairs went down to the two-lane road that ran past the building. Concrete pylons sat alongside what had been a large open area in front of the building. The Syndicate safe house was a one-story faded orange structure with large, boarded windows. The side of the building said *Bridge Pavilion*. The center of the roof held a domed skylight.

Mom laid at the edge of the half-wall, rifle stuck out, using the scope to see if the building was occupied. She shook her head.

Dad motioned us back to the bus stop. Mom filled us in, once we were all under cover. "Nothing is moving. There are cameras on the outside corners, but I'm not sure they're active."

"Mr. Wizard, you got anything from your end?" Dad said.

Marcel's voice came through loud and clear. "There's electricity running to the building, but I don't have anything to see inside. I reviewed the security cameras and saw lights on. My guess is someone is there."

Dad nodded. "Once again, this is by the numbers. Warden, can you pull up a storm but hold off the rain? I'd like a way to slow down any pursuit. Snapshot, keep us in your sights, but don't open fire unless a fight breaks out or I give the signal."

"Got it," she said.

He turned to Blaster and me. "I'm going to go high. You two head for the front door and scout. Do not enter. Report back what you see. If no one is in there, we'll enter, collect any intel we can, and get out via the translocator. Does everyone understand the plan?"

We all nodded.

"Warden. When you're ready, you call the ball, and we execute."

"On it, Ranger." She closed her eyes. Wispy clouds dotted the sky overhead, but as she worked, more and more dark, angry clouds scudded across the sky. The distant roll of thunder rattled the windows of the bus stop. After five minutes, she said, "Calling the ball."

Marcel's voice came into my ear. "Warden has the ball. Good luck."

Dad launched into the air as Blaster and I took the stairs down into the dimly lit area under the overpass. I looked up to see Mom was stationed so she had a clear view of the front door. We stepped out into the wind from Warden's storm.

Waxenby's memory overlaid the real world. They'd pulled him into the safe house from this direction. Just below us, another building with the same orange paint stood off to the left. Most of the silver letters were present, spelling out *Bridge Café*. The doors and windows were gone. From Waxenby's memories, I guessed they had a way into the area from that building. There must be tunnels connecting it, if they brought him this way.

Debris skittered across the open pavement as the winds increased, but the rain held off.

"What do you see?" Dad asked. With all the dark clouds overhead, he was difficult to pick out. The massive remains of the Golden Gate bridge loomed off to our left.

Blaster and I stalked toward the building, heads on swivels as we watched for trouble. I kept looking at the destroyed bridge.

"Reclaimers blew it to keep people out. Not that it worked. The Underground built a translocator here, and we moved in." Blaster still wore the sunglasses, even now with the sun hidden behind the curtain of clouds.

We closed to fifteen feet from the target, separating so any Syndicate people couldn't take a direct shot out the door.

The seawater's odor was strong, but underneath it something tickled my nose. I couldn't place what it was, couldn't put my finger on what was bothering me. "Does anyone smell something off?" I asked

Blaster responded. "Nah, just the ocean and dead fish. We're fifteen feet out. Are we a go to close in on the target?"

"You're good. No signs of life," Mom said. "Keep your eyes sharp. I've got a bad feeling about this."

I did as well. What was I sensing? Or was it just my paranoia messing with me? "Closing in."

Step by step, we drew closer to the building. The plywood had been removed from the right-hand door, exposing a glass center. The room inside was dark, and my vision couldn't penetrate the gloom. I wished I had my helmet; the heat vision would have come in handy.

Fire. The scent reminded me of a burned-out building or a left-over campfire. That's what had been triggering me. Why would it smell like that? I glanced around but didn't see any signs of one.

The door swung open, and Tenji stepped out.

Even though I knew there could be someone here, he shocked the crap out of me.

"I'm surprised you found this place, but I'm not unprepared for your arrival."

"Where's Reaper?" I said, pulling the swirling energy inside me into a ball, ready to strike.

Tenji's Gift summoned and controlled flames. The burning smell must have come from him.

"Reaper is on business for Yelena," Tenji said, casually leaning against the building, looking at his nails. "She left a present for you, in case you showed up."

"Great. We'll be leavin' your corpse for whoever Yelena is," Blaster said, as he struck a fighting stance.

Tenji laughed. "It is not me you should be worried about."

A loud series of growls filled the air.

"There are five dogs on the roof. I repeat five dogs on the roof," Mom said.

But they weren't dogs. Five hellhounds watched from above, snarling at us.

"Abort," Dad said, just as the lead hellhound leapt at me.

No time to abort. The fight was on.

14

When a hellhound the size of a small horse jumps at you, moving is a great option. Too bad my body didn't get the message fast enough.

I spun to my left, but the hellhound moved faster than expected. Its front paw clipped my shoulder, throwing me off balance. I crashed to the ground, attempted a roll, and ended up face down on the cracked concrete. The skin on my palms scraped when I hit. I'd be feeling that for a while.

Mom opened fire, cutting off Tenji's laugh. A bullet nicked his shoulder, sending up a spray of blood.

I rolled to my side. The hellhound pounced, missing me by inches. I swung my foot hard, striking the thing in the side and knocking it away from me.

As I climbed to my feet, Dad raced in, unleashing a cyclone at one of the hounds circling Blaster.

The wind grabbed the dog and threw it into the side of the building. Blaster opened fire on the beast, but mostly took out the corner of the building behind it.

Another set of shots rang out as Mom laid down support fire.

Three bullets impacted the downed hell beast. It fell to its side, geysers of flame spurting from the holes.

"Warden, bring the rain," Mom said. "They bleed fire."

"Inbound storm. Two-minute ETA," Warden's voice said in my ear.

Two minutes! We had to hold our ground. I raced over to Blaster, who'd been fighting off two of the beasts. The closest one lunged toward his unprotected back. I kicked it before it could strike Blaster. Its head snapped up as my boot slammed into the underside of its jaw, snapping it shut. It yelped and moved out of range.

The larger beast dove at my side, but Blaster moved to intercept. His hands came up, and he unloaded on the beast at point-blank range. Cone-shaped translucent force bolts left his arms. Sound exploded across the wind-swept area. Once he finished firing, Blaster slumped against me. Flames dripped from the larger beast's chest where the shots had struck it.

Tenji's fireball flew at us. I pushed Blaster flat, so it went over us and struck the beast instead. Its injuries closed over, and it grew larger.

"Fire heals these things!" I yelled as I pivoted around the rapidly expanding hell beast.

Blood ran from the wound in Tenji's left shoulder. Lightning arced from my arm, flashing across the distance between Tenji and me. He flowed around the bolt with the grace of a dancer.

"When I finish you, I am going to burn your sniper to death slowly for injuring me," Tenji said as he lobbed another fireball at us.

Another shot struck inches from his head. "If he'd stay still for a second, you wouldn't have to worry about him," Mom said with a huff.

"I've got him," Blaster said. The sounds of him firing came from behind me.

Dad sped in, releasing a wide spread of lightning aimed at Tenji. Without missing a beat, Tenji rolled under the arcing electricity and tossed two fireballs at Dad. He dodged the first, but the second struck him in the leg, exploding on impact. Above us, Dad did an involuntary forward somersault in air as the force knocked him off balance. He righted himself and flew straight up, avoiding the third fireball Tenji shot. The fire Gifted ran for the building's corner.

"Damn." Mom said when Tenji ducked out of sight. She put a shot into the larger hound who circled us.

Another dog threw itself at me. I wrapped a ball of energy around my fist and punched it. The hound hurled backward and struck the building with a thud. It yelped, hitting the wall. It dragged itself upright.

I grabbed Blaster, who devoured beef jerky. "You're eating now?"

"Reloading," he said around the massive mouthful of dried meat. He chewed, swallowed, and shoved more in.

Thirty seconds might have gone by, and we still had three healthy and two wounded hellhounds to deal with. Add in a very fast, fire-throwing Gifted, who could also heal these things, and it spelled trouble. Where was the rain?

The beasts circled us. I moved to put my back to Blaster. "Are you re-loaded?"

"I'm about half full. What kills these things?" he asked around the jerky he chewed.

"We killed them before, but these are much tougher. Just inflict maximum damage and hope the rain gets here soon." I ducked as a burst of flame shot at us from Tenji's hiding spot. A bullet shattered the brick next to his head. The flame ended abruptly.

"Wind is wreaking havoc with my aim," Mom said, anger in her voice.

Another shot hit the building, keeping the fire-wielder out of the fight.

The nearest hound darted in. I kicked it in the head, letting the momentum carry me around to punch the larger one on my right flank. The pack instinct was strong with these things. It made them far more dangerous than if they all just charged in attacking.

Blaster, using short bursts, drove one of the smaller hounds back as it pushed to get to us. Their attacks increased, forcing us to be defensive.

The wounded hellhound leapt. I stepped under it and punched

upward into its exposed abdomen. It jerked higher into the air from the force of the blow. Dad flew in, catching the beast and propelling away from us.

"Let's see how they like to swim," Dad said, as he flew the hellhound over the building and toward the bay.

The massive beast crashed into me, knocking me to the ground. Pain shot up my leg as it wrenched under the weight. I got my hands on the hound's neck to keep it from poisoning me. Its forepaws raked at my chest and belly, but the reinforced suit held; it wouldn't for long.

With a sharp twist, I pulled the creature off balance. I grabbed onto its ears and yanked, moving its head farther away. It yelped and tried to free itself, but I held on.

Thunder erupted next to me as Blaster hit another hellhound at point-blank range. Its head evaporated in a brilliant display of pyrotechnics.

Over the comm-link I heard a loud splash as Dad dropped his passenger in the bay. "They can't survive water. Where is the rain, Warden?"

As if he'd summoned them with his words, large drops spattered over the concrete. The storm quickly increased until we stood in a wall of water. The hellhounds whimpered, convulsing as the water dissolved them. Blaster whooped. The beast he'd been fighting turned into a puddle of goo.

I dropped hold of the hellhound. It melted away before it could try to run.

*Tenji.* He was still here. I ran to where he'd been shooting flames at us and saw him headed toward the back of the building. He had to be stopped, one way or the other. I ran as fast as I could, intent on catching him. My boots thudded across the wet, cracked pavement as I chased him.

The loud pounding of my pursuit must have warned him. He spun and lobbed a fireball at me. His aim was off, and the fireball soared over my head and fizzled against the rain-soaked pavement. He dodged around wrecked cars and an overturned bus, making a clear shot impossible. He ran down the road, away from the building and the rest of the team. I followed, my breathing ragged in my own ears.

"Tommy, where are you?" Dad asked.

"Following Tenji. He can't get away," I said as I dodged around a three-car accident.

A fireball hit the nearest car as I cleared it. Tenji swore and ran on.

I needed to be careful. The impact of the fireball wouldn't do any permanent damage, but the fire would burn my skin like anyone else's.

The rain increased as I pushed myself for every ounce of speed. I wasn't letting another of the Syndicate get away to kill someone else I loved.

Tenji turned down a road marked "one way," and I realized why he'd run here. A small boat bobbed in place, moored to an old concrete dock. If he reached the boat, I'd lose him for sure. I doubted Dad would find him in the storm Warden had pulled in. I jumped into the ankle-deep water. In a few more seconds, Tenji would be on the boat and gone.

I thrust my hand into the water and unleashed every ounce of energy I could. It raced across the surface, dancing over it like water on a hot griddle. The arc hit Tenji's legs, and he stiffened and fell.

I cut the juice and ran to catch him before he could recover. He had pushed himself to his hands and knees. I flipped him over and grabbed him by the front of his shirt. The rain plastered his long, jet black hair and beard against his face.

I pulled him in close. "Where's Reaper?"

He laughed. I let a jolt of lightning flow into him.

He shuddered and groaned as the electricity raced through his body.

"Next time, I won't be so nice. Where's Reaper?"

His eyes closed, as he coughed. "He's gone. Yelena took him. He's not himself anymore." He opened his eyes and stared into mine. "Soon, you'll be just like him: her puppet."

"Never. Why did you take Waxenby?"

Tenji smiled a weak smile. "Yelena wanted him. He's not what you think he—"

He coughed. His body shuddered. His mouth opened wider, green foam pouring out. I rolled him to his side to help clear his airway, but the foam turned from green to red. Tenji vomited blood, splattering it across the pavement and me. He convulsed on the ground. The blood slowed to a trickle.

I checked his pulse. Dead.

I left him lying in the pool of water and returned to the building. The rain slowed to a drizzle. Warden must have decided the hellhounds were done. Was I becoming like Reaper? I was fighting to save my family, but was he too? Maybe Tenji was right.

Dad landed in front of me. "Are you hurt?"

I looked down, noticing the blood on my hands and arms.

His voice softened. "What happened?"

"I'm fine. I caught Tenji." I saw his eyes widen slightly. He must be thinking, given the amount of blood covering me, I'd killed him. "I questioned him until green foam poured out of his mouth. He vomited blood until he died."

He put his hand on my shoulder. "It was probably a poison pill. The Syndicate are known for using them in case they're captured. What did he say?"

I sighed. "He said Reaper was gone and wasn't acting like himself, and Waxenby wasn't who we think he is. He died before he could finish answering."

"For a has-been wannabe, Oliver certainly has a lot of people after him," Dad said softly. "We might need to look at him a bit closer. Are you okay?"

I shrugged. "I wanted to kill him, and I might have. He said I was turning into Reaper." I looked Dad straight in the face. "The funny part is, I think he's right."

"No, Tommy, he's not." He put his arm around my shoulders. "Reaper lives for the kill. It's his drug of choice. It drives him. It bothers you to hurt people, and you were angry because you want to protect the people around you. Reaper would have let

Tenji die before he risked himself. Would you let Marcel die to escape?"

"No," I said glumly. He made sense, but I'd been excited to catch Tenji and willing to torture him to get the information I needed. None of it sounded heroic.

"Let's get back to the team. Reaper may have left information behind." We returned to the building. "Mr. Wizard will have a field day if we find anything good."

It took us a couple of hours to search the building and package up all we found. The gold mine was two laptops, which Marcel hoped contained information we could use. Once we completed our search, we used the portable translocator to travel back to San Francisco Underground base.

Blaster shook my hand, as he said to Dad, "Call me if you ever need another man. It was a good fight."

"We will. You did great out there." Dad clapped Blaster on the shoulder. "You were a real professional today."

Blaster's face lit up. "Cyclone Ranger just complimented my fighting. Wait until I tell the guys. They'll never believe it."

Warden shook her head dramatically. "Blaster, report to Atlanta. I'm going to need your assistance there. I've got a couple things to discuss with Ranger."

"Yes, ma'am." There was a happy jaunt in his step as he crossed the room and headed out the door.

"You know, his ego is going to be out of control for a while," Warden said with a smile. "He already had a high opinion of himself. God help us all now."

"His ego will help him get through what's coming next." Dad said, seriously. "Mr. Wizard is working on finding a spot for your people. I'm hoping the information we uncovered will give us enough to stop the death ray once and for all."

"Let's hope so. For all our sakes."

We shook Warden's hand and translocated back to Harker with all the materials we'd taken from Reaper's hideout. We stepped into our room to find Marcel sitting on a box, a frown set on his face.

"Hey Marcel," I said. "What's up?"

"I need you guys to see something and let me know what you think." He shook his head, sending shock waves through his fro. "I don't know, but this could be really bad. Follow me."

Marcel led us up a flight of stairs and into the armory. We went to the black door in the back of the room. He keyed the entry lock, and the door slid open. Inside looked exactly like the machine Mr. Fix-it used to make our combat suits, and I said as much.

Marcel's frown deepened. "It is. I dug into the code, and his name is all over it. If Mr. Fix-it built this, he must have been in the Dark Brigade."

"Mr. Fix-it in the Dark Brigade? No way," I said. "There has to be another reason. Maybe they forced him to build it."

"Doubtful," Dad said. "Mr. Fix-it was embedded with various teams for his protection. It would be close to impossible for him to be coerced into building a device he didn't want to."

Marcel opened the panel under the keypad and pushed a series of buttons.

"Welcome." Mr. Fix-it's voice came out of the speaker. "Step inside and the device will create a custom fit combat suit for you."

"That's his voice. He definitely built it, bruh," Marcel said.

It was Mr. Fix-it. Was one of our allies a Dark Brigade member? Could today get any worse?

15

Dad called a meeting on level two, including Pepper and Mimi. We sat around the table as Marcel reviewed what he had found out about the machine.

"I'm not sure what, if anything, it means, but it would be good to know if Mr. Fix-it was a member of the Dark Brigade. He might be able to tell us the location of the remote station."

Pepper rolled her eyes. "I've known Fix-it for years. He's an upstanding guy and wouldn't work with terrorists. Geez, guy even refused to sell to the Patriots since Titan kept killing innocent bystanders."

"This is stupid," Mimi said. "Why don't we ask him?"

"He'll just admit to it, if he is a member?" Dad asked. He sounded curious about the answer.

Mimi shrugged. "People make mistakes. Once he's confronted, he might own up to it, so he could stop carrying a secret around."

"Well, it couldn't hurt," Mom said when Dad looked over at her. "People confess to the craziest things in court. I can't see why it would be different here."

Marcel pulled up the video conference, and a few minutes later,

Jinx answered. Her hair was frazzled, and she had bags under her eyes.

"Are you okay?" I blurted out before anyone else could talk.

"Harold has been taken. We went to the grocery store yesterday, and a van pulled up and snatched him. I swear it was Reaper driving. I'm gonna kill him when I get my hands on him."

"Slow down," Dad said calmly. "We'll find him. How did Reaper even locate you? You're off the grid, as far as Gifted go."

"If I knew how, I'd tell you. None of this is getting my Harold back. If they remove his dampening unit, he'll drift back into his vegetable state. He's no good to anybody like that. They'll kill him for sure." Jinx hovered on the verge of hysteria.

"This is important to us finding Harold. Did he ever work for the Dark Brigade?" Dad asked her, carefully. "We found a device he created in one of their bases."

Jinx's face became the dictionary's definition of incredulous. "Are you stupid? Harold never worked for those bastards. Back before the Storm, he was kidnapped and forced to build a bunch of stuff. I got him out, but they had his toys still. Now, if you're done askin' stupid questions, we need to find my husband."

Dad cleared his throat. "I'll handle—"

"Oh, no you won't. What you'll do is find a way to get me, and we will rescue my Harold, or I'll jinx your ass into next year. Screw the consequences."

Dad held up his hands. "Yes, ma'am. Let me figure out how to get you, and I'll call you back."

"You better." Tears welled up in her eyes. "I don't know what I'll do if they hurt my Harold."

"They won't hurt him. We'll make sure of that," Dad said softly. "We'll be in touch."

The line disconnected. The woman who'd been on the other end of the line wasn't a Gifted hero fighting for survival, just an old woman who wanted to live in peace with the husband she loved.

I wondered if her time as a hero had brought her as much pain as it did me. She'd lived through terrorist attacks, being hunted by the Reclaimers, and watching her friends get killed.

"Michael, we need to get Jinx and keep her with us. If Reaper finds out who she is, he might kill her to keep her from helping us," Mom said as Dad rubbed his forehead. "Reaper needs to be dealt with."

It dawned on me how Reaper found Fix-it. "Jon was with us in Charlotte. He must have led them to Fix-it."

"Bruh, good call. I never liked that asshat. We need to blue screen him in a hurry." Marcel's fingers flew across the screen to the point they almost blurred. "If Reaper was in Charlotte yesterday, he's still got to be within driving distance. My guess is in DC, because Atlanta is crawling with Underground and Reclaimers."

"We need to fight fire with fire," I said. "It's time to force the Council to take a side. Yelena's making us look like chumps. If we're going to beat her, we need magic of our own."

"I agree with Tommy," Mom said, clicking into lawyer mode. Her back straightened as she locked on to Dad. "The fight with the Brotherhood is a long-standing conflict with the Council. Therefore, they are duty-bound to assist and defend parties the Brotherhood attacks in pursuit of their agenda. Under these circumstances, they cannot and will not be allowed to stand idly by while we wage war against an aggressor they should have long since dealt with."

Dad gaped openly at Mom for a minute. "That's a lot of words to say, 'Get off your ass and help us.'"

Mom sniffed. "If you'd like to be imprecise about the statement, then you should present it to the Council. If that is the case, please continue on without my assistance."

Marcel and I laughed.

"We usually give up here, Ranger," Marcel said. "She's got you locked down."

Dad shook his head. "I'll leave the lawyering to my brilliant wife, while I sit in the corner and drool." He chuckled. "We need to get Alyx to convene the Council, and Susan can state our case. In the meantime, Marcel, any ideas on how to track down Jon or Reaper?"

"I'm working on the two laptops you brought in, and Pepper is reading through the loose materials for me. I'm also running a search program to locate a suitable spot for the Underground, since we need to relocate them. I'll have more resources to use once the decryption program finishes tomorrow. Then I'll have full access to Harker's systems and online storage."

I saw Marcel had removed his Gift dampener. How long could he burn at this rate before his powers took a toll on his mental state?

I waited until Mom and Dad were caught up discussing our strategy to deal with the Council.

"How long has your dampener been off?" I asked him, keeping my voice low. Mom would insist he put it back on, but I knew he wouldn't since we needed all his skills more than ever.

"Two days, but I put it on when I sleep. I figure I can make it through the Harker system decryption finishing before I put it on again." He rubbed at his goatee. "Maybe a bit longer if I put it back on once I finish hacking Reaper's laptops."

"Alright, but be careful. If Mom notices, she'll flip out." I punched him lightly in the arm. "Besides, I don't want to have to water you daily when you turn into a vegetable."

He laughed. "Bruh, I'd be dead in two days with you taking care of me." He returned to working on whatever he was doing. In a lot of ways, Marcel was the backbone of this team. He'd saved our butts more than once. We'd have been captured at Castle if not for him.

"Tommy, you up for a jaunt to Atlanta tomorrow?" Dad asked after he gave Mom a quick kiss. "Marcel, can you leave word with Warden? We'll be there tomorrow at noon and we'd like Alyx to meet us there?"

"Sure thing, Ranger." He didn't even look up as he worked on the screen. "Done. Should have a reply for you later."

"Get some sleep. We need to stay fresh."

I decided now was a good time for a trip to the armory and the suit creation machine.

Deep gouges decorated the front of my suit, thanks to the hell beast. With a little extra time on my hands, I could get a new combat suit. I entered the armory and realized I didn't know the keypad combination. A yellow sticky note with Marcel's scrawl was affixed to the door—the code. I punched it in, and Mr. Fix-it's voice welcomed me. A screen lit up in the middle of the door, and the suit construction wizard appeared.

"If you are ready to begin, say 'Yes.'" A female computer-generated voice had replaced Mr. Fix-it's.

I said, "Yes," and followed the prompts, answering all the questions. I chose black for the color after seeing all the grief Dad had taken over his gold Cyclone Ranger suit.

When I finished answering questions, the door slid open, and I stepped in. I remembered this from last time. The lights ran over my body, measuring me for the suit. When the lights stopped, the door opened, and I stepped out.

The display read, "Time to Completion: 20 minutes." Below, it asked if I wanted to create another suit. *Might as well.* Selecting "Yes" put me back to creating a new suit. I decided having my Saturday Showdown suit wouldn't be so bad, so I selected the blue and red color combination. The display now showed progress bars for both suits. In twenty-five minutes, I'd have two new suits and could throw out the one I wore.

I dropped on the floor to wait and fell asleep, waking to the display alarm going off. Next to the door, two panels had opened, revealing my new suits. No helmets, but I'd gotten used to going without one, and with an expected lifespan of ten minutes with me wearing them, I didn't mind. I pulled the suits out and exited the armory. Everyone had left the meeting room, so I decided to return to my room.

I tried on each suit, and they fit perfectly. No surprise there. Where my old suit had panels incorporated between the layers of mesh, this one consisted of a thicker material, but no extra pieces. Maybe this machine was an older model and didn't have all the advanced features of the one in Charlotte.

I tossed both suits over the end of the bed and took a long hot shower. The fight in San Francisco had worn me out. Energy still swirled within me, but I was drained on a level I'd not experienced before. I wanted to feel bad for Tenji, but I kept thinking he deserved what he got for working with Yelena. Did he think she'd spare him if they ended the universe?

Some people never learned.

---

I got up, ate breakfast, and then got dressed for our trip to Atlanta. Since this wasn't a night mission where the colors would stand out, I threw on the blue and red suit. I might deal with some remarks, but the suit reminded me of Wendi. She'd been proud, strong, and fierce the night we fought on Saturday Night Showdown.

To think she loved me when I wasn't any of those things. I missed her still, but my memories tended to be of the good parts of being with her, not how it ended.

Our translocation room was empty when I arrived, so I took a seat on a crate to wait. I really wished we could have cell phones again, but the security risk far outweighed playing games while I had downtime. A few minutes later, Dad came in dressed in a new suit as well.

"Great minds think alike," I said as he strode in. His suit was dark navy blue with a single lightning bolt up each leg. He looked every inch the hero he was.

"Marcel told me when I saw you go into the armory. You were asleep when I came in, so I went back later. You ready?"

"Yep."

I stepped over to the silver disk, and Dad activated it. A moment later we were in Atlanta.

A slight girl with short, platinum blond hair sat behind the control console. As she approached us, I noticed a crossed lightning bolt tattoo running down her arm. "Welcome. Warden is out by the main doors, so do you need an escort?"

"No, thank you," Dad said. "We know where we're going."

"Excellent." She smiled. "It's an honor to have you both here with us."

"Thanks. I like your ink," I said. Mom hated tattoos, but I thought they were cool if done well. The artist had put a lot of detail into the image. I hadn't noticed from a distance.

She blushed. I started to apologize, but she spoke before I could. "Do you? The Underground had adopted it as the symbol after you both beat the Gauntlet. It's a reminder we have to fight to be free."

It was my turn to blush. "Really?"

"Totally. No one thought beating the Gauntlet was possible, but you did it. My parents are in the Block, and it gives me hope you'll be able to free them one day." Her blue eyes were full of optimism I'd long since lost. I wanted to promise her we'd free them, or stop the death ray, or anything else to encourage her, but nothing came out.

Dad saved me. "What's your name?"

"Darcy," she said quickly. "I can't believe I'm actually talking to the two of you."

"It's great to meet you." Dad smiled at her. "Keep up the good work. We've got to meet with Warden now."

Her eyes widened. "Oh, I'm so sorry. I'm keeping you from saving the world with my babbling." She scampered off to her seat behind the control panel.

"Just what we need. Groupies," he said with a laugh. He steered me out of the building and down the street.

"They're tattooing themselves with lightning bolts because of us?" I was stunned at the thought that anyone would want to commemorate the Gauntlet. Wendi had died, and we'd been on the verge of losing until Marcel broke in.

"Sounds like it. Be glad she had them on her arm. I've seen people tattoo bolts in very, um, inappropriate areas. It gets uncomfortable fast when a fan drops their pants in the middle of a restaurant to show you their dedication."

"Wow." I'd experienced some weird stuff, but I'd never had fans before. I walked along with Dad, noticing more lightning bolt tattoos in various designs as we moved through the streets. I heard cheers a couple of times. We were famous?

Warden and Blaster stood surrounded by people, most likely the engineers working on fortifying the defenses of Atlanta. The group parted as we arrived. I noticed two of the people had the tattoos.

Warden saw me staring and glanced over to see what had caught my attention. "Saw the new artwork? We've been fighting the Protectorate for over twenty years, and I've never seen anything take hold so fast."

"People need hope," Dad said, nodding to the group. "With the death ray going, they have to believe we'll save them." He shook Blaster's hand and exchanged greetings.

"Well then," Warden said. "We better find a way out of this mess. Have you found a new location for us? I need time to—"

The main doors of Atlanta began to open, something that wasn't supposed to ever happen.

Reaper stepped through. "Atlanta, I have returned home!"

So much for a nice visit. It was time to take out the trash.

16

As if Reaper weren't enough, Jon and Armageddon strolled in behind him, along with ten lizard monstrosities. The monsters were the color of a dead body left to rot. They had long spikes growing from their backs and squared off jaws with shark-like teeth protruding from their lipless mouths. Each had eight legs ending with a three-taloned foot and long tails tipped with a wicked barbed hook. People screamed, running from Reaper's invasion.

Above us flew three winged humanoid creatures that appeared to be crosses between a dragon and a human. Their wingspans must have been at least fifteen feet, with long talons coming out of the wings.

They circled near the ceiling, gouts of flame coming from their mouths as they roared.

Dad turned to Warden. "Get as many people out as you can, while we try to hold them."

"Forget it. They aren't taking our home base from us without a fight." Warden pushed forward, but Dad restrained her.

"You can't summon a storm in here. Move the people to San Francisco. They can come back once we've dealt with Reaper. Send your fighters here."

She looked ready to argue but didn't. "Get them out of my base." She turned and ran, calling for people to follow her.

I helped people move toward the translocator.

Blaster stepped in next to Dad. "What's the plan, Ranger?" He almost bounced on his toes as he stood there.

Had I been like him at my first fight with Brunner? I doubted it, since I'd been scared to death. After all this time, combat still frightened me. Anything could happen once the fighting started. I'd lost too many friends to be excited about it.

"I'll take the three fliers," Dad said. "You two hold the ground until we get reinforcements." He launched himself into the air.

Blasts of lightning illuminated the dimly lit recesses of the ceiling thirty feet above us. The dragons screeched their challenge as they dove toward Dad who flew far faster than the bulky-winged creatures. He threw lightning at them, but it didn't stop their pursuit.

"Stay close. Yell if you need help," I said as I ran toward Reaper. The ground between us held the giant lizard monsters. They lashed their tails back and forth, like angry cats waiting for their chance to pounce on us.

I knew Reaper would hide behind the reptiles and wait for a chance to strike. He'd never risk a fair fight. It was time to end him, once and for all.

The lizards scuttled forward to meet us. I unleashed a bolt of energy into the closest one. The blast dug into the gray-green skin but didn't slow it down much. Blaster followed up with a quick burst to its head, which split apart like an overripe melon. The stench choked us as it billowed off the carcass.

"You always show up where you aren't wanted, boy!" Reaper yelled as I knocked back a lizard who'd tried to take a bite out of my arm. "Too bad I'm gonna have to kill you this time."

"Like you killed Gabriella?" I called back, using the information Pepper had given me about how Reaper had murdered his girlfriend as a weapon.

I wrapped force energy around my foot and booted the closest lizard in the side. The impact threw it across the space toward Reaper. He scrambled out of the way as the eight footed reptile bounced across the ground at him.

"How could someone so pretty ever love a loser like you?"

Reaper screamed incoherently. Jon aimed and fired an arrow that I barely had time to dodge. It burst behind me, releasing a gas I was sure wouldn't be good to breathe.

"Watch the arrows," I told Blaster, who was busy taking down a second lizard. "Jon's full of tricks."

I fired an arc of lightning at Jon, who easily avoided it, but it also kept him from taking aim. I kicked another reptile in the face, breaking a whole lot of teeth.

The odor from these things smelled like rotten eggs and blood buried in a sewer in the middle of August. Every hit released more of the stench. Blaster killed his third lizard, casting even more of the reek into the air.

Blaster had gotten too close and fell to his knees, retching. I held my breath and ran to get him.

The lizards charged Blaster. I fired an arc of electricity in front of the attacking reptiles. They backed up, but one forced its way through. With a lash of its tail, it hooked Blaster through the leg, knocking him over. He scrambled to escape while the lizard dragged him along the ground toward the others.

I dove to grab Blaster's outstretched arm and fell short. He shouted as the lizards converged on him. Izanami leapt over the prone Blaster and brought down a machete, severing a lizard's tail. She wheeled around, striking another across the face before latching on to Blaster and flinging him from the fight.

He bounced across the ground with blood seeping from his pierced leg, but he coughed and pushed himself up. I wanted to get him to safety, but taking my focus off the fight would be bad for both of us.

While I was distracted, more lizards pushed closer. A bolt of lightning shattered the ground in front of me as Dad swept by, two of the winged dragon-men on his tail. I backpedaled as fast as I could, getting to cleaner air. Izanami lifted one of the lizards and flung it at Reaper, whose sickly green scythe made him easy to find.

Where was Jon? I put both hands out and made a web of lightning in front of me. It had barely formed when two arrows burst against the shield and disintegrated. I needed to watch him more closely. He was gunning for me.

We'd killed half the lizards, and I saw the crumbled form of a gray dragon-man on the ground near where Jon stood. I threw a ball of energy at him, forcing him to retreat. We were holding our own, barely.

Blaster was on his feet again.

"Can you fight?"

He nodded a bit unsteadily. "I can, but I can't eat. The gas makes me sick."

I fired another blast at Jon and then one at Reaper, to keep him from flanking Izanami. "See the guy in green?"

He nodded again.

"Shoot at him any time he tries to fire his bow. Keep him off balance until we get more help."

"Got it." He held up his arm and fired a single shot, barely missing Jon, who threw himself flat to avoid the blast.

Izanami had four lizards around her. She kicked at the closest, only to have another slam into her. While her power lasted, she was invulnerable, but based on her coughing, the toxic stench was affecting her as well.

"Ranger, we need a cyclone," I said.

"Incoming."

I fired a blast of lightning over the group of lizards, knowing Izanami would be immune to the electricity. I had to get her out of there fast.

As the reptiles scattered, she ran through the opening between the lizards to where Blaster leaned against a wall. His face had gone ashen. He struggled to stay upright. His leg seeped blood where the barb had pierced it. He needed medical help now.

With a roar, a cyclone spun up in the center of Reaper and his crew. One of the winged creatures got sucked into the whirlwind, flapping helplessly against the funnel of air.

I pulled Blaster's arm over my shoulders and dragged him toward the translocation room. Izanami helped, and we carried him to safety. Once we turned the corner, the whir of the cyclone lessened enough to yell over it.

"Take him to Warden before he dies," I shouted to be heard.

She nodded and helped our injured companion down the street.

I ran back toward the fight. I didn't get far. An arrow exploded near my feet. I tried to jump, but found a cord had wrapped around my legs, preventing me from moving. As I landed hard on the ground, I felt a flood of energy from the jolt I'd taken. Jon stood before me, an arrow nocked and ready to fire.

"Tommy, I want to talk," he said, the bow never wavering in its aim. I'd never get out of the way of any shot he took. He knew a normal arrow wouldn't hurt me, so he was up to something.

"You come in here with Reaper, and you expect me to listen?" He must have hit his head on something if he thought I'd ever trust him again.

"Balthier can resurrect Wendi. He needs you to help, but she'll be alive again. We don't have to be enemies. You can help me get her back." His tone was pleading, and it hurt, but I knew the truth about the Brotherhood.

"Whoever Balthier is, you can't bring people back from the dead. I know what happens when you try. They aren't alive. I saw it firsthand. They live in excruciating pain, screaming and crying as they thrash on the ground. Do you want Wendi to live like that?"

Jon's eyes glazed over, like Mom's had when she used Alyx's mind necklace. Someone had control of his mind and nothing I said would change it. "Tommy, you loved her. She loved you. I have to save Wendi. It's your fault she's dead, so help me undo the wrong you caused."

He'd accused me of causing her death before. Lying on the ground with my legs strung together, I couldn't fight. I might get a shot off, but Jon was fast enough to dodge anything I threw at him. The Reclaimers had needed three soldiers to take him out after they'd inhibited his Gift. I had one shot, and it would have to be enough.

"Jon, set the bow down, and I'll take you to the Council. If anyone can bring her back, it's them. Please, I don't want to fight you." I knew it was futile, but I owed Wendi and would try to spare her brother.

"If the Council had stopped the Reclaimers, none of this would have happened. They are useless. Decide. Are you helping me or not?"

A knife struck Jon in the shoulder, spraying blood as it buried itself to the hilt. He tumbled to the ground, rolled, and ran between the two buildings he had stood in front of.

Nico Desiderius, the Gladiator, strode down the street, sword in hand. His gaze swept the area as he came to me. A single slash of his sword cut the cord wrapped around my feet. "Are you hurt?"

"No. Are you here with Alyx?" I asked as the big man pulled me to my feet.

"Yes, Warden told us you'd be here. It looks like you could use some help, my friend." He ran down the street with me close on his heels.

Dad threw lighting at Reaper, who used the scythe to deflect the bolts. The last dragon swooped in to slash at Dad with its barbed wings but missed.

The remaining three lizards charged us as we came into the open area by the doors, but Gladiator dispatched them easily. I pulled him back from the stench. Jon was nowhere to be seen.

Armageddon stood near the door, looking like he was ready to run. Reaper looked unsure as his head jerked to the right.

I turned to look. Alyx floated in above the ground, which was littered with dead lizards and winged dragon men. A blast of blue energy hit the last flier, and it winked out of existence. "Reaper, give up. There's no one to save you this time," Alyx said, as he floated out of reach.

Yelena's laugh echoed through the open space.

## 17

T hat is amusing," Yelena said, entering through the still-open door. She cast a withering glance at Armageddon, who followed behind her like a whipped dog. His head hung as he stomped his feet like a spoiled child. She wore a gold gown and a tiara, like she was a princess. "Oh, you've brought Gladiator for me to play with. How I love short men."

Gladiator glowered at her but said nothing. Alyx and Dad landed next to us. I still hadn't spotted Jon. The knife wound would slow him down, but I didn't count him out.

"This place is under my protection, Yelena," Alyx said, his voice tinged with anger. His walking staff emitted a bluish-white light. "Leave now or suffer the consequences."

She laughed. "Dear boy, you aren't strong enough to blow out the candles on my birthday cake, let alone make me do anything. Send Thomas over, and I'll retire without harming any of your pets."

Now it was Alyx's turn to laugh. "Tommy is staying right where he is. Now leave."

Her face grew more serious. "Reaper, bring me the boy."

Reaper started toward us, scythe glowing in front of him. Gladiator stepped forward, testing the swing of his gladius. The blade glowed faint blue as he moved into a ready stance. Under different circumstances, this would have been the fight of the century. Today, it was a distraction.

Reaper lunged, sweeping the scythe low, aiming for Gladiator's legs. The attack failed to even come close. Gladiator leapt back out of range, advancing in the wake of the scythe's swing. Reaper switched his grip and blocked the over-hand swipe Gladiator brought down on him.

The weapons rang with the force of the impact.

Nico kicked Reaper square in the gut with the sole of his boot. Reaper stumbled backward, striving to avoid one of the dead or dying lizards. The smell from the dead lizards still lingered all around us.

Gladiator pressed his advantage with quick strikes to keep his opponent off-balance as Reaper retreated toward Yelena. Reaper reversed his grip and swung again, only to have Gladiator duck the blow and open a slice across his opponent's belly. It wasn't deep, but it must have shocked Reaper, since he rarely got much of a fight from his victims.

Reaper swung his scythe again, reversing it in mid-swing, but it wasn't an agile weapon. Gladiator neatly parried the blow and nicked Reaper's arm. Blood trailed off the sword's tip as it whistled through the air.

"I'm not a helpless woman or an old man, Reaper. You'll have to do better to kill me." Gladiator unleashed a fury of blows, forcing his opponent back.

Reaper's swings became more frantic and wild.

"I grow bored of this," Yelena said, throwing a bolt of red magic at Gladiator.

He blocked the blast with his sword, but Reaper took advantage of Gladiator's distraction and swung the scythe into his chest. I screamed as I watched the tip of the blade bite into my friend. Gladiator grabbed the shaft of the scythe in his left hand. He looked down at the glowing blade protruding from his body.

Reaper laughed. "Not so high and mighty now, are you?" He pushed against the blade, but it didn't move.

Gladiator flicked his sword upward and caught Reaper in the groin.

Reaper released the scythe's handle to grab his crotch, screaming in an octave usually reserved for choir boys. His knees buckled. He slowly toppled like a melting snowman.

Gladiator casually pulled the blade from his chest and threw it next to the writhing Reaper. A small trickle of blood ran where the edge had cut him "Your disgusting weapon does not work on me." He kicked the groaning man in the chest.

I stood there, stunned. Reaper's scythe had killed so many people, but Gladiator had stopped the blade before it cut into his body. Why hadn't it sucked his soul out like it had mine?

He addressed Yelena. "Come now, witch. I will sever your head like I did the one who cursed me."

Yelena sighed. "Why do men always disappoint me?" She flicked her hand at Reaper, and he vanished from sight.

Even after she'd done the same in Dallas, her taking Reaper from us still pissed me off.

She floated up, out of reach of the advancing Gladiator. "You are vexing me." A single ring of yellow light wrapped around Gladiator, immobilizing the big man in his tracks.

Alyx cast a band of blue at Gladiator, but the warrior didn't move.

Yelena's laugh sounded cold and menacing. "See? You can't even undo one of my simplest spells. Hand over the boy, or you will face my fury."

"I will not," Alyx said.

Dad stepped forward, arms raised to let loose on Yelena.

Alyx stopped him. "This is my fight." His hands moved in a fluid motion and a ray of blue light covered Gladiator, who faded away.

"Oh, good. You sent your pet home." She settled back on the ground, peering around. "I do so hate a mess." She spread her arms wide, and the lizards and winged dragon-men disappeared. "This is between us. No distractions. I will show you the true meaning of power. Shall we dance?"

"I'd be delighted." He rotated his hands, spoke one word, and shot a beam of brilliant blue at her. The shield around her shimmered as the magic dissipated against it.

Yelena responded with a fierce bolt of red. It impacted against Alyx's shields but didn't penetrate.

Dad pulled me back out of the way.

I leaned over to him. "Jon is still here. Keep an eye out for him."

He nodded before launching into the air. The mages ignored Dad as he swept the perimeter, looking for Jon.

Alyx threw a series of blue orbs across the intervening space that transformed into the small, stocky water golems I'd seen when we fought the Kra-kelal. They launched a barrage of swirling marbles at Yelena. The spheres stuck to her shield as they hit. More and more covered her shield, pounding it.

She screamed and unleashed a blast of pure red magic. The orbs and golems smoldered as the red light hit them until they evaporated away to nothing.

Alyx renewed his attack by throwing a disc of blue light at her. It sheared through her shield when it struck, but she avoided it before it hit her.

"You've improved since our last encounter. I'll make sure to finish you this time." Yelena said.

"You can try, but I'm stronger now than I was," Alyx said.

Yelena cast a bolt of ruby red at him, which he deflected into the building to his right. It collapsed as the explosion tore it apart. Dust billowed out from the site, obscuring my vision for a few moments and causing a minor coughing attack.

Alyx spun his staff, spoke a word, and two blue dragons the size of Great Danes flew at her with a crackling energy.

Yelena countered with a viscous slicing attack. The streak of red slashed the first dragon's head clean off. It transformed into motes of blue dust and fell to the ground.

The second dragon banked sharply, avoiding her attack. Electricity raked her shield. Alyx fired a bolt of energy at her, neatly parting her shields and knocking her from her feet.

She stood, face flushed red with anger. The tiara hung from a clump of her silver hair, which had come undone. Her golden gown was torn along her side, the fabric dangling from the waistline. "I will destroy you and all those you love. The earth will burn with my rage."

The dragon swooped in from behind her, launching another attack. Her shields held as she blasted a wave of red magic at Alyx. He spun his staff before him so fast it blurred. Blue energy spread out from him. As the wave of Yelena's magic hit, he stumbled from the force, but held the barrier in place.

Yelena dispatched the dragon and renewed her attack against Alyx. She fired repeatedly at him. He struggled to hold the barrier in place. Sweat dripped off his face as he rotated the staff like a plane's propeller, deflecting shot after shot.

Debris and dust filled the air as the magic blew apart anything it touched. I dove out of the way of a ricocheted bolt. The building behind me fared no better than the others.

The onslaught continued until Alyx fumbled his staff. He caught it, but the momentum was gone, and the barrier dropped. Two bolts lanced through him. His phantom legs vanished, sending him sprawling on the ground. It saved him having his head blown off by the third blast. He knelt on the ground, trying to use his staff to rise again.

Yelena cackled. "You thought you could best me?" Her arm shot out, and Alyx fell on his back from the force of her blow. "I am the breaker of worlds, and you think to be my equal? The Council will shudder when they remember your fate this day."

"Do your worst," Alyx said as he pushed himself to a seated position. "If I fall, another will rise to take the Summoner's mantle and stand against you."

"Fool. The Council has been betrayed from within, and soon the Brotherhood will end this reality and bring forth a new one created by the masters." Her hands twisted in a swirling motion as she chanted her spell.

I had to save Alyx. I ran toward him, realizing I couldn't reach him in time. I dove to push him out of the way of her spell.

That's when the whole world came apart.

Yelena's spell struck me in the side as I shoved Alyx with a blast of force. He tumbled across the ground like a rag doll, but I didn't have time to worry about him.

My Gift absorbed her spell, turning my vision red. Every molecule in my body wanted to explode from the energy transformation inside me. I thrashed on the ground. My power fought to convert the magic's energy even as the spell tried to destroy me. The magic tore at me, forcing a scream of agony.

I became aware of Yelena standing over me, a smile plastered on her haggard face. "I offered you the world, and you refused me twice," she said in icy tones. "Now, you will see what happens to those who cross me."

"Screw you, lady." I pushed the words out of my mouth like shoving a truck tire through tar with my nose. The magic slipped through my fingers while my Gift struggled to coalesce it into a usable form. My skin burned from the inside out. Energy sought to escape the prison my Gift built around it. I'd transformed the death ray's force into a form I could use. Why would magic be any different?

"Defiant to the end." She put her hand over her heart, giving me a pitying look. "So tragic to die so young. I will remember you fondly as I torture and kill your family."

The magic pulsed within me. I pulled at it, forcing it into a familiar ball shape. Slowly, I clawed at the foreign substance of her magic until my powers synced with the rhythm of the spell I'd absorbed. The building blocks broke down as my Gift used the raw power to craft a new type of energy. A maelstrom of power and fury combined into a single creation. My vision cleared, and I took control.

Yelena's eyes widened. "It's not possible. You aren't a mage."

"Bite me, bitch." I unleashed her magic, amplified tenfold back at her. She shrieked. The impact blew her across the clearing, slamming her into the door meant to protect Atlanta from the Reclaimers. Her body broke with a sickening crack. Armageddon ran to her and fell to the ground before cradling her body in his arms.

I forced myself to my feet. The energy still thrummed inside me, but most of it had been consumed by the shot. I crossed the space between us. Armageddon whimpered as he held her lifeless body. The vision of a beautiful woman had fled, leaving an old, wrinkled face behind. Everything with Yelena was a lie.

Time passed as I stood there. Dad settled down next to me with Alyx in his arms.

"You did what you had to do," Dad said. He set Alyx on the ground.

Words wouldn't come to me. I stood there, mutely staring at the woman I'd just killed. Even though she'd deserved it, it tore me up inside. There was more blood on my hands. Would I ever get used to the killing? Gladiator had told me people who got used to it ended up monsters. I took some solace that I still held on to my humanity, for now.

A green glow surrounded Yelena's body.

"I told her you were far stronger than she gave you credit," a man said from the doorway. He strolled into Atlanta's base, a look of disdain firmly affixed to his face. His short, salt-and-pepper hair was slicked back over his scalp. He had a long black mustache which he'd heavily waxed. He wore a blue and scarlet overcoat with arcane symbols along the collars. Dark pants and boots trimmed in the same red completed the outfit. He carried an ornate staff with a fiery gem at the top. "Yelena always did overreach."

Dad pushed me back. "Who exactly are you?" Lightning arced across his knuckles as he waited for an answer.

The man gasped. "How rude of me." He bowed low to us, with a magnanimous sweep of his arm. "I hadn't realized Alyx here hadn't told you of me. I am Balthier Caligari, High Priest of the Brotherhood. I've come to retrieve Yelena's body."

"Balthier, you are not welcome here," Alyx said, pointing his staff at Caligari. "Take Yelena back to your masters and leave this place in peace."

Balthier's eyes glowed as he stared down at Alyx. "You are growing tiresome. I came to speak with young Thomas and retrieve my fallen compatriot. Cease your idle threats. I'll be gone shortly."

"We aren't interested in speaking with you," Dad said, stepping forward. The lightning intensified around his hand as he spoke. "Take her body and leave now."

"Ah, the infamous Cyclone Ranger, always thinking with your power and never using your wits, few that you own." He flicked a dismissive gesture at Dad. "I tire of all the bravado."

With a pop, Alyx and Dad disappeared, prompting a serious WTF moment.

"What did you do to them?" I asked, trying to keep the panic out of my voice.

Caligari studied me for a moment before he answered. "Nothing. They are safe, though they will find coming back here troublesome for a few hours. I would speak to you. Will you do me the civility of listening, or will I be forced to use violence against the good people of the Underground first?"

I'd never dealt with Balthier Caligari before. At least with Yelena I had intel enough to fight her. As Mom told me growing up, listening costs you nothing and sometimes gives you everything. "Go on. I don't want any more people hurt today."

The High Priest smiled at me. "I fully concur. Yelena, shall we say, was overenthusiastic in her pursuits. You are aware of the trouble the world is in?"

"Trouble? You mean the death ray?" I wasn't following, but after absorbing Yelena's magic, my brain was a bit scrambled.

He sighed. "No, my dear boy. Gifted like yourself are caged like animals. Civilization has been built on the backs of the oppressed minorities since the beginning of time. There is hatred, death, and disease. All these things are rampant across the universe. Does any of this sound fair to you?"

"No." I hated to agree with anything Balthier said, but the world *was* a mess. With the death ray and the Protectorate, it would get worse.

"Exactly. My brethren want to replace this flawed reality with one where all beings are equal. Humans are just the tip of the iceberg. There are species across the universe living in much worse conditions. In our new reality, they will all be at peace."

"And you'll rule over everyone, correct?" I saw where this was going, but the longer I kept him talking, the more likely Alyx would bring help to fight Caligari.

He spread his hands before him. "All people need leaders, and who better than the one who controls the power to create a utopia?" He held his hand out, and a galaxy spun over it. "This is just one galaxy. In it, trillions of souls live and die every day. We will end all of it and bring about true peace for all the beings who inhabit the universe."

He sounded like the Protector going on about the purity of humanity, how weeding out the Gifted made them stronger and united. They must teach this crap in Dictatorship 101. "What does any of this have to do with me?"

The galaxy winked out of existence. "Your ability is extremely rare. You amplify the energy you absorb. With you as our focus, we believe you can increase the magnitude of the spell to a level that will bring about the new reality we've discussed. Of course, you will be one of the chosen ones. The leaders of our new society."

"Believe? You don't know if it will work?" *Alyx, hurry up. How much longer can I listen to this crap before I laugh in his face?*

He was spinning a tale, but Caligari spoke his version of the truth. All beings would be equal, as slaves. Power-hungry tyrants never were good for the people they ruled over. I'd seen it time and again in Redemption.

"Nothing is absolute, until you test a theory. My offer to you is this: join us, and we'll leave your loved ones alone, or dismiss my offer, and you'll find Yelena was soft as a blanket compared to my wrath. What will it be?"

"I don't get time to think it over?" I asked, trying not to laugh. The idea of destroying the universe was ludicrous. "This is a big deal. Destroy the world or not. Become part of an evil organization or fight against them. Tough decisions."

Caligari frowned. "Yelena warned me of your impudence. I will take your sarcasm as a no, and bid you farewell." The green glow around Yelena increased and then vanished. "I will leave you with a reminder of your foolish decision."

"You've got a business card?" My brain may have snapped when I absorbed all the extra energy. Was I punch drunk? Or just plain stupid to antagonize Caligari this way? My mouth had a mind of its own.

"You could call it that." He smirked at me. "Armageddon, finish your mission." A green sphere encompassed the big man as he stood up and started toward the middle of Atlanta. "Don't you hate dilemmas? Do you try to absorb all his energy and possibly end your life, or allow him to destroy the Underground's home? I'll be interested to see your choice, Mr. Ward." He stepped through the portal and vanished.

"Oh, shit." I opened fire on Armageddon, but the green shield diverted all the energy.

He ambled, eyes half-shut, as if he were asleep.

I fired in front of him, but he simply stepped around the hole I'd made. I keyed my comm-link and got nothing but static.

Nothing worked. I had to stop Armageddon, but how? I fired a sustained blast to his right, moving him in front of an office Yelena's magic had weakened. Running between the two buildings, I unleashed a force bolt against the back. The structure swayed but stayed up.

Concentrating the energy within me, I used both hands to deliver a solid blow of force to the back of the building. With a loud groan, it fell forward, sending up a huge cloud of dust as it hit the ground, pieces raining down on me. My mouth and nose filled with dust, plaster, and who knew what else, causing me to gag. Breathing became difficult, forcing me to hold my breath to run out of the cloud.

With an effort, I stumbled behind the neighboring building and into clean air again. Gratefully, I took a few deep breaths, coughing out as much of the dust as I could. I headed back toward Armageddon.

The building landed on him. After a few moments, the pile shook as the big man fought his way free of the tangle of wreckage. Soon, he would release himself and be climbing out. I might have bought myself a couple of minutes.

I crossed the street and repeated the process of knocking down another weakened building, but I kept my mouth and eyes shut this time as the walls collapsed. I knew it wouldn't hold him forever, but it would have to be enough.

I ran for the Underground's translocator. When I reached it, I found Warden pacing in front of the device, while the tech from earlier sat at the desk.

"Where have you been?" she demanded as I ran into the room. "Where are Alyx and Ranger?"

"Caligari sent them somewhere. Armageddon is here and is going to destroy the city." It finally occurred to me no one else was here. "Did you translocate everyone out already?"

"Yes. Alyx and a couple of the mages opened portals to other bases, and we evacuated the city in under ten minutes. I waited for your team to return, but I'd hoped it would be with better news."

It annoyed me to admit I never had better news. At least Armageddon wouldn't be killing over a thousand people when he blew. "You two get out of here. I'm going to try to divert the blast."

Warden grabbed my arm. "What are you talking about? The city is empty. You aren't throwing away your life to save a rundown base. For God's sake, we've already been compromised. Do you think Reaper won't come back here to settle the score?"

The Underground had lost so much, I refused to let them lose their home as well. We could replace the doors, create new ways into the city after collapsing the old. We didn't need to lose Atlanta after I destroyed Dallas. If I lured Armageddon into the translocation room, we could send him to one of the abandoned cities where he couldn't hurt anyone. I knew my plan would work. "Reaper won't be bothering anyone for a while. We can fix the security issues. Your people have lost enough already. I can stop Armageddon."

Warden took my face in both of her hands. "Tommy, it's an empty city. The *people* are the Underground, not the places. We will fight from another city, but you are coming with us. Understood?"

Darcy yelled from the control desk. "Big guy is pulsing red and is about a block away. I think we're out of time."

"I know I can do it," I said weakly. Her stare held me in place. "You've got to let me stop all this."

She smiled. "I know you can. I'll stay with you then, if you're going to try. We both live or die together."

As much as I wanted to save the base, I knew I couldn't jeopardize Warden. Darcy joined us. "I believe in you, Tommy, but Warden is right. There's nothing left here worth dying for."

I nodded. They were right. I was so fixated on my need to save something or someone from all the bad stuff we'd been through that I'd lost track of what was important. "We go."

"Good choice. Darcy, set the self-destruct on the translocator and let's get out of Dodge before Armageddon brings the roof down." Warden pulled me to her, and we waited for Darcy.

After a few seconds, the self-destruct warning came over the speakers. Darcy ran to us as the ten-second countdown started. The machine whirred to life, and a moment later we stood in Harker.

Mimi was waiting for us. "Everyone is upstairs." We followed her up to level two's conference center. Marcel had the Atlanta feed on the main monitor with Mom, Dad, Pepper, Alyx, Gladiator, and Izanami seated around the table. Mom ran over and hugged me, but my eyes stayed locked on the feed.

Armageddon reached the translocation building and everything went solid white before dissolving to static. Marcel flipped to an external view. I watched as the abandoned city of Atlanta crashed into the giant hole Armageddon had created under it. No one could survive a collapse of that magnitude. Balthier had sent him to his death.

He was just another in the long line of people the Brotherhood had thrown away in their pursuit of a new universe.

After checking on Blaster in the med bay and relating my conversation with Caligari, I did what every normal seventeen-year-old would do. I headed to bed. The next morning, I got ready and strolled to the commissary to get my Mountain Dew and Wildberry Pop-Tarts.

Mom sat at a table with a cup of coffee and a patient expression. I sighed. Let the lecture commence. I considered turning around and going back to bed, but it was better to get it over with than run from it. I grabbed breakfast and took the hot seat. "Good morning, Mom."

"Good morning, honey. How did you sleep?"

I smiled at her. This game was as old as I was. "Fine. You?"

"I slept well. Thank you for asking." She took a sip from her coffee. "I wanted to talk to you—"

I held up my hand. "You spoke to Warden, and she told you about my lame brain scheme to divert Armageddon's attack away from the base, and you're worried it means I have a death wish, or I'm stupid, or more likely both. Points?"

"Am I that transparent?" she asked, taking another drink from her cup.

"Only to me." I took a couple bites of pastry and a gulp of liquid bliss and savored it for a minute. "So, what happened was, I absorbed Yelena's magic, then killed her with it. By the time I got to Warden, I was frantic. My system overloaded on high test energy and guilt over not stopping Yelena's plan in time to stop their home from being destroyed."

"This isn't the normal mother-son talk, is it?" She peered into her coffee, probably waiting for the oracle of parenting to guide her through uncharted territory. I doubted it happened. "I worry about you. You are my child. Your Gift protects you from a lot of things, but it doesn't stop them from affecting you. Seasoned warriors have broken under mental pressure far less than what you've been exposed to."

I ate in silence for a minute. "Seriously, I don't know why it was so important to me, but it was. I felt horrible, but at least none of us died. You always taught me to protect those who can't protect themselves. Sometimes, I take it too far."

"I'm very proud of the man you're becoming," she said. She reached out her hand to take mine. "You've saved more people than you know. Beating the Gauntlet gave hope to all of us. A hope that had died long ago, in most cases. Warden told me she'd never seen such energy in her people before. Just remember to take care of yourself."

I squeezed her hand and shot her a quick smile. "Roger that, Mom." I finished off my breakfast, ran to get another drink, and then Mom caught me up with all the news.

Gabriel had patched up Blaster. He would be back on his feet soon. Warden, Darcy, and Izanami were staying on until we could figure out our next move. Marcel had cracked the encryption on the Harker systems.

Mom gestured over my shoulder. Alyx entered the room, phantom legs restored. Instead of his Summoner's robes, he wore an old Storyteller's t-shirt, baseball cap, and jeans. He pulled up a chair and sat after Mom waved him over.

He looked tired as he sat there. "Well, Tommy, you did something

I'd not been able to do. I'd yell at you for pushing me out the way, but her spell would have killed me, so instead I'll just say thank you."

"I owed you after you got us out of the zoo. Oh yeah, and I still owe you one, since you got us out of the Megadrome."

He shook his head. "You never cease to amaze me. Are you okay after all that?" He glanced at Mom, who nodded slightly.

"I'm sitting right here. I'm good. Sleep definitely helped." I took a long pull from my drink. "What can you tell me about Balthier Caligari?"

He scowled before answering. "Not much, I'm afraid. He's always stayed in the shadows, pulling strings, unlike Yelena, who preferred a confrontational approach. He's a time mage like Maya. Tricky to nail them down, though I'm surprised he's working with Reaper."

"Why is that?" Mom asked.

"Reaper is far too blunt in his approach for Balthier to use as an agent. My guess is he'll keep him around as a backup to whatever plan they are trying to execute."

"He said I was needed to amplify their spells to create a new universe." I picked up my glass, but it was empty.

"It might work, but I'd be surprised if it did. Magical theory isn't my thing, but the power needed to recreate the universe would be far more than any one person could handle."

"Only if you're concerned with the person surviving." I doubted the Brotherhood cared if I survived the procedure or not. If they got their way, who carried the cost? Especially given they were killing every being in the universe.

"Good point, but I still don't buy it. Caligari wouldn't divulge his plans until it was too late." Alyx stared at me for a minute. "No, I can't see it working. He wants you to join them but not for the reason he suggested."

"What other reason could there be?" I asked.

"I don't know, and that scares me," Alyx said, his forehead wrinkled as if he were thinking really hard.

I got up and refilled my glass. "Do you believe Yelena about the traitor on the Council?"

His face clouded over. "Yes, I do. She had me beat. No sense lying to a dead man."

"So, who can you clear on the Council?" Mom asked. She tapped her finger on her lips as she thought. "There has to be a way to narrow it down."

Alyx shrugged. "Charles, our elemental mage, still hasn't recovered from the fight with the Kra-kelal, but is he really injured? I'd like to think Makeda is trustworthy, having healed Blaze. Your guess is as good as mine."

Mom wasn't done yet. "Is there a way you can verify if they are working with the Brotherhood?"

I thought back to the day I met Charles, when he attacked me, thinking I was a demon.

Alyx frowned. "No, there—"

"Sir Charles," I said. "His staff reacted to me after I'd been in contact with Eiraf. Can we use it to find out who's been in contact with the Brotherhood?"

Alyx opened his mouth to answer, then closed it. After a minute, he responded. "The barrier around the Council's stronghold would make communication with outside forces nearly impossible. I could ask Charles for the staff and then make each of the members touch it."

"You'll tip your hand by doing that. Who would be the most useful to have on our side?" Mom asked.

"With Charles injured, Makeda would be the strongest and most resourceful," Alyx said after a short pause.

I wanted with all my heart to believe Makeda would never betray the Council, but my wishes weren't taken into account very often. "If you have the staff in his room when she checks on him, you'd know."

"Yeah, it should work." He turned to Mom. "Why not unmask the traitor now? We would be much stronger with five mages working together."

"Then how are you going to feed Caligari false information? Unless we need a specific mage, you should continue to act as if nothing is wrong. When the chips are down, we can relay bad intel to the Brotherhood and hopefully play it to our advantage." She smiled sweetly at him.

"Susan, did you ever lose a case?" Alyx asked, his eyes wide.

"Not often, and never from being outplayed."

Alyx left to get Makeda and Jinx. Mom suggested he take Dad along for backup. We still needed to find Mr. Fix-it, and I had no idea if Caligari would ignore Jinx as Yelena had. Once everyone was in one place, we would decide on the correct course to take.

A few hours later, we were ready. Pepper decided to stay in the med lab, along with Mimi. They wanted to be there if anything happened to Blaze or Waxenby. We gathered around the table on level two. Makeda had passed the test and sat at the far end of the table with Alyx. Warden and Darcy huddled together, representing the Underground. Jinx was next to Mom and Dad while I sat with Marcel as he manned the control to the wall display.

Dad stood and addressed the table. "We have a lot of issues facing us, and we felt it best to discuss them as a unified team instead of in smaller groups. Not everyone is affected by each of these problems, but together we are stronger than apart."

"Stop your blathering and tell me how we're going to find my Harold," Jinx said. "That bastard Reaper took him, and if he forces Harold to work, his mind will be gone in a week."

Mom jumped in. "That's as good a place as any to start. Marcel, can you give us an update?"

Marcel's gaze darted around the room at all the new people. I nudged him to get him started. "Hi, um, some of you know me as Mr. Wizard. Um, I hacked into the retrieved laptops and found a location outside of Atlanta that may be the place Reaper is working from. I don't have any way to get eyes on it, but there's a high probability Mr. Fix-it is being held there."

"We can send a small team down to rescue Harold" Alyx said. "If there's nothing there, we can keep looking."

Jinx clapped her hands. "Well, you young'uns get going and get my Harold back."

"Being the middle of the day, sending people in now wouldn't be our best plan," Warden said gently. "We want to get Mr. Fix-it back as much as you do, Jinx."

"Huh, if that don't beat all. You want to get my husband back as much as me? You are crazy. Been livin' underground for too long if you believe that."

Warden clamped her mouth shut and leaned back in her seat. Darcy's eyes bugged out a bit as she stared at Jinx. I doubted she'd ever heard anyone talk to Warden in such a way before. I know I hadn't.

Dad plunged on, ignoring the interruption. "We'll send a small team with Alyx tonight to scout the locale Marcel uncovered, with an eye toward rescuing Harold." He glanced down at the paper on the table. "The next topic is the death ray and the Underground. Warden, can you give us a quick update on your preparations?"

Warden gave Jinx a sidelong glance before she spoke. "We've evacuated all the Asian continent bases on Mr. Wizard's—"

"His name is Marcel, not Mr. Wizard, just like Harold ain't Mr. Fix-it. I know you live in a hole in the ground, but at least have some manners," Jinx said. Warden looked like she was about to have a fit.

Makeda stepped into the fray. "Ma'am, please, we are trying to work together to save your husband along with numerous others. If you—"

"You can go right on ma'amin' me, but when I have Harold back, I'll be on my way, and you all can handle whatever mess you've gone and created."

"Enough." All eyes turned toward me as I realized I'd been the one to speak. "Jinx, we are going to get Harold back. So, for now, please let everyone talk. There's a lot at stake."

"Now, Tommy. I don't kn—"

"I'm the one who got Harold back from his vegetative state. When I met him, he could barely speak. Because of me, you've had your husband back, and because we are all willing to risk our lives, we'll hope to have him back again. Don't you think that deserves your respect?" All the stress boiled out of me as I lectured Jinx, a woman who was old enough to be my grandmother. "I'm sorry."

Jinx cleared her throat. "You've got a way about making a point that makes a soul listen up." She turned to Warden. "I'm sorry. I'm so worried about my Harold, I've lost all sight of my manners. I hope you'll forgive an old woman."

Warden nodded. "We are all worried about him, Jinx. He's a good man, and we'll do everything we can."

"I know you will." Jinx looked at Dad. "I won't interrupt again."

"Thanks." Dad checked his notes again. "Warden, you've evacuated the Asian bases. Is that correct?"

"Affirmative. Marcel advised the station could hit several sites from its given location, and we are relying on it using the same pattern as before. My people have moved all essential equipment and set fail-safe devices on the translocators, in case the Reclaimers make a move to take them."

"Excellent. Marcel, do we have an ETA on the next city to be attacked?" Dad asked, glancing at Jinx to see if she was going to comment again. She sat with her hands folded in her lap.

Marcel tapped at his keyboard before answering. "The last two strikes have been at a decreased time interval. This will be the ninth city the weapon has fired at. If my calculations are correct, we have six hours until the next strike."

Before Dad could reply, the warning siren started, giving the standard ten-minute countdown to the weapon firing.

"Well, I guess your calculations were plumb wrong," Jinx said.

Marcel pulled up the Moscow cameras, and the assembled group sat waiting for the beam to strike. When the countdown ended, we watched the death ray hit the city, killing anything living within. *At least it will kill the giant rats if it gets to Washington, D.C.*

Jinx spoke into the silent room. "Ranger, you might want to get on stoppin' that."

Mom rubbed his back as he put his head on the table. "Why don't we take a break? Tommy will show you where the commissary is if you're hungry or thirsty."

Pepper ran into the conference room. She'd obviously been practicing since I'd been away. "The machine is done. Blaze will be out in twenty minutes."

"Please make yourselves at home. We need to attend to this first." Dad said. Our team followed Pepper back to the stairs.

I hoped the regeneration chamber worked to cure Blaze, not kill him like the Death Ray had the people of Earth.

As we entered the med bay, Gabriel stood by the machine.

"What is Blaze's status?" Pepper asked. She walked over to study the hologram.

"The sequence is complete, and he is being brought back to consciousness. In five minutes and twelve seconds, the lid will open." Gabriel flickered slightly as we moved in to stare at Blaze's bearded face through the window. A slight fog covered a portion where his breath hit the glass.

No one moved as Gabriel counted down to the machine opening. For the first time since the death ray started firing, we had the possibility of good news at the end of a countdown. At least, we hoped so. I wasn't sure how Pepper would take it if Blaze died as he came out or had been deformed to the point of non-survivability. The fact he breathed encouraged me, but anything could happen once the lid lifted.

"Please step back from the device. The lid will open quite rapidly."

With a sharp hiss, the top of the machine popped up, revealing a very naked Blaze. Mom grabbed a hospital gown and draped it over his exposed parts. Pepper leaned over Blaze as he opened his eyes.

"We need to do a full diagnostic workup. If you could move him"—

Gabriel flicked out of existence and appeared at the opening to the examination room—"here."

"Blaze, can you hear me?" Pepper had her hands on his face.

He wasn't focused on her. He mumbled something before his eyes rolled back in his head. He started to convulse. Pepper wailed as she begged him to stop.

"Convulsions happen in 46.2 percent of patients. Please move him to the exam table so I may treat him before he perishes."

Dad pushed the grief-stricken Pepper away and scooped Blaze into his arms. He ran through Gabriel and placed Blaze on the operating table. Robotic arms descended from the ceiling, placing heart monitors and other electrodes on his temples. Other appendages pressed injection guns against Blaze in various places. They emitted a pneumatic hiss. Medicine was pumped into his system.

I stepped closer to get a better look as another arm swung down. It struck me in the back of the head before stopping.

"Please exit the operating theater until the patient has been stabilized."

The heart monitor showed his heart beating rapidly. Two paddles pressed against his chest, shooting a jolt through his body. After the second time, they rose into the ceiling as the monitor displayed a more normal heart rate.

"We have stabilized the patient. It is normal for cardiac incidents to occur on completion of the molecular reassignment device."

The machine elevated Blaze's arm and inserted a line into it.

"We will keep him sedated and hydrated as is necessary. Initial scans are encouraging. There are no external maladaptation or gross deformities. His internal organs scan as normal. The tumors are gone, but spots of tissue remain. This is normal but can lead to a rapid regeneration of the cancer if the DNA has not been re-written correctly. Odds of survival are 72.09 percent. If the patient lives twenty-four hours, the chances of revival are at 91.1 percent. After forty-eight hours, success is expected."

Pepper hugged herself, as she stood crying. Mom had her arm

around Pepper, whispering in her ear. Dad, Marcel, and I stood off a bit.

Blaze had always seemed indestructible, but as he lay on the table, stuck full of tubes and wires, he appeared small and weak. Would he be himself after all this, or would the procedure leave him a shell? I wondered if he'd thank us for reviving him if he was an invalid or worse. Only time would tell, and we had less of that now than ever.

Once Gabriel assured us Blaze was stable and resting comfortably, Dad led Marcel and me back to the conference room. Dad gave a brief update on Blaze's condition. Blaster had joined the group, not wanting to miss the mission to find Harold, but Dad refused him going on missions until Gabriel greenlit him as ready for action.

It was agreed that Makeda would take Warden, Dad, and me to the outskirts of what had been Atlanta to scout out the location. Alyx argued, but after the beating he'd taken from Yelena, he was overruled.

It had been three days since Mr. Fix-it had been taken, and I didn't know what kind of shape he'd be in if we did find him. Marcel ran us through the specifics of the location. It had been an old factory before the city had been hit the first time. Most of the communities around the dead zones had vanished as the locals moved away, fearing contamination and anything that came out of the cities. Given the armorgators and giant rats, I couldn't much blame them.

We ran through the possible scenarios we might encounter, but with Reaper and Jon injured in the last battle, how much resistance would we face? Even with Gifted healing, Reaper wouldn't be fighting anything stronger than a cold for the next few days. Jon would fare better, but not tonight.

Dad finished briefing everyone on the challenges we faced, and then we broke for dinner. I ate but don't know what. My mind kept wandering back to Blaze lying on the table. Maybe he'd survive, maybe not. I'd imagined he would wake and be fine, not struggling for his life with a seventy whatever percent chance of survival. Part of me kept waiting to see Mom leading a devastated Pepper in from the med bay. After all we'd gone through to get to this point, there was still no guarantee he'd make it.

At nine, I readied myself, recharging my stores from the black box. I wore my new suit and found a box of night goggles, which I took to Dad, Warden, and Makeda. The mage declined, saying she had better ways to see in the dark.

I hated to admit it, but I was glad Makeda and not Alyx was accompanying us. After talking to Pepper, I had reservations about Alyx, even though I knew it was unfair, not having heard his side. In the end, I'd rather trust Pepper and owe him an apology than not listen to her and regret it later.

As I walked to meet up with the team, Marcel stopped me in the hall. "Bruh, you might need this." He handed me a dampening watch. "If they've been working Fix-it hard, he could be slipping into his vacant state. You'll need to get this on him."

I checked his wrist and saw he wore his. When he noticed my puzzled expression, he said softly, "It was Wendi's. I thought she'd want us to help Harold."

I placed it around my wrist, making sure it was off. "She would. She adored Harold and Alicia." A fresh wave of embarrassment washed over me, thinking about how I'd spoken to Jinx this afternoon.

Marcel punched me in the shoulder. "Bruh, you were *epic*. We'd have ended up in a screaming match if you hadn't set Jinx to rights."

"Great. Being an asshole makes you epic now."

He laughed. "She told me after that you reminded her of herself at your age. 'Full of spit and vinegar and ready to take over the world' were her exact words. You did good, Tommy. You always do."

I smiled at him and returned the punch to the shoulder. "Thanks. I'll be talking to you soon." I pointed at the comm-link in my ear.

"Mr. Wizard, at your service."

I met up with the rest of the away team, as Marcel called it, in the translocation room. Makeda opened a portal to a moonlit street near the factory. Tree roots punched through the asphalt in places. Nature always took back deserted areas. Even in the dead zones, mutant plants and animals survived in the harsh environment.

Warden summoned up a storm, blotting out the moon with a thick layer of clouds. The winds picked up, but this wasn't one of the gale force storms from Dallas—more of a springtime shower. The clouds drizzled as we moved down the dark street. No streetlamps shone, only the empty eyes of deserted buildings. Some were covered with graffiti, others had been burned down, and nothing was as it had been.

Dad took the lead as we came into sight of the old factory. All the windows had been boarded up, but light leaked through the cracks. Someone was in there. With Yelena dead and Reaper injured, we had no idea which members of the Syndicate were guarding Mr. Fix-it, if he was here at all.

"Mr. Wizard, do you have eyes on the target?" Dad asked, more as a formality than anything since Marcel was blind here.

"Negative, Ranger. Call the ball."

"I'm calling the ball." Dad said. He signaled to move forward.

"Good luck team." I could hear the concern in Marcel's voice. For all the geeky terms and casualness, he worried as much as Mom when we were in the field, especially when he couldn't watch out for us.

Using the cars as cover, we crossed a small parking lot. Once Dad spotted the door, he stationed Makeda and Warden behind a rusted-out Buick, providing them a direct line of sight into the building. The two of us moved around the car, him on the left and me on the right.

Dad reached the building ahead of me. I took the other side of the door while Makeda watched the building. She gave the all clear. I swung around and booted the door, throwing it open with the first kick. I may have put a bit too much force into the strike, since the door tore free of the hinges and flew across the room with a loud crash.

"So much for subtle entrances," Dad said commenting on my entrance technique.

Before me was an ancient industrial shop. Lanterns hung from long chains, unevenly lighting the factory. Rows of rusted-out machines stood in lines next to an old conveyor belt. Rats skittered away in the darkness, and I cringed. After the giant rats in Washington, I couldn't stand any rodent.

I gave the signal. Dad slid in behind me and moved past me, lightning rippling across his knuckles. I caught a whiff of burning flesh as he passed. I stepped behind the first row of machines, staying low so I could use them for cover as I crept down the length of the factory floor. In the center of the room stood an old metal staircase leading to a walkway that ran around the building. At the top of the staircase was what looked to be an old office. Brighter light shone from within.

Dad launched himself up to the second floor, where he landed gently outside the door. I ran to the bottom of the stairs but didn't climb since my boots would make a huge racket on the old metal treads.

Dad cracked the door and peered in. He gave the all-clear and entered. I went up the stairs as quietly as possible, sounding like a bear tap-dancing on a metal stage. I reached the top and found Dad kneeling in front of Harold. The older man cried as he spoke to Dad.

I stepped in and took Harold's hand. "Hi. This will help," I said, keeping my voice low. I gently snapped the dampener I'd worn on his thin wrist and turned it on.

He looked me in the face. "Tommy, I knew you'd come for me. I'm so sorry. They made me build it. They would have killed Alicia if I hadn't."

Dad barely shook his head. He didn't know what Harold spoke of. "What did you build?"

He sighed. "They made me build them a thirty-foot lens structure to focus the energy from the death ray to a meter-wide beam." He smiled at me suddenly. His grin was huge to the point I worried he'd been hallucinating the whole thing. "I pulled a Death Star on the bastards, I did."

"Death Star?" Dad asked, a confused look on his face. "You mean like in *Star Wars?*"

"Damn right," he said. "I built in a defect so you can destroy it. They'll never find it until it's too late."

"Way to go, Mr. Fix-it," Marcel said in my ear. "Stick it to the sick bastards."

Dad nodded. "Let's get you back to base. Alicia has been worried sick."

We half-helped, half carried Harold out of the building. Makeda opened the portal to Harker. It was a good ending to a very trying day.

And it wouldn't be the last hard day, by far.

21

We'd arrived back at Harker much sooner than anyone expected. Why go through the trouble to kidnap Mr. Fix-it then leave him locked in a room unguarded? Reaper and Jon had probably gone to ground instead of facing us if we found their hideout. I doubted either would be in shape to handle Dad and me after the fight with Yelena.

We deposited Harold in the med bay, giving Gabriel the chance to look him over. With his dampening watch on, any effects of overwork should recede in a few days.

Mom escorted an overanxious Alicia down the hall to see her husband. For once, I was glad to not witness their reunion. Not that I wasn't happy for them, but most of my reunions hadn't been overly joyous. I knew it was childish, but I didn't want to deal with other people right then. I headed down to the communications room to talk to Marcel.

"Hey, bruh," he said as I entered. "Totally epic finding Mr. Fix-it and no Syndicate. Nice to max out the gains for a change."

"Yeah." I slumped into a chair, leaning my head back, trying to relax. At seventeen, I felt like seventy. "Not sure what happened, but

I'll take it. Dad's going to talk with Harold and see if they can piece together any intel for where the remote station is or what it does."

"As close as I can tell, the remote station was designed to operate the death ray from Earth, but I haven't found any place with coordinates or any other location data." Marcel scratched at his chin. "From what I understand, only the twelve leaders of the Dark Brigade knew where the site is. Even with Harker's systems decrypted, I haven't clued into anything new."

"Harold said he built Reaper a lens to focus the death ray's energy, and they took it before Yelena attacked Atlanta." Nothing about Yelena's plan made any sense. "Why build a lens without anything to use the energy and then leave Fix-it unguarded?"

Marcel's fingers ran over the keyboard in front of him. "Because they implanted a tracking unit in him."

"What?" I sat up so fast I got a head rush. "We brought him back bugged?"

"You did, but Harker was built to neutralize any transmission devices. There's a tensor field around Harker that restricts most communication bands," Marcel said. "The oscillating frequency of the magnetic pulse array makes standard protocols inoperable."

I took the opportunity to close my eyes and pretend to snore.

"You have to match the…" He kicked me, interrupting my pretend nap. He tapped on the keyboard some more. "Sorry. Gabriel has been alerted and will remove it. Anyway, the comm-links are specially designed to work around the fields."

I leaned back, rubbing my sore neck. "You certainly know how to freak me out."

Marcel buffed his nails on his shirt. "Grand Master Bruh, at your service." He turned back to the monitor. "Freaked myself out as well. I wasn't sure if the field would restrict the tracker or not."

"We should have been more careful. Alyx warned me Caligari's style was to play from the shadows. If they located Harker, I'm sure the Reclaimers would love to get even for Castle. One call, and there would be a battalion here in a few hours."

"The self-destruct is wired, and I can activate it from just about anywhere," Marcel said. Boulder had died setting off the explosion that kept the Reclaimers from capturing our base.

"It wasn't your fault," I said into the quiet. "Boulder tipped the Reclaimers off to our location."

Marcel's eyes grew wide behind his glasses as he stared at me. "How did you find that out?"

"Warden told me. I didn't tell anyone else, but you need to hear it. My guess is Parasite left behind a compulsion to betray the Underground, but he fought it long enough to get away. You didn't screw up. He betrayed us."

Marcel sputtered as he tried to talk. "I can't believe I've been blaming myself when he turned us in."

"Yeah. Parasite messed him up bad, just like Waxenby."

"Absolutely," he said, with an energy I hadn't heard in a while. "Thanks for telling me, bruh. I appreciate it. Now, let's find Reaper and fatality his ass."

I left the room as Marcel tore into his search with a renewed sense of purpose. I hit up the commissary for a pre-bed snack and called it a night. I needed to think about how the tracker tied into all of this. Tomorrow would bring its own headaches.

---

The next morning, I headed downstairs to the meeting room after finding the commissary empty. Warden, Alyx, Mom, and Dad sat around the table discussing the situation at hand. Dad waved me over, so I grabbed an empty chair to listen in.

"After talking with Harold, which took far longer than it should have, I got my answers." No doubt, Jinx had made it much more challenging. Regardless of the state of the world, she looked after her husband first. Everything else came second. "Reaper and Caligari were discussing a trial run of the lens in Cairo when the weapon fired there. We should plan a strategic assault. We've killed Yelena. If we can take down Caligari, the Brotherhood should be set back."

Alyx nodded. "Without Balthier in charge, the Brotherhood's leadership on Earth will be eliminated, but not permanently. It may take years for the next leader to emerge from the succession fight, but by then we'll have destroyed the death ray."

I cleared my throat. "Excuse me. Marcel found a tracker had been embedded in Mr. Fix-it, but it's been neutralized. My guess is that once they had the lens constructed, they left him for us to find so he would lead them here."

Warden leapt on the information like a hungry tiger. "Bugged? How do we know it didn't transmit our locale before Marcel eliminated the threat?"

"He says there's some field surrounding us, making communications out impossible. He called it a tractor field or something like that." Damn if I remembered all the technical details Marcel spewed out. "The comm-links are specially built to work around the field."

Mom shook her head. "It's a tensor field. Marcel is looking into how we could deploy it at the Underground bases once this is over. With Mr. Fix-it here, they'll probably be able to make one."

"We certainly need the extra security," Warden said. "When the Protectorate needs a scapegoat, they come looking for us. I'm sure you all know the feeling."

After being blamed for killing a lot of kids on a field trip, I certainly did. The Protectorate stopped at nothing to keep the population scared of Gifted. Without the imaginary threat, the people would realize how much freedom they'd given up to stay safe from us.

"At least we dodged the bullet with Mr. Fix-it," Dad said with a sigh. "We need to be more careful, but I still think attacking Caligari in Cairo is our best play. We can coordinate a strike against the Syndicate and the Brotherhood while Reaper and Jon are injured. It may be our best chance to stop him once and for all."

"Caligari isn't going to fall back on the Syndicate for his troops." Alyx leaned forward, placing his elbows on the table. "He can summon a far wider range of creatures than Yelena. Even alone, Balthier is vastly more dangerous. I hate to think about what nightmares he can release on this world, if provoked."

"Then what's stopping him from summoning an army of creatures and taking over?" Warden asked in her no-nonsense way. Going from fighting Reclaimers to magical hellhounds hadn't seemed to faze her. Dealing with all the mutated animals in the dead zones had probably prepared her.

"Time and energy," Alyx responded. "Magic takes both, and Balthier has used a lot of each already. Yelena couldn't have summoned the beasts in San Francisco by herself. My guess is he can control ten or less creatures."

"Can we ambush him?" Mom asked. "If I got a clean shot, he'd be done without risking any of our people."

"Except you," Alyx said with a wry smile on his face. "You are one of our people, Susan. Balthier Caligari is too careful to allow such a mundane threat to down him. He'll have shields up against physical attacks for just such a reason. He's far older than any on the Council except Pimiko. This isn't the first time we've tried to rid ourselves of him."

"It was worth a try," Mom said, somewhat defeated. I was sure she'd like nothing better than to have all of us sitting safely here while she gunned down the threat to her family.

"We have seven, eight including Susan, if we need long range fire-power, to go to Cairo and attempt to eliminate Caligari," Dad said. "If we get to the Underground base there, Marcel can give us the go signal when Caligari shows. If the weapon activates, we can translocate back and wait for another opportunity. Anyone think otherwise?"

"I do," I said. Marcel discovering the bug on Mr. Fix-it had given me an idea. We were constantly one step behind, and we needed to stop chasing and start setting the rules. "This is a setup. Caligari spoke about his plans in front of Harold and then put a bug on him and left him unguarded. Why? Because he knew we'd find the factory after we raided the Syndicate house in San Francisco."

Dad's brow furrowed. "I doubt they planned on Reaper and Jon being injured enough to not guard him. My guess is we caught them undermanned, and he decided to leave Harold behind."

"I'm not so sure, Ranger," Alyx said. He studied me for a moment. "Balthier is crafty. I can see Tommy's point. Leaving Harold with their plans and bugged gave them the chance to either attack us here, with us unaware they'd found us, or plan to counter our obvious attack to stop them."

Warden agreed. "If Cairo is a trap, then what is the correct course of action?"

"The bug," I said. Four sets of eyes stared at me like I'd lost my mind. "They're expecting the bug to tell them where we are. Why not let them find us?"

"Honey, there are other bases around the world, but we've already lost a handful of them. Exposing Harker would be a mistake, even if we neutralized the Brotherhood," Mom said carefully.

I smiled. "Who said anything about Harker? We go somewhere we can set up an ambush. It doesn't matter where. What matters is they show up, and we are waiting for them."

"Makes a lot of sense," Warden said, a smile creeping across her face. "If they buy it, we hold the cards. We can set them back with a concentrated strike."

"So, what about Cairo?" Alyx asked quietly. "Do we let them fulfill their plans?"

"If Cairo is a trap, we'd be better off avoiding it," Dad said. "We do take a chance they are planning something. I hate the cloak and dagger games. Give me a straight up fight anytime."

Alyx shook his head, his long hair waving side-to-side. "Balthier is all about the misdirection and stabbing opponents from the shadows. I agree with Tommy. Lay a trap and whatever happens in Cairo happens. We can clean it up later."

"If there is a later." Dad didn't look happy, but he finally agreed to the plan.

Marcel would find the location, and we'd set a trap. If we got lucky, Caligari would be done, and we could destroy the death ray once and for all.

Pepper entered the room. "Blaze is awake and is asking to see you guys."

The noise of the chairs was deafening as we all leapt to our feet.
Finally, maybe we'd get some good news.
At least I hoped so.

2 2

We raced to the med bay and into Blaze's recovery room. A long gray beard covered his gaunt face, and he was thinner than before he went into the machine.

Gabriel stood by his side. "It appears the procedure has been a success. The medical scans show no signs of cancerous nodes in the lungs or other previously affected organs. Heart functions are stable and minimal damage occurred during the cardiac incident. The patient should recover fully."

Blaze sat propped up by the adjustable bed. He smiled wanly as he greeted us. "Good to see you dudes." His gaze flickered back to Pepper; a warm smile lit his face as their eyes met.

She took his hand in hers. "You know, I come back from the dead, and first thing you do is try to leave me," she said, tears mixing with her smile. "Do it again and I'll smack ya upside the head."

He chuckled. "Sorry about being such a nuisance. I will say, I haven't felt this well in years."

Mom hugged Blaze to the point I worried his ribs would crack. "Eugene, we are all so glad to have you back. We'd thought we'd lost you."

"Me too, Susan." His eyes held a haunted expression as he looked past us all. "Me too."

When Mom released him, each of us took a turn welcoming him back. His head hung down by the time we finished.

Gabriel broke into the celebration. "The patient needs his rest. Please adjourn for now. Glenda will establish visiting times until the patient is back to full health."

No one wanted to go, but the crowd moved out of his room. As I went to leave, Blaze called to me. "Tommy, hang for a minute, dude."

Mom patted me on the shoulder and indicated I should stay behind. Pepper sat next to the bed, still holding his hand. I sat on the edge of the bed and really looked Blaze over. His hair hung down to his waist while his beard only reached his chest. His eyes shone clear and bright, although dark circles ringed them. The grin was pure Blaze.

"Pepper says you returned her body. It's a bit trippy for me but fill me in on what went down."

"You sure? A lot has happened since you've been sick." Watching him, I saw how exhausted he was, but Blaze, being stubborn, wouldn't wait.

"Give it to me, dude."

I started back at Castle with Makeda trying to heal him and continued from there. Next, I described the events with the Underground, Jon and Turk, the collapse of Dallas and Castle. I talked about Reaper stabbing me in the back, and Pepper moving into my brain. Then I talked about the escape to Harker and putting him in the molecular reassignment device and told him about the death ray. I spoke for most of an hour, answering questions and elaborating on certain parts.

Blaze leaned back against the mattress. "You've certainly been busy. Explain to—"

"Excuse me," Gabriel said. "You have exceeded the parameters of what is healthy for a person in your condition. Please rest now, or I will administer a sleeping agent to assist you."

Blaze glared at the holo-doc. "Fine. My questions can wait. You'll come back later?"

"Sure thing. Glad you're doing better." I stood and left the room. After all we'd been through, the world felt right with Blaze back in it. I hoped he'd recover enough to resume training with us. The daily work and his steadying presence stabilized me. I hadn't realized how much I'd missed him until now.

On returning to the meeting room, I took my chair, gave a quick update on Blaze, and listened as Dad, Warden, and the mages discussed options for ambushing Caligari. I doubted anything we did would trap the mage. He seemed far too intelligent to fall for the bug trick, but Reaper or Jon might.

They discussed plans long into the night, and when I nodded off, Mom sent me to bed. On my way to my room, I thought about how close we'd come to losing Blaze. It scared me to think of another person dying.

In the movies, the good guys always won and rarely did any of them get hurt, let alone die. The bad guys cornered the market on movie deaths. I wished life could be so simple. But I might as well wish for fairy wings.

I climbed into bed and was asleep before my head hit the pillow.

---

The next morning, I checked in with Blaze. Pepper had him up walking short distances, though he grumbled about it the whole time.

"I'm not an invalid, Raychel," I heard him complain as I walked toward his room. "How can I get stronger on a liquid diet? I want something solid. It's not like I'm asking for a greasy burger, just a banana or an apple."

"Fine," she said, as I stuck my head into the room. "Tommy will keep an eye on you while I get you somethin' to eat." She winked at me as she passed.

I nodded to her before checking on Blaze. "How are you today? From your appearance, I'd say somewhere between grumpy yeti and constipated grandpa." I laughed as Blaze's face twisted in shock.

"Dude, harsh much? I come back from death's door, and my favorite student throws me in the rip current." The gleam in his eye was unmistakable. Blaze hadn't acted like this since we'd left Redemption. The smile faded. "I still can't get over Turk turning Protectorate. Hate is a bad trip, man."

"He was full of it," I said, then tried to change the subject before it brought us both down. "You realize they have a food replicator here? You can order anything you want."

"Dude, Raychel told me. Pretty rad. I'm sure Marcel had a good time figuring out how it works." His smile flickered back into place, but with everything that'd happened, he had a lot to process.

"Mom told me last night Gabriel said light exercise would be okay. I can't wait to get back to learning more martial arts."

He held up his hands. "Whoa. Give me time to get back on the board before we go for a ride. I'll teach you, if I'm able." He checked the doorway for about the fourth time. "Where is she with the food? I'm flippin' starvin'."

"Now you sound like me," I said, with a laugh.

A minute later, Pepper entered the room with a tray full of food. Every type of fruit was there. Some of them I'd never seen before.

"I'll let you eat."

He mumbled something around a mouthful of banana as I left. Pepper waved. She chewed on a piece of something green. I think it was fruit.

I grabbed my own breakfast before heading back to the meeting room. By now, Dad should be conferencing with the others. I wondered how long it'd be before we sprung the trap on Caligari. We'd made progress in stopping the Brotherhood, but we needed to destroy the death ray and eliminate the head mage if we were to have any peace.

Only Dad and Marcel sat at the table. "Where is everyone?" I asked, flopping into the chair next to Marcel.

Dad looked up from the screen he'd been reading. "Alyx, Gladiator, and Makeda are moving the planted tracking device around so Caligari can't pinpoint the location. We've got an abandoned warehouse on the outskirts of Ottawa where we'll spring the trap. We couldn't have the device not broadcasting for a long period, or he'd realize we'd found it. Hopefully, the few hours Harker blocked the signal weren't noticed. Your mother is with Warden and her team in San Francisco, organizing the Underground." He gestured toward Marcel. "Mr. Wizard found a subterranean military installation in the northern reaches of the North American Zone the Underground can inhabit. Warden has her people removing the translocator in Dublin to use at the new base."

Marcel grinned. "Warden actually smiled when I told her about the place." He returned to his work on the screen in front of him.

"Alicia and Harold are staying here until we can relocate them, but Warden is pushing for them to move with the Underground." Dad shrugged. "We'll see. Jinx has never been an easy person to deal with."

I understood the sentiment very well. I'd dealt with a lot of strong-willed people, but Alicia "Jinx" Reynolds topped the list. According to Mom, people like her could give mules lessons. I was happy Dad had dealt with getting her settled.

"What is the plan for Cairo then?" I asked. "Are we going in to try to stop the Brotherhood?"

"No," Dad said, with a quick shake of his head. "Not convinced it's the right decision, but everyone wants to wait to see what Caligari is up to."

"There's a lot of chatter coming from around the area. At this point, the death ray is almost certain to fire soon." Marcel tapped a couple of times, and a map appeared on the wall display. He zoomed in, showing the Cairo area covered in red dots. "The red dots are Reclaimer units the Protectorate deployed. There is no reason they should be fortifying a city with an event this close unless they've been tipped off by whoever is directing the death ray."

I stood so I could better scan the map and noticed none of the troops were inside Cairo. "If Yelena moved the Reclaimers into Beijing to change them, why is Balthier keeping them outside?"

Dad came to stand next to me. "Marcel, can you monitor the transmissions between Cairo and the Protectorate military liaisons? There has to be something we don't know about going on."

Marcel worked without comment as the dots continued moving to a spot south of Cairo but outside the strike zone for the death ray. After about ten minutes, he patched a communications feed into the main display. A familiar voice came over the speaker: Reaper.

"I'm not going to argue with you commander," he said with all the disdain I'd grown accustomed to. "The Protector himself has signed off on this."

"You are nothing but a traitor to your kind. Why anyone listens to you is beyond me," the other voice said.

"All that matters is the Protectorate wants Ranger and the rest. They will be at the coordinates as promised. It's up to your men to bring them in," Reaper said.

"Reaper, the Protectorate has agreed to amnesty for you and your Syndicate but only if we take down the fugitives. If they don't show, I'll hunt you down personally." I knew the voice but was having trouble placing it.

"General Mahady, my employer assures me Ranger and his team will be here. Caligari has gone to great lengths to draw them to Cairo." Reaper said, though his accent was gone. "Ready your men. The death ray will fire in twenty minutes. The fugitives will be here to retrieve the device Mr. Fix-it built."

"They'd better be." The line died with a click.

"So, Cairo was a trap. Interesting," Dad said. He still stared at the screen. The red dots were gathered in one location now, forming a singular large red dot on the display. "If we hadn't ascertained the nature of the bug and the information they fed Harold, we would have blundered right into the trap."

Marcel split the screen to show an overlook of the Cairo skyline on the right and the map on the left. A countdown started in the corner, matching the estimate Reaper had given. "I don't know who spoke to Mahady, but it wasn't Reaper. Vocal patterns are all wrong, according to the voice analyzer."

"One of his personalities?" I asked. On occasion, one of Reaper's victims forced their way to the top and spoke through him. That could have been why he sounded so weird.

Marcel stroked the stubble on his chin. "Possible, but they don't tend to stay on script. Either Reaper is dead, incapacitated, or being used to deliver the message. It would be nice to think Reaper has gotten his, but I doubt it."

When the counter reached ten minutes, the siren wailed through Harker. Marcel dropped the map and scanned through the Reclaimer cameras.

A spark of light caught my eye as he passed by one camera's view. "Go back."

"What did you see?" Dad asked, stepping up to get a closer view of the screen.

I did the same as Marcel clicked backed up one. "Can you zoom in on the highest tower?"

Marcel did, and I froze. The lens Mr. Fix-it created had been attached to the tower.

Marcel whistled. "Good eyes, bruh." He brought the image in closer. "It's on the south facing side. What do you think they're doing with it?"

"Testing," Dad said, as he watched. The lens swayed back and forth. "When the death ray hits, it will direct the beam into the Reclaimers. We've got to stop it."

I caught Dad's arm. "We can't. The troops are waiting for us, and by the time we get there, it will be too late, or we'll be caught in the ray."

Dad pulled his arm free. "Thomas Ward, I will not stand by while innocent people are slaughtered. We are the only ones fighting to save all the people from the Protectorate, not just the ones we like."

"You stood by while the Gifted were hunted, imprisoned, or killed. Those troops are there to kill us. Didn't we lose enough already? How many of us do they need to kill before you stop protecting the killers? What if they killed Mom? Would that be enough?"

He slapped me, turning my head to the side and sending a jolt of pain through me. The iron tang of blood seeped between my teeth.

Anger and betrayal surged into my mind. I clenched my fists, ready to fight. Energy pulsed within me, and all I wanted to do was lash out, but something held me back.

Dad's carefully constructed mask cracked, showing the anger underneath. "You've got no right to speak to me like that."

"I have every right." I clenched and unclenched my fists, fighting the urge to punch him. How dare he put Reclaimers above our safety? "Dominion killed those men, and you turned yourself in instead of protecting Mom and me. You can't save everyone, but maybe you can save us."

He stared at me, veins popping out of his forehead as he shook with rage. I waited, but he didn't make another move.

Finally, he said, "Marcel, can you send a message to Mahady? Warn him Reaper is going to attack them in eight minutes."

After a few seconds, Marcel said, "Done. I coded it from Protectorate command."

The map appeared again. A few seconds later, the massive dot broke into smaller dots and moved away from their location. When the beam struck, a single ray burst across the city and slammed into the Reclaimers' post. They lost a lot of their troops, but it would have been much worse if they hadn't been warned.

Dad still hadn't said anything, but when the death ray finished, he stormed from the room without a word to me or Marcel. I wandered over and dropped into the chair next to my best friend.

"Bruh, that was brutal," he said, not looking at me.

"What else could I do? He would have run in to save the day and died. I'd rather him be mad at me than dead." I put my feet on the table. My brain ran in circles, replaying the events. Had there been a way to stop him without the fight?

I wondered if it had been an excuse to say the things I'd thought all those years in Redemption. He'd never been there for me, and now that he was, he tried to run off and die again.

Marcel sighed. "You did the only thing you could, but I doubt he'll thank you for it."

No, but Mom would. At least, I hoped so.

## 2 3

I stayed out of sight for the next couple of days. FNN blasted the scenes of a Dissident attack on a training exercise in the North-east African Zone. They trotted out the affected spouses and their children to show the human toll those attacks had. Once again, the Gifted were the villains in the never-ending news cycle coverage of the Protectorate's personal propaganda channel.

The training rooms became my new home while I waited for word on our next move. I spent hours going over the stances Blaze had taught me. Mimi and I had started training together. Since her Gift had manifested, she needed to be ready in case of a fight. Her powers were incredibly strong, and I felt bad for anyone who crossed her.

Moving through the motions cleared my head and focused me in a way I'd never experienced before. Hours passed as I moved from form to form, adjusting small details: the angle of my foot or where to stop on a punch. Each piece integrated into the previous one and set the stage for the next.

Late on the second day, I was working through a series of blocking moves when I heard, "Dude, square off your block. Your forearm isn't vertical. You'll end up with a broken wrist if you block like that."

A beardless Blaze stood in the doorway next to Pepper. He'd

pulled his hair back into a ponytail which hung to his belt, but he looked strange with the naked face. He still leaned on her, even though he was mobile. He crossed to me and moved my arm, twisting my fist so it fully faced me. "Now, you're in correct alignment."

"Thanks, Blaze," I said, grinning like an idiot.

"Ya think you should wait fer me next time?" Pepper asked. From the size of the smile on her face, she was excited to see Blaze up and around. "If you fall on yer ass, it's yer own damn fault."

"Only been back a couple of days, and she's harshin' my vibe." Blaze's smile matched Pepper's. After all the years apart, I was glad they were together again. He turned back to me. "We'll go slow, but watch my movements."

Blaze stepped clear and centered himself with a slight wobble. His body flowed from position to position as he glided through the routine. The whole time, he gave me pointers: "Right arm snaps into place" or "move your foot farther out to maintain balance."

As he spoke, I followed along, mimicking the poses and adapting to the suggestions he offered. The second time through, he only commented twice.

As we finished, Blaze flickered in my peripheral vision. I stopped and looked at him, but he stood there nodding. *No flicker. Must have been the lighting.* "Dude, you've gotten a lot better. Just remember the punches snap out, and your feet need to maintain your center. By the time I'm stronger, you'll be ready for more advanced work."

Pepper sat cross-legged on the floor. "It's like watchin' ballet when you two work together." She stood and got ahold of Blaze's arm. "Now that you're done showin' off, can we eat?"

"I'm starving. I haven't eaten this much since I was in high school." He held onto Pepper's arm, though I doubted he needed to or that she minded at all.

Blaze had always been on the short side, but now he reached my chin. "Blaze, you're taller."

He regarded me as if I'd hit my head one-too-many times. "Dude, don't pull an old man's leg. I stopped growing a long time ago."

"No, you only came up to my chest before. Now you're taller. Not by much, but you are."

Gabriel had said people coming out of the cellular regenerator had a chance to develop Gifts. Was it possible for Blaze to have gotten a power from his time in the machine?

"Your eyes are playing tricks on you," he said. With a laugh, they left the room.

I guess time would tell if he developed a Gift. Many people had powers, but their Gifts never manifested or were so minor no one noticed. Before testing became available, many of the world-class athletes were unrecognized Gifted. They were stronger, faster, and healed better than their peers.

I spent the next few hours practicing the forms as close to the way Blaze had taught me as I could. After a mistake, I'd stop, make an adjustment, practice the form, and then start all over. I'd used a lot of these moves in combat, but I'd grown sloppy. A well-placed strike meant the difference between finishing off an opponent and leaving yourself open.

I'd lost track of time when the sound of someone clearing their voice brought me back to reality. Dad stood inside the training room doorway. He wore a faded Storytellers brewery sweatshirt and a pair of sweatpants. He didn't look much like the world's greatest superhero.

"I can leave, if you want to work out," I said. I released the form I held and returned to a normal standing position.

He stared at me for a couple of seconds.

I guessed we weren't on speaking terms at all. I threw the towel over my shoulder and grabbed the black box I used to recharge my Gift off the mat. I headed toward the door. "Sorry, I'll get out of your way."

"I'm not good at this," he said, as I came even to him.

I stopped but didn't look at him.

He sighed. "I never thought I'd be a father or a husband. As far as abandoning you, I had no intentions of it." He stood perfectly straight, the consummate soldier.

"Point taken, but that's not what happened."

With military precision, he pivoted to face me. "You have put yourself in harm's way more times than anyone, but you call me to task for wanting to save lives? Where do you get off judging me?"

"Judging you?" I barked out a harsh laugh. The hurt welled up from my feet and threatened to drown me, but years of anger boiled it away, leaving only rage. "Really? You strut around here like you're the general and we're your lackeys. I've done everything I can to live up to your colossal expectations and fall short every time. I get it. You deserve better than the kid who got the crap kicked out of him daily, or the one who got Mom pulled into the Gauntlet."

His face reddened. "You aren't a failure, nor was anything that happened in the Gauntlet your fault. If I've given you the impression that I'm disappointed with you, that's on me. Lord knows I've failed enough for both of us."

"Kind of like when you didn't destroy the death ray? How many people died because Omega Squad failed its mission?" I regretted the words as soon as they left my mouth, but I was too hurt and angry to stop them. The last person in the world who should be bitching me out was Michael Ward, the man who gave up.

Mom entered the room. "What's going on?"

We both ignored the question, too consumed by the fight.

"When you've lost as many people as I have, then you can discuss my failures," Dad barked. "Until then, keep your opinions to yourself." The words sliced the air into ribbons with the deadly edge they carried. "When the time comes, I hope you can live up to your expectations of me."

"Sure thing, Mike." The black box was in my hands. My Gift required pain, and for what? I threw the box at Ranger's feet. I walked past Mom, shrugging off her hand, and without looking back, I said, "I quit."

# 24

I spent the next few hours walking through knee-high snow.

*"When the time comes, I hope you can live up to your expectations of me,"* echoed in my mind as I stomped through the snow, sticking to tracks left over from the last vehicle that had passed through.

Lights came into view as I made my way into town. Given the cold weather, I'd had time to cool off, but the hurt and anger wouldn't let me turn around and go back, even as part of me knew I should.

I stumbled into Haynesboro, cold and tired. The town consisted of a blinking yellow light with a diner on one corner and a gas station on the other. The diner sign's lights were off, and from the drifts of snow reaching the roofline of the building, nobody had been there for a while.

*Gladstone's Service and Bait Shop it is.*

After passing the one fuel pump, I pushed open the heavy door and entered the dirty confines of the "convenience" store.

Two rows of shelves separated me from the cashier. On them was an assortment of cheap candy bars to cans of oil to things I couldn't readily identify. Over a wall case filled with soda, a TV sat on a shelf with FNN showing, though the sound was off.

I carefully crossed the wet linoleum floor, my boots sliding a couple of times from all the snow stuck in the treads. Behind the counter sat a bald old man with a Chevy hat perched on his head. He smiled, revealing yellow teeth with a couple of major gaps. He had a parka over his shoulders. As I got closer, I noticed he wore a mechanic's jumper with the name Merle barely legible through the grease. "Where the hell you come from? I didn't hear no car."

"It broke down a couple hours back," I said. I rubbed my hands together to warm them. "I was hoping a bus would come through so I could get to Albany or Syracuse."

Merle laughed, slapping the counter with a dirty hand. "A bus? Out here in the dead of winter? You've got a better chance of Santa showing up and givin' you a lift, boy."

"Oh." I hadn't planned this very well. "Where's the closest bus stop?"

He chuckled to himself. "Closest bus stop, he asks. Now that's grand." He pulled a map out. He unfolded it until he found what he was looking for. He stabbed a greasy finger at the paper. "We're here." His finger traced a road for at least five inches until it stopped. "You can probably catch a bus in Utica. Only take you a month to walk in this weather, lessen you freeze solid 'fore then. You might want to call someone to come get ya."

"No buses come up here?" I asked quickly, ignoring the phone call suggestion. Once again, I was making a mess of this.

"Once in a while, in the summer." He spit a stream of something black into an empty soda bottle. "Rich folk drive armored vans up here to fish or hunt. Most of the locals are survivalists, off the grid to stay away from the Protectorate. We're still loyal to the United States of America up here. Reclaimers will make sweeps to collect the young'uns, but never find any."

"Really? So, you don't send your kids to Redemption?"

He scratched under his cap for a minute. "Oh, you mean the town where they lock away all them special ones? Nope, sure don't. We still live in the land of the free and the brave. Up here we still follow the old ways. Screw Mr. High and Mighty."

This sparked my interest. Maybe I could join with another resistance group and make a difference. "Do you fight the Reclaimers?"

He laughed so hard that black tar gushed out of his mouth. "Now that be funny." He wiped his chin with a grayish cloth I guessed had been red at one point. "With what, sticks and stones? Nah, boy. We mountain folk up here. We live and let live unless they come stickin' their noses in our business round here."

"Makes sense," I said as casually as possible. "I guess I should walk back and see if I can start my car."

"Probably froze up." He pushed a bag across to me. "My wife made enough chicken to feed an army. You take it with you. Grab a couple sodas from the cooler. We're supposed to get a warm spell tomorrow. Engine might start once its above freezin'."

"Thanks, Merle. I've got a cooler with food in the car, but I wouldn't mind a soda."

He pulled the paper sack away. "Suit yerself. Long walk back."

I grabbed a bottle of Mountain Dew and opened it. As soon as I took the first drink, I regretted my decision. When I glanced at the sell by date, it was over two years old. I screwed the cap back on and closed the glass door.

My uncertainty must have shown on my face. "Might be a bit old, but the dates don't mean nuthin'." Merle said. He switched his attention to the TV. He thumbed a remote and sound filled the store.

"The Eastern European Zone is on high alert tonight, after Protectorate intelligence issued a warning of more terrorist attacks." Hannah Fulbright, a newscaster with long brown hair and cool glasses was on the set. "The Underground has issued a statement taking credit for the attack on Reclaimer troops outside of Cairo and are threatening more violence in the days to come. Stay tuned to FNN for more breaking news as it happens."

I wondered where I'd have to go to get away from the world when it followed me to a backwater stop in the middle of nowhere. Was there a place on Earth I could get away from the propaganda and fearmongering? The scenes from around the globe of people taking shelter against possible death ray strikes filled me with anger. You couldn't hide from a weapon when its main purpose was to dissolve all living materials to goo.

I hated to admit it, but Dad was right. We needed to save everyone from the Protectorate, and his need to save the troops was an extension of that belief. I wanted to pound my head into the wall. All this time, I thought I was acting like an adult, and really, I was just a spoiled brat. I needed to go back and make things right.

"You listen to old Merle," he said, using a drumstick to point at me. "People are people."

"Unless they are dissidents," I said trying not to sound snarky. I failed.

Merle shook his head. "I met one of them Gifted when I was a kid. Flew in an' saved a whole bunch of people from a fire. Wouldn't take nuthin' from the town. Just like any folk, there was good ones and bad ones. Now we're stuck with this Protectorate clown and his bullies. I'd take the old days anytime. People need to be free, not scared every day of their life." He glanced out the window. "You'd best get walkin' 'for the sun sets. I don't want to be findin' your body come spring thaw."

"Thanks, Merle." With effort, I pulled open the door and headed back to the place I belonged. Merle was right, people deserved to be free to live their lives—which was exactly what Dad was trying to do.

It would never happen under the Protectorate's rule.

If we fought long enough, maybe we'd give them a better solution.

Stranger things had happened.

## 25

I'd pitched the expired Mountain Dew down a hill for a burial in snow as soon as I was out of sight of Merle's. It had suffered enough and deserved an honorable end to its tragic life in Merle's cooler. Since last I passed, the tracks had frozen, making each step of my return trip sound like I was eating a bowl of Cap'n Crunch.

Mom met me in the cabin as I returned. She wanted to talk, but I hugged her and excused myself for a real Dew, a plate full of chicken tenders, and a long hot shower.

It had been a long day, and I was tired, angry, and hurt. I thought about what Merle had said about people needing to be free. Even now, there were still people who remembered a time before the Protectorate and the Reclaimers. Would they rise and fight for what they lost if they knew the truth?

I stayed in my room for the rest of the night until sleep took me, though it brought me no peace. Now that I'd quit the team rather than deal with Ranger anymore, I didn't know what to do with myself.

I'd waited my whole life to meet him and this was what I got: a man willing to throw his life away and abandon us again to save the Reclaimers.

No one came to check on me, so I went about my business. A

quick trip to the commissary for food, down to the training room to work out and practice my moves, followed by a shower.

When I emerged from the bathroom, Mimi sat on my bed.

"Good thing I got dressed before I came out."

"I would have stopped you if you'd tried to come out naked." She laughed and patted the side of the bed next to her. "We need to talk, Tiger."

I didn't move. "If this is about Ranger, I'm not interested." I crossed my arms over my chest and waited.

"Funny. He said the same thing when I spoke to him earlier." She patted the bed again. "You can sit, or I can make you. Your choice."

The thought of being forced to sit was embarrassing. I wondered if she'd planted the thought in my head and then realized it didn't matter. I dropped on the bed, putting my back against the headboard. "Go ahead."

"Hostile much?" She moved so she faced me dead on. "Normally, I don't interfere in—"

"Great. We're done then." I stood.

"Sit down." Mimi's power tickled my mind, but nothing else happened.

She regarded me for a second. "I can hear your thoughts, but you don't respond to my commands. I wonder why?"

"Alyx warded me against Yelena. Must work on nosy waitresses too," I said with a grin.

"Would you please sit?" she asked, waiting until I complied. "I'm worried about you and thought we should talk."

"I'm fine," I said, not wanting to deal with it.

"You're not, and we both know it. You're upset, and it's like blasting music in a confined space." She set her hand on mine. "Tiger, you can't let this stuff fester. It'll eat you alive."

"I had a fight with Dad is all."

"And?"

"And what?"

She leaned back. "Spill it, Tiger. I won't do anything to make you tell me, but you need to. You'll feel better."

I sighed but launched into it. I told her about the original argument over the Reclaimers, the fight in the gym, leaving Harker, and talking to Merle. She didn't interrupt the waterfall of words; she just let me talk.

When I finished, she asked, "What are you going to do now?"

"I don't know," I said with a shrug. "I guess I should apologize."

"Why would you do that? Were you wrong?"

"I could have handled it better, I guess, but I was so angry." I hated feeling this way. I loved my Dad, but I still felt betrayed and abandoned by him.

Mimi nodded. "Tiger, you could have, but Ranger should have known better than to pick a fight with you. He's a grown adult and owes it to you to listen when you're upset."

"So, what do I do then?"

"Give it time. He'll come around. When they get back, see how things are."

"Wait. Where are they?" Panic stirred at the edges of my brain. What if something happened and I wasn't there to help?

"The team went to trap Caligari," she said.

Heat burst through my mind. "They left without me?" I leapt off the bed. "Caligari will be ready for anything, and they're shorthanded."

"Warden brought in some extra help, but you might want to touch base with Marcel. He's the brains of the operation."

I ran to the communications room. I threw the door open, making Marcel jump. "Bruh, what the hell? You scared me half to death."

"Sorry. Mimi said Dad had taken the others to trap Caligari. How's it going?" I asked, trying to feign indifference.

Marcel had reorganized the communications room. The console hadn't moved, but he'd slid the extra desks against the wall with their chairs arranged to face the displays he had attached to the wall above the communications gear. He had parts scattered across the desktops, each grouped by whatever project it was.

He shook his head. "It's been four hours, and Caligari is a no show. We're about to call it."

A red light started blinking on the panel in front of Marcel. He swiveled his chair and pulled up a new screen. "Well, now I know why." He flipped a switch while lowering his headset's microphone to his mouth. "Ranger, we've got a report of an attack on a Reclaimers' supply warehouse outside of Paris. Looks like Caligari had other plans for the morning."

"Roger that. I'll have the details ready and meet you in the conference room. I've got Player with me." He paused before answering. "Roger. I'll tell him."

"Tell me what?" I asked, as I spun his chair so he faced me. "What did he say?"

"Bruh, relax. You'll make me barf, and I won't be able to tell you." He smiled his normal goofy smile at me. "He said your vacation is over and to get your ass ready to deploy with the team."

I didn't wait to answer. Instead, I ran back to my room, pulled on my combat gear, shocked my finger for a recharge, and headed to the conference room. Alyx was closing the portal as I arrived. Makeda, Warden, Gladiator, Izanami, Blaster, Mom, and Dad were scattered around the room.

"Nice of you to join us," Alyx said with a grin, though he shot a look at Dad's back. "Caligari is a tough one to outmaneuver, I guess."

Mom came over and hugged me. "I was worried about you."

"I know." My cheeks flared with heat as the embarrassment of what I'd done set in. "I'm sorry. I was so angry. I should have thought it through instead of storming out."

"We can talk later. I'm just glad you're here now." She didn't let go of my arm, and I didn't mind in the slightest. The one constant in my life had always been Mom, and when I needed her the most, she was there for me.

Marcel sat in his normal chair with a map pulled up on the screen. "Mostly the site holds stuff the Reclaimers looted from Paris. The depot supplies the local border guards as well as the other Reclaimer bases in the area. I can't get a video feed from their system."

"What are the Reclaimers saying on their comm channels?" Dad asked. He moved to be next to Marcel. "I don't want to walk into a shootout."

Marcel played a clip of a Reclaimer officer's frantic voice. The screen translated the French into English for us. "Don't know what these things are, but they've killed four of my men. We are sealing the containment—" The message stopped scrolling as the line went dead.

"All I got before the comm channel died." Marcel pulled up a new map, showing the nearest bases. "The closest reinforcements are over an hour from the warehouse. From the records I could quickly find, there might be forty soldiers stationed there to guard the place. My guess is they aren't a crack commando squad."

"Have they called in reinforcements?" Gladiator asked from where he stood next to the wall display. He wore pants and a thick sweater under his combat jacket. All were black. His sword hung from his side, as always. "To Ranger's point, we do not want to involve ourselves in a three-way battle."

Marcel spoke while he pulled up data from the Reclaimers' systems. "The orders were sent, but it's night, and the closest base with combat troops is in Lyon. It's almost five hours to get their troops up to Paris by transport, but a small team could be there by helicopter in an hour and a half."

"We need to put him down ASAP," Blaster said, bouncing with excitement. "After what he did to us, we need to drop this motherf—"

Warden stared at him, eyebrows raised.

"To Blaster's rather enthusiastic point," Warden said, her eyes still locked on Blaster's, "we might not get a better chance."

Dad glanced over his shoulder at me. "Tommy, thoughts?"

"We should go. It gives us a shot at Caligari, and we might be able to save any civilians in the area from whatever he's brought with him." I hoped Dad read the apology in my words, if not my expression.

He nodded. "I agree. Alyx, can you get us there?"

Alyx shook his head. "Never been to this place. I can open a portal at the Paris Underground base, but we'd have to exit the city to get to the warehouse, since it's outside the dead zone. Balthier would be long gone by then."

Makeda moved to examine the map. "I have been to a location near here, possibly two miles or so. I can open a small portal for Alyx to go through, then he can establish a larger portal for us to use." Her finger touched the screen. Marcel winced. Smudges on the displays was a big pet peeve of his.

"We leave in ten. Everybody use the bathroom. Blaster, make sure you have food on hand. We need to make this one count." He stepped over to me. Mom squeezed my arm and followed the others to the commissary.

"I'm sorry," I said, but he held up his hand.

"Tommy, as your mother pointed out in loud, unreasoning tones, you and I are a lot alike." He grinned like a schoolboy as he poked fun at mom, who looked back over her shoulder at him. "She's right. You and I have a lot of years to make up for, and I am not the best father."

I didn't say anything, just listened.

After a few seconds' pause, he continued. "I never stopped to consider how my decisions impacted your life, and I am truly sorry. Susan told me about what it was like growing up in Redemption. I always wanted to believe I did the right thing, but I was wrong, and you paid the price for it. I deserved every word you said to me, and I'll try to do better. For what it's worth, I'm proud to have you as my son."

The words cracked the wall I'd built around those feelings. Part of me was happy to hear his apology, part of me embarrassed that I'd lost it on him. My stomach churned as all this hit my system at once. A tear rolled down my cheek. I wiped it away and saw tears gathered in Dad's eyes as well. He pulled me into a rough hug.

"I'm sorry," I whispered into his ear, but he just hugged me tighter. Relief that I hadn't lost my Dad again surged through me as we stood there.

We separated, and both awkwardly laughed. "You're right about Mom being loud and unreasonable."

"I was married to her before you were born. Not much has changed." His eyes lit up, and he hurriedly added, "Except she's even more beautiful than the day I met her."

"Yeah, right," she said with a laugh, though I noticed she blushed a bit. "Are you two good now?"

I looked at Dad and nodded. He smiled at me, relief in his eyes. "Yeah, I'm pretty dense. Sometimes I need a sanity check from my boy."

I grinned like an idiot.

"Good." She retrieved her sniper rifle from where she'd left it against the wall. "I've got a bullet with Caligari's name on it."

"Let's hope it finds its home," Dad said.

The rest of the team assembled as Makeda opened a small portal for Alyx. A few seconds later a larger one opened into the French night.

"Bonjour," Alyx said. "Let us hunt ze madman down, shall we?"

Blaster strolled through the portal. "Don't quit your day job," he said as he passed Alyx.

"Everyone's a critic."

I stepped into the night air, ready to fight.

It was time to take out my anger on someone who deserved it: Caligari.

26

Makeda led us down the streets of Palaiseau. The moon was high in the sky, partially obscured by clouds that increased rapidly with Warden here. The winds picked up as we followed Makeda. We reached a road named Avenue de la Vauve.

Across the street from us stood the huge warehouse. A fifteen-foot wall surrounded the building and parking areas. Tractor trailers and smaller trucks filled the lot outside the loading bays. Two access gates were the only ways in or out. Guardhouses flanked the gated entrances. The compound took up the entire block. Whatever it held, Caligari wanted.

Off to the right, I saw a fifteen-story building branded with the Reclaimers' logo. It had the generic look of an office building. Lights illuminated the lowest floor, but the rest of the building sat dark.

We crouched behind a row of decorative hedges across the street. I doubted the landscapers ever realized they gave great cover for studying the Reclaimers' warehouse

Mom peered through the scope on her rifle. "The guard post is empty, but I see a puddle of blood by the door, and the gate is open. We're in the right place."

"I'm going to take Snapshot and Warden to the top of the high rise so they have a better vantage point," Dad said. He gestured to them. "We should be able to spot where Caligari entered the building. The rest of us will move out once we've established the target."

"Nothing coming over the comm-link, though two helicopters launched from Lyon five minutes ago. You're on the clock, Ranger," Marcel said over the comm-link. "Inbound in seventy-two minutes."

"Understood, Mr. Wizard." Dad scooped up Mom and flew to the top of the neighboring building. A minute later, he returned and repeated the process with Warden.

I watched the warehouse, seeing nothing out of the ordinary. But if Caligari were here, something bad was going on.

Dad settled down next to us. "There's an open loading bay door marked 743 about halfway down. My bet is we'll find the mage there. Mr. Wizard, can you see if you can locate what's in bay 743?"

"On it."

"By the numbers," Dad said. He pushed through the foliage and crossed the deserted street, the rest of us following. Anyone looking down from the adjacent buildings would see us, but it was late enough that we should be safe.

Dad and Gladiator took the lead with Izanami and Blaster flanking them. Makeda and Alyx took the center, and I brought up the rear. Once we passed through the gate, Dad signaled to spread out. We moved between the trucks like ghosts, sticking to the shadows until we reached the open loading dock.

The door had been raised to the top, not blown off the tracks as I would have expected from Caligari. A short set of stairs ran from the parking lot to the top of the dock. Large black bumpers were attached to the concrete to stop collisions. Nothing moved as I watched from the cover of a parked semi.

"No one is on the dock." Always good to know Mom was watching over us.

The wind picked up steadily as we readied ourselves. Landing a helicopter in a Warden-induced storm would not be advisable.

"Calling the ball," I said, as I ran to the edge of the dock. I stayed below the rim to lessen the chances of being spotted. Grunting noises came from within the building, but I couldn't identify them. Without waiting, I leapt over the handrail of the stairs and dashed to the side of the opening. I could see inside now, and I thought we were in the right place.

The warehouse had rows of metal shelving running back deep into the darkened space. Boxes and pallets of every size filled the shelves. A light shone through the stacks, giving me a pretty good idea where Caligari might be.

Caligari's screaming voice carried from beyond the shelving. "Push, you great louts! We need to be rid of this place."

If there was an answer, I couldn't hear it.

I pulled back so my voice didn't echo. "Confirmation. He's here." I leaned back in. A loud scraping noise filled the warehouse. Whatever they were moving was heavy.

"Let's move. Alyx and Makeda in the center. Everyone, fan out but watch your fire," Dad said. "We don't need any self-inflicted wounds." Dad soared across the lot, through the door, and into the rafters.

Shields popped up around Alyx and Makeda, as they readied for the battle with Caligari.

The scraping noise continued.

Makeda and I walked in, going to the left, Alyx and Gladiator to the right. Gladiator had his sword out, ready for action. Blaster and Izanami moved to our flanks as we crept through the stacks. After fifteen rows, we found the light source and our target.

Caligari, still wearing the long blue coat from our previous encounter, stood with his back to us. A portal was open as a group of huge, man-shaped beasts pushed a wooden crate up a shallow ramp toward it. Caligari paced back and forth as the package inched toward its destination.

Alyx and Makeda moved as one. Each released a stream of magic at Caligari's back. Energy splashed off his shield in all directions. The portal closed as Caligari rounded on them.

"I wondered if you'd be smart enough to leave your ambush to pursue the real objective." Caligari said in his mocking tone.

Dad flew in, laying down a barrage of lightning, which glanced harmlessly off Caligari's shields as well.

"So predictable. Would you like to retreat now, or shall I unleash the Urtourans on you?" Caligari sneered.

"We're here to stop your insane plan, Balthier," Makeda said, the steel in her voice unmistakable. "Submit yourself to Council justice. You were one of us once. You know what's at stake."

"Saving the pitiful humans? I spent eons protecting them, and for what? They backstabbed me as soon as they saw an opening. Now I will end Earth as repayment for their treachery."

"Those people are long since dead," Alyx said. "Stop now before it goes too far."

"Stavenous, destroy these intruders." Caligari's hands twisted, and Makeda's shield burst into brilliant shards. She screamed, collapsing to the ground.

The closest of the beasts pushing the crate stood straight. While not tall, he was wider across than anything I'd seen on two feet. Huge horns like a bull's curved around until they pointed up and forward. Red eyes set into a coarse face did nothing to alleviate my fears. Arms the size of my waist unlimbered a giant axe from his back. Tattoos covered every inch of his skin. Leather armor with metal plating attached protected his torso.

"Holy shit," Blaster said. "What is that thing?"

"Stavenous is my guess." I watched his band spread out to face us.

Alyx and Caligari exchanged magical attacks, while I focused on the giant cow in front of me swinging the axe from side-to-side. Dad sped in, laying down a stream of lightning, hitting two of the Urtourans. The second one roared and struck Dad with his club, sending him spinning across the warehouse.

I fired a bolt of energy at Stavenous, who blocked it with his massive axe head. He bellowed and charged.

Blaster opened with a quick blast at the rampaging bull, who deflected the shots with a gauntleted fist. Stavenous swung his weapon much faster than I thought possible.

I threw myself to the ground, letting the axe pass over me. I bounded to my feet, ready to throw another bolt of lightning.

Izanami took her shot, landing a wicked elbow to the face. Green blood spurted from the creature's nose. He batted her away with the butt of his axe, sending her crashing into the wall behind us with a solid thud.

Gladiator advanced, swinging his sword at the monster. "I've dealt with your kind before," Nico said. Stavenous blocked the sword with the axe handle.

The monster reversed his blade, missing Gladiator as he spun out of the way. Another round of attacks rang out.

Dad rose above the mages and unleashed a blast at Caligari. Arcs of lighting penetrated his shield, striking the mage. Caligari screamed in a rage. Before he could counter, Dad shot back into the rafters and out of sight.

Izanami returned. Dirt covered her suit, but she didn't seem harmed. Invulnerability had its perks.

"The rest of you, stop them!" Caligari yelled.

Four huge bull-men left the crate, pulling clubs out. They headed for us.

I signaled Izanami and Blaster. "We take those four!" I shouted over the clang of metal from Gladiator's fight.

The closest bull pushed a shelving unit over, toppling them like dominoes. He swung the massive club at me. I ducked under the weapon, firing an arc of lightning straight into his face. He reared back as it struck. The Urtouran's long beard caught fire from the strike, blisters appearing on his skin.

Blaster unleashed another burst into the second bull, driving him back as Izanami kicked a knee out from under the third.

If it had been three on three, we'd have been doing fine, but the fourth Urtouran charged, slamming into Blaster. He flew past me with a sickening crunch and landed in the middle of the collapsed shelves.

As far as I could tell, Blaster was down, but I couldn't stop to check on him. I grabbed the horns of the bull who'd run over Blaster and, using his momentum, swung him in front of his comrade. The club meant for me slammed into the unprotected back of my foe. He roared in pain and dropped to the ground.

"That's for Blaster!" I stepped onto his back and fired a bolt of energy at the smoldering Urtouran I'd hit earlier.

An arrow struck, pain exploding in my shoulder. It knocked me sideways, sending my shot wide of the mark. Energy bloomed within me from the impact.

My heart sank. Jon was here.

Izanami retrieved one of the fallen bull's clubs and threw it at Jon. He stood on top of the crate the bulls had been pushing. Jon jumped over the improvised projectile as it spun by. He fired an arrow at Izanami. She pivoted away from the attack and used the momentum to deliver a kick to the head of the Urtouran whose knee she'd broken.

Dad raced in and fired at Jon, who dove off the crate and into a roll. Jon got to his knees, launching an arrow. It struck Dad in one leg. He cried out.

The arrow shaft exploded, launching two filament wires. One wrapped around his legs. The other anchored him into the rafters above. Dad swerved like a fish on a line as his momentum worked against him. He cartwheeled through the air, the wires entangling him even further.

"Dad!" I screamed. He hung limp in the wire.

"What happened?" Mom asked over the comm-link

"I'm trapped in one of Jon's damned arrows. I'll be fine. Finish these guys off."

A club crashed into my ribs, driving the breath out of me. A torrent of anguish exploded through my brain. The blow lifted me off my feet and sent me sprawling on my back.

As soon as I hit, I rolled to the left, avoiding Jon's follow-up shot. The arrow hit the concrete floor and skipped away. The wires fired off harmlessly. I threw lightning three feet to the right of him and was rewarded with a curse as the bolt clipped Jon's leg. He always moved to his left after shooting.

Makeda, who'd fallen ten feet to my right, struggled to rise as I stood. She'd gone ashen from whatever Caligari had done to her. Her eyes blazed with fury, but she stumbled, trying to walk. I didn't spot Jon from where I stood but could see Dad fighting to free himself from the wire trap.

Another roar caught my attention as three more Urtourans stepped through the now-open portal.

"They've got reinforcements." I fired a spray of lightning at the new arrivals, but they ignored it as they began to push the crate back up the ramp. I didn't know what was in there, but I didn't want Caligari to have it.

Izanami was being beaten by the two she fought, clubs raining down on her from both sides.

I wrapped my hand in energy and drove it into the back of the nearest bull. My fist sunk into his flesh with a spray of green blood. He roared, dropping his club to grab his wounded back. I twisted around.

An arrow sped across the open space, taking the bull-man in the chest. A puff of smoke burst from the arrow.

I backed up, staying away from the smoke as the cow staggered from the noxious fumes surrounding its head—some sort of knockout gas.

Jon had learned not to attack me straight on. It only made me stronger. I rolled away from the swaying bull. I landed a kick on the other beast, setting him off balance.

Izanami grabbed both horns and landed two feet into his face. The horns broke off from the force of the impact. The Urtouran howled in dismay, falling onto his back, bleeding from multiple places.

Gladiator traded blows with Stavenous, both bleeding from cuts they'd taken during the fight. Alyx exchanged magical attacks with Caligari, though neither side made much progress.

More of the Urtouran came through the portal, some joining in moving the crate but more headed toward Izanami and me.

Izanami got to her feet, horns held before her like daggers. "I don't know how much longer my invulnerability will last," she told me. Five more of the giant bull creatures headed our way. I fanned out a blast of energy, making a shield to keep any arrows Jon fired away from us.

"More of these damn things?" Blaster said, crashing through the wreckage of the fallen shelves. "Time to make some hamburger."

Another arrow sped in but died against my energy shield. The crate was almost to the opening. Even if we beat Caligari's forces, him getting the package would be a loss for us. "We need to destroy the box at all costs," I said. "We can't let him have it."

Dad pulled free of the wire and flew to us. "We need to focus our attacks on the crate."

He was right. More of the Urtouran were moving the package toward the portal. We couldn't let it cross through.

"We heard you needed some help hunting seals!" a jovial voice announced over the fight.

Yutu and Abby stood behind us, both wearing big grins. Abby cracked her knuckles and charged.

Abby slammed into the Urtourans like a wrecking ball. She towered over the shorter bull creatures, punching and kicking them aside as they tried to surround her. She grew larger with each passing moment. Izanami attempted to join them, but I grabbed her arm.

"Fall back. If your Gift runs out, you'll be dead."

Izanami hesitated.

Over the comm-link, Warden made her opinion known. "Izanami, fall back. That's an order."

The invulnerable warrior flushed, but she ran from the fight. She'd have to deal with her injuries later, but at least she'd be alive.

Abby threw a punch that knocked the bull she struck across the room and into a pallet of boxes. They burst from the impact, showering the floor with oil. The bulls tried a coordinated attack, but Abby's onslaught scattered them.

I turned to Blaster. "How do you like your burgers cooked?"

He smiled. "Well done, son." He opened fire on the closest bull. It stumbled away from Abby. The bolts hit the Urtouran full in the chest, shredding his armor and knocking him to his knees. He grabbed at Blaster, who danced out of his reach and unloaded another series of blasts. The whole time Blaster screamed, "Welcome to the bar-b-que, bitches!"

Caligari yelled to Jon. "If you ever want to see your sister alive again, stop her."

Abby grabbed an Urtouran by the horns and swung him into the others, giving her a clean space. "Jon, Wendi's gone. Come home. We miss you. I miss you. Please, stop listening to this asshat."

"Do it, or I will never bring your sister back." Caligari blinked to a new location next to the portal. "I have to keep the way open. Do it now!"

Jon stood behind the crate, but I didn't have a clear shot at him. With one more push, the crate would move through the portal and everything would be for nothing.

"Stop the crate!" I yelled as I unleashed a stream of lightning into the Urtourans who pushed the box.

"I'm sorry, Abby." Jon fired an arrow that burst into a powder on impact.

Abby coughed, and then her body convulsed. I ran toward her, but Gladiator's fight with Stavenous blocked me. I force-punched the creature in the side, feeling bones snap under my fist.

Gladiator seized the opportunity. His sword whistled through the air, slicing the bull's head completely off. A fountain of green blood shot from the severed neck as the body fell to the ground.

Abby writhed, her features elongating as her metamorphosis took over. Within a few seconds, a giant bear roared in her stead. Yutu yelled a word I didn't understand, but he didn't finish. Caligari hit him in the face with a sphere of green energy. Yutu fell to the ground, pulling frantically at the substance, which bound itself to him like glue.

Now a bear, Abby tore through the Urtouran warriors line and headed directly at Jon. She reached him and a mighty paw pulled back to strike. Even Jon couldn't withstand a blow from her, but he didn't flinch. Abby trembled as Jon held her in his gaze, speaking to her, but I was too far to hear.

I fired another blast; it scorched the wooden crate, but missed Jon.

Abby's head hung low for a moment before she moved behind the crate and used the top of her head to push the crate into the portal. Caligari laughed, as he stepped through and closed the portal, leaving the Urtourans behind. The ones remaining roared as they saw the portal shut, stranding them on this side.

Dad landed next to me. The bull warriors milled around, confused but not hostile. Alyx joined us as Makeda went to assist Yutu.

"Can you get the Urtourans out of here?" Dad asked Alyx.

He nodded. "I think so." He muttered some words before he called out in a guttural tongue several times. One of them approached us. It grunted at Alyx and he answered in kind. "They want to know if you will kill them for trespassing on your area."

When Dad started to answer, Alyx cut him off. "They are asking Tommy. They are calling him Hands of Death and will only accept his answer."

Dad looked at me, eyebrows raised. "So, Hands of Death, will we execute them?"

I shook my head. "Tell them—"

"I'll translate, but you need to talk. Speak up so they all hear you." Alyx said, keeping his voice low.

I cleared my throat, suddenly aware of all the warriors staring at me. "We have no issue with the..." I looked at Alyx in a panic.

"Urtourans," Alyx said softly.

"Oh right." I raised my voice. "With the Urtourans. My wizard will open a portal so you may go, but you are to never return here."

Alyx spat out a long growling speech which I assume was what I said. The leader bowed and spoke to Alyx. "He says you are very wise, and his people will never cross us again in payment for your mercy. He wishes to take his dead."

"Take your dead and be at peace." I felt like I should be in a bad western on TV.

Alyx repeated what I said, and they all bowed to me before collecting their dead and using the portal Alyx created to leave. The leader returned and knelt before me. He grunted at Alyx for a moment. Alyx responded, but the grunts grew more insistent.

"He tells me as the victor, you should take his head as payment for the incursion. He is quite adamant on this point," Alyx said. He chewed his lip for a second. "I don't think he'll challenge you to a duel or anything, but if you'll pardon the pun, they are very bull-headed about matters of honor."

Of all the times for bad humor, this was the least appropriate. I walked past the spokes-cow and took the head of Stavenous from the warrior who held it and dragged it back. "Tell him I have the head of the leader who caused me harm, and I am satisfied with that."

Alyx repeated my words. The warrior nodded to me and led his people back to their home world. I dropped the head as soon as the portal closed.

"Nicely handled," Dad said to me, as he squeezed my shoulder.

"Thanks, too bad we didn't stop the Caligari."

Dad nodded. It had been that kind of day.

Alyx summoned a portal for us before anything else could go wrong.

After food and a shower, everyone, except the unconscious Waxenby, met up in the conference room to talk over what had happened. We discussed what could be in the crate and while there were a lot of guesses, no one really knew. The only thing I was certain of is we were on the wrong side of whatever was in the crate.

FNN was running live footage of the attack on 'innocent Reclaimers' and showing off the bull head as proof of satanic activities amongst the Dissidents. The cameras showed ambulances being loaded with body bags of the dead soldiers. Smoke trailed from the high-rise next door, telling me where they had gotten the bodies.

General Mahady appeared on camera behind his usual lectern. "Another Dissident attack on the brave men and women of our armed forces."

Live footage from the scene played over his right shoulder as the rescue crews pulled dead bodies from the warehouse. "Be assured, the Protectorate has every intention of stopping these attacks. In an effort to curb the ease with which the Dissidents are striking various targets around the globe, all non-essential travel has been banned and martial law declared. A mandatory curfew will be enforced in all urban centers. Anyone out after ten p.m. local time without a work visa will be arrested and detained as a threat to the Protectorate and our citizens. We do not take these steps lightly. The eradication protocol is in progress to eliminate the Underground faction of the Dissidents. The Protectorate will do what is necessary to ensure the public's safety." He closed the folder he carried and walked off screen.

Marcel muted the display. "Wow, they just slapped the entire planet with martial law. Do you think people will stand for it?"

Mom shook her head. "People are scared. As long as Caligari is stirring up trouble, the Protectorate has every reason to move to a complete dictatorship. Soon they'll close the courts, like they did the newspapers and anyone else who questioned their authority."

Merle's words came back to me. *"We live and let live unless they come stickin' their noses round here."*

There wouldn't be an uprising or protests. The Protectorate pushed the aggressive members of society into the Reclaimers and left the sheep to support them. Unless General Mahady staged a coup or a new leader emerged to show people they could fight and win, the Protectorate would grow stronger until no one cared. It was the way it was.

"So, what can we do?" Pepper asked, clearly annoyed. "How do we stop this prick?"

"Good question," Dad said, as he lifted his cup of coffee. "The population would have to rise up and demand their freedom, but then who do they follow? A Gifted? They followed the Protector, but he collared himself to become normal. We've been portrayed as evil for so long, people wouldn't trust us."

"It would have to be a Norm who the people trusted. Someone like Mom," Marcel said. His fingers were still flickering across the screen in front of him.

Alicia snorted. "You best kiss her goodbye then. You think anyone who challenges the Protector himself is gonna live?"

"She's right," Mom said. Marcel gaped at her for agreeing with Jinx. "People tried early on to form a resistance party, and every one of them ended up dead. All opponents were 'accident prone.' The job is 100 percent fatal."

"We could keep you here and use tech to rally the people," Marcel said, grasping for a reason to launch an insurrection. "They'd never find us."

"Honey, they aren't really looking for us, but if we become a threat, they will find us. Even if they have to nuke the whole area to remove us."

Everyone stopped speaking. What do you do when there is no way out? We could live in Harker indefinitely, but Alyx couldn't shepherd us around the world forever, though the Brotherhood was his responsibility, not ours. We were lending a hand to keep Caligari from destroying all life on the planet.

Gladiator cleared his throat. "If I may ask, what happened to Abigail? She is a fierce warrior, and it is not like her to be so easily manipulated."

All eyes went to Yutu, who studied his folded hands. "Abby had made strides in her training. We returned to find you all locked in a battle with the Brotherhood and thought our assistance might be the thing to defeat Balthier, once and for all. It was foolish and reckless of me to expose her to such a situation. Most of her kind spend years training in order to maintain the control needed."

"She just followed Jon," I said. "There was no way she would join up with him against us."

Yutu nodded. "In human form, you are correct. In animal form, Jon's Gift must have taken control of her. It is the only reason I can think of for such a change."

"His Gift?" I asked. Jon was an amazing marksman and moved like the wind.

How could that possibly hypnotize a bear?

"We've seen it before," Makeda said. She put her hand on Yutu's arm. "Most Gifted with Jon's particular talents can influence animals. Davey Crockett from the old west had the ability to run off animals or bend them to his will. Jon evidentially has a similar skill and used it to calm Abby and make her follow him."

"Is it permanent?" Marcel asked, his voice going up a level or two. "He can't force her to do what he wants forever, can he?"

Yutu shook his head. "No, unless he keeps his focus on her, she will break free. If he uses her against you, say the word 'Inuk' to her. It will trigger her conditioning and return her to human."

I repeated the word over and over. It sounded like *ee-nook*. I would be ready when the chance came to get Abby back. Jon had done a lot of rotten things, but this was unforgivable.

"He's one messed up dude," Blaze said. "If this magic man is promising Wendi in return for fighting you, it's not fair to hold Jon responsible."

"How do you figure that?" I asked, a bit more hotly than I should have. "He's stupid to think anyone could bring her back!"

"As stupid as the boy who asked me to do the same?" Makeda said. Her tone was gentle, but her gaze pinned me down like a bug at the science fair.

I sputtered, as I fought to find an answer.

Blaze took care of it for me. "Yep, he's just that stupid, but he doesn't have the people around him to help him through this typhoon."

"Jon isn't in his right mind, honey," Mom said. "Grief can do terrible things to you, so when a person tosses you a lifeline, you don't really care who's holding the other end." Mom squeezed my arm, and I realized she was right, as usual. Just once, I'd like her to be wrong. Not about anything major, but *something* would be nice.

"You ask me, he wasn't right back when he was at our house. Boy's a loose cannon." Alicia added, ending the sympathy-for-Jon segment of the evening.

"So what is our next step?" I asked, to change the subject before Jinx elaborated on Jon's shortcomings. "How do we get Abby back and stop Caligari?"

Alyx sighed. "We wait, and when he makes his next move, we hit him with everything we've got. In the meantime, we need to find the remote station. I doubt Reaper has stopped looking for it."

I'd have loved a better answer, but there wasn't one.

When the time came, we couldn't afford to lose again.

The next morning there was a knock at my bedroom door. I pulled on my shirt and opened to see a smiling Blaze. "Dude, how bout we do a little sparring?"

I laughed. "Less than a week ago, you were having a cardiac arrest, now you want to spar?" I had to admit he looked healthy and full of energy, but men his age didn't heal this fast normally. The idea of Blaze being Gifted might not be so far off.

"I feel great." He gave me a sideways look. "Unless you're scared of an old man?"

"Fine." I rolled my eyes in an exaggerated manner. "Mom always told me to respect my elders, and you're the oldest elder I've got."

Blaze feigned a hurt expression. "For that, I'm not taking it easy on you. Come on, Sparky."

Great. Pepper must have told him about my code name screw up. I'd never live it down now.

We took the stairs to the training room. Blaze had set out light gloves and mouth guards.

"Where's Pepper?" I'd expected her to be here since she barely left Blaze's side these days.

Blaze tossed me a pair of gloves. "She accompanied Warden,

Blaster, and your Dad to check out the base Marcel found. With any luck, we'll be able to move the Underground up there and help them get established."

I stretched my arms, limbering up for sparring. "Are you two going to stay with Warden's people?"

"Yeah, not much call for over-the-hill martial arts instructors here. Pepper and I are going to help train Warden's people. Jinx and Harold are going as well. Once the hydroponics units are producing, the base will be self-sufficient."

I grabbed my mouthpiece case. "Why don't you stay here and help us, even if it's just training?"

"Dude, I'm too old to fight. I would have retired fifteen years ago, if I'd stayed with Stryke Force. Besides, it looks like the Dark Brigade removed Pepper's built-in weapons. She can still fight, but she'd be a lot less effective." He moved to the first form. "Start with Sparrow Through the Forest?"

I nodded, taking my place next to him. For the next twenty minutes, I should have been concentrating on the forms, honing my motions until they were fluid, shifting from one to the next without any seams.

Instead, my mind tumbled over Pepper and Blaze leaving. Warden would take her people as well. Abby captured, Jon under Caligari's influence. All that would be left were Mom, Dad, Marcel, Mimi, and Waxenby. Assuming Mimi and Waxenby even stayed. He hadn't come back to consciousness yet. How could we fight the Brotherhood and the Reclaimers without the additional people?

More than once, I missed a move or stumbled with footing I'd long since mastered. Blaze didn't comment, just kept moving as we'd done so many times before. I fought to calm my mind and focus my energy, to tighten the control over the chaos raging through me as my body relaxed and took over. Slowly, my thoughts calmed until my worries were a faint hum in the back of my brain. My movements became surer, and by the time we finished, I moved in time with Blaze.

He bowed to me. "Excellent! Control is everything. You can't master the external until you've calmed your internal conflict. When you are calm, you'll notice the mistakes your enemies have made and can exploit them."

I returned the bow. "I don't know if I'll ever have the kind of control you do."

Blaze sat cross-legged on the mat. "Please." He waited for me to comply.

*Old man, my foot.* He'd dropped into a seated position in one move. It took me a bit to get my gangly legs in the correct position.

"You watched my memory of the fight with Reaper," he said. "I lost my focus, and you saw what happened. When you calm your mind, time slows for you. You'll notice the way Turk overextended his punches or that you don't lock your wrist when you block. Those minor things can be exploited. Leaning away from Turk pulled his balance forward and made it easy to toss him, using his own momentum."

"When you don't lock your wrist, you can force your way through the block?" I hadn't thought of it from that angle before. "So basically, we're exploiting people's weaknesses?"

"In a fight, yes. In life, it depends on the situation. Reaper uses his mouth to distract from the truth in front of your eyes. If we hadn't been watching him, Alyx and I might have seen Ruby Lash early enough to have changed the outcome. Knowing your Dad will always do what's right, his enemies bait him into becoming predictable. During the Reclamation Wars, Titan always grabbed the biggest weapon, which was his downfall."

I hadn't heard this story before. "How so?"

"The Reclaimers rigged a bus with a power cancellation device like what was in your old collars. He picked up the bus, and they activated it. The bus crushed him on the spot. Never even knew what happened. If he'd fought with his fists, he wouldn't have been as strong, but he'd be alive."

Interesting. I hadn't lived through the rise of the Protectorate or fought the Reclaimers in a world where the Gifted had been at the top of the food chain. "So, they out-thought him."

Blaze chuckled. "Didn't take much. He was as dumb as a post. The point is that when your mind is consumed with all the static of life, you miss opportunities, don't take chances, or take foolish ones. Control is the key to a productive life."

"You make it sound so easy."

"No," he said, shaking his head slowly. "It's simple, not easy. You'll find the simple things are often the hardest. It's like cooking. Scrambled eggs are simple. Eggs, milk, and heat. Simple. Yet making incredible scrambled eggs is difficult until you've discovered how to do it."

"What's the secret?"

"You'll have to discover it on your own," he said with a smile. "Enough talking. While we're sparring, practice calm, control, and pay attention. I'm rusty, so I'm sure you'll spot mistakes if you are in the moment."

He fired off two quick jabs. I blocked the first. The second landed. I ignored the hit and saw his foot twitch. When he kicked, I had moved out of the way and struck at his anchor leg. I would have scored against anyone else, but Blaze shifted his weight and pivoted, avoiding the attack and delivering a round house kick. I blocked it and rolled left, avoiding his follow-up.

"Good," he said around his mouth guard. He launched a swift kick to my chest, but I caught his foot and twisted. He rolled the direction I twisted, wrenching his foot free. A quick bounce had him back up and on the attack again. I blocked his jab, reset to block his second, and spun out of the way of his roundhouse.

I'd forgotten how fast Blaze was, not having sparred with him for a while. During the training sessions at Castle, we'd practiced against each other or training dummies. Abby said either way she was hitting a dummy.

*Time to change it up.* I went into an aggressive stance and attacked with a series of punches. He knocked them away, but a bead of sweat trickled down his cheek. I brought my foot up, feigning an attack. He pivoted to avoid it, and I punched instead, catching him in the shoulder harder than I should have.

Blaze spun and lashed out with a back-handed punch I barely blocked. He sped up, strikes coming faster and faster until he virtually blurred, and then he was behind me. The blows stopped. We stood back to back.

I pivoted around, and Blaze stared at me. "Dude, how did you do that?" Blaze asked in amazement.

"Do what? Get my ass handed to me?"

"No. One second you were facing me. The next you went through me. Is it part of your Gift?" He looked puzzled as he stared at me.

"I didn't do anything. You were punching so fast. Then you blurred and were behind me. I think the machine gave you a power of your own."

Blaze dropped to the ground. "I'm too old for this shit."

When Dad and Pepper returned, we recounted the story in the conference room. Pepper looked like she'd seen a ghost.

Dad shrugged it off. "Welcome to the team, Blaze. You always wanted a power. Now it would seem you've got one. You'll have to practice until you can control it."

"Marcel can help you. He came up with ways to figure out what my Gift was. If anyone can figure it out, it's him." I said.

Blaze blanched. "What if it's speed? They die sooner because of their Gift." His eyes went to Pepper. He'd finally gotten Pepper back, and a speed Gift would age him at an accelerated rate, and he was significantly older already.

"I don't think it's speed," I said, as I worked it out in my head. "Wendi blurred but you could see her afterimage for a split second after she moved. You were there, then you were behind me."

As he came to the table, Marcel said, "Sorry, I overheard you. When I researched Tommy's Gift, I found a sub-group of Gifted called Jumpers. They use a form of limited teleportation to move short distances. A hero named Jumping Bean was referenced as an example."

"I've heard of him," Blaze said, slowly. "Worked in New York for a while. Fought with a couple of knives. Would slash up his targets."

Pepper laughed. "I remember the schlub. He wore a yellow and red wrestling suit to fight in. I saw him land on a hydrant one time. Hit him right in the nads. Laughed so hard I almost peed myself."

"Nads?" I asked. Pepper's use of slang sometime left me clueless, like she spoke a foreign language.

She pointed to her groin. "Nads. Balls. Whatever you want to call 'em."

My face decided to superheat at that moment. "Oh." *One day, I'll learn to keep my mouth shut. Maybe I should wear a mask to hide my face. Probably save me a lot of embarrassment.*

Marcel came to my rescue. "Anyhow, Ranger, one of my surveillance hacks picked up this outside of D.C." He slid a photo across to Dad. "I can't be sure, but it looks like Reaper. If it is, he's alive and moving around."

Dad showed me the picture. It was grainy, but there was no way it wasn't Reaper. He had a short dark beard now. He carried a small box under his arm. "Wonder what he's doing in D.C.?"

"The Syndicate still has a strong presence there. My guess is he needs backup after Yelena took him and his team. With her gone, he's more dangerous than ever," Dad said. He handed the picture back to Marcel. "Snoop around and see if you can spot where he's going and if he's contacting the Protectorate."

"On it, Ranger. I'll let you know as soon as I know anything." Marcel stored the photo and returned the way he came. Probably back to the communication center, his official lair.

"Nothing we can do now but wait." Dad said.

As it turned out, we didn't have to wait too long.

I spent more time with Blaze as we waited for Reaper to show or Caligari to make his presence known. I wasn't sure which one would be worse.

After two days, Blaze could manage to teleport short distances once out of every twenty times he tried. Mostly, it happened when he worked against a training dummy. His fists would blur and then *poof*, he was somewhere else. He'd gotten the hang of reappearing facing the target, which was a major improvement.

We had broken for lunch as Marcel came into the commissary. "We've got a lock on Reaper. He went into an old building in the center of D.C. about twenty minutes ago."

"What did the building look like?" Blaze asked, setting down his coffee cup. "Long, rectangular, with lots of columns?"

"I don't think so. Lots of windows. There might be a raised roof. Hard to see from the camera angle." Marcel shrugged. "Everything is overgrown and broken. Hard to tell what was what. The team is assembling in the translocation room."

Blaze pushed away from the table. "Where do I get a combat suit?"

"Nowhere," I said, hesitantly. Blaze was my friend, teacher, and mentor, but he wasn't ready to fight Reaper. Practice dummies were one thing, but the scythe-wielding psycho was another. "You aren't ready to go up against Reaper."

"Dude, I fought Reaper before you were even born. I know I'm ready, and this time I have a Gift to even the score." Blaze glared at both of us, daring us to disagree with him.

"Blaze, you aren't goin'" Pepper's voice cut through the silence of the commissary. "Tommy's right. You ain't ready to deal with him. Believe me, I was stuck in Reaper's head for way too long. I just got you back, I'm not losing you to his damn scythe."

I motioned with my head to Marcel. We motored away from the upcoming fight.

I hit my room and got ready, reloaded my energy, and secured the comm-link. I snuck past the happy couple arguing over Blaze going and took the stairs down to the translocator room.

Dad, Blaster, and a very bruised Izanami stood waiting by the machine.

"Marcel, are you online?" Dad asked over the comm-link.

"Affirmative, Ranger." Marcel had taken to the military lingo like a gamer to Mountain Dew. It didn't hurt that Dad approved and made mention of it, a lot. "You're clear for translocation to the D.C. base."

Izanami activated the portable device, and moments later, we stood in the evacuated base.

"Izanami, take the lead. Tommy, Blaster, and I will bring up the rear. This is not a combat mission. If we run into the Syndicate, we retreat. I'll lay down cover while you get back to the egress point. Understood?"

"If I get a shot at Reaper, I'm takin' it," Blaster said before quickly adding, "before I follow Izanami back here."

"Just make sure you do," Dad said, giving Blaster the look. I had to give Blaster credit. He didn't step backward.

Izanami set out at a quick pace, leading us through an old access door and into a series of tunnels below the city. Fortunately, we didn't have far to go before we climbed a set of stairs up, out of the gloom, and into the cold, dreary morning. Nothing had changed since I'd been here the first time, but I hoped we could skip the rats. At least my Gift worked now, so fighting back was an option.

A light drizzle of rain and snow greeted us as we wove through abandoned and wrecked vehicles. Thick ropes of green grew over everything in this area of the city, giving the air the scent of rotting vegetables. We slowed our pace to minimize stepping on the vines. After the killer moss, I didn't want to take any chances.

An hour and many more turns later, we reached the building Marcel had spotted Reaper entering. We crouched behind old rusted-out cars, surveying the site.

"You're on target. Ranger, call the ball." Marcel sounded so happy, safe and sound at the base. Water trickled down my back as we made our way through the thickening precipitation.

"I've got the ball," Dad said. He signaled Izanami, who slid from behind the blue car and moved to the doorway. She waved, and I followed her, standing at the other side of the doorway. Nothing moved inside. I gave the all-clear, ducked in, and took cover behind a broken statue. At one time, it had been a woman holding a globe, but no more.

Dad crouched beside me as I saw the others getting into position.

The place was enormous. Patterned tile lay under the dirt that had accumulated from being abandoned for so long.

Dad gave the *follow* signal and moved into the gloom of the interior. Large desks flanked the entry, covered with vines growing from the balcony overhead.

The room beyond held a ton of old shelving units filled with books. A sign read "Fiction" and "Non-Fiction" with arrows pointing right and left. In the center of the second room, tables had been pushed together, and papers, books, and equipment lay scattered across every horizontal surface. The smell was atrocious, a mix of acid and mold. If Reaper was here, I didn't see him. It didn't make me breathe any easier.

A draft blew in from above. Drifting snowflakes settled on the floor in front of me. I was sure whoever built this place hadn't imagined it would end up this way. A layer of black lay across the floor, intermingled with the snow coming through the cracks above.

"Stay together, and watch your backs," Dad whispered over the comm-link. "He may have left, but we don't need any surprises."

"I'll move into the center while you cover me," I said, readying myself.

Dad nodded to me. "Izanami, protect the rear flank. Blaster, you cover right. I've got left. On three."

Marcel counted down. When he reached three, I stood and crept toward the tables. Nothing moved around me as I entered the open area. My gaze moved up to the second-floor balcony, and I froze. Crows the size of Great Danes perched on the marble railing. I spun in place slowly. There must have been at least fifty of them. "There are massive birds all over the place."

"Bruh, they don't call it a murder of crows for nothing. Get out of there." Marcel's fingers pounding the keyboard. "They shouldn't bother you, unless you provoke them."

"Right, leave the nice birdies alone," I said, standing still and watching. They seemed to be sleeping or frozen in place. It kind of creeped me out.

Out of the gloom, Reaper appeared, a scowl frozen on his face. "I wouldn't wake them. They'll tear you apart, Gift or no Gift." He wore a black leather jacket, jeans, and heavy boots. Under his arm, he still carried the box we'd seen in the photo. "I've got scores to settle before I deal with you, Ward, but I will end all of you before I'm done."

"It's just you and me. Let's end it now," I said, feeling the energy build inside me. A squawk from above stopped me from firing.

Reaper grinned. "Smart boy. Crows are very sensitive to electric current. You go throwin' your lightning around here, and they'll tear your eyes out." The grin faded. "You get in my way, and I'll make you suffer."

"In your way of what?" I asked, hoping Dad and Marcel had heard what Reaper said.

"Don't play dumb with me, Tommy. I know you. You're looking for the remote station, same as me. I'm going to use the ray to wipe out the Protectorate. Nobody double crosses the Syndicate."

"Funny, you sound like Yelena." I said, trying to get a rise out of him. "Too bad she's dead now. You'll need a new owner."

Reaper's face darkened, and he sneered at me. He'd done this to Jon a hundred times, pushed him until he did something stupid. "You'll pay for her death soon enough, Ward. Waxenby can tell you all he knows, but I've already found the code book. Once I find the Siren, I'll have control of the most powerful weapon around and will finish off the Protectorate scum. Then it's your turn."

"What code book?" Marcel asked as Blaster said, "Who the hell is Siren?"

I had to answer fast and not give away my ignorance. "Waxenby told us where to find a copy of the code book. You think the Brigade only had one? There were two teams."

Reaper fumed. "I told Parasite *el pendejo* lied about one book." Reaper's eyes narrowed as he studied me. "Then you know all about the key?"

I knew Reaper well enough not to fall for the trap. "Key? I guess you got the fake manual. Looks like you aren't a threat, after all." I turned to walk away.

His growl was loud enough to unsettle the birds above. One singular solid black feather, long as a forearm, floated to the ground.

"I'm always a threat, *chico*," Reaper said. "We'll see who gets to Siren first. Once I've got him, the game's over."

I smiled back at Reaper. "We'll see who gets him first."

Marcel groaned in my ear. "Siren has to be female. It's in the name."

I'd thought of siren as in "horn," not a mythical creature who lured men to their deaths.

"You don't know shit." He laughed, backing up. "Nice try, but you're a fool, boy." He reached the last of the book stacks and threw something, which landed on the table.

A second later it exploded. Flames shot in all directions, engulfing the table's contents. My ears rang from the loud noise, but not enough to miss the chorus of angry squawks erupting from above.

The birds launched from their perches. They flew, circling the domed ceiling. One dove in my direction. I froze.

Dad didn't. One second, a large bird descended; the next, a burst of lightning slammed into it, throwing feathers in every direction like a torn pillow. The body cartwheeled across the room before it destroyed two old bookshelves. Paper flew everywhere, mimicking the snow that fell.

A second plunged in my direction. I backed away from the cacophony of squawks and shrieks. Blaster fired on the birds closest to him. More birds dove in ever-increasing numbers.

"Get to the doors," Dad said. "We can't fight them all."

I did as told and moved back the way we'd come. The fire engulfed the table, destroying any evidence Reaper had left behind. This had been a wasted trip.

Izanami broke a chair over a bird stupid enough to get too close to her, tearing the wooden chair in half. I wondered if all her fighting technique came from pro wrestling. As long as it worked, I really didn't care.

She bludgeoned more birds with the remnants of the chair until all she had left was kindling. She'd be unstoppable with a metal folding chair.

Blaster continued to fire, breaking to shove food into his mouth as fast as possible. Dad unleashed wave after wave of lightning arcs, setting feathers on fire as he went.

Two birds descended on me from either side. I fired on the one to the right as the beak of the second one jammed into my shoulder. Energy burst within me, but damn did it hurt! Anyone else would have been impaled by the razor-sharp beak. I loaded up and force-punched it, driving it back into the whirlwind of avians.

"We've got—" The comm-link went silent.

"Mr. Wizard?" I asked, but there was nothing. *Perfect time to lose our connection.* I bumped into Dad, as I retreated farther. Blaster ran to join us. Izanami punched a bird in the side of the head, dropping it on the spot. The others cawed, straining to reach her.

Dad yelled, "Izanami, come on!"

She heaved a bird that stabbed fiercely at her back into the murder and ran. I laid down a series of energy bolts to dissuade the others from following. Fire would come in handy for situations like this. I needed to practice creating flames.

The birds, whether from the smoke or incensed by our fight, tore at anything in their way to get out. The fire had spread to the books and old carpet, turning the abandoned library into a bonfire. They flooded the main hall, blocking the doors we'd come through. They pushed toward us as they sought an escape.

All of us opened up on the front row, dropping many of the birds, which stood as tall as me, in their tracks, but it made no difference as they backed us into a corner of the building with no exit at hand.

"Out now." I blasted the wall and tore a hole straight to the outside. My energy dropped to where I felt lightheaded, but we had an exit.

Dad leapt through the hole, followed by a rapidly chewing Blaster and Izanami. She scooped up a few chucks of concrete, which whistled past me as I dove out of the building to avoid the rampaging birds. As soon as they hit the snowy air, wings extended, they took off.

I fell to the ground, taking a deep breath of fresh-ish air. The destroyed cities had a unique mix of death and rot which I'd never describe as smelling good.

Dad crouched down next to me. "You okay?"

I bobbed my head. "Yeah, just took a bit out of me. I thought we had Reaper."

"Me too. There's a reason it took so long to catch him, and even then, the Protectorate couldn't hold him," Dad said, with a frown. "I should have taken him out before I turned myself in."

Back when I was in school, Reaper killed twelve guards breaking out of the Block. Reaper was strong, cunning, and extremely dangerous. He'd also tried to sell us to the Protectorate. Ending him would save a lot of lives.

Dad was helping me to my feet when we heard the bullhorn.

"Reaper, we know you're in there. We've got the area surrounded. Put your hands up and come out quietly."

The Reclaimers had entered the fight.

## 3 0

"Marcel, the Reclaimers are here. How do we get out?" I said, forcing my voice to stay calm. It almost worked.

The only answer I got was static.

"They're jamming transmissions," Dad said. He looked around for the source of the interference. "We've got a head start of a few minutes. They don't know we're here. If we can make it back underground, we can slip the trap and return to Harker."

"Follow me," Izanami said. Like everything else she did, she ran with a graceful efficiency. No wasted motions. We raced down the street and away from the library.

The Reclaimers had pushed old cars together to form a barricade across the intersection on the way to the exit. An idea popped into my head. "Hit the ground and roll under something!" I yelled, increasing my speed. Dad stopped but didn't get out of the way. "Now! I have a plan."

He did as I asked or told, however you want to look at it. I kept running at the Reclaimer line, darting between cars since they'd have inhibitor bands ready for any Gifted they found.

"Stop and put your hands up," came from a bullhorn one of the

217

soldiers had. There were about twenty weapons pointed at me, including at least two with the dreaded inhibitors.

I didn't stop. Instead I yelled in my craziest voice. "You'll have to kill me if you want me to stop."

On cue, two soldiers fired. One bullet hit me in the chest and resupplied my energy levels. It hurt like hell, but I didn't have time to recharge any other way. The shooter's eyes widened, seeing the spent bullet drop to the ground at my feet. Two more hits topped me off. I swore as they struck. There were much less painful ways to gain power, and I should use them more often.

The power rippled across my hands as I fanned a wide spread of lightning, making them duck. I leapt over the hood of an old Mercedes and shouted before rolling under the car.

Bullets followed me as I crawled between two of the abandoned cars. I focused my energy and lashed out with both feet, sending the car rolling into the startled Reclaimers. It smashed into their lines and scattered them. I repeated the maneuver, sending the troops fleeing from the flipping cars.

I scrambled for cover near where the rest of the team waited. I found them a minute later crouching and watching the demolition derby I'd created.

"Nice job," Blaster said. I pulled up next to him. "Just like the Gauntlet. Nice."

Dad grinned. "The distraction won't last long. Let's go."

Izanami signaled, and we followed her into a building. Before the Darkest Storm, it must have been a government building, given we entered a large, spacious foyer with a metal detector stationed in front of the elevators and an eagle logo set into the floor. We ran across the broken tile floor and tried to exit onto the street. A group of ten Reclaimers sat behind a barricade down the street from our position. Bullets ricocheted around us as they opened fired.

"Shit!" Blaster yelled. His hand grabbed his leg. Blood leaked between his fingers from the wound on his calf. He dropped to the floor.

Dad dragged him back into the lobby while I provided cover fire.

Dad pulled Blaster's hand away from the wound. "Punched clean through. Bite on something, and I'll get you patched up."

"Do it," Blaster said, then jammed a piece of beef jerky between his teeth.

Dad cauterized the wounds on both sides of Blaster's calf as he groaned.

"It will hold until we get out of here." Dad wiped his hand across the floor to get most of the blood off it. He stuck his head out to get a peek and retracted it quickly as bullets slammed against the concrete. "Any way out of here?"

Izanami shrugged. "Through them?"

We didn't have time to wait. If we didn't get free soon, we wouldn't be. It was only a matter of time before they got an inhibitor on one of us and everything would break down from there.

"Count to five and follow me." I charged out into the street far enough to draw fire, but out of range of the inhibitor bands, though it didn't stop one from being shot at me. It fell about fifty feet short.

A loud voice screamed not to waste them.

I pulled as much energy together as I could and fired a steady stream of lightning down the street. The closest Reclaimers dropped, as the current burned through them. Bullets struck me, building my power.

Dad shot out of the front of the building, adding to the lightning flowing down the street. Blaster hobbled through the door, his force bolts joining the fight. The Reclaimers died or ran as we moved down the street; Izanami came behind, watching our backs. We reached the corner, and she ran ahead, indicating we should follow. The Reclaimers standing behind the barricade at the next intersection shouted with surprise at seeing their buddies headed toward them.

We ducked in and out of buildings, avoiding the Reclaimers, until we reached the downward stairs that led to the Underground. Blaster's limp had improved, his enhanced healing having taken effect. In a couple of days, he'd be good as new.

We took our time navigating the tunnels beneath the city. With all the activity above, lots of things had descended into the tunnels. The squeaking of rats echoed through the dimly lit underworld, setting my nerves on edge.

The fight with the giant rodents still gave me nightmares.

Loud thuds from above made me wonder if the Reclaimers were demolishing buildings or had brought in heavy armor for the fight. Either way, I was glad we'd gotten out before the reinforcements arrived.

As we walked through the murky tunnels, I wondered how many more people I'd killed. Those people had families who'd blame us for their deaths, furthering an already rampant hatred of the Gifted. At least this time we deserved it, unlike all the times the Protectorate killed and then blamed us for it.

An hour later, we emerged at the Underground's base. We slid into a blind room to wait for a while, in case we were followed. No sense showing the Reclaimers where the translocator was. When Izanami was satisfied it was safe, we entered the base.

We sealed the doors so they couldn't be opened from the outside and rigged the self-destruct systems as Warden did now in all the abandoned bases. The translocators were too important to be allowed to fall into the Protectorate's hands. If they managed to figure out how to use them, the Protectorate could eliminate the Underground and us in one quick sweep.

Warden sat at the entrance to the command bunker. "Marcel freaked out when he lost contact with you, so I wandered down to assess the situation. Other than a slightly damaged Blaster, you all look to be in one piece."

"The Reclaimers heated up the area, but they were after Grim Reaper, not us," Dad said. He rubbed at the back of his blistered hand. Blood oozed from the deeper burns. Every fight left him looking like an intensive care patient after a fire. "The Protectorate wants him bad. I wish I knew why."

She shrugged. "Most likely the Protectorate is working with the Brotherhood. I doubt they understand the Brotherhood's mission is to destroy the universe, but as long as the Protector is in power, what does he care?"

"You're probably right." He turned to the rest of us. "You did good, especially against Reaper. It could have gone sideways fast."

Blaster laughed. "You mean a murder of angry crows trying to eat your face doesn't count as sideways?"

"You walked, or in your case limped, away from it," Dad said. He clapped Blaster on the shoulder. "So no, it could have been much worse. Let's get back to Harker."

Five minutes later, we were seated around the wall display, watching the Reclaimers' attack on Washington. I stopped looking when the cameras panned over the dead bodies left in our wake. Why everything came down to people dying bothered me. I'd seen up close what waited for us if we were captured, and being dead wasn't high on my priorities. Redemption would be a walk in the park in comparison to the Block or, worse, death.

I'm not sure how long we watched the newscasters. Mom was still at the new base with the advance team, trying to get the systems working. Mr. Fix-it had joined her, and from Warden's accounts, it might be habitable before the death ray reached Boston, but not by much.

San Francisco wasn't large enough to hold all the Underground's people. London, Madrid, and Dublin would be hit in the next few days. After that, there were the nine cities in the western hemisphere. Two of those were already destroyed, and Washington had been abandoned. With twenty-five thousand people to move, we were running out of time, but sending masses of people to the base without sustainable food and heat was a death sentence.

After dinner, I went down to Waxenby's room. Mimi sat next to him, as always. Her eyes were closed. At first, I thought she was asleep, but they flickered open as I stepped into the room.

"Hey, Sport," she said with a grin. "Trying to get Waxenby's brain back together. I think I'm close to a breakthrough. He's starting to be able to piece together what happened while he was with Reaper, but there's a block I can't get around."

I took the chair across from Mimi. "What kind of block?"

She pondered for a moment before answering. "I thought it was something the Syndicate did to him, but now I'm not so sure. They were brute force all the way, and this is much more subtle."

Interesting, but it wasn't getting us any closer to the code book or Siren. I told her about the conversation with Reaper.

"Why would Ollie know anything about a Dark Brigade code book?" Mimi asked, a puzzled expression on her face.

"A lot of Gifted entrusted their secrets to him before they were killed or captured. My dad did. Same for the Patriots and Crusaders. He became a living backup."

"Along with the data Blaze kept in the Lair." She shrugged. "Makes sense. I'll keep trying, though knowing about the Dark Brigade stuff gives me a different angle to explore."

We talked for a couple of more hours before I excused myself and headed to my room.

We needed to destroy the remote station before Reaper got to it. I wondered if Caligari was a distraction to keep us off Reaper while he found the station and took control of the death ray. More lies wrapped in deception and sold as the truth. It made my head hurt thinking about it, but I worried at it until sleep finally took me under.

---

The next morning, I found Alyx with Dad and Warden in the commissary.

"Tommy, glad to see you," Alyx said, as I approached the table. "Why don't you join us?"

I flopped in a chair. "Hey, Alyx. What brings you here?"

"The Council has spotted Balthier's people in and around the London dead zone. We think he'll make his next move there." He glanced at Dad before continuing. "I'll need backup if I'm going to stop him once and for all."

Dad shook his head. "I'm not sure it's a sound tactical move to go head-to-head with Caligari again. We caught him unaware, and he still beat us, and we lost Abby. He'll be expecting us this time. Who knows what he'll be planning?"

"Really, can he be beat?" Warden asked. Her long red hair was pulled back in a bun today. "You and Makeda couldn't take him down, and Yutu even showed up to help. We can't keep risking our people to fight your war."

Alyx's features tightened. "It's not our war. Balthier is using Gifted to fight us as well as magic. Without your help, we can't rescue Abby or free Jon from his control. There is a lot at stake if we don't defeat him. Who knows where the weapon will strike once it finishes the pre-programed sequence?"

Warden huffed. "Honestly, who cares? We've been fighting against the Reclaimers since the Darkest Storm. Let Reaper destroy the Protectorate, then we can take control of the government and establish a new one."

"You sound just like the Brotherhood," Alyx said, his face flushing red. "What happens if Balthier's plan kills all life on Earth?"

"Then I won't be here to worry about it, will I?" Warden said. She leaned into the table. "You sit at the Council, safe from all of this, and expect us to do your fighting. It's no different than the Brotherhood. I'm tired of being a pawn in your game."

"Queen," I said, drawing blank stares from the three adults at the table. "Warden moves around too much to be a pawn. You'd have to be a Queen or maybe a rook. Marcel would know better."

"What?" they all asked at once.

"Never heard of chess?" I asked, putting on the bewildered act like when I got in trouble for something when I was little. "Hmm. I thought you'd have heard of it."

"We've heard of it. What are you trying to say?" Dad asked. He was looking at me like I was crazy.

I shrugged. "Talking about chess makes as much sense as sitting here arguing about why we're fighting or whose war it is. Bottom line is Caligari has Abby, and we need to get her back. If he's in London, then so are we. End of story. I'm getting a Dew. Anyone want anything?" I stood and got a drink and a couple of Pop-Tarts. Might as well have breakfast while they argued.

No one said a word as I sat down and started eating. I looked at each of them in turn. "What?"

"Will you still go to London if I take Blaster and Izanami with me?" Warden asked. Her normal calm had reappeared, which was a good thing. When she was being a fiery hothead, she didn't listen.

"Yep," I said. I popped a piece of wildberry goodness into my mouth and chewed noisily. Mom would have killed me, but it was all part of the plan.

Alyx decided to rejoin the conversation. "What are you thinking?"

"We go to London and kick Caligari's ass. You bring Gladiator, Makeda, and Yutu. Warden brings Izanami and Blaster. Dad and I join you. We hit him hard and fast."

"What happens if we fail?" Alyx asked. "As Warden pointed out, we don't have a great track record against him."

"Then we die, except for Gladiator."

Dad stared at me still. "That's your plan?" I knew it sounded crazy to him, but what other choice did we have?

"I might be able to help," Blaze said from across the room. With the argument in progress, no one had noticed him enter.

Dad looked at him. "What are you thinking, Blaze?"

He took a low bow and said, "Introducing Pepper Spray, version two."

Pepper entered from the hallway wearing a new combat suit. She struck a pose like a video game fighter. "Gabriel got my cybernetic arsenal back online. The bad guys won't expect me at the party."

She was right. Caligari wouldn't be expecting Pepper, so he couldn't plan for her.

Things were finally turning around. At least I hoped so.

We fell into a routine over the next few days: morning training with Blaze and Pepper, break for lunch, afternoons spent reviewing possible locations in London that Caligari might use to make his next move, dinner, and then downtime for the evening.

The strike team consisted of me, Mom, Dad, Warden, Blaster, Izanami, Pepper, and Blaze. We'd handle any non-magical threats. Alyx, Makeda, Yutu and Gladiator were to take down Caligari, or at least keep him busy enough to allow us to stop his plan. It was the largest team we'd used. Warden wanted to bring in more Underground Gifted, but it was decided that too many people created the possibility of friendly fire or a hostage situation. We'd go with the people we knew.

Marcel had gotten his estimates on the next firing down to an hour plus or minus thirty minutes. He was projecting a ten a.m. London time weapons fire. He'd spotted activity near the old Jubilee Garden site near the rusted Ferris Wheel that overlooked it. We assembled in the meeting room at four a.m., armed and ready.

"Overnight, Caligari placed a machine in the center of Jubilee

Gardens," Marcel said. He stood next to the wall monitor with the live feed from one of the Protectorate cameras on the screen.

"The Reclaimers' surveillance cameras ringing London aren't close enough to get a good view of what it is, but there have been people moving around in the park. He has to expect us to try to stop him."

Dad stood on the other side. "Marcel, can we have the overhead map?"

Marcel changed the view from his tablet. An overhead shot showed a walking path around the center where Caligari was. There were four exits, two onto the street on one side and two on the Thames river side.

"Thank you. Alyx will open a portal here." Dad pointed at an old playground on the side of the main section. "There is enough over-grown equipment there to cover our arrival. We progress through to this area." He indicated a path from the playground to the center of the gardens. "Makeda will take Susan and Warden to the roof of the building overlooking the garden from the north. Tommy will lead, following the walkway to the edge of the open area. Gladiator will stay with Alyx and Yutu on the right side while I take the rest of the team left. We destroy the device and then focus on Caligari until the one-minute mark. At that point, we extract back to Harker. No one stays behind. We don't know what the ray will do to Gifted. It might kill you or mutate you. Questions?"

There weren't any. After three days, everyone had a pretty good idea what was involved. "We leave in five."

Dad spoke with Alyx as the rest of the group broke into their assigned teams.

Marcel approached me. I drank my Mountain Dew, waiting to hear what he had to say. It would be better to fight in the afternoon after I'd slept in, but it was always early mornings or late nights.

"Bruh, be careful today. I've got a bad feeling about this one." Marcel wasn't normally nervous before a mission, so I tended to listen when he was. "This is all too easy. Caligari hasn't tried to hide anything he's doing in London. We only caught Yelena's plan with hours to go. It has to be a set up."

I agreed it was, but we had to take the bait to stop Caligari and hopefully get Abby back. "I've been thinking Yelena, and now Caligari, have been covering for Reaper as he looks for the remote station. Why else would the Brotherhood be so up front in their attacks?"

Marcel rubbed his chin scruff. "Makes a lot of sense, bruh." He laughed unexpectedly. "Look at you thinking and everything."

"I think Pepper broke something while she was in there."

"Alyx, open the portal. Tommy, you lead, and then it's by the numbers."

Marcel punched me in the shoulder. "Luck, bruh."

"Thanks." I headed over, stopped for a Mom hug, and then I went through the looking glass and straight down the rabbit hole.

As my feet landed in London, a light flared below me, and I dropped straight through another portal and onto faded red bricks. Cold hands grasped my neck before I had the chance to rise. Tendrils of acid drove their way into my brain. I screamed. My arms shook and my knees buckled, dumping me on the ground. A weight crashed on my back, pressing into me.

"Parasite, do you have him?" Caligari's voice came from behind me, but I couldn't turn to see him.

"Yes, Balthier." The words came out of my mouth. This surprised me since I hadn't said them. I tried to speak. I'd been pushed to the side behind an invisible wall. "He is fighting me, but I have him."

"He bested Yelena. Do not lose focus."

My body stood, allowing me to see my surroundings. We weren't at the garden. Instead we were in the center of a square of buildings. The high walls contained numerous windows and doorways. I was sure it had been an impressive sight back before the Storm. Over us sat the lens structure Mr. Fix-it had described. It covered most of the open sky between the buildings and ran down to a narrow focusing lens above a massive engine.

Jon, with Abby in bear form following behind, approached. "Just remember our deal, Balthier. As soon as this is over, you bring my sister to me."

Abby growled and pushed forward. Jon touched her shoulder, and she laid down. I had to break her free, but I couldn't exactly do anything at the present.

Caligari sniffed. "Of course. I am a man of my word. You'll rejoin your sister today." He returned his focus to me. "Parasite, get him hooked to the machine. The ray will fire in a matter of minutes."

"Yes." I walked across the courtyard to the device. Jon snapped metal canisters over my hands. Each had a conduit running into the base of the machine. The focus lens sat directly over my head.

Caligari sauntered up to stand in front of me. "Jon, go scout and make sure none of his people have located us. They have certainly been a nuisance, and I don't want any interruptions. Be back here in five minutes. I doubt you'd survive the ray outside the protective lens."

Jon grumbled as he loped off. Abby's head swung back to look at me. Anger and frustration filled her eyes, but then she followed.

No matter what, I had to free her. She'd been stuck in animal form as a child, and it haunted her to this day. Being locked into it again must be horrifying to her. I beat against the walls separating me from my body. Parasite tightened his grip on my throat. I struggled to gain control, but he was too strong.

"Can you let the boy speak without losing control of him?" Caligari asked after Jon was gone.

"Yes, but he strong."

A portion of the wall retreated as I watched. There were sections blocking different aspects of me. Some were open, like the ability to think, but my power lay behind a faintly pulsing piece. If I broke through it, I'd have control of my abilities.

"Today, I win," Caligari said to me. "I retrieved the lens even though you fought me. Now, in a few moments, Parasite will use your power to drive this sonic drill into the Earth's core. After that, the world will shatter, and the magic contained within will be mine to control."

"Delusions of grandeur much, Caligari? My team will be here before the ray fires and will end you." I hoped. The comm-link had a location tracker Marcel could use to find us. As soon as I'd vanished, he should have been able to pinpoint me and send the rest here.

"So much power at your disposal yet so naive," Caligari said, picking a piece of lint off his immaculate jacket. "You don't see what is right before your eyes. You could be king, but instead you hide like a scared mouse, waiting for the Protectorate to hunt you down. But, alas, it is too late for you."

"I'm going to kill you and then Jon for betraying us." We should have killed him rather than allow him to inform our enemies about us. Once again, my softness had cost us. If I'd killed him, Abby would be free, and we wouldn't be in this mess. I'd have to start taking matters into my own hands before another person I loved died.

The mage laughed in my face. "You'll be dead along with the rest of the pathetic humans on this rock. It's been a millennium since I've enjoyed the prospect of watching someone die."

"What about me?" a small voice asked from over my shoulder. "I want to live."

"Parasite, I told you. Once the boy has powered the drill, you'll come with me. You're far too important to leave behind."

Caligari started to say something until Jon yelled from across the courtyard. "They're searching for him, but I don't think they'll make it here in time."

Caligari hissed. "You weren't seen, were you? If you fail me, our deal is off, boy."

"They didn't see me, though Abby tried to interfere. Once we're out of here, I'll let her go back to her human form. She'll see the light once we're done." Jon ran his hand along Abby's back, petting her like a dog.

I didn't say anything, just waited. Caligari hadn't told Parasite to stop me from talking, so he didn't. I needed to convince Parasite to let me go, and for that I had to be able to speak. For once, patience won out over my mouth.

"How long do we have left?" Jon asked, continuing to soothe Abby. She slumbered on the courtyard bricks, like she was hibernating for the winter. Jon's Gift must have been strong to control Abby in animal form. If I had to kill Jon in order to release Abby from his grip, I'd do it and hope Wendi would understand.

"Three minutes or so," Caligari said. He returned to checking the drill. "Once the ray starts, stay back. There will be debris flying as it pierces the Earth's crust. Once it hits the core, we will portal out of here. Understood?"

"It's not a hard plan to follow," Jon said to Caligari's back.

The mage spun around. "You can stay here if you'd prefer, Mr. Stevens. The lack of your company wouldn't bother me at all."

Jon held up his hands as Abby lumbered to her feet. "No need to get upset. Once I get my sister back, I'll be out of your hair."

A growl rumbled from Abby's chest. She took a step forward. Caligari had magic enough to stop her, provided he could cast it fast enough. I wanted to laugh as the mage's face lost all color as the giant teeth bared at him.

"Get the beast under control. I doubt your former team would be happy to see you again. I know Mr. Ward wasn't."

Jon glared at me. "He'll get what's coming to him when you've destroyed him and his family, like he killed mine." He turned and walked away from the drill, taking a seat against a column. Abby dropped down next to him, her eyes open and watching.

Caligari finished whatever he was doing, but I was more focused on the wall between me and my powers. I probed the barrier until I located the edges. If I found a way to hit the barrier at its weakest point, it might shatter, giving me control long enough to rid myself of Parasite and get Abby away from Jon.

The mage stood in front of me. His lip curled in a sneer as he studied me. "To think you killed my beautiful Yelena, but you'll pay for it today. The Darkest Storm will be but a footnote after you've destroyed an entire planet. You've failed for the last time, Mr. Ward."

I kept my mouth shut. He moved so he stood next to Jon. Parasite tensed. The time grew near for the ray to strike. His hands trembled on my neck as I stood immobile, unable to move any part of my body below the neck. I continued to probe against the invisible wall that boxed me into my own brain.

"You not break free. I too strong," Parasite said into my ear. His grip firmed on my neck, though I hadn't attacked or done anything to provoke him.

"Caligari is leaving you to die." I let the words sink into my captor's head. He'd already been worried, but anything to get him to lose focus would help me.

"No, he take me. He say so. You hear him."

"I heard him, but how can he take you? As soon as you let me go, I will try to stop him. He's got to leave you until the job is done. By then, we'll both be dead."

Parasite paused. I felt the anxiety through our connection. "No, he magic. He save me." He said the words uncertainly. I'm sure Parasite knew Yelena and Caligari lied to the many people they betrayed.

"Reaper means to kill him."

Shock ran through me. The words hit me like a gut punch. "Reaper is dead. Caligari say so."

I had him now. "Can you see my memories?"

"Yes," Parasite whispered.

I remembered meeting Reaper in DC, noting the beard, his clothes, and every word he said. Parasite dug through the details, pulling out trivial things I'd missed during the encounter. He ran the memory back and forth, zoomed in on certain details and ignored others. He went on this way for what seemed like an eternity but was probably a few seconds at most.

"Reaper alive?" Parasite asked, like a child would. Emotion flooded through the bond we shared. I caught glimpses of his memories of Reaper. Some were cruel, but most were shining moments in his life. Reaper was family to him, though I doubted the feelings were mutual.

"He won't be if Caligari's plan works. We'll all be dead." I pictured Reaper burning as the world tore itself apart. Images of his hair flaring into flame, his face melting away. The little man lived through the death of Reaper. Parasite's sorrow and anxiety flooded my brain. Then it stopped, and Parasite resumed control.

"You lie." Parasite tightened his grip "Reaper hate you. He no tell you kill Caligari."

I needed to break his grip if I had any chance at all. "You saw the memory. He said you got the information from Waxenby. Do you remember him?"

"No remember." Parasite paused for a second. I felt the confusion in his mind. "You mean Stonewall? The one he took from you?"

Now it was my turn to be confused. "You took Commander Gravity. We called him Oliver Waxenby."

Parasite laughed. "No, we took Stonewall. You stupid."

I was about to argue, but the death ray hit London, and I couldn't think anymore.

Earth was about to end, and there was nothing I could do to stop it.

The lens funneled the death ray's energy into me, blurring my vision out to a solid whiteness. Agony shrieked through every atom of my body. My Gift absorbed the power, amplifying it. The larger lens took up most of the open air above the courtyard, focusing it until it struck only me.

Being inside the lens's area, Parasite was shielded from the death ray's beam. My body fought to retain its form as the mutagenic beam slammed into me, condensed into a single, thin ray.

The beam tried to rewrite me at a molecular level and change me into something new, but slowly my Gift absorbed enough to stop the process. The energy burned its way down every nerve in my body, sending me into convulsions. I couldn't utter a sound as the death ray fought to undo me.

Invisible hands manipulated the power that flowed through me. Parasite triggered my abilities and pumped the newly converted energy into the tubes connected to the sonic drill. My convulsions quieted with the release of the built-up force. The drill began to turn, digging into the ground, throwing pieces of red brick around the courtyard.

The ray magnified within me. My Gift amplified any energy I

absorbed, and if I didn't release enough, I would overload. My body pulsed, trying to expand, stretching my skin and muscles like I was on a medieval rack. My shoulders and hips strained to not be torn loose, shooting spasms though my limbs.

Parasite, unused to dealing with my Gift, didn't release enough to balance the energy. Every molecule in my body wanted to break apart, straining my Gift to its limit to hold me together. Soon I'd go super-nova and destroy a large section of the West European Zone and maybe more. I gritted my teeth and held on.

"It's working!" Caligari screamed. The sonic drill bit deeper into the earth, spraying dark soil now. He ran closer to the drill, Jon and Abby coming to stand next to him. The large lens kept the energy from touching them.

This was the only chance I'd get, so I took it. "Inuk!" I yelled at the top of my lungs.

Parasite slammed a shield down. My mouth still moved but no words came out. He'd hit the mute button.

Abby's head jerked up at the sound of the word. Jon reached out to touch her, but she lashed out with a giant paw, raking the long talons across his face. Blood sprayed as he screamed and dropped to the ground.

Caligari made to cast, but Abby batted him into the side of the drill, knocking it so a shower of rock and dirt exploded over the struggling mage.

Abby's form shifted until she stood naked in the center of the courtyard. Parasite panicked at the sight of her and loosened his grip. It was the break I needed. With all the mental force I could muster, I slammed into the barrier and cracked it enough to access my Gift.

I covered my body with energy, shocking the unsuspecting Para-site. With a yelp, he let go and fell to the ground. I was in control of my body again.

"Abby, run!" I shouted as I funneled more energy into the drill before it burned me out or sent me supernova. It had been close, and it felt like my body was about to explode. With the shackles still on my hands, I couldn't do much, but I reached up and grabbed part of the drill, failing to budge it.

Jon pulled out his bow. Abby grabbed him by the arm and flung him against a wall. He hit with a loud thud and fell limp to the ground.

"Help," I said to Abby as she ran to me.

She was over eight feet tall and easily reached the top of the drill. With a loud grunt, she pulled it back, bringing the bit out of the ground in a shower or rock, dirt, and bricks. She shoved her shoulder into the side of the housing and wrestled it until it pointed at Caligari.

The spinning end of the drill bit shot the sonic blast across the courtyard at Caligari. A green shield snapped into place, diverting the blow over the startled mage. The building behind him crumbled as the deadly sonic waves struck the structure.

The ray finished, but I continued to pump every ounce of energy through the drill and into the shield protecting the Brotherhood's leader.

"You'll never break my shield with a blunt, little weapon such as that, boy." Caligari sneered at me. "You may have interrupted this attempt, but I'll never stop until I've destroyed the Earth and claimed her magic as my own."

"By the time I run out of energy, the Council will be here. I don't need to kill you. Just hold you long enough to let them deal with you," I said through gritted teeth.

Abby laughed.

Motion out of the corner of my eye caught my attention. Reaper stepped forward from the building next to where Jon lay on the ground. He pulled the wooden box I'd seen him carrying earlier, opened it, and extracted a glowing red orb. He bounced it in his hands as if gauging the weight. "Yelena sends her regards," he said to Caligari.

"That trollop is dead. You can do nothing to me, boy!" Caligari screamed, panic thick in his voice as his eyes took in the sphere.

Without a word, Reaper threw the red ball of magic at Caligari. It burst as it struck, sending tendrils of red through the glowing green shield.

The mage fumbled to cast another spell, but the shield shattered. The sonic drill's blast struck and shredded him to bits in a puff of red haze and torn meat. I stopped the flow of energy, but not before it blew through the building behind it, collapsing a large section. Debris and dust billowed out from the demolition.

Reaper grabbed Jon's arm and dragged him into the building on the right. Blood still ran from the wounds Abby had inflicted on Jon earlier. He wouldn't be so pretty anymore, assuming he survived the damage she caused.

Abby broke apart the canisters that held my scalded hands.

I flexed my newly freed hands, wincing at the blisters that covered them. "Thanks. You okay?"

She dropped to the ground, pulling her hair over her exposed chest. "I will be. Jon forced me to stay in animal form somehow. He slept next to me so I couldn't change. Yutu's trigger worked though. I just wish I'd ripped his head off instead of only slashing his pretty face."

"I've missed you. I'm glad you're safe."

A blue light cut through the still air of the courtyard. Alyx's head peeked through. "Tommy's here. Abby is, too." He stepped out of the portal and swung his cloak over Abby.

"I'm going to have to buy you a new one," Abby said as she wrapped herself in it. He helped her to her feet. I noticed she'd returned to normal size as she stepped through the portal to cheers.

Alyx extended his hand to help me up. I took it, grimacing as a couple of blisters burst, and got to my feet. His gaze flicked over my shoulder just before his arm shot out, throwing a blast of blue magic.

I pivoted to see Parasite floating toward us, encased in the spell Alyx had thrown. The small Gifted struggled and thrashed in an attempt to get free.

Alyx grinned. "Looks like we caught a live one." He opened another, smaller portal and pushed Parasite through.

Even after Parasite had killed Salvo, injured Waxenby, and tried to use me to destroy the Earth, I felt sorry for him. He'd done as he was told by terrible people. He didn't belong in the middle of a war.

"He'll sit in confinement until we need him. Let's get you home."

I stepped through the opening and back into Harker. Mom tackled me with a hug, going on about how she thought she'd lost me. Dad pulled me in as soon as Mom let go, and the pass-the-Tommy-line was on. I guess falling through a portal freaks people out.

When everyone was done, we moved to the meeting room, but not before I grabbed a huge Mountain Dew for myself and a Pepsi for Abby. I was sure she needed something stronger, but Mom frowned on underage drinking. Like we were going to go drive around the mountains after a few beers.

I set Abby's Pepsi on the table and dropped into a chair. I sipped at my drink while my team filed in and we waited for Abby. She came in dressed in a baggy sweatshirt and jeans, with her hair pulled back in a ponytail. She shot me a quick smile as she grabbed the soda and drank. Fighting evil wizards is thirsty work.

Dad started the proceedings. "We are all glad you're safe, Tommy, and happy to see Abby back at home. Let's review the plan—"

"Forget the plan," Blaster said. "What the hell happened? You stepped out of the portal and fell into a hole that wasn't there."

Dad shrugged and sat down. "It might be better to have Tommy start."

I launched into the story, going over falling through the portal and Parasite latching onto me. When I reached Reaper throwing the orb at Caligari, the dam burst with a flood of questions, most of which I couldn't answer.

When I told them about using the drill to kill the mage, the room burst into applause and general mayhem for a minute. One more of the Brotherhood had fallen, and they needed to celebrate our win. I silently added Caligari to the list of people I'd killed. Not for the first time, I wondered if I'd ever be free of this guilt.

Once it quieted, I turned the floor over to Abby, who explained about Jon keeping her in animal form. What had once been Abby's secret was out in the open. Angry mutters followed her description of Jon using her as his personal weapon.

More cheering ensued when she got to the part where she ripped

Jon's face open, but I knew it was eating at her. She'd been as close to Wendi as I had been, and hurting Jon would have hurt Wendi as well. When our eyes met, we shared the pain together.

Once our tales were complete, Dad resumed his earlier tact. "We arrived at the garden to find a device built of old boxes and metal poles. From a distance it looked real, but up close we realized we'd been set up. My question is: how did they know where we would portal?"

Makeda answered. "Anyone can create a portal if they have line of sight. Balthier knew we'd come in close with the time running short."

"There was an aura around the fake device," Alyx said. "Most likely, it was a scrying spell to alert him where we were when I opened the portal. I never thought he'd grab one of ours from that distance."

"After we'd established it was safe to move, we fanned out, searching for any clue to help us find you," Dad said. "Marcel called off the search at the one-minute mark, and we came back here. Once the death ray fired, we spotted your location."

Confused, I said, "How did you know where I was? The ray blotted out the entire city every time we've watched it."

Marcel grinned. "The lens distorted the pattern of the energy signature for the death ray. I used an electro wave analyzer to find the varied pattern in the frequency of the disbursement pattern." He stopped and looked around at all the blank stares. "Never mind. I'll tell Mr. Fix-it. He'll get it."

"Once Marcel found the pattern, he pinpointed you on the map," Mom said, shooting Marcel a smile. "He was right. You were at Buckingham Palace."

"I used the sonic drill on a palace?" Even though the city was deserted, guilt gnawed at me that I'd destroyed an important building.

"Honey, you did, but I doubt anyone will be upset with you." Her eyes danced with mischief. "If they do, you've got the best lawyer around."

I laughed. I didn't just have a great lawyer. I had the best mom around. "I don't think the Protectorate will be suing me any time soon."

"They might," Marcel said. He pushed the FNN newsfeed to the monitor.

"Today, the Dissident terrorists have struck again. We are live outside the Reliance Military Installation on the outskirts of the London dead zone. Hundreds of Reclaimer troops and their families were viciously attacked by this man." A picture of Reaper appeared in the upper right corner of the screen. "He is armed and dangerous. Citizens are to contact their local Protectorate patrols if he is spotted. Do not attempt to apprehend this man. We're going live to Hannah Fulbright, who is waiting for General Mahady to make a statement. Hannah, over to you."

"Thank you, Skip," Hannah said, adjusting her glasses. "General Mahady has promised a full statement on the events outside of London today. To be sure, the Protectorate is under attack from subversive elements of our society."

There was a bustle of activity behind the reporter. "It looks like the General will be giving his statement." The camera moved to center on General Mahady, freshly shaven, in a perfectly pressed uniform, standing at the podium.

"Good morning," he said, looking into the camera. "The Dissident faction called the Syndicate has launched an all-out attack on the people of the Protectorate. Early reports confirm the group, led by the terrorist known as the Grim Reaper, attempted to destroy a Reclaimer military base with a sonic weapon. Details are unclear, but the wreckage is quite evident."

Footage of a burning base rolled on a screen next to the General.

"These cowards attacked, killing hundreds of brave and loyal troops as well as their families. The Protector himself has asked for all citizens to be aware of your surroundings. If you see anything out of the ordinary, report it to the authorities. While we are at war with the Dissidents, mandatory military service will be instituted to ensure we have enough forces to defeat this insidious foe. All able-bodied candidates between eighteen and twenty will be called up to fulfill their duty to serve the Protectorate from her enemies."

With that, he turned and left the podium. Hannah returned to the screen, but Marcel muted it.

"More military?" he asked as he set down the remote. "Who are they going to fight? They own the whole world."

"It's a show of force. Outlying areas have started to rebel against the Protectorate policies. They need the threat of the Gifted to keep the populace in line," Dad said as he got up. "Soon they'll have to bomb civilians to keep the fear levels high."

Merle had said as much to me.

"Why does the Protectorate always resort to violence?" Makeda asked. "Even when they have everything, they want more."

"They want control of the death ray," I blurted out. "Reaper is looking for it, so they are hunting him down. They can have a Darkest Storm any time they need an attack to scare the populace into submission."

"Bruh, they said they had control of it. Nobody would believe them." Marcel scratched at his scruff. "But if Reaper stole the station, he'd be responsible for all the deaths."

"And they are running out of time," Blaster added. "Once Frisco is hit, they don't know where it will fire. Could be right at them."

"We have to find Reaper and fast," I said.

How do you find someone as elusive as the Grim Reaper?

## 33

I 'd left one major piece of information out of my version of the day's events. Parasite had said Waxenby was actually a hero named Stonewall.

Waxenby told us he'd been Commander Gravity, and Dad had vouched for him. I needed to discuss it in private with Dad. If someone was leaking info to Reaper or the Protectorate, I wanted to keep the information away from whoever the leak was.

Mom was huddled up with Abby, who needed her now more than ever. I didn't want to disturb them, so I headed for Dad. He'd know what to do with the information far better than I would.

I waited until he finished speaking with the Council members. He faced me as Alyx left with Makeda and Yutu. "You had us worried," he said. Dad put his arm around my shoulders. He'd been trying harder to be a father since our blowout. I appreciated the effort, but now I needed Cyclone Ranger.

"I was worried about me, too," I said with a grin. "Can we talk about something, privately?"

The last time we'd had a "private conversation" it ended in a fight. Concern reflected in his eyes as he said, "Sure. Let's go to the training room. Less likely to break anything in there."

He was half joking, so I played along. "Yeah, Marcel gets upset if you damage his tech." I fired up a big smile, hoping he'd get the message.

He regarded me for a second before the light bulb popped on over his head. "Upsetting Marcel would be a bad thing. Last thing I want is a lecture from someone when I can't understand half their words."

Message delivered and understood. I laughed because it was true and with relief that he'd gotten the message. This wasn't a heart-to-heart. This was business. We took the stairs down to three but walked into the more secure translocator room instead of the training room. He closed the door behind us.

"Something happened, and you don't want to announce it?" Dad asked as he sat on a crate near the portable translocator. "Usually you go to your mother with these things."

I'd never realized going to Mom with everything would be an issue. I fumbled around for the right words. "It's a habit. For most of my life, she was all I had, though there wasn't a day I didn't wish you were there. I guess we both have something to learn about being a father and a son."

He nodded. "We Ward men are hard-headed. Sometimes it takes a while to get through to us. We'll figure it out. You didn't call me down here to discuss family relations is my guess. What happened?"

I took a seat on a crate across from Dad. "Parasite took control of my powers, but he said they'd taken Stonewall, not Waxenby. With us being bound together, I know he told the truth."

A sharp intake of breath informed me this was as important as I thought it might be. "He definitely said Stonewall? You're sure?"

"Absolutely," I said. For Dad to be this freaked out was bad news. "I'd never heard of Stonewall before."

"You wouldn't have. He was a terrorist in every sense of the word. He disappeared right before the Darkest Storm, and no one has heard from him since." Dad stood and started pacing. "Waxenby looks nothing like Stonewall. This makes no sense."

"You knew Waxenby before the Storm, didn't you?"

"I met him the night he quit being a hero wannabe. I didn't run into him again until the Reclaimers captured Dominion. Blaze and Oliver collected information on locations and technology from the remaining Gifted so it wouldn't be lost."

"Could they have replaced Waxenby with Stonewall?" None of this made sense. Even if Waxenby was Stonewall, how did Reaper know it was him? Waxenby had been at Dresden with us.

"Anything's possible, I guess." He stopped pacing. "Go get Marcel. We're going to need his help. Don't even whisper the name outside of here. Warden would kill Waxenby if there was even the slightest suspicion he could be Stonewall."

"Why?" Warden was no-nonsense and ruthless when needed, but "cold-blooded killer" didn't really fit her.

"Stonewall killed her husband. It was long before Molly, but I can't see Warden just letting it go." Dad considered for a second. "Come to think of it, your mother might decide to help her."

He wasn't wrong. Mom had a strong sense of justice and didn't mind getting her hands dirty to enforce it. "I'll go snag Marcel and meet you back here."

"Sounds good. I'm going to go talk with the others. No sense getting everyone riled up wondering where I went." As I turned to go, he said. "Tommy, good thinking about keeping this quiet. I'm proud of you."

I grinned like a video game addict getting a collector's edition of his favorite game. "Thanks, Dad."

With the stupid smile still plastered on my face, I jogged up to level two and found Marcel in the communication room. He was working on the terminal when I came in. "Bruh, what's up?"

"I need to talk to you," I said, glancing around to make sure we were alone. "It's important. Can you spare an hour or so?"

Turning away from the screen, he rubbed his chin. "I always have time for you. You alright? You seem antsy."

"Dad wants to discuss something I found out, but it needs to stay off the radar. We're supposed to meet him down at the translocator room."

"Hmmm, very interesting." He retrieved his tablet and stood. "Let's go. No sense keeping the Ranger waiting."

Turned out, we waited and waited and waited.

An hour later Dad returned. "Sorry. Trying to get away from Warden's things-to-do-list is difficult. Did you fill Marcel in?"

I shook my head. "No, I wanted to tell him with you here, in case he had questions." I gave him the update on what Parasite had said.

Marcel whistled sharply. "Stonewall was one bad mamma jamma. Seriously, he'd give Sauron a run for his money in the evil department, and you think Waxenby is him?"

"It's a definite possibility," Dad said. "I doubt Parasite would lie, given his limitations."

"Limitations?" I asked. "He was extremely strong."

"Don't get me wrong. Parasite is a world-class talent," Dad said. "But he has the mind of a five-year-old. Reaper broke him out of a mental institution, which is another thing he has to answer for."

"Wow, that's ice cold," Marcel said, clearly upset. "We've got to fatality Reaper's sorry ass."

Dad looked confused but went on. "We need to find any references to Stonewall in Harker's systems. We need to get to the bottom of what's going on."

"Mimi said she found a block in his memories. She tried to get around it but hasn't yet."

"Interesting. Tommy, you need to get Mimi away from Waxenby before she breaks the block. We don't know what the block does. We don't want Stonewall roaming around Harker uninvited."

Marcel held out his arm, pulled back his sweatshirt, and undid his watch. "Put this around his ankle, under the covers, so she doesn't notice it. If he does break free, at least he won't have his Gifts."

"Good. I can fuse the metal clasp so he can't take it off," I said, liking the idea even more. "We can cut it off if it isn't necessary."

Dad nodded. "Now I see how you two ended up rescuing me. Good work, gentlemen."

Marcel laughed. "We aren't gentlemen. We're epic gamers. Learned everything we know on the tough digital streets."

"Just when I think I understand you…"

"I like to keep you guessing, Ranger." Marcel winked at me. "I'll go see what I can uncover. When I find something, I'll ask if you tried the peach cobbler. Then we meet down here."

We adjourned our meeting and returned to the main section of Harker. The commissary was empty, and Mimi wasn't in Waxenby's room. A few quick seconds and I had the watch around his ankle and the clasp fused shut. Without his Gifts, he's never get it undone. I turned the dampening field on and broke off the pin to keep it from being turned off.

I wandered back to the commissary and grabbed a piece of pie and a Dew. Mom came in as I sat snacking. Fighting an evil mage had given me an appetite.

She sat down across from me, stealing a piece of my pie crust.

"Hey, get your own pie, lady."

"I carried you for nine months, and you used my bladder for a soccer ball. I'll eat your pie anytime I want, Thomas George Ward." To prove her point she took another piece, ignoring my howls of protest.

After a good laugh, she asked, "How are you doing? I was so worried about you."

"I'm fine. Sorry you were worried, but at least Caligari is gone, and we can concentrate on stopping Reaper."

"I'm just glad you're safe. You know, I'm beginning to think your father's right, hiding out and waiting until things get better. At some point, the Protector will fall, and the government will collapse. Maybe then we can help rebuild what was here."

"You've never suggested giving up, ever." I took a bite of pie and listened.

"Honey, when you disappeared, I almost lost it. If something had happened to you, I'd never forgive myself. You should be graduating, worrying if the pretty girl will go to the prom with you, and getting ready for college, not saving the world from a death ray and evil magic. You're seventeen, and you've seen more fighting than most military vets ever do."

I shrugged. "It helps keep me young." From the glare I received, joking around was over. "Seriously, you taught me that justice requires sacrifice. How can I sit here and watch innocent people die? If Reaper gets control of the weapon, he'll destroy the government, and we'll have chaos. If the Protectorate gets it, they'll destroy any rebellion before it even starts. We have to stop the death ray. After, if you want to hide out here, I'll listen."

She stared at me for a moment before answering. "You sound just like your father. You're right, but every time you leave, it might be the last time I see you. All I wanted for you was a normal life, a wife who loves you as much as I do, and children you adore like I adore you. Is that too much to ask?"

I took her hands in mine. "No, and after all this is over, I'd like those things too, especially kids, so I can call you Grandma."

She laughed, tears spilling down her cheeks. "I want to be called Nana. It's what I called my grandmother. We'll call your dad Pop-pop. It will drive him crazy."

"Good to see you're thinking ahead." I pulled her up and hugged her. What would I do if something happened to her? I needed to finish the mission, so she wouldn't have to fight anymore. Hiding might not be too bad, after all.

Mom pushed me back to arm's length. "Thanks, honey. Go talk to Abby. She's been asking for you."

"I will." After a quick peck on her cheek, I whispered, "I love you," in her ear before heading for Abby's room.

I knocked on the door and heard a muffled, "Come in," so I entered. Mimi sat on the bed next to Abby.

"Ah, so this is where you're hiding," I said to Mimi. "I checked on Waxenby, but you weren't there."

"Hey, Tiger. Can't get anything by you." She gave Abby a quick hug. "I'll check in on you tomorrow." She punched me lightly in the shoulder as she passed.

I dropped on the bed. Abby's eyes matched the red side of her hair. "Mom said you'd been looking for me. Sorry, I thought you might need some rest."

"Do you have any idea how many hours a day a bear sleeps? Most of my time away, I was unconscious." She paused for a second. "Unless Jon was forcing me to sleep. I should have ripped his freaking head off."

"From the amount of damage, you came pretty close. He's not going to be pretty anymore, unless the Brotherhood has a great plastic surgeon."

Her shoulders slumped. "I tried. Wendi made me promise to protect him, but I'm not anyone's slave. He used me, and he wanted me to hurt you. As hard as I fought, I couldn't transform back."

I didn't know what to say. It hadn't been her fault. No one realized Jon had the ability to control animals. I just let her talk. Sometimes, it was better to listen.

"He kept saying we'd tear you apart, because you'd never raise a hand against me." She shuddered before continuing. "I think he read my thoughts. When I'd refuse, he'd make me do tricks like a common animal to prove his control over me. Caligari promised he'd rejoin Wendi, but the idiot didn't see the mage meant to kill him. How do you save someone from themselves?"

"You can't."

Her head drooped; her hair covered her face like a veil. "No, you can't. I loved Wendi, but Jon has gone to a dark place, and I don't think he's ever coming out."

That made two of us.

3 4

Abby charged at me.

"Inuk," I said.

She shuddered and changed back into her human form.

Thanks to the bracelet she now wore, she was covered from view by a virtual outfit. Mimi had spent hours perfecting the look. A long black coat hung over a purple and red-striped shirt. Jeans and knee-high boots completed the outfit. If you didn't know it was a visual construct, as Marcel called it, Abby appeared fully clothed. It wouldn't keep her warm in the cold or help if she ran over glass, but it gave her time to find real clothing after she changed.

We'd contacted Mr. Fix-it to see if an adaptable combat suit could be made for her. Harker's suit generator could make her a regular one, but it would tear apart when she transformed. The version in the lab under his house could make a suit which would transform with her, but it had been sealed away to keep prying eyes from finding it, and he wasn't up to the trip, regardless. His health was fading after being forced to labor for Caligari. At least I'd settled that score with the mage.

The training room had a large open area in the center for sparring or anything else requiring space to move. On the left side, a variety of machines, from treadmills to weight machines, sat. The other side had free weights and stations with dummies to punch or practice on with assorted weapons. Two doors in the back led to locker rooms with showers, saunas, and automated massage tables. The training room wasn't as extensive as Castle's and didn't have a Gifted combat room, but it was good enough for what we needed.

Abby straightened as the transformation completed. "Damn, I'd had it, then it slipped away. Let's try it again."

She cracked her neck and then began to elongate as her animal form took hold. Her skin changed to a solid black coat as she lurched forward, her arms rotating as they became legs. In a matter of seconds, a very large panther stood in front of me. She snarled, exposing a mouth full of sharp teeth. Her claws dug into the mats, leaving deep cuts in the foam.

She leapt at me, huge paws knocking me on my back. The force of her weight bore me down until I was flat on the ground. A long, rough tongue lapped at my face, leaving trails of saliva behind.

"Gross!" I yelled, as I tried not to laugh. She kept at it, ignoring my screams. "Enough. I give up."

In a single move, she bounded over me, circled and transformed back into herself. I wiped the goo off my face as she laughed. "Gotcha."

"Thanks. I took a shower."

She cocked her head at me. "Really? You tasted like day-old sweat."

I flicked my hand, showering her with her own cat saliva.

She just laughed harder at me. "Poor Tommy, cat got your tongue?"

"Weren't you the one who asked me for help?" I grabbed a towel from the treadmill where I'd left it. After two days of practice, I'd had to mop up blood, sweat, and tears. This was a first for saliva.

"I appreciate it. It was so easy to transform when Yutu trained me, but now I'm scared I'll get stuck in animal form. I'm glad you have the trigger word handy. Every time I think I've got it, I get stuck."

"Do you want to try a different form? Maybe don't use the bear for a while. How about a gorilla or a wolf?"

"I need to conquer my fear. If I can't use the strongest of my forms,

I'm at a disadvantage in a fight." She rolled her shoulders. "One bear, coming up."

I watched, fascinated by the process. Unlike her cat metamorphosis, this one wasn't smooth. Her snout extended only to retract again. Sweat beaded across her face as she fought to obtain the form. After a full minute, a giant grizzly bear lumbered up to me. She roared, but it wasn't the fierce sound of a warrior—more the hurt sound of a wounded animal.

The door behind me opened. "Bruh, have you tried the peach cobbler, yet?"

Abby charged as Marcel entered her space. "Inu—" my words stopped as she bowled me over and headed for my unsuspecting best friend.

Marcel froze as the huge bear bore down on him.

"Inuk!" I screamed as she closed the distance between them. Nothing happened. I fired a bolt of lightning into her back flank, eliciting a painful sound.

She spun to face my attack. Her head rose with a roar that shook the room. She lowered her head and charged.

"Get out of here!" I yelled. I ran at Abby.

The door slammed behind a fleeing Marcel. I didn't have time to check to see if he really left.

Abby lunged at me.

I jumped over her head, landing on her broad back, grabbing handfuls of fur to keep my position.

Abby bucked at the unexpected weight on her. When it didn't work, she rolled, but I flipped myself to the side and jumped back on when she righted herself. This time, my head was near her ear. "Inuk."

The bucking stopped. I slid off her.

Almost two minutes later, a sobbing Abby lay on the floor. "Is Marcel okay?"

"He's fine, but he may have a few gray hairs in the fro."

She didn't look at me. "It's not funny. I could have hurt him."

I dropped onto the floor next to her. "But you didn't. What happened?"

She didn't answer at first. I just waited until she was ready to talk. Slowly, she said. "He startled me, and my instincts took over. I hadn't expected anyone to come in. I knew it was Marcel, but I didn't have control."

"We just need to keep working on it."

"Yutu said it took years for some metamorphs to fully control their changes. I guess I've got a long way to go."

I nudged her with my foot. She looked me in the face. "I'm here to help. We'll get through this together. Just like everything else. Got it?"

She nodded. "Thanks, Tommy."

I gave her a hug, which felt weird. My brain saw her clothes, but my arms felt the skin in her back. I let go quickly.

"I guess I should get some real clothes on."

I helped her up and went to find what was left of Marcel.

M arcel sat outside the training room door, visibly shaken. "Bruh, what the hell happened?"

"Abby is still working on her control issues. You startled her." I reached out my hand to help him up.

"I don't think I'll do that again." He took my hand, and we set out toward the translocation room in silence.

Dad sat off to the side as we entered. "You've got news?"

Marcel nodded, his fro rocking forward and back with the motion. "There wasn't much, but I found a reference to Stonewall. It said, 'In your house I long to be room by room, patiently.' Whatever that means."

"It sounds like a song lyric, but I can't place it," Dad said.

Marcel and I grabbed seats on the crates we'd pushed into a circle. "So, what do we do with it?" I asked. "Is it a clue on how to find the remote station, or is it the key to releasing him?"

"It's the only reference I found of him in the entire system. Dublin was hit last night. We don't have much time left before the death ray starts hitting cities with Underground people still in them."

Dad sighed. "Warden is evacuating Boston and New York today to the new base, but with over six thousand people, she can only feed them for a little over a month. It's better than the alternative, but not by much. Los Angeles and San Francisco are the last two. Each has over seven thousand people." Dad sounded exhausted as he went over all the logistics.

"Then we need to get whatever information Stonewall has and fast," I said. Now wasn't the time to play it safe. We needed to know how to locate the remote station and shut it down. "I say we go read the line to Stonewall and see if it does anything."

"I'm thinking bringing the bad man back isn't such a great idea," Marcel said. "If he's as strong as Ranger says, we might not be able to control him."

"It's a calculated risk, to be sure." Dad didn't say anything else for a few moments. "We'll move him through the DC base and set him up in an external safehouse and then try it. If he comes to, he isn't a security threat to us or the Underground."

"But what if the death ray hits there before we retrieve him?" Marcel asked, a look of shock on his face. "We can't just leave Waxenby there to die."

"We'll know rather quickly who he is. If he's really just Oliver, we'll bring him back. If not, I'd just as soon kill him as risk releasing him."

"But Mr. W—"

"Marcel, if it is Stonewall, he killed Waxenby a long time ago and replaced him. In that case, we never knew him," I said, hating the idea of Waxenby being a ruthless killer, but we needed answers and soon.

"He still helped us when we needed it. Doesn't that count for something?" Marcel asked, his voice shaking. "We'd all be dead if he hadn't gotten us out of Redemption."

"Marcel, if this is Stonewall, anything he's done is because someone layered a personality over his. Once we remove it, he'll be a killer again. I hope we are mistaken, and it's Oliver Waxenby lying on the table down there, but we have to know." Dad didn't look pleased, but he'd stated his case, and I agreed.

A thought occurred to me. "What about Mimi? We could use her to read his mind so we can find out what he knows once the block is gone. I doubt he's going to just explain the whole thing."

Dad looked concerned. "He's a terrorist, so he's not going to tell us much unless we make him. You think Mimi would be willing to help?"

"She'll do it if we ask her," Marcel said to me. He regarded Dad. "When are we going to move him?"

"Tonight," Dad said after a few seconds. "Warden and the others will be back at the new base, and I'll ask your mother to keep an eye on Abby. We can slide out, test our theory, and return with an answer."

"Shoot for seven?" I asked. That left me most of the day to talk to Mimi. I might need significantly more time than I anticipated.

Dad nodded. "Seven it is."

We went our separate ways. I set course for Waxenby's room and my talk with Mimi. I wasn't dreading it, but it wasn't in my top thousand things I wanted to do today. Wrestling Abby in bear form had been more fun.

Mimi sat in her normal spot, playing a game on one of Marcel's spare tablets. I was pretty sure he was going crazy knowing he was months behind the newest gadgets, but Harker didn't lend itself to runs to the store. At least Castle had had an exit down the mountain to the local retailers.

"Hey, Sport," Mimi said, as she set down the device. "Come to keep me company?"

"Can we talk in the next room?" I asked, trying to keep my mind blank.

She quirked an eyebrow at me but exited without comment. We entered the next exam room, and she sat on the table.

I took a chair, trying to figure out how to say what I needed to say.

"We need to talk, and you aren't sure how to start?"

"Yeah, have you made any progress with Waxenby?" I asked casually. I might as well have pointed a gun at her child.

"Why? What exactly do you have planned?"

*Damn mind readers.* I held up my hands. "Hear me out, please." I waited until she leaned back, folding her arms across her chest. The unfinished tattoos peaked out from under the cuffs of her sweatshirt. "When I was in London, Parasite said Waxenby wasn't who we think he is."

"How stupid do you have to be to believe any of Caligari's people?" She shook her head. "You can't honestly expect me to buy this crap?"

"No, which is why we want to move Waxenby to a secure location and test him. Marcel found some information, and we think it might remove the mental block you've been dealing with. Most likely it's nothing, but we need to try. New York will be hit with the death ray in two days. If we don't find the remote site, a lot of people will die."

"And how is a catatonic man supposed to tell you anything?"

"Reaper found the code book for the remote station based on what they got from Waxenby. I don't like it either, but it's all we've got."

"If I go along, what's the plan, Tiger?"

I walked through the details, answering questions as I told the story. Finally, she nodded. "I'm going, and if I say stop, we stop. Agreed?"

"Agreed." I wasn't sure if Dad would approve, but an on-board Mimi would be a lot easier to deal with than one who fought us every step of the way. "We're leaving at seven."

"I'll see you then, Sport."

I had the gnawing suspicion this was not going to be a fun event.

# 35

At seven, Dad and I met outside Waxenby's room. Marcel showed up a few minutes later carrying a syringe gun. Mimi stepped between Waxenby and Marcel. "What do you think you're doing? Last time I checked, you weren't a doctor."

"Gabriel's autonomics are having an issue, so I retrieved the sedative the auto-doc requested. Ask him if you'd like." Marcel waited, tapping the gun in his open hand.

Mimi's eyes narrowed a bit. She didn't like being challenged. "Gabriel, what are your directives on moving the patient off-site?"

Gabriel's holo form flickered into view. "I recommended a one milligram dose of Lorazepam be administered to the patient to ensure they are incapacitated during movement."

"Why didn't you administer the shot?" Mimi asked the virtual doctor.

"I'm experiencing a systems issue with the calibration of the rotator guidance system. The issue has been escalated to the system admin, one Marcel is da Bomb. I am awaiting a correction before administering any injections. There is no ETA for a fix."

All eyes shifted to Marcel. "Da Bomb? Really?" Mimi asked him incredulously.

"Admin one was lame. I needed to spice it up. Don't harsh on my style." Marcel might have sounded confident, but his face reflected more embarrassment than anything. "Anyhow, I need to figure out what the issue is, so I got the manual injector."

Mimi took the gun and verified the dosage before injecting Waxenby's arm. She set the gun aside. "How are we moving him?"

"Fireman's carry is about all we've got." Dad said. "We need to move fast, in case we run into bogeys. I'm open to any other ideas."

Gabriel was the one to answer. "There is a Zero-G transportation stretcher in the main section of the med bay. I will meet you there to explain its use, if you'd like."

"I'll go get it," I said, and jogged down the hall to where Gabriel stood by an open locker.

"This is the stretcher in question." Gabriel said. "On the handles are controls to raise or lower the height of the apparatus. Simply push on it, and it will glide."

I pulled out a metal frame with a red fabric mesh interior. Three sets of straps were coiled along the side. "This will work great."

"Yes, it should meet the parameters requested." He flickered out of view.

Returning to Waxenby's room with the stretcher, I found Gabriel had reappeared. "If you depress the power button, we can begin moving the patient."

After ten minutes or so, we had Waxenby strapped to the stretcher, maneuvering him down three flights of stairs and through the translocator. We followed the same path out of the base and into DC. Scurrying noises pursued us as we pushed Waxenby through the deserted streets of the city. I quickened my pace, not wanting to meet up with any more giant rats.

"You should see the safe house on your left," Marcel said over the comm-link.

We stood in front of a narrow gray building with faded blue shutters. The bottom windows were boarded up, but the top floor still had glass panels intact. Dad led while Mimi walked next to the stretcher that I pushed.

At the door, Dad keyed in the number Marcel read to him. A low beep announced his success, and the door hissed open. Dad entered first and looked around quickly before giving the all-clear.

I maneuvered the stretcher into the house before closing the door behind me. The seal hissed as it re-pressurized the building. Warden had planned ahead.

"On the third floor, there is a safe room," Marcel said. "You should probably set up there. According to Warden's records, there's nothing of value stored here." His voice lowered once we entered the house. The Underground must have set up an anti-surveillance system.

We got Waxenby to the third floor, where a solid metal door greeted us. Marcel gave the code, and we entered. I seriously hoped Warden never found out we'd raided her files to get this information. I set the stretcher to hover in the center of the room.

"We got him here. Now what?" Mimi asked, annoyance thick in her voice. "You got some magic trick to bring him back?"

Dad read the quote to the unconscious man. Nothing happened.

"See, I told you. He's Oliver Waxenby," Mimi huffed.

"She might be right," I said. "We don't know he's Stonewall for sure."

Mimi hissed. "You think Ollie is that bastard Stonewall?"

Waxenby's eyes twitched and then stilled.

"Mimi, can you check the block again? If he's Stonewall"—his eyes twitched again—"you might be able to break through knowing it," Dad said.

"I can try." She stepped to the head of the stretcher, placed her hands on his head. Waxenby's eyes flickered open and closed rapidly.

"The block is still in place, and he's still Ollie. We should probably take him back to base."

"Let's give it longer," Dad said as he looked on. "If someone buried Stonewall inside Oliver's personality, it won't be easy to remove."

Mimi put her hands back on Waxenby's head. Her face twisted in concentration.

I repeated the phrase Marcel had found. Waxenby thrashed against the restraints as I spoke the words.

Mimi's eyes flew open. "The block is dissolving. He's still under because of the Lorazepam, but he'll come out of it. I can see he really is Stonewall. I'll be damned." Her mouth pinched until it was nothing but a thin line. "There has to be an explanation. He was Oliver Waxenby."

Dad shook his head. "We need to know what's in his head."

A pang of loss hit me. I wondered what had happened to the real Waxenby, the one Dad had sent home to keep him safe.

We waited for an hour for the sedative to wear off and for Stonewall to regain consciousness. Slowly, he shook his head, as if trying to clear it. After another five minutes, he glanced around the room, his eyes settling on Dad. He fought the restraints but went nowhere. "What did you do to me? I can't use my power."

Even though they were in the same body, the transformation from Waxenby to Stonewall was startling. Where Waxenby had sad eyes and a small smile affixed to his face, Stonewall's eyes blazed with anger, and he sneered at Dad.

Meet Dr. Jekyll and Mr. Hyde.

Dad stood over him. "We disabled your Gift. Can't have you causing problems. You'll answer my questions, or I'll leave you here to die when the death ray strikes."

Stonewall spit at Dad and then laughed like it was all a big joke. "Cyclone Ranger. You finally caught me. Where are we?"

"I'll ask the questions, Stonewall." Dad's tone was steady but with heat just under the surface. It wouldn't take much for him to explode. "Where is the remote station for the death ray?"

"Don't know."

Mimi nodded. "He doesn't know."

"Get out of my head, bitch," Stonewall growled. "Tired of you mental freaks. Siren was bad enough."

"Who's Siren?" Dad asked, still holding back his temper.

"You gone stupid? She's a hot blonde chick. Since when do we swap real names, Michael Ward?"

Dad placed the palm of his hand against Stonewall's chest and arcs of electricity coursed through the terrorist's body.

"Stop it!" Mimi screamed. "You'll kill him. Ollie could be in there still."

Dad stared at her, causing her to take a step back. "No, I won't, and I will get answers one way or the other."

"So now you're stooping to their level? You're going all Protectorate on him? I thought we were better than that?" she asked, though I noticed she kept her distance.

"In under a week, thousands of innocent people will die and our only way of finding them is lying right here. Do you want to dig through the cesspool of his mind to find what we need?"

Her eyes went wide as she rapidly shook her head.

"That's what I thought. If you'll monitor his thoughts, I'll make him talk. You don't need any of his filth stuck in your brain." I'd never seen this side of Dad. He'd gone from hero to vigilante, but I wasn't sure we had any other options.

"Mimi, you okay?" I asked. She'd turned pale and her bottom lip shook as she chewed it.

She nodded.

Dad studied her for a minute as she pulled herself together. "Mimi, Stonewall killed Oliver and took his place. Don't pity this piece of human garbage."

Stonewall laughed. "Boy, he squealed like a stuck pig when I—" He didn't get to finish. His body convulsed, and he shrieked in pain as Mimi's hand touched him.

"Don't make me have to hurt you worse. Answer the fucking questions, or I'll make the last one feel like a love tap. Ollie was my friend..." Mimi didn't finish as the tears streamed down her cheeks. She nodded at Dad to continue.

*What the hell is going on? I've never seen Mimi like this before.*

"Do you need to step out?" Dad asked. He looked a bit rattled.

"Just get what we need from him," she growled.

"What was the code book you sent Reaper after?" I asked, remembering what Reaper had said in the old library. "What's so important about the book?"

"Nothing. I sent Reaper on a wild goose chase. He wouldn't stop torturing poor Waxenby, so I gave him the pieces he remembered. The code book was a decoy Siren placed in Ollie's head."

Mimi nodded. "What do we need to access the remote site to shut down the death ray?"

He opened his mouth but closed it as his eyes widened.

I held a globe of energy in my hand just over his face. "Think before you answer. You know what raw energy does to people?"

He nodded, his eyes gone frantic with panic. "No need to get crazy about it. There was a bunker just outside Boston. It's in the Blue Hills Reservation at the Randolph Ave. entrance. Techno had an old white house we used as a secret base. In the basement, there's a hidden door down into the bunker. You'll find what you need about the death ray there. I swear to God, I'm telling the truth."

We looked to Mimi to verify. She nodded.

I repeated the line Marcel found in the Harker system. His eyes flickered again, but he didn't answer. "What does it mean?"

"I...I don't know. It sounds familiar, but I can't place it."

Mimi jerked her head toward the door. We left the room as Stonewall screamed that he'd answered our questions and that we had to let him go.

I closed the door behind us.

Mimi said, "There is a block on the memory associated with the message. I don't think he can access it. There's a chance I could break it, but it could take weeks."

"Our best chance is to get into the bunker and find out what's there," Dad said. "I doubt he's got any more useful information to give us."

"What do we do about him?" I asked, knowing I wouldn't like the answer.

"We leave him here," Mimi said, her eyes as cold as Dad's. "He pushed the memory of killing Ollie so I could see it. He's beyond evil, and leaving him here to die is a mercy compared to what he did to that poor man."

"Tommy, you okay with it?"

"I'll have to be. The only other thing is to kill him ourselves, and I've killed enough people for one lifetime."

"Me too," Dad said. "Me too."

An hour later, we stepped out of the translocator. Marcel was there waiting for us, tablet in hand. "Hey," he said as we entered the room. "That was a rough one."

"It was," Dad said. "Did you find anything on the bunker?"

"Yeah. You aren't going to like it, though." He turned the tablet around to show us a white house. It sat at the corner of two intersecting roads, but instead of being alone in the woods, buildings had been constructed all around it. People in Reclaimer uniforms went about their business, unaware we were watching.

"Seriously? It's inside a base?" After all the crap with Stonewall, and now we needed to raid a Reclaimers stronghold to find how to stop the death ray. Of course, I was assuming the bunker was still in the basement and hadn't been found.

One step forward, and two you've-got-to-be-kidding-me moments.

We spent the next day mapping out a plan to get into the base, down to the basement, and retrieve what we needed, all without getting caught and knowing the death ray would hit Boston within twenty-four hours.

Nothing like a strict timeline to keep us motivated.

A cold front had moved in, dumping a few inches of snow, but more importantly, dropping the temperatures below freezing. We used the suit creator to make winter camo combat suits with thicker insulation to handle the extreme temperatures. This would have made my walk down the mountain feel like a summer's day at the beach. We only had one shot at this, so it had to work.

Boston's Underground had been a relatively small base, so the inhabitants had been shuttled to the new location. Word was the Underground had dubbed it Wendigo. Crews worked around the clock to get the facilities back online to accommodate the refugees from the bases around the world.

With the death ray scheduled to strike in the early hours of the morning, we'd have to hit the base tonight. We'd agreed on a midnight departure, since the trip out to the Reclaimers site would be a couple of hours on foot. Warden sent us Blaster since he'd spent time in Boston and knew the layout well enough to navigate.

Marcel packed us a tech kit with USB drives, tools, and an electrostatic-proof pouch in case we needed to retrieve anything. We also stopped in the storage lockers for ski masks and night vision goggles. We looked like bugs by the time we'd donned the extra gear.

The next few hours were spent traversing the frigid landscape of snow-covered Boston. Our combat suits were well insulated, but the cold still crept through. I was glad Blaster had suggested the masks. The snow was ankle-deep but hadn't frozen so it made for easier, and quieter, going. It's a strange sensation to have sweat trickling down your back while you're in the cold, but it's what happens.

Blaster motioned us down as we reached the fence dividing the dead zone from the rest of the world. There wasn't a watchtower in sight, so after a minute, we slid through a hole in the fence and continued toward the target.

"The Reclaimers have pulled back from Boston after the previous attacks," Marcel told us. "Most of the troops have moved to the New York zone. The base is still guarded but not as heavily as normal. You should reach the target in twenty minutes."

"What's the ETA on the next death ray?" Dad asked. We entered a wooded area between us and the base.

"Eight a.m. It's two now, so you should have time to get out."

"Assuming we don't run into any complications," Dad said.

I heard Marcel's apprehension on the other end. "Don't run into any."

Dad chuckled. "Sure thing, Mr. Wizard."

We finished the trek in silence. The base's spotlights came into view as we crouched at the edge of the tree line. There was a three-hundred-foot clearing between us and the fence. Nothing moved. Most of the Reclaimers would be huddled around heaters in the gatehouses, or asleep. The cold was helping us.

"Blaster, you stay here. If we give the word, create as big a diversion as possible and then head back to the translocator. Tommy and I will follow. Mr. Wizard, do you have the camera feed?"

"Affirmative. It's on a three-hour loop. As far as I can tell, there aren't any patrols. They are having issues with the cold weather."

"Let's move out," Dad said.

I followed him as we crept across the open space. While I believed Marcel, the whole time I had a feeling we were being watched. Fifteen excruciating minutes later, we reached the fence, cut our way through, and we were in.

"No alarms, Ranger. You're good to go."

We snuck through the deserted streets of the base, sticking to areas without as much light. Judging by the smells and the dumpsters full of garbage, we had reached what I guessed was the mess hall. The cold killed most of the stink, but I was glad not to be getting it full force.

From our spot next to the fragrant mess hall, we could see the white house. No one moved at this time of the night, and the surrounding buildings sat dark. We only needed to cross the road and enter the house.

"Target is in sight," Dad said over the comm-link once the white house came into view. "Do you have eyes on it, Mr. Wizard?"

"Affirmative. Looks like two guards and the commander, according to the duty roster. Proceed with caution."

Dad gave the ready check. I nodded to acknowledge. We slid across the space and took our places next to the house's door.

I turned the handle, only to find it locked. *Damn.* Shielding the door with my body, I created a thin line of energy and sliced through the lock.

The door swung open. I stepped into a tiled walkway with an opening on my left and glass-paned doors on my right. The hallway ran straight until it opened out on a living room, judging by the couch and chair I saw in the dimly lit space.

I motioned for Dad to go left. Glancing through the glass doors revealed a cluttered, unoccupied office. Dad gave the thumbs up, and I moved down the hall. An old, beat-up kitchen with a metal table and six chairs sat off to the left. From the smell of it, the only danger there was if you were eating something.

The living room was no better. Serviceable furniture sat around the room, but there were magazines and books strewn all over the place. Mom would have had a fit. Doors on either side of the room were probably sleeping areas, so we headed for the opening at the back of the room. A washer and dryer stood on one side of the long room, but a set of stairs led down on the other side. *Bingo.*

Slowly, I descended into the basement. A light was on at the bottom of the steps. I crept down and peeked around the corner. The only things sitting in the room were an old couch and a large TV. The basement had roughhewn rock walls that bore the marks of the tools that built them. Empty cans of Storyteller's Earl Grey covered the coffee table in front of the sofa. A heavy-set man dressed in boxers and a stained white t-shirt, probably one of the guards, snored on the couch. I stepped onto the shag carpet, motioning for Dad to join me.

He entered the room. The guard snorted and twisted into a more comfortable position. When the snoring resumed, Dad moved over and shocked him. The guards body convulsed once, and then he flopped back onto the couch.

I gave the kill sign, wondering if he'd just killed the guard. He shook his head. Just knocked him out. Even though the Reclaimers fought against us, a drunk guard in the basement of the commander's house wasn't a threat.

I grabbed the remote and turned off FNN news anchor Cassidy Zollinger and her riveting report on a talking chicken, plunging the room into semi-darkness. With the bare bulb behind us, we could see enough to move by. After a moment, I saw a faint outline in the wall behind the TV. Dad and I moved the furniture to allow us to access to the door.

It took a few moments to find the latch to unlock the door. Once I'd pushed the correct stone, the door swung open silently. We stepped through and resealed the door. No sense inviting someone to stumble across it. A black, steel, spiral staircase descended deeper underground.

We followed it down. Dim tread lights marked our way. When we reached the bottom, another door waited. This one opened without issue.

Lights came on as we entered. Dad pulled the door closed behind us. "Welcome back, Techno," a soft female voice said over hidden speakers. "No one has entered since your last departure."

We pulled off our ski masks and goggles. I stuffed mine behind my belt so I wouldn't accidentally leave them. It would be a cold walk back with an exposed face. The room was thirty feet to a side. One open door stood across from us. A series of computer terminals covered the left wall. The right had a wooden desk and floor-to-ceiling bookcases packed to the point of breaking.

"How will we find anything in here?" I said.

"Easily," the disembodied female voice said. "If you give me what you are looking for, I can locate it by its RFID tag."

"We need the manual for the—" Dad stopped, uncertain.

Marcel came to the rescue. "It's called the molecular reassignment device."

"We need the molecular reassignment device manual," Dad said.

"Accessing location now."

I moved a couple books from a chair and took a seat at the first of the old computers. The tiny screen lit up as I pressed power. The Windows logo sat center on the desktop, though I'd never seen this designation before. "What the hell is Windows XP?"

"Bruh, he's got XP machines?" Marcel asked, excitement bubbling across the comm-link. "Man, I wish I was there. I've never seen an actual installed version. See if you can download it onto the USB drive."

I looked at the front of the machine and didn't see a slot for a thumb drive. "No ports on the machine."

"They're probably on the back." Marcel wouldn't be deterred. "If there isn't one there, pull the hard drive."

I rocked the PC forward and found the slot. After inserting the USB, I copied the C drive onto it. "It says it will take four hours, and there are three computers here."

"Damn," Marcel said. "See if you can pull the drives."

"Won't that turn off the assistant?" I asked.

"No, it's on a mainframe."

I pulled the screwdriver from the kit Marcel had sent and set about removing hard drives. I had unplugged the computer and removed the side and two hard drives. I did the same for the other two machines, placing the drives in the protective pouch Marcel had so thoughtfully provided. Too bad he didn't include a snack. I was hungry. I put the drive-filled pouch into a leather backpack I found lying next to the desk.

"I've got six hard drives for you."

"Is there a manual around here?" Dad asked the virtual assistant.

I needed to work fast if Marcel was going to get any data.

"Searching. The name is not listed as such. Cross referencing titles for possible matches."

Marcel whooped over the comm-link, earning me a headshake from Dad. "Bruh, awesome. I can actually boot Windows as well as search for any relevant data. You are da bomb!"

The female voice spoke up again. "In order of keyword comparison scores, there are three books. The first is in the first bookcase, second shelf from the bottom. The title is Molecular Rearrangement Protocols."

Dad sorted through the books until he found the correct one. He tossed it to me, and I added it to the bag. "Next."

"Three cases to the right, top shelf. The title is Molecular Rearrangement, Theories and Practice."

Another search and another book. "Next."

"First shelf, third shelf down. The title is Molecular Devices Field Manual."

Dad found it, and I placed it in the bag.

"Anything else?" he asked Marcel and me.

"Ask her if you left any messages behind," Marcel said.

Dad repeated the request.

"Yes, Techno, you left orders to transfer all data to the remote site. That task has been completed. Are there any other requests?"

"Where is the remote destination?" Dad asked, hesitantly. If we could get the location, we could get there before Reaper and shut down the weapon before it reached the rest of the Underground.

"I sent the data to the IP address. It was received and verified."

Marcel gasped. "Repeat the address."

Dad asked her to repeat the numbers, and he read them off to Marcel.

"I'll start a search and see if I can locate the destination. It might lead us to the site."

"When did you compete the transfer?" I asked. It must have been years ago, before the Reclaimers' base was built over top of the bunker.

"Techno, you requested the transfer three days ago."

"Three days ago," we all said in unison.

"Is there anything else we should know?" Dad asked. I pulled the rather hefty backpack on and donned my ski mask and goggles.

"The Reclaimers have been notified of the breach and are in transit to apprehend the intruders." With that the door locks snapped shut. "I have locked the exits."

From overhead, mist started spraying into the room.

"Sleep gas!" Dad shouted, pulling on his mask. "We need to get out of here."

"Oh, man," Blaster said in my ear. "There are two trucks of Reclaimers pulling up to the main gate. Should I set off the diversion?"

"No. Stay under cover until we get out of here. No sense giving yourself away." Dad covered his mouth as he came over to me.

The door was locked, but not for long. I pulled together all the energy I could force into an energy knife. I slid it through the door and down, severing all the metal bolts. With a hard shove the door swung open.

"Get out of there," Marcel said, his voice on the edge of panic.

We charged up the stairs, and I sliced open the second door. No time for stealth now. The guard was still out on the couch. I followed Dad out the door. I shoved it shut, hoping the Protectorate didn't find it. I shouldn't have bothered. A plume of flame hit the other side of the door as the bunker self-destructed.

Dad reached the stairs ahead of me. "Leave it. We've got to get out of here," he said. He waited, waving me on.

I let go of the door, which burst outward in a gust of smoke, heat, and fire. I flipped the couch over, knocking the guard to the floor. He grumbled, but at least he might get out of the burning building. "Run!" I shouted at him.

He reached for his gun, but he only wore his underwear. He yelped as his brain focused on what was happening. The fire had spread across the floor. The flames reached the bottom of the couch, releasing plumes of smoke. He lumbered to his feet, stumbling toward me.

I followed Dad, who raced up the stairs. If anyone was asleep before, they weren't now. We reached the main floor and ran into a woman, messy-haired and wearing a nightgown. She screamed and ran for the front door. Dad started to go after her, but I grabbed his arm. "This way."

I gathered pure force between my hands and hit the back wall, which then ceased to exist. Cold air flooded into the house. We dove out into the night. The woman wailed for help from the porch. I looked back in time to see the basement guy stumble out behind us. He swore when his feet hit the snow.

We ran the way we came.

"Where are the troops?" Dad asked over the comm-link.

"They are at your nine o'clock. You've got a clear run if you hurry," Blaster said. "They're offloading now. I'm gonna slow 'em down."

"Stay put," Dad snapped, but it was too late. The sound of Blaster's firing echoed through the night before something exploded off to our right. A fountain of flame lit the night sky. Heads down, we ran to the hole in the fence. Blaster held it open long enough for us to edge through.

Shouts came from behind as we ran. Dogs barked, and we had a long way to go to safety.

The race of our lives had begun.

It seemed like we'd been running for hours. My legs hurt. The cold sapped my energy. By the time we reached the fence around the Boston dead zone, the dogs were close enough for us to catch glimpses of them in the woods. They were far too close to lose them.

We pushed through the hole in the fence and headed for the nearest building. Our tracks would give us away, but we needed to see how many pursued us. I punched out a boarded-up window, and we watched as the dogs reached the fence.

"What are you doing? You've still got to get back to the translocator before the death ray fires," Marcel said.

"If we have to fight, better to do it once and be done with it." Dad didn't respond further, just watched the massing of troops and dogs as they met at the fence.

"What are they waiting for?" Blaster asked. The soldiers milled around outside the barrier. No one had crossed into Boston yet. There must have been forty heavily armed soldiers at this point.

A few minutes later we got our answer, and it wasn't good. "Fall back," the Reclaimers' leader yelled. "The Protectorate's sources are reporting the death ray will fire in an hour. They aren't going anywhere. Establish a ten-foot perimeter along the forest line. Shoot anything crossing the fence."

"Marcel, they're saying the weapon will fire in an hour. Are you tracking the same?" Dad asked as he motioned us away from the window.

I heard Marcel's fingers on the keyboard. "I'm recalculating, but the station is moving faster than before. You've got fifty-seven minutes until Boston is hit."

Blaster gnawed on his beef jerky. "It took us three hours to reach the fence from the translocator. I guess we're blastin' through these chumps. We'll never get out of here in time otherwise." His mouth was full, making his words slurred, but I got the picture.

"No way," Dad said. "From their uniforms, those are elite commandos out there. They set a trap for us. It's lucky we got this far."

"Lucky?" Blaster asked, pieces of meat flying from his mouth. "Dying in the middle of a dead city isn't exactly lucky."

"Dad, can you fly out of here?" I asked, knowing full well he could.

"Yeah, but I'm not leaving you two." His jaw was set, ready to argue away our remaining time.

"Take Blaster and get out of Boston. Get to New York and take the translocator back." I held up my hand. "The blast in London didn't kill me. I'll just have to funnel the energy out as it hits, but I'll live."

He shook his head. "No, you had Mr. Fix-it's lens between you and the death ray. It must have changed the ray somehow."

"No, it concentrated it down to a single beam. I can ride out the blast here, but you've got to go. We can keep in touch over the comm-link."

"Tommy, if you—"

"I'll be fine, but I can't protect you two." I pulled the bag over my head and handed it to Blaster. "Get this to Marcel. We've got to find the remote station. They're speeding up the firing. There are only six cities after New York. We have no idea how long we've got."

"Ranger, he's right. By the end of the day, we don't know how many more cities they'll have hit. We're out of time, and I need the drives." Marcel said, selling it far better than me.

Dad hugged me tight. I whispered, "Tell Mom I love her, and I'll be back soon."

He nodded. "I will."

"Dad, I love you too. Take care of Blaster."

He smirked. "Love you too, Tommy."

"If we're done with your Hallmark moment, can we get out of here before we're turned into atoms?" Blaster said.

A second later, Dad tossed Blaster on his back and flew out through the door and into the night. I followed him out and sent bolts of lightning over the heads of the gathered soldiers. Last thing I needed was another stray bullet breaking Marcel's tech. There weren't any backups this time.

I ran back the way we came while Marcel chatted in my ear to help pass the hour. After the death ray fired, I'd still have to get back to the translocator and return to base. Marcel announced the five-minute mark, as Dad came on the comm-link. "We're back at Harker. Good luck, Tommy."

"No worries, Dad. I've got this." I looked around and found an open area. I didn't want to collapse a building on top of myself. I stepped into a nearby shelter to get out of the wind, which had taken to gusting. "Marcel, give me the one-minute mark, please."

"Will do."

I wanted to be scared, but all my mind focused on was how much trouble I was going to be in when Mom found out. It wouldn't matter that Dad and Blaster were safe. She'd be on me about my reckless behavior and that I didn't appreciate how much she worried. I saw her face as if she were there.

And in a way, she was.

"One minute, bruh. Good luck. May the Force be with you."

I shook my head and stepped back into the cold. Marcel called the thirty-second mark as I reached the center of the open area. The clouds blotted out the night sky and snow began to fall harder than before. I'd need to move in order to find our tracks to get back to the translocator.

"Ten seconds." Marcel counted down in my ear. When he got to one, he said. "Take care, Tommy."

The ray hit me like a typhoon.

My Gift absorbed the energy, and I felt the familiar sensation of the beam's mutagenic properties battling to break me down into component parts. I fired a sustained blast of energy away as the death ray was absorbed and amplified inside me. I heard the impact in the distance, but I concentrated on maintaining an equilibrium where my stores were full of the ray's energy. Too much and it would eat me alive.

In London, I'd exhausted every bit of the energy I'd taken in and drained myself to nothing. Maybe it had been the fight with Caligari or Parasite's influence, but I was calmer now and rode the edge of Armageddon as my body did what it was built for. As the death ray lessened, I stopped firing and took in the last of the swirling mass of energy.

"I'm fine," I said into the comm-link and heard shouts of joy from the other end. Smiling, I traced my steps back to where I'd diverted earlier and resumed following our tracks back to the Underground base. I wondered if I glowed, holding this much energy, but I couldn't tell.

An odd sensation mingled with the normal flow of energy I maintained. It felt like a ball of the mutagenic power still resided inside me, even though I thought my Gift had converted it. Residual feedback was a possibility. I'd been too worn out to have noticed. Still, it was strange.

Walking through the city of the dead, I considered if I were closer to Wendi in this place without any life but me. I remembered all the good times we had together. I pushed aside the painful ones and kept her firmly in my head as she'd been to me. Fierce and beautiful. She stood her ground when she had to and loved me, even when I made stupid mistakes. I felt her forgiveness here, and it made me happy.

3 8

My stomach informed me it was dinner time, so instead of continuing to enjoy the relative comfort of my bed, I ended up eating while Marcel caught everyone up on the day's events. Mom, Dad, Abby, Mimi, Pepper, and Blaze sat around the table as Marcel spoke.

"The Protectorate has claimed they are speeding up the attacks to rid the world of the Underground. Warden barely got New York and Rio evacuated in time. The space can't support many more while the systems are still being brought up and, in some cases, fixed."

He sighed. "More bad news. Stonewall escaped DC. I'm not sure how, but he's headed west currently."

"How do you know where he's going if he escaped?" Mimi asked. She glared at Marcel as if she suspected the answer.

"Um." He looked around sheepishly.

"Out with it," Mimi snapped.

"I put a nanotech transmitter in the sedative we gave him, just in case he escaped. Figured we'd track him to wherever he went, if he got away. I couldn't tell you, since you thought he was Waxenby and not Stonewall."

"And if he had been Ollie?"

"The transmitter will get filtered out in a couple of weeks. No harm, no foul. Plus, he really was Stonewall, so I didn't hurt Mr. W."

Mimi rolled her eyes. "Never argue with a nerd."

Marcel's eyes gleamed. "Thanks for the compliment."

"Anyhow, where is he going?" Mom asked.

"He's headed west, but I don't know to where. As fast as he's traveling, he must have stolen a car. Once he stops for a while, I'll be able to pinpoint his location. I've been going through the manuals, and we can remote detonate the weapon by overloading the energy supply and ordering it to…" He looked around at the group. "We can make it go boom."

Dad snorted. "Important technical details are fine."

"At the current rate of the station's movement, it will hit populated Underground cities in two days. If we don't find the remote station by then, Warden will lose a lot of people. They've started evacuations, but she can't move sixteen thousand people to Wendigo in that amount of time."

We'd come so far, but we were still short of stopping the death ray in time. The worst part was no one knew what would happen after the previous targets completed. Would it turn itself off, or was someone in control of the weapon?

If Reaper had found it, he'd start hitting Protectorate government centers. Millions of people would die as he enacted his revenge against the government.

I had no idea on where the Protectorate would strike if they controlled the station. Their first target might be where we were since the locals didn't follow the laws.

"Marcel, what do you need?" Pepper asked. "Is there something we can help with?"

"Right now, I need to concentrate on the hard drives retrieved from the bunker." He rubbed his chin while he thought. "Anyone going to fight at the remote site should look over the manual. I'll leave it in the commissary. If the place is protected, we might only get one shot at shutting it down."

"Good idea," Blaze said. "Ranger, who do you want going?"

Dad shook his head. "I'm not sure until we find out where we're going and how many people the Council can provide." He turned to mom. "Can you and Abby go to Wendigo? Check to see if Alyx is there. If you can, help Warden get things moving faster."

"Of course," Mom said, after checking with Abby, who nodded. "We'll be back before the mission goes. You're going to need as many bodies as we can muster."

"Let's hope not," Dad said, but didn't sound convinced.

I gave Mom and Abby hugs before they left for Wendigo. The meeting ended, and I went to the commissary. I grabbed more food while I waited for Marcel to bring up the manual.

A few minutes later, he wandered in, carrying the book with him. He slid it over to me. "I marked the parts you'll need to read. Mostly how to shut it down. I put instructions on how to overload the weapon, but if we can shut it off and destroy the remote site, over-loading it is a moot point.

"Have you gotten any sleep?" I asked.

Dark circles hung like old laundry under his eyes. His hair drooped down instead of its normal style. "Not much. If I can make it through destroying the damn death ray, then I can sleep." He stole my Mountain Dew and drank most of it. "Thanks. I'm hoping the drives have the location of the remote station on them. Following Stonewall might be a snipe hunt."

"Let me know if you need anything."

"Thanks, bruh. I will."

I watched as the most unlikely hero of all time staggered back to his tech hut to find the one thing that could stop the destruction.

Marcel never got enough credit.

39

The next morning, Blaze and I met in the training room to spar. He'd come a long way in controlling his powers; more than once, he punched me in the back. He'd always taught me to watch my opponent for their tell. Blaze stuttered just before he teleported.

As I threw a punch toward his head, I caught the stutter and spun with my arm extended. The momentum carried me around, striking Blaze as he came back into view, knocking him to the ground.

"Dude, nice move." Usually during training, Blaze adopted a strict instructor poise, but now with me training him on how to use his Gifts, he was his normal self.

Pepper laughed from where she was seated against the wall. "He cleaned your clock."

"You stutter to the right before you leap. Try coming in at a different angle or back farther. You've got to vary your attacks, as my old instructor told me. Repeatedly."

He feigned indignance. "Dude, I'm not old, just very seasoned."

"You're old as dirt, but I'll keep ya," Pepper called out to him. "Tommy's right. You're becoming predictable."

We kept at it for another hour, until he could move around more. "Do you guys have suits yet?" I asked, taking a breather.

They both shook their heads. "Nah, Ranger isn't about to let us fight," Blaze said, though I could tell it bothered him. He'd filled out a lot since his Gift had manifested and looked years younger.

"We should get you suited up. You never know." I took them to the armory and walked them through the screens. Pepper pushed Blaze aside to start designing her new suit. I went to find breakfast while they worked.

Pop-Tarts and Mountain Dew in hand, I headed down to the meeting room. Dad and Mimi sat at the table, watching the news feed. I took a seat and lost myself in the disaster FNN showed on the screen.

Hannah Fulbright reported on the latest targets of the death ray. Her hair looked different, but her glasses were the same cool ones she usually wore. She said that the Protectorate had taken control of the death ray and was using it to eliminate the terrorist Underground once and for all. We'd thought we had two days, but by nightfall the attacks would be over.

General Mahady, looking more worn since the last announcement, gave Protectorate updates as to wiping out the Underground. If they'd really been in control of the station, they would be enthusiastic, which made me believe they knew Reaper had control of the weapon.

Marcel stuck his head in periodically. Stonewall hadn't stopped anywhere for more than a few hours, so either he hadn't reached his destination, or he wasn't headed to the remote station. Either way, Marcel delved into the hard drives looking for any clue that would point us at the remote station and how to stop the death ray.

Mimi wiped tears from her eyes as we watched. "Will this never end?"

"It will be over soon," Dad said softly. "One way or the other."

Dallas had been hit and the best estimate was a three p.m. attack on Los Angeles. Alyx showed up around eleven a.m., and he didn't look pleased as he strode into the meeting room.

Dad muted the display as he greeted the mage. "Glad you're here.

We're going to have to move out as soon as we locate the remote station. We have under four hours to get there and shut it down before sixteen thousand Underground people die."

"That's what I came here to tell you, Michael." Alyx's gaze dropped to the floor. "The Council has forbidden any of its members from assisting you in stopping the death ray."

Dad was on his feet. "What? How can they do that? We've fought side-by-side to stop the Brotherhood. Now you're abandoning us?"

"I don't like it any more than you do, but my hands are tied. Pimiko enacted the coven. The Council only involves itself in strictly magical conflicts where humanity can't defend itself. I've been told any attempt to help destroy the weapon will forfeit my place on the Council, and I'll be immediately censured."

"Sometimes you have to pay a price to save lives," Dad said. The veins in his forehead bulged on his reddened face. "If it costs you a spot on the Council, so be it. You can join with us here."

Alyx shook his head. "You don't get it. Censure means I lose all my magic. They can block me from ever using it again. I'm useless without my magic."

"What about Gladiator?" I asked, trying to give Dad a chance to calm down. "Can he help us?"

The mage's face flushed a deep red. "Pimiko's men arrested him after an outburst in the proceedings. Charles hasn't recovered. Makeda and Yutu are gone, and Maya agrees with whatever the dreamer says."

The memory from the Oracle crashed into my brain. "The dreamer?" I asked.

"It's an old term for a seer. I just meant Pimiko is in control now."

I thought back to my first meeting with Eiraf. She had given me a prophecy.

*"Listen to the cursed one, the phoenix, and the doppleganger. They will help you choose. If you fall to the dreamer or the trickster, all is lost. The way is fraught with danger, fire, and death, but choose wisely or it is all for naught."*

"Eiraf warned me not to fall for the dreamer's tricks. Don't you see? Pimiko is the traitor Yelena told us about." Understanding finally dawned on me as the pieces fell into place.

Alyx crumpled into a chair, his head in his hands. "We've been outmaneuvered. I can't help you without her stripping away my magic. We've lost."

"I'd have to say I agree with him," Marcel said, as he entered the meeting room. He took a seat at the controls and pulled up an image on the display screen. "This is Siren."

Tracy Stevens's picture filled the screen. Jon and Wendi's mother appeared to be in her early twenties. It was from years ago, but it was definitely her. We'd met when Wendi had run away and again at Wendi's funeral. Wendi looked just like her mom at that age.

"How?" I asked, at a loss for words.

Marcel did something and the screen split into five panels. Tracy Stevens was labeled Siren. The man next to her was Stonewall, though the rugged, good-looking man had been replaced, as we now knew, by a replica of Oliver Waxenby. Next was Jon's dad, "Igniter" in bold under his photo. Two others, a woman with the name of Stiletto and a young man named Twitch, completed the set. The last two had red slashes across their faces. The original Dark Brigade.

"Stonewall is sitting at the Stevens's farm as of ten minutes ago. Once I saw this, I checked, and he was there. To make matters worse, if they could get any worse, the Wendigo translocator broke. Mr. Fix-it is trying to restore it, but every minute it's down means more people are going to die when the death ray hits Los Angeles," Marcel said, keeping his voice level as he spoke.

"Alyx, you've got to help us," I said. "We have to stop the death ray before it fires again. You've got friends in both places."

"I know, Tommy. You think I don't? What the fuck do you want me to do? If I lose my magic, I'll literally die. I'm over eighty years old. Without my magic, I'll return to my normal age."

"So instead, you'll live with the blood of all those innocent people on your hands?" Mimi asked. She sat next to Marcel. "You'd rather live for centuries with that knowledge?"

Alyx laughed. "Innocent, my ass. Those people are just like the rest.

They'd stab you in the back to save themselves. If being a mage has shown me nothing else, it's all people are petty and self-centered. Don't think otherwise."

Mimi shrugged. "Sounds like you're already dead to me."

"Alyx, can you do one thing for us?" I asked, cutting off his retort. "As my friend, can you do one thing for me?"

"Tommy, I'd like—"

"How about for me then?" Pepper asked. I don't know how long she and Blaze had been standing there. "Would you do something for me?"

"Pepper, you know I'd do anything, but..." His eyes wandered to Blaze and back to her.

"Open a portal to the farm. That's all we need," I said, staring at Pepper. "We need to stop this now, and an open portal won't cost you anything."

Alyx hung his head. "How long have you been standing there?" he asked Pepper, though I'm sure he knew the answer.

"Long enough to know I was right about you. You don't love anything but your magic."

Alyx's head came up. "I loved you. I swear."

"Then you'd want me to be happy. Give us ten minutes, open the portal, and leave." The look she shot him could have punched through solid carbinium.

His head drooped again. "I'll do it. You have ten minutes. Then I have to go."

***

Eight minutes later, I stood in my blue and red combat suit. If I was going out, I'd do it in style. Mimi wore a black combat suit with bright red accents across the chest and legs. Dad had his standard Cyclone Ranger suit. Pepper wore her white and orange, while Blaze wore black and bright blue.

Dad pulled me aside. "Here, you might need this." He put the black recharging box into my hand. The case was dented from where I'd thrown it at his feet.

"Thanks," I said, embarrassed that I'd behaved that way. "Ummm…"

Dad held up his hand. "We're good. Just stay safe."

I nodded and walked over to the team. "You got a name picked out?" I asked Blaze. "Maybe Poof?"

He groaned along with the rest of the team. The tension was like a noose around our necks, and we needed to break it, or it wouldn't go well for us.

Dad handed Pepper, Mimi, and Blaze comm-links. "I thought Bamf would be suitable," Dad said.

"I told him to go with Repeater, but he's stuck on the name he picked," Pepper said, rolling her eyes.

"You killing us? What did you pick?" Mimi asked, sounding quite amused.

"Blaze. It worked then. It'll work now."

"Perfect," I said. "Alyx, open the portal."

"I'm sorry. I want to help, but I can't risk losing my magic." His voice was low and morose. "Pepper…"

"Just open the portal, Alyx. Don't make this any worse than it has to be."

"Comm check," Marcel said.

"Cyclone Ranger."

"Pepper Spray."

"Blaze."

"The Mechanic," Mimi said on her turn; it fit her.

"Tommy." The Dark Brigade all knew my name, and I wanted to make sure they remembered it after we were done. One way or another, we were shutting down the death ray.

"I'm sorry, but you understand, right?" When no one answered, the portal opened. Dad gave the signal, and we moved out. Alyx had dropped us on the main road leading to the entry of the farm. Rain sheeted down as we exited the portal and established our location at the Stevens's farm.

Trees blocked the farmhouse, keeping anyone watching from

seeing us. Dad led us through the trees. He signaled to crouch down as we reached the edge of the woods. A fence divided us from the farm. In the distance, the house stood at the top of a gentle upslope. The red barn sat farther away. Two cars were parked outside the barn. One was an old, beat-up brown car, the other was a brand-new, blue sports car.

The rain swirled around us as the storm picked up. I'd gotten used to fighting in rain with Warden around, but I wondered about the others. Pepper and Blaze hadn't fought in years, and Mimi had never used her Gifts in battle. We weren't the elite commandos we needed for this mission, but the fate of the Underground rested on our shoulders.

"I can't get eyes on the target, but Stonewall is in the barn, if the GPS location is correct. Good luck," Marcel said.

This time it wasn't a game show, but we'd punch the Dark Brigade's ticket to nowhere today. Or die trying.

40

We watched for a few minutes, but nothing moved on the farm. Mimi tried to sense anyone with her psychic power but came up short.

"I don't see anything, so they're either hidden or don't know we're here," Pepper said. She had enhanced vision, which was nice since we didn't have binoculars.

"Ranger, we are T-minus twenty until Los Angeles gets attacked, and the translocator isn't online," Marcel said.

Dad grimaced. "Tommy, you take the lead. Blaze and Pepper, flank him. Mimi in the middle, and I'll bring up the rear. We shoot to kill, people. We can't take any chances."

I set out at a trot. With twenty minutes, we couldn't creep across the field, peer into windows, and devise a strategy. "I'm heading to the barn. Watch my left for anyone coming out of the house."

"Got your flank," Pepper said. We continued to cover the distance to the barn.

The structure was huge—thirty feet wide and two hundred feet long. At one time they'd managed a herd of cows, according to Jon. Now it held farming supplies and maybe a secret base to control an orbital death ray.

Tracy Stevens being a member of the Dark Brigade would have never occurred to me. At worst, I thought she was a mother who'd sent her kids to Redemption alone.

It made sense now, though. If she were guarding the remote station for the Brigade, kids popping up with Gifts was the last thing she needed.

I paused when I reached the edge of the driveway. No one moved around the cars. The winds picked up as the storm intensified. Lighting flashed and thunder shook the earth under the massive storm.

I crouched, moving quickly across to the nearest car. It was a beautiful blue sports car with a ragtop. The owner must have been pissed when it was stolen. I kept it between me and the house as my team followed suit. Three large overhead doors and a smaller entry door covered the front of the barn. Rolling up one of the big doors would make a lot of noise and take forever, so I headed to the smaller one.

I peeked through the glass and saw nothing. The handle turned with a click, and the door opened on the barn's massive interior. A waft of cut grass and manure boiled out of the barn. To my right, a huge stack of hay bales sat behind the first of the garage doors, a forklift parked next to it. On the left were stalls for livestock. They appeared deserted. Large overhead light fixtures lit the area, but also threw a lot of shadows.

Keeping low, I moved across to the nearest stall and crouched out of sight of the rest of the barn. Mimi and Dad joined me there. Blaze and Pepper sped across to take cover by the haybales. The rain slapped out a rhythm on the tin roof thirty feet overhead. If we'd had a guitar and a bass, we'd have a band.

Still nothing moved. "We're at the target. No bogeys in sight," I said.

"He's there somewhere. His signal hasn't moved since I spotted it." I heard the tension in Marcel's voice. He was watching the countdown back at Harker while we searched the farm. "The Reclaimers have moved lots of troops around Los Angeles. Someone tipped them off. The Underground wants to fight, but they are outmatched."

"Understood." Dad's voice was cold, professional. "Move out. We've got to find the device."

I stood and walked to the center of the barn. An arrow whistled across the space at me. I threw myself into a forward roll, but it struck my shoulder. I got myself into a kneeling position and fanned electricity in front of me. A second arrow burst as it hit the shield.

Jon dropped from the top of a covered horse stall. His face bore the scars from where Abby's paw had struck him.

"I guess your modeling career is over, huh?"

He stared at me, as if his vision could bore through me like a drill bit. "Always with the jokes, Ward. Did you laugh after you killed my sister?" He snapped off another shot, which I easily sidestepped. "Where's Abby? I owe that bitch for this." He pointed to his ruined face. Gifted healing fixed a lot of injuries, but her paw had removed half his face. "Where is she?"

"Not here, but she sends her regrets that she didn't tear your head off." I threw a bolt of lightning at him.

He dodged it and shot another arrow over my head. It burst, cascading powder over me. I gasped for air as my throat began to constrict. Panic set in, knowing my Gift couldn't compensate for suffocation. My lungs spasmed as I tried to breathe.

"Time to pay for your sins, Ward," Jon said.

A blast of air struck me from behind, knocking me down. The wind streamed past me, taking whatever Jon hit me with. Oxygen began to flow into my lungs. The cloud of dust blew toward Jon.

From the far end of the barn, I caught the green glow of Reaper's scythe. He led three others, running toward where I sat.

I fired a shot of energy at Jon's feet, making him move as he tried to aim his bow.

He collapsed, grabbing his head as he rolled on the floor. "Get out of my brain!" he screamed. Mimi must have gotten to him.

I needed to eliminate Reaper before he could use his scythe on any of my friends. I refused to lose anyone to the wasteland of his mind.

Blaze and Pepper moved in from the right, closing in on Stonewall.

Jon's father, Igniter from the pictures, threw a flaming orb, striking Mimi. She collapsed. Dad sped in, stopping Igniter from finishing her off.

Stonewall fought against Blaze and Pepper. Blaze flickered into and out of view as he attacked. According to Dad, Stonewall's shields could block anything, but it had to have limits. Pepper unleashed lasers out of both forearms. I'd never seen her fight, but now wasn't the time to watch.

Reaper headed directly for me, Parasite running behind him. I fired a series of force bolts at Reaper, who deflected them with his scythe blade. If nothing else, he was fast with his weapon. He swung it in a wide arc, forcing me to dive forward. I grabbed Parasite and sent a shock through the little man. He howled before he collapsed into a heap.

Reaper pulled back his scythe over his shoulder, preparing to strike. I'd miscalculated how far Parasite was and overextended, leaving me lying on the ground in front of Reaper.

"You're not getting away this time, boy," Reaper growled as he swung the blade toward me. Blaze flickered into view and kicked Reaper in the side.

Reaper stumbled, the scythe hitting the floor. He regained his balance before I could get up.

"Get away from him!" I shouted at Blaze.

He flickered and was gone as the scythe passed through where he'd been a moment before.

I pushed myself up and shot an arc of electricity into Reaper's face.

Reaper screamed, grabbing at his face with his left hand. He swung at me one-handed and half-blind, almost hitting me, but I danced out of range in time.

Dad swooped by, driving Igniter before him with a volley of lighting. It was one thing to fight an opponent on the ground, but Igniter missed repeatedly as Dad flew circles around him.

An arrow struck my leg like a hard punch. Wires wrapped around my legs, sending me crashing to the floor. I tried to electrify myself, but the wires conducted the electricity away from me.

"Not so funny now, are you, Ward?" Jon said as he crossed to where I struggled to free myself.

Mimi lay on the ground, unmoving.

Reaper lifted the scythe. Without being able to use my Gift, I was a sitting duck. My only hope was the scythe not working on me.

Jon grabbed his hand. "Go kill Pepper again if you want, but Ward is mine."

A mixture of relief and anxiety rose. Jon knelt before me. I knew he hated me, but Wendi wouldn't want me to hurt him. There was more on the line than Jon's vengeance.

Reaper spit on me as he ran past, toward the fight between Blaze, Pepper, and Stonewall.

Jon pulled a long bowie knife from his hip sheathe. He held it up before me, twisting it back and forth. "I should just cut your throat, but I want Abby to know I carved you up before I killed you. Before I'm done, I'll make sure you look like I do."

"Wendi would be so proud of you."

Jon punched me in the mouth. Power coiled inside of me, replenishing my energy. I was pretty sure I'd need everything I had for this one.

I silently begged Wendi to forgive me. "You should be glad she died, rather than watch you become this monstrosity."

He took the knife and slashed it along the side of my face. Warm blood trickled down from the cut as he dragged the blade down my cheek. I tried not to cry out at the anguish of the slicing knife, but I didn't succeed.

I needed to free myself before Jon could carve me up like a Thanksgiving turkey. Try as I might, the wires were too tight for me to do much. My mind scrambled for ideas, but nothing came to me. I was done.

"By the time I'm done with you, you'll look like the monster you are. Reaper told me as long as the knife moves slowly, you'll cut like anybody else."

"Since Abby didn't finish what she started, I will," I said, but my confidence was fading fast.

Dad still fought with Igniter. Reaper and Stonewall pushed Blaze and Pepper back. We weren't winning, especially with me immobilized, while Jon carved me up.

Jon moved the blade to the other side. "Too bad she isn't here. I'd make her eat the scraps I cut off you." He grinned. "Should probably cut your tongue out, so I don't have to listen to you." He grabbed my chin and squeezed, trying to force my mouth open. His hand jerked once and then again. Jon staggered like he'd been kidney-punched. He swayed, stumbling as he backed up. With a loud groan, he fell to the ground.

Mimi started pulling the wires off me. "Somebody knocked me for a loop." She was sporting a pretty serious black eye and burns across her face. She released me from the last of the wires. "There ya go, Tiger."

At the far side of the barn, a short, squat guy wearing all black threw pieces of stone at me. I launched a bolt of lightning at him, driving him back.

How many people did the Brigade have here? And we still hadn't seen Siren.

Jon had fallen to the ground, twitching. I ran to him, broke his bow in half, and retrieved the knife he'd used on me. *Let's see the archer work without his weapons.*

Another, thicker piece of stone struck me in the head, dazing me and blurring my vision. I threw a bolt of lightning at the ape and was rewarded with a yelp. He charged at me, rocks enclosed in his fists. Boulder had been a lot more intimidating. As he reached me, I hit him with a force-amplified uppercut and immediately wished I hadn't.

My fist struck and the arm stopped with a massive jolt. I wondered if my shoulder had torn free from the force.

He grinned at me. "I'm made of rock."

*Wonderful.* He swung at me. I danced out of the reach of his punch. I fired a force blast at his feet. The ground gave way, and he fell flat on his face. Mimi ran in and grabbed his head. He wasn't going anywhere for a while.

"Tommy!" Pepper yelled from across the barn. Reaper had her pinned against the stacked hay bales, pushing the tip of the scythe closer and closer to her face.

I couldn't fire into his back. It might cause the scythe to hit her. The blade inched closer as Pepper struggled. Her panicked screams echoed around the barn.

I threw a bolt of lightning next to them. The hay exploded outward in a shower of dust and flaming stalks. Reaper flinched away from the strike.

Pepper fired a laser into Reaper's throat, burning him.

"You bitch!" he screamed, dropping the scythe to grab his injured neck.

Pepper punched him in the side of the head as he tried to get away. "God, I've wanted to do that for so long." She struck again. "And that's for Gabriella. She loved you, you stupid bastard, and you killed her." She punched the reeling man over and over, reciting a litany of wrongs he'd committed while she was trapped inside him.

Stonewall fought with Blaze as he teleported around. Stonewall's power protected him but couldn't eliminate Blaze either. They fought to a standstill.

I fired a force bolt into Stonewall's back. The shield absorbed the blow but allowed Blaze to slide inside and punch Stonewall in the jaw. The big man dropped like he'd been poleaxed.

More people ran from the back of the barn toward the fight, now that we'd beaten their first string. Jon was nowhere to be seen. Reaper lay on the ground, as Pepper kicked him.

"T-minus ten minutes until Los Angeles is hit."

"Stop." A woman's voice rang out across the barn, her figure emerging from the back of the building.

Dad landed awkwardly, while Mimi stepped next to me. My hands were behind my back, so I wiggled my fingers, checking to see if she controlled me. Her power rippled across my brain but didn't seize hold like Yelena's had. I was free of her influence. Alyx's block must be in place. I stood still, not wanting to give away that I could move.

The rest of my team, as well as the Brigade, marched to stand in a line, even Jon, who'd been out of sight. We were in elementary school again and had pissed off the teacher.

Tracy Stevens strolled up before us. Behind her, Yutu and Makeda were blindfolded and gagged. Two guys held each of them in place. "Tommy, how many minutes until Los Angeles is destroyed?"

"Ten," I answered but didn't say more.

I'd get one shot to take her out. If I missed, she could turn my friends on me, and I couldn't risk that. I waited as Mrs. Stevens, aka Siren, paced in front of the line.

"Reaper, you assured me you could take care of this." She waved down the line. "Yet, here they all are. Why?"

"Señora, they are stronger than I'd believed. Their new members are fierce and powerful, but free me, and I will end them for you."

She tittered at the suggestion. "How gallant you are to kick immobilized opponents. Almost as bad as my worthless son." She stopped in front of Jon. "Just like your inept father. Caligari taught you nothing. You spent your time tormenting your opponent instead of killing him outright."

"He killed Wendi!" he screamed in her face, but she silenced him with a flick of her hand.

"No, stupid boy, Powell killed Wendi. Cutting up her boyfriend is a waste of time. Until you can control your rage, you're useless to me. Go to the console and fire the weapon now."

"I want to kill Ward."

"You'll do as told, or I'll let Mr. Ward even the score. The sight of you sickens me. Go!"

Jon lurched forward as if he were a puppet, each leg stick straight as he walked toward the console.

Siren approached me again. She ran her finger down my torn cheek. "It will heal. Some girls like a few rough edges on their men. I know I do. The only smart thing Wendi ever did was pick you. It's a shame Jon didn't die in her stead."

"Why do this?" I asked, haltingly, like it was an effort.

"Yelena said you were strong and indeed she was right." Siren said. Her fingers cupped my chin and pulled me forward. "The Protectorate drove us underground like rats. After we eliminate the Protectorate and the Underground, we'll fix the system and turn the rest of the population into Gifted. We will be powerless no more. Once all people are equal, we will establish a new world order."

"It won't work."

"Tommy, my love, it will. Pimiko delivered us two of the Council. Charles will never recover from his wounds, and Alyx has been stripped of his magic and will be dead. We'll kill Pimiko and Maya, and no one will interfere with Earth again."

"I don't think so," I said, now more confidently.

A blue strip of light appeared, opening out into a portal. Alyx and Gladiator came through.

Now it was a proper party.

# 41

S iren spun. "What are you doing here? Pimiko eliminated your magic."

"My large friend here rallied the Council's troops. Pimiko decided to vacate the premises, as it were," Alyx said, as he bowed to Siren. "It is time to end your charade and bring order back to the world."

Gladiator's sword whistled from the sheath. "Pimiko has fled, and we are here to free the others." He advanced on Siren.

"If you want me to fight, let me go." Reaper snarled. With a stutter-step, Reaper lurched out of line, hefted his glowing green scythe, and attacked. Gladiator blocked each of the slashing blows as Reaper engaged his foe.

A second portal popped into being, allowing Pimiko entrance to the barn.

"What are you doing here?" Alyx asked, shock evident in his voice.

Yellow currents swirled around her, as she sent waves of magic at Alyx. "I will kill you for your interference."

Alyx diverted her magic, but it took effort. It appeared Pimiko was far more powerful than the others had told me.

"Been holding back all these years. To think of the good we could have accomplished," Alyx said.

"All I seek is the release of death," Pimiko said. She rapid-fired yellow ribbons at Alyx. They turned to large hissing snakes as they landed.

He scattered blue marbles in front of him. The spheres elongated, forming into ferrets. The animals fought between the two mages. A series of brilliant blue bolts arced from his hands, striking the golden-shielded Pimiko.

Siren yelled. "Alyx, stop!"

"I'll take care of you in a minute," Alyx said to Siren with a laugh.

Pimiko pushed a wave of pure golden light which spread out from her. As the wave passed over them, the ferrets poofed into smoke, drifting away from the fight.

Alyx's staff burst into the brightest blue I'd ever seen and sliced through the wave. Pimiko stumbled but righted herself in time to deflect Alyx's bolt of magic.

Pimiko threw a solid ribbon of golden magic that hung between the mages like a tug-o-war rope. Neither moved as they silently fought for control.

"Alyx, cease your fighting!" Siren yelled at him.

"You'll have to do better than that," Alyx said.

Now was my chance. I gathered my energy and fired into Siren's back. Double arcs of electricity struck her. She screamed. Her body flew across the intervening space, striking the golden magic. She crumpled.

Her control vanished, releasing both sides simultaneously. Jon fell to the ground ahead of us, only to right himself again.

I had to stop him from firing the weapon at Los Angeles. I broke into a run. There were only minutes until the death ray fired.

Pimiko's yellow magic spiraled around me, tangling me in threads of gold until I couldn't move.

Alyx's spells hammered away at her, but she resisted his attacks.

I waited for an attack of some sort, but nothing happened. I stood encased in the weave of her magic.

Chaos ensued around me as Stonewall and Igniter battled against Dad, Mimi, Blaze, and Pepper. The light show was amazing as bolts of lightning, laser beams, and flashes of fire flew around the barn. For all of that, I could have been at a rock concert.

With a whoosh, a fireball struck the hay bales. The flame spread out of control and burning debris lit more of the area on fire. Smoke billowed into the contained space.

Gladiator and Reaper fought to a standstill in the center of the open area. Gladiator's skill couldn't penetrate the sheer speed of Reaper's scythe. Evenly matched, the first one to make a mistake would pay for it.

Jon descended into the floor at the other end of the barn. *There must be a stairwell there.* If I didn't break free, I'd never stop him in time. I attempted to force my way out, but no energy would come.

"No energy to spare?" Pimiko asked, dodging a blue sphere from Alyx. The wall behind her ceased to exist, leaving a huge hole in its place. She chanted, and the world fell away for me.

I stood in a field like I'd never seen before. Vivid pink grass dotted with orange and purple flowers ran as far as I could see. In the center of the field, on a pile of chocolate cupcakes, a yellow pheasant the size of an elephant perched next to a bucket of squirmy things. The head bobbed down and plucked some writhing mass from the container and devoured it.

The sky roiled with red clouds as blue lightning bolts flashed across the sky. I wandered toward the bird, but my mind wouldn't focus correctly as my gaze swam across the unreal landscape. Screams echoed in the still air, but I couldn't concentrate on them.

The pheasant regarded me for a moment. "Welcome to my home." Her tone was soft and reassuring, the kind of voice you'd expect from a giant bird. "You are safe here from the strife of the other planes. Stay and be content." The massive bird swallowed more of the wriggling mess. I moved forward, trying to see what she ate, but the contents stayed a mystery.

"I have to go back," I muttered, though why I needed to leave slipped through my mind like sprinkles over an ice cream cone. "They need me."

"You were dreaming. Here you may have anything you desire," the bird said to me as it ate more from the giant bucket. "Lie down and rest. It will be over soon."

Over? What was going to be over? I walked to the base of the cupcake hill and climbed. Sprinkles clattered down as I ascended the mound, reaching the pheasant and her food.

The screams of sorrow and fear were clearer up here. In the bucket were people, begging for help or mercy. The beak dipped in and snatched up more, ending their struggles.

My mind snapped back into place.

Pimiko shimmered into existence before me "Yelena warned of your strength, but you will not best me. You stay here until your people are dead. Then I bend you to my will."

I'd broken through Yelena's control before. I racked my addled brain, looking for clues of how to end the dream.

*"Do not fall for the dreamer."* I heard the Oracle Eiraf's voice in my head.

This was a dream, an illusion. I tried to gather my power, but nothing happened. Another illusion? I went through the motions of firing a lightning bolt, throwing my hand out at the giant bird.

The bolt struck her. She screamed, falling off the mound of cupcakes. She bounced down the side of the hill.

The dream shattered.

In the real world, Pimiko dropped to the ground, her side blackened by the bolt.

Chaos reigned. Blaze fought the four men, who kept him away from Yutu and Makeda. They bore electric cattle prods. Anytime Blaze moved, one of them struck him, disrupting his teleport.

He lashed out with every move he'd ever taught me and a few I'd never seen. He caught one guard in the kneecap, staggering the man. Blaze followed up with a punch to the next guy's head, propelling him into another guard where they collapsed in a heap.

Dad and Igniter battled in an epic showdown of elemental fury.

The barn showed signs of the fight. Fire from the hay bales had spread across the floor, igniting the wooden animal stalls. The flames grew higher, licking at the ceiling supports. If the barn took much more damage, the roof would cave in.

Pepper and Stonewall fought against each other. Her right hand flipped back against her forearm and shots tore through Stonewall's shields as he struggled to contain her. He bled from numerous spots around his face and torso. He grunted, stopping the pulse blasts, only to have her left arm laser tear through his shields.

Every time he switched his shields, Pepper hit him with something else, including a nasty kick to the balls when he got too close. Somehow, he shifted the shield in time to keep her from punching his lights out.

Gladiator was on Reaper. Blades whirled. The two strained to pierce each other's defenses.

I didn't know how long I'd been gone, but I needed to hurry. "Time check, Mr. Wizard."

"The official time is under six minutes, but the weapon appears to be charging, so any minute is my best guess." Marcel held it together, but the strain was etched in his voice. I'd worry about him later.

As I ran to the stairs I'd seen Jon take, I asked Marcel, "Will it fire when the charge is ready, or will Jon have to manually do it?"

"According to the instructions, he'll have to trigger the shot to get it to discharge earlier than scheduled. Once the timer reaches zero, the death ray will automatically fire." Marcel sounded more agitated than normal. "Warden is worried Molly is in Los Angeles. Nobody can find her at Wendigo. The Reclaimers have surrounded the city and are shooting anything that moves."

"Shit," I said. Molly had a habit of being at the best or worst possible place at any given time. Today, it was definitely the worst. Warden had only one daughter, and now she was in the target of the death ray. I had to stop the weapon. I owed it to Molly, especially since she'd freed me from Dr. Goat. "I'm almost to the stairs."

"Shut it down. We can overload it after we crash it into the ocean. Good luck, bruh."

I found the stairs and descended them as fast as possible. I reached the last turn and swung myself over the railing, dropping the last ten feet and landing in front of the open door.

Jon sat in a chair with his back to the door, hands on the control panel.

I fired a force blast, hard enough to hurt, but not enough to knock him into the controls. It struck him in the center of his back. He hit the edge of the console and spun around to face me.

"Too late as usual, Ward," he said, his disfigured face twisting grotesquely in a sneer. "I've set the death ray to wipe out the Underground's base. Soon Gifted will rule the world, as we were meant to."

I entered the room, headed for the console. Siren stood to the left of the door, Mimi held in front of her. She pressed a gun to the back of Mimi's head. I flinched when I saw them.

"Tommy, you touch the controls, and Mimi dies while you watch. Jon, when the death ray is at full power, fire it. We'll reset it for San Francisco and finish off the Underground," Siren said.

"They aren't there. We evacuated them to a new base," I lied to distract them so I could free Mimi and shut down the death ray. Panic raced through my brain as I struggled to see a way out of this mess.

"Really?" Siren said with a smirk. "Even after Pimiko destroyed the translocator? How exactly did the refugees get to Wendigo? Carrier pigeon?"

My heart sank, but I didn't let it show on my face. If she knew the base name, we'd been betrayed. "Eiraf opened a portal. She said the balance wasn't served by the slaughter of all those innocents." I edged closer to the console.

Siren pulled back on the gun's hammer, locking it in place. "One more step and you'll be seeing your new girlfriend's brains, just like you saw my daughter's. I guess you've got a knack for getting the women in your life killed."

Jon's eyes widened. "How can you say something like that?"

"Shut up," she snapped at him. His jaw audibly clacked shut. "Your sister should have stayed where I put her, and she'd still be alive."

I shook my head. "Powell would have killed her in the woods the night we broke free. Brunner wanted her, so Powell handed Wendi over to him to do as he pleased. Some mother you are." I filled my words with every ounce of anger and hate they'd hold.

Here was a woman who'd had two beautiful, Gifted children, and she'd shipped them off to Redemption to rot.

"I guess they were a nuisance. I guess it would have been more convenient if Jon had died in the Gauntlet along with Wendi, or is he useful now because you can control him?"

"Shut up!" she screamed.

The power of her words was like a sledgehammer to the brain, but they didn't stick.

Alyx had warded my mind from Yelena's magic.

I kept my mouth shut, noticing the flashing red "ready" light on the console.

"I gave up everything for the Dark Brigade, and the leadership sold us out. The government came for us. Stiletto and Twitch didn't make it away from the ambush. We were hunted by our own people and theirs. We had to hide. Stonewall and Igniter used a face-altering device at the safehouse to change their looks. We had killed Waxenby, so I turned Stonewall into him and hid him in Redemption when it was built. Igniter and I stayed here, and I raised my dead lover's children."

Jon, unable to speak, stared in horror at his mother. His mouth popped open, and the words tumbled out. "You aren't our parents?"

"No. Twitch was your father, but he died in a hail of FBI bullets as we arrived at the launch site. Igniter is an idiot, but he was handy to take Twitch's place. I lost the man I loved and got stuck with you two in return. I sent you away rather than risk being found."

"If you aren't my mother, who is?" Jon asked.

"She was a nobody, and I killed her to keep her away from Twitch. You remind me of her. Weak." Siren's face twisted in hate as she spoke. "I should have killed you both, but Twitch made me promise to raise you if anything happened to him."

Jon's injured face fell, as his whole world crumbled beneath his feet. "How could you do that to us? We had the right to know."

"Leave!" Siren screamed at him. Her power took hold of Jon. "I don't want to see your mangled face again. Never return here. You are an orphan, Jon Stevens."

Jon's body jerked upright and ran awkwardly from the room. The heavy clatter of boots on the stairs echoed in empty space.

"Now, Tommy. You will press the button and wipe out Los Angeles. Then we'll do the same to San Francisco and Wendigo. After all of that, I'll turn you over to the Protectorate, so they can proclaim you a hero before they put you to death for being Gifted. A fitting end, don't you think?" Siren shoved the gun into the side of Mimi's head. "Push the button."

4 2

Another wave of telekinetic control hit me, but nothing happened. I moved my hand in fits and starts as if I were fighting and losing to her control.

I had to stop her without hurting Mimi. Time was running out, but I was done burying my friends. Even though I hadn't pressed the manual-fire control button, the automated schedule would still fire on Los Angeles in a few minutes. Without Marcel, I didn't know how long I had.

Her power surged around me. "Push the button!"

*Tommy, she's not controlling me,* Mimi's voice said in my head. *She's distracted so I can make her move the gun, if you can stop her.*

*I can. Count to three.* I used my Gift, remembering how the death ray's pulse had felt. The energy signature resisted my attempts to modify it, but I pushed and pulled until my Gift began to change the structure and it mirrored the core of death ray energy I'd absorbed.

*One.*

My body responded to the change. The mutagenic properties began to coalesce as my Gift reformed my stored energy into the death ray energy matrix.

"Push the button, or I kill the girl!" Siren's face mottled with red

301

patches. She pushed her Gift to the limit to make me obey, heedless of the fact it didn't affect me at all.

*Two.*

The matrix snapped into place, and I held the power of the mutagenic ray in me. My Gift amplified and transformed it, resisting its urging of my cell to mutate. I'd mastered the energy signature of the weapon Siren intended to kill everyone I knew and loved with.

*Three.*

It all happened in a flash.

Mimi commanded Siren to drop the gun. The weapon clattered to the floor. An ear-splitting report of the weapon firing deafened me for a second. Beside me, the console threw up sparks and a wisp of smoke from the bullet hole. The screen flickered, then went dead.

Mimi dove after the pistol and out of my way.

The energy flowed from me like a hungry swarm of piranha to attack Siren. Her mouth worked silently, the edges of her power flickering against my senses. Gruesome forms bulged and writhed under her skin, pushing against it like new life fighting to break free. Blood trickled out of her eyes and ears and down her face. Convulsions seized her, racking her body as green pus poured from her mouth and on to the floor.

I pulled Mimi up and pushed her behind me. She clutched the gun like a holy relic of protection.

A crushing sadness lay on my heart as I watched the woman Wendi thought of as her mother dissolve on the floor before me. Her hair withered and turned black. A few seconds later, Tracy Stevens, aka Siren, was gone. Nothing remained to mark her passing but a puddle of viscous liquid. I stared at the empty space. Gone, just like the millions who'd suffered the attacks in the Darkest Storm.

I pulled myself back from staring at where Siren had been, realizing the weapon would still fire. "We need to shut this down."

Mimi didn't respond. Her eyes focused on the patch that had been Siren.

I pulled her to face me, breaking her view. "Are you okay?"

She nodded and handed me the pistol. I shoved it under my belt to free up my hands. I hoped Blaze didn't see it there. He was a fanatic for gun safety.

"It's still active," Mimi said, her voice tinged with panic.

The red light flashed, so the death ray hadn't fired. I sat at the console, and Mimi stood next to me.

"The weapon is already charged. We need to shut it down," I said as my mind went blank. Panic set in. I drew a blank at the sequence to shut down the death ray. Of all the stupid things to do. This wasn't a "forgetting to pick up milk" kind of mistake. "I can't remember how to stop it."

Mimi pushed me aside, all business. "I've got this. Hopefully the console is still working after being shot." She twisted two knobs and depressed a button. "That shuts down the death ray."

The red light still flashed. "Shouldn't the light be dead if it's turned off?"

"Yes." Mimi repeated all the steps. "Nothing is working."

Without the console, we couldn't stop the machine from firing on Los Angeles. Thoughts of Molly intruded, but I pushed them away. I needed to find a solution, not worry about what happened next.

Mimi pushed her hair back out of her face. "Let me try to overload the weapon. It will be a mess when it goes, but better than it firing." She moved through a series of buttons, knobs, and levers. The red light still flashed. "I've got no idea," she said, slumping in defeat.

"Until it fires, we aren't done yet." I grabbed her arm and dragged her after me. "We need Marcel."

Up the stairs we ran, like we were running from the Reclaimers. We reached the top and entered the barn. The fight was still going as the place burned.

"Marcel?"

"Bruh, you've got thirty-five seconds."

I ran outside into the pouring rain. Last thing I needed was getting caught up in the fighting. "The console is damaged. We can't shut it down from here."

"Shit." The line silenced for a second. "Can you spot the satellite dish?"

Mimi and I looked around frantically. She hit me and pointed at an old-style dish. "I've found it," she told Marcel.

"Great. You two need to overload the generator. If the signal stops, the station goes into lockdown. Hurry. You've got twenty-six seconds."

We ran to the satellite dish. A gray box sat next to the receiver over a hundred feet in the air. "So, destroy the gray box?" I asked.

"Yeah. It's insulated so you'll need to fatality it, bruh."

"Got it." I pulled the energy from my stores and barely got a trickle. Hitting Siren with the death ray had drained my supplies. "I'm dry. I've got the recharging box."

"Good. Juice up and fry it."

I pulled the box from my suit's pocket. The case was worse for wear from the fight, but I slid my finger in and pressed the button.

Nothing happened. No jolt of current.

A wave of panic seized me. I kept clicking the button getting the same result.

"What's wrong?" Mimi asked, barely keeping her composure. "Why aren't you destroying the satellite generator?"

"The box isn't working. I'm tapped out."

"What?" Marcel and Mimi both said. Mimi looked on the verge of tears, and Marcel's voice was full of panic.

He recovered first. "Find a power source. You've got thirteen seconds."

We looked around, but the closest power was running to the front of the house. We'd never reach it in time.

I twisted back the other way and bumped the gun. "Oh, man, this is going to suck." I pulled the pistol and handed it to Mimi. "Unload it into my back."

"What? Are you freaking crazy? Tommy, it will kill you," she said, her voice of the edge of hysteria.

"He absorbs energy. Shoot him then run!" Marcel screamed.

I barely had time to turn around before thirteen bullets slammed into my back in lightning-fast succession. Energy burst through me. I fired every drop into the satellite's transmission box.

Nothing happened. The metal box swayed under the impact of the beam. My heart dropped. I doubled my efforts, knowing I'd tap out soon.

Slowly, the metal box glowed red and then white. I forced more power through until a loud crack and a puff of smoke appeared. The box shattered into a million pieces, setting off an explosion that could be seen for miles. My ears rang in the aftermath.

Marcel whooped in my ear. "The death ray powered down. You did it!"

The death ray was dead.

An hour later, we'd freed Makeda and Yutu and captured the rest of the Dark Brigade. Pimiko had escaped, and Jon was long gone. Everyone bore marks of the fight, but no major injuries.

Reaper was being held by two of the Council guards Alyx had brought in to secure the Brigade. "Tommy, I need to say something to you," Reaper said, his normal accent missing.

Dad put his hand on my shoulder. I saw the deep burns and places where the blood had cauterized during the fight.

"I want to hear what he has to say," I told Dad.

He nodded but followed me over.

"You may have beaten my puppet, Tommy," Reaper said in a low whisper of a voice. "But I'm not done with you."

Pepper had taken over Reaper in the zoo and freed us. Was another personality doing the same now? "Are you one of the people Reaper killed, like Pepper?" I asked.

"No, boy. I took Jose from his home long ago and have used him to further my plans. He's of no use to me anymore, so you may have him as a gift, so to speak." The voice had a tone that made my skin crawl.

"Who are you then?" I asked, not sure if I wanted the answer.

"You may call me the Puppeteer. Rest assured, I will be coming for you."

Dad pushed me back. "We killed the Puppeteer years ago," he said, sounding confused. "We saw his body."

Reaper laughed. "You see what you want to see, fool." Reaper clenched his teeth like he was having a seizure. A green gas swirled out of his nose and mouth as he began to cough.

"Poison gas," Dad said, pulling me away from Reaper.

The Grim Reaper's knees buckled. Tears streamed down his face as the gas did its work. His body fell to the ground.

***

We buried Reaper at the edge of the field where Wendi was buried. I said a few words, mostly about the times we'd had before he betrayed us. Pepper added in a few thoughts of a man haunted by the ghost of the woman he loved. We returned to Harker to rebuild the Underground and make plans for the future.

I found Marcel seated at the meeting room table, watching FNN's Daniel Higgs' reporting on the end of the Underground, as the death ray removed the dissident threat from San Francisco and Los Angeles.

"I don't know why they bother," Marcel said, sipping on his Cherry Pepsi. "They'll have to have a new bogeyman to scare the Norms into being sheep."

"I don't care," I said, as I pulled up a seat next to my brother. "Can we watch something else?"

He grinned at me. "I thought you'd never ask." The screen flipped over, and the scrolling words of *Star Wars* took over the screen. "Always good to go back to the classics."

I couldn't argue with that.

Over the next few weeks, things returned to normal. Blaze and Pepper joined Warden's group at Wendigo. Mom and Abby came home. Mimi decided to stay with us for a while. None of us knew what to do next, but Harker was secure, the Brotherhood had been disrupted, and the Council was on the hunt for Pimiko. For a while, we just wanted to be a family.

And I, for one, was in full agreement.

Since leaving Redemption, I'd lost Wendi. I wasn't sure if I'd ever truly be over the pain of her loss. My memories of all the death and destruction haunted me.

I'd changed in ways I didn't like, been ruthless when I'd had to, and yes, I killed people. The quiet solitude of Harker sounded like heaven —a place to deal with the demons and maybe, one day, learn to live with the loss and regret of choices I'd been forced to make and people I might have saved. When I looked in the mirror, I saw a killer, not the hero I'd always wanted to be.

Dad had said heroes always fall the hardest, and now I understood it all too well.

I wish I didn't.

**THE END**

ACKNOWLEDGEMENTS

The book (or device containing said book) you hold in your hands is the end of a journey for me. I started writing Tommy's story when my children were four and nine. Emily is now 22 and Nicholas just turned seventeen. A good portion of almost two decades has passed since I had the first ideas for Storm Forged and began my writing adventure. Turning in Storm Shattered was a great thrill and a bittersweet moment for me. These characters grew up with me as I went from a noob writer to a published author. While there are many more stories to be told in the Darkest Storm universe, Storm Shattered, ends the first trilogy in a way I hope you find satisfying.

Back to the dedication. I'd be still sitting on an unpublished book if it weren't for John Hartness, the publisher at Falstaff Books. He believed in me before anyone else and regardless of anything yet to come, I will always be grateful to him for taking a chance on me. Melissa McArthur, associate publisher at Falstaff is amazing and always there when I need a pep talk or to run ideas by someone. Venessa Guinta took over the editing on Storm Shattered and did a fantastic job with helping to hone and deepen the story. Paul Barrett did a great job getting my copy edits - done in the middle of a pandemic no less. Thank you to Alicia Grace for proofreading. At the end of the day if anything was missed it falls to me since I do the final check, but I couldn't do it with the team.

The cover of this book is gorgeous. It amazes me how Davey Beauchamp takes my rambling ideas and turns it into such a piece of art. There is a reason my walls are cover with his artwork.

A big thank you goes out to my beta readers old and new. Cat, Cheri, Chuck, Joe, Jon, and Regis. If I've missed anyone, it was unintentional. You've stuck with me through early drafts, awful grammar, and all the rest of the general weirdness. You've all had my back through my writing, and I appreciate a LOT!

Finally, I want to thank my wonderful family. This whole series started when I was watching Power Ranger with Nicholas. After three thousand episodes, I started thinking they should just kick the Power Rangers out of Angel Grove and Darkest Storm was born. A lot of the slang and mannerisms of teenage boys come from watching Nick and his friends interact. My daughter Emily's suggestions and personality are woven throughout Molly's storyline. She was my original beta reader before Storm Forged even had a name. Both kids are a constant source of inspiration and pride.

Emerson left us two years ago and we got Blaze a year later. Both have laid under my desk as I write into the night, occasionally reminding me to take a break to let them out or get a treat (for me, or one of them, or both).

My last thank you is to my wonderful and lovely wife, Hope. Not only does she put up with late-night writing sessions, traipsing to conventions, listening as I work through book plots, being reassuring and supportive me when I get a rejection letter, but she also is the first line of defense in stopping you from getting bad books. She reads everything in draft form, which can be fairly awful. Seriously, she is always there to celebrate accomplishments and commiserate when things go awry or I'm having a crisis of talent. I'd be lost without her.

I'd be remiss if I didn't thank you, the reader. I've met or emailed many of you over the past few years. All of you have been wonderful, gracious, and a lot of fun. Every time I interact with you, I come away feeling great. I couldn't ask for a better group of readers.

What's next? I'm not sure if this is the end of the line for Tommy and his friends. We'll see what the future brings. What I don't want to do it put out books just to continue a story that has reached its natural ending point. There are other books in other worlds. I hope you'll join me on those adventures.

Patrick Dugan
    May 2020

# ABOUT THE AUTHOR

Patrick Dugan was born in the far north of New York, where the cold winds blow. This meant lots of time for reading over the long winters. His parents didn't care what he read as long as he did and thus Patrick started with a steady diet of comics and science fiction novels.

His debut novel, Storm Forged, Book One of the Darkest Storm series, was published by Falstaff Books in May of 2018. Unbreakable Storm followed in 2019.

When you start out as an author, nobody tells you about all of the other "jobs" that you take on in addition to writing novels. Being a full time technologist has led Patrick to start a blog on the uses of writing technologies and how to apply them to the writing process. He delves into software, hardware, social media, and all things web related.

Patrick resides in Charlotte, NC with his wife and two children. In his limited spare time, he's a gamer, homebrewer, and DIYer.

You can find out more at www.patrickdugan.net, https://www.facebook.com/patrick.dugan.3781, https://www.instagram.com/patrickduganauthor/

# FRIENDS OF FALSTAFF

Thank You to All our Falstaff Books Patrons, who get extra digital content each month! To be featured here and see what other great rewards we offer, go to www.patreon.com/falstaffbooks.

## PATRONS

Dino Hicks
John Hooks
John Kilgallon
Larissa Lichty
Travis & Casey Schilling
Staci-Leigh Santore
Sheryl R. Hayes
Scott Norris
Samuel Montgomery-Blinn
Junkle